THE CRYPTOS CONUNDRUM

THE
CRYPTOS
CONUNDRUM

Τηε Χρψπτοσ Χοννυδρυμ

Chase Brandon

A TOM DOHERTY ASSOCIATES BOOK
NEW YORK

THE CRYPTOS CONUNDRUM

A Forge Book
Published by Tom Doherty Associates, LLC
175 Fifth Avenue
New York, NY 10010

www.tor-forge.com

Forge® is a registered trademark of Tom Doherty Associates, LLC.

Library of Congress Cataloging-in-Publication Data

Brandon, Chase.
    The cryptos conundrum / Chase Brandon. — 1st ed.
        p. cm.
ISBN 978-0-7653-1877-0 (hardcover)
ISBN 978-1-4299-4464-9 (e-book)
1. United States. Central Intelligence Agency—Fiction.   2. Intelligence officers—
Fiction.   I. Title.
    PS3602.R3597C79 2012
    813'.6—dc23

                                                            2012009271

First Edition: June 2012

Printed in the United States of America

0 9 8 7 6 5 4 3 2 1

For my wife, Jamie, and my son, Greg

ACKNOWLEDGMENTS

Special thanks and everlasting memories go to my late friend and agent, Marty Greenberg, who took my manuscript to the publisher's front door; and to my first editor, Denise Little, who helped me learn to write, and made sure my pages were well dressed when we rang the buzzer at Tor/Forge Books. There I later met Cynthia Merman, the best copy editor I could ever have hoped to find. All of her professional touches and amazing attention to detail were greatly appreciated.

I genuinely appreciate the opportunity of a lifetime provided to me by Tom Doherty and especially Robert Gleason at Tor/Forge Books. They opened the door to their publishing house and allowed me and my story to come in, where Whitney Ross, Elizabeth Curione, and other Tor/Forge staffers provided invaluable assistance in getting this story into print. Bob Gleason has continued to encourage and tutor me from the moment I stepped across his threshold. His help in turning me into an author has meant everything, as does his friendship. Deeply grateful for Bob's support and hospitality, I hope to be not merely a one-time guest, but to become a member of the Tor family over the course of many published novels.

Time will tell on that score . . . as it ultimately does for *The Cryptos Conundrum*.

AUTHOR'S NOTE

True facts involving people, places, and events described in this book inspired the broader, fictional story that unfolds through the pagination of time.

One part of the truth is that a *real* metal sculpture stands in the courtyard at CIA headquarters, and it contains an *actual* coded message that is displayed in plain sight. It is an enigmatic, beautiful work of art, commissioned to commemorate an expansion of the original headquarters building popularly and publicly known as Langley. At its unveiling, the CIA director challenged Agency employees to decipher the message.

In fact, the director had earlier authorized CIA's chief cryptographer, a man referred to as Langley's *Wizard of Codes*, to assist the design artist with basic code construction. The beguiling sculpture and the sophisticated variant code that was created have been an enduring mystery and challenge for all who've seen or puzzled with it. After almost a quarter century, no one, not even experts at the National Security Agency, has fully deciphered the message.

Although inspired in part by the CIA's real work of art, nothing that follows should be construed to reflect the actual sculptor's *craftsmanship or authorship* with the format or interpretation of the Agency's sculpture. The description, meaning, and authorship of the sculpture in this work, called *Cryptos*, is purely fictional. The fictional sculpture's title is derived from the cryptographic method used by the fictional artist to construct the coded message in concert with the central character, both of whom will be introduced in due course.

Cryptos is a towering, furnace-charred slab of oxidized steel, bent in half at a ninety degree angle. The L-shape structure is set in a granite base and flanked by massive, shiny aluminum columns.

Both wall-sections of *Cryptos* are perforated with two thousand and six alphabetic letters cut out with a hand torch. At different times during the day, the traversing sun casts a total of four thousand and twelve back-lighted letters as *reverse shadows,* which slowly drift across the large disk of black granite that rings the sculpture at ground level. Everyone has always believed the coded message was to be found in those *projected* shadow patterns, if not in the scalpelled letters themselves.

They were wrong. Turns out most everyone has been wrong about almost everything.

Even the Mayans.

Truth is so hard to tell, it sometimes needs fiction to make it plausible.
—**Francis Bacon**

Coincidence is God's way of remaining anonymous.
—**Albert Einstein**

GALACTIC GLOSSARY

ENTITIES

Ga'Lawed—Galactic savant, an omniscient supreme being

Headmaster—Head disciple, historian, and spokesman for Ga'Lawed

Samaritans—Twelve GoodWill apostles for Ga'Lawed and his Headmaster:

Won	Vor	Sa'ven	Tenyah
Tu	Fieva	Aigh	E-levi
Tha'Ree	Sixkt	Nie-nun	T'wel-va

LOCALES

Tutorium—Cosmic classroom for the Headmaster/imprimatur's syllabus

High Stasis—Cosmic plateau from which Samaritans monitor their venues

VOCABULARY

Ascension—Elevation to the next cosmic realm

Chalmerian—Samaritan reference to the Chalmers family

Fiverians—Civilization under the GoodWill influence of the Samaritan
Fieva

Iris Portal—Event horizon for the Meg'etheral

Meg'etheral—Transition to another eternal dimension

Missions—Services performed by Samaritans

Voracians—Civilization under the influence of the Samaritan Vor

Part I

THE RISING SUN

1

VERDUN, FRANCE. FEBRUARY 26, 1916

The cordite-clouded sky flashed sparks of primordial fire. And Earth's anvil shook with concussions that pounded his body and soul as though smithed by Thor's angry-red hammer. In terrified awe, Dr. Jonathan S. Chalmers Jr. watched as blinding artillery bursts and dismembering detonations reinforced the enemy's specter of Death that he felt already overshadowed him.

Cold, wet, wounded, and a lifetime's distance from his family in New York, Chalmers gripped the steel barrel and bloodstained stock of his 8mm French Lebel, but he would gladly have swapped the rifle for a crystal brandy snifter.

A brilliant mathematician, Chalmers was a scholar and gentleman completely out of his affluent Long Island element. Against reasonable odds or definable logic, he was also a private in the U.S. Army and at present trapped in a gash of dangerous dirt between France and Germany known as the Western Front. Here, a form of human slaughter called trench warfare raged unabated with the rising sun of each new day in a world at war with itself.

Chalmers knew that the gruesome horror of this historic killing zone was already immortalized in the battlefield term *no-man's-land*—a realm that his knotted guts and analytical mind told Chalmers was nightmarish beyond even his own vivid imagination.

THE TRENCHES. 0215 HOURS

Chalmers clutched his circular ID tags, their cool metal a talisman for him. He surveyed the trench to his left and right. Flanked by shattered bodies, he saw his dead friends as harbingers of his own anticipated fate.

Chalmers had been sent up to reinforce the 407th French Rifle Regiment two weeks ago with a platoon of American volunteers, including longtime friend and fellow New Yorker Paul Baker, as well as some British regulars. He'd been under siege and without sleep for so long that he'd lost all track of time.

"So tell me again, John," Baker said. "What the hell are we doing here?"

"Saving the French by holding this line. Didn't you listen to that lieutenant's briefing, *le bâtard* who sent us into this rats' nest?"

"Yeah, right. Guess I overlooked the part about the Krauts trying to wipe us out."

Both men were scared, though they tried not to show it.

They winced, recoiling again from the thundering bombardment now under way to destroy fortifications and trench systems along a twenty-mile front from Bois d'Avocourt to Étain.

German Krupp howitzers, called Big Berthas, should have finished the demolition in a matter of days. But both of them were still here, still alive and holding this line—even though the French fortification at Douaumont had been captured by German infantrymen.

Chalmers knew it was only a matter of time until the Krauts pushed them back or overran the allied stronghold here in Alpha Sector. If they survived the night, their orders were to go over the top at first light and claw across a five-hundred-yard-wide strip of barbed-wire hell. And if they made it to the other side, fight the Fritzies man to man with bayonets, and then bare hands.

The killing zone, Chalmers thought. *A suicide charge into no-man's-land.*

Chalmers touched his heart, then pulled a photo of Margaret from his tunic's breast pocket. He could make out her features in the sudden glare of a bomb's blast. He loved her deeply and felt this was probably his last chance to look upon her face.

Chalmers felt his friend nudge him. He quickly replaced the photo.

"Seems like an eternity since we enlisted, huh?"

Chalmers nodded. "Maybe longer." He scoured mud from his rifle breech with his sleeve. "Sorry I snookered you into this latrine. Rotten thing to do, Paul."

"Aw, it's all right. I've always been your shadow. You couldn't have come without me . . . just don't *leave* without me, okay?" he said with a weak grin.

⊷

Chalmers and Baker had been neighbors and inseparable pals since they were still in short pants. Two years older, Chalmers had always been like a big brother to Baker.

Tall, lanky, and with angular good looks, Chalmers had excelled in lacrosse in his early years but quit the sport in favor of academics.

Baker was short and stocky, and though quite smart, he tended to muscle his way through life's challenges, having eventually earned his law degree and joined his father's practice more through sheer grit than a scholar's grasp of jurisprudence.

A year ago, they'd been safe on Oyster Bay, Long Island, secure in the warmth of their parents' love and their families' wealth, power, and influence. Although he'd recently married, Chalmers still lived in the stone mansion that had housed generations of Chalmers families. Baker still lived just down the road with his parents as well.

It was a near perfect world they'd willingly left in favor of this deadly trench.

Even more than Baker, Chalmers had been born and raised in privilege, with every advantage of wealth and sophistication his parents could give him. Chalmers's father, the man he'd been named after, was a successful ship line attorney and investment banker. Chalmers's French mother had always been a tender caregiver to her son. She was a consummate homemaker and devoted wife.

She'd told her son, when he was just a young boy, that she'd met his father on one of his business trips to the Continent. They'd fallen in love at first sight. He was their only child, and he'd always tried his best to live up to their love and expectations. He had set a high achievement bar for himself as well, especially in the field of education.

Most who knew Chalmers described him as being blessed with extraordinary, if not incomparable, intelligence. When Chalmers was only a few months old, he'd already begun to demonstrate awareness, physical prowess, and nascent communication skills that astounded his parents and the family physician.

৯৯

Now twenty-six years old, Chalmers held doctoral degrees in mathematics and engineering physics from Columbia University. Before enlisting, he'd been a professor, head of his department, and the youngest man to hold that job. His students and university colleagues believed Chalmers was a true savant, the most brilliant individual they had ever known.

He'd never set a foot off the path his parents had planned for him, nor his own pursuit of knowledge, until the day he'd seen the recruiting poster. Its patriotic message spoke to his idealism and sense of adventure, and constituted what Chalmers called the *convergence of coincidence*—a force majeure of unrelated events that shaped one's life, that perhaps defined the concept of life itself. He believed in the power of that force.

Chalmers Senior believed that his son's abrupt decision to enlist would, "in hateful fashion," as he'd put it, change the young man's life, and he had argued vehemently against it. Jonathan Chalmers had stood his ground—and now occupied it in the soggy bottom of this trench.

Baker was here too, having followed Chalmers's lead by signing up the next day. Both of them now faced another moment of convergence, waiting for the only thing they knew could ever end their friendship . . . Death.

2

"I thought we'd be a part of a gallant army that would save France from the heel of the Huns," Chalmers said, his voice flattened by disillusionment.

"If this is gallant," Baker replied, after spitting out the mud from the trench wall that oozed into every orifice, "I'll eat this stinking, ass-dirty uniform."

"Paul, truth is I wish I'd never gone to town, never seen that goddamned poster."

"We probably would've volunteered anyway, just to prove that we were men."

"Maybe it was just rebelling against following in our fathers' footsteps. Me probably more so than you." Chalmers shrugged. "Doesn't make much difference now."

"We should've swiped your dad's boat again . . . sailed around the world instead."

"Yeah . . . Father told me I'd rue the day I volunteered."

"And . . . ?"

Chalmers surveyed the corpse-strewn trench. "He was right . . . about everything."

Chalmers had made impetuous decisions that had landed him in hot water before. Like the time he'd decided it would be exciting to cross Long Island Sound in his father's sloop-rigged daysailer during a fierce summer squall. Baker had been along for the ride then, too. The boat had capsized and sunk half a mile from the pier.

Chalmers rescued Baker from certain death in the whitecaps that day.

However, he wasn't nearly so sure he'd be able to save them both from his disastrous impulse to join the army.

They'd been assigned to the 101st Infantry, slated for an elite "exploratory" assignment in France. He'd promised Baker it'd be a memory maker to last a lifetime. He promised his parents and his young wife that he'd come home in one piece as soon as they whipped those Germans into shape.

FIRE BAY. 0330 HOURS

Concussive artillery shells and ratcheting machine gun fire shattered the night. Chalmers was positioned with others in his unit, including Baker, on the Alpha Sector fire bay, which was a cutout in the trench with an elevated platform where Allied riflemen stood to fire on enemy positions.

"You have to admit, John, there's a certain orchestral quality to it."

Chalmers, who'd been trying to distance himself, at least mentally, from this nightmare, cast a sideways glance at his trench mate.

"Sure. Like a concerto of death."

Chalmers knew he was smart. He had the degrees and titles to prove it. Right now, though, he felt like the dumbest jackass alive—the *alive* part being a condition he feared would end soon enough.

"Yeah, I want you, too," he muttered, remembering the poster with Uncle Sam's finger pointing at him. All Chalmers wanted now was to go home.

‌‌‍‍ᵼᴀ

President Woodrow Wilson wouldn't have his congressional declaration of war against Germany and its Central Power allies until a year from now, although Chalmers' political sense told him that bill would have to be passed. In the interim, a few small units of American volunteers had been shipped overseas as a show of good faith to America's future Allied Power partnership with Britain, France, and Russia. Chalmers and Baker were here in this trench as part of that "show."

Chalmers believed the adage that those who failed to learn from history were doomed to repeat it.

He realized he'd enrolled himself in the front line of a brutal class.

Fear told him that something far worse than the school of hard knocks was about to start.

3

Chalmers, with Baker next to him, stood high point on the elevated fire bay. Other Americans in the unit were positioned alongside them at shoulder width.

"Close in! Heads down!" Chalmers yelled as he heard the distinctive *ka-plumpt* of shell casings dropped into the German "beer-barrel" trench mortars. Everyone hugged the wood-reinforced dirt wall and braced for impact. Mortar rounds struck them, and their screams became painful arpeggios to Death's concerto.

Hot shards of metal blasted some of the men to Chalmers's left completely off the bay. They fell into the trench, dismembered and dead before they hit the ground.

A chunk of searing shrapnel ripped into Chalmers's left arm. He saw that Baker had tumbled backward into the bottom of the trench. His best friend's pants were shredded and smoking, his skin seared by hot metal. Chalmers jumped into the trench, gathered Baker in his arms, and wiped mud from his friend's face.

"How bad is it?"

Baker clenched his teeth and pulled a tight smile. "Flesh wounds. Just a piece of my ass shot off. How 'bout you?"

"Red stains on my Doughboy tux, but I'm still at the party."

"Ah . . . me too. Care to dance?" Baker said, clutching Chalmers's tunic sleeve.

One look told him that Baker was in bad shape, his wounds more extensive than Baker had let on, or probably realized. His legs were broken and bleeding profusely. Calves, thighs, and buttocks were ripped open, with muscles and bones showing.

As Chalmers lifted his friend, Baker cried out, one anguished voice among the others who lay gravely wounded in the death-filled trench.

What could he do for the rest of them? Nothing. There was time and strength only for Paul.

"Sorry I dragged you into this," Chalmers said as he pulled Baker down the line in search of medical assistance.

"I'm sorry you're dragging me now," Baker gasped. Shudders ran through his body with each step.

"Hang on. We'll make it. I promise."

Baker coughed, and blood dribbled from his lips. "I don't . . . think so."

"Yes we will, Paul. I've got you. Just keep going."

"John . . . your arm . . . it's a mess."

"Doesn't matter. We're going home together."

Chalmers looked at his own wounds. *Severe lacerations. Fractured forearm. But no real discomfort . . . yet.*

Like Baker, he knew he was in shock and doped by his own adrenaline. He also knew that when the shock wore off and the adrenaline ran out, the pain would be unbearable for Baker, and probably him, too.

He figured they'd probably both lose limbs, assuming they lived long enough for their wounds to become infected.

THE STATION. 0405 HOURS

Chalmers hauled Baker along the duckboards—planked trench flooring coated with mud and slathered with gore too horrible to describe.

"Up in there, Paul," he told Baker as they took shelter in the medic station Chalmers had finally located.

It was nothing more than a crude, sandbag- and timber-reinforced cave dug high on the main trench wall. There was a handmade Red Cross sign hanging from a bayonet to mark its function, and there were also a couple of dead French soldiers.

"Hold on, I'll make some more space," Chalmers said as he rolled the cadavers down the incline to the trench bottom. He looked around. No sign of the medics. Maybe they were the dead French guys.

He surveyed the space and found some rags and a bottle of "antiseptic" cognac. Chalmers poured it on Baker's legs, ignoring his screams. In apology, he offered the rest of the bottle to his friend, who sucked it down, gasping at the burn in his throat.

Chalmers began to wrap Baker's legs with gauze strips.

"What's this, a dirt sarcophagus?" said Baker with a chuckle to mask his moan. "You said we'd make it outta here, now you're wrapping me for a burial."

"You can joke at your own funeral later. I'm making sure it won't happen tonight."

Baker began to hyperventilate.

"Slow, deep breaths, Paul. Compression bandages will keep the blood in and the mud out." He stroked Baker's forehead.

Hyperventilation turned into convulsions. "It hurts bad. I'm s-sa-scared, John."

"I know. Me, too." Chalmers tenderly wiped mud from Baker's anguished face. "Paul, I never intended—"

"It's all right."

Baker tried to smile. It was a failure. He coughed up more blood and squeezed his eyes shut against the searing pain.

Chalmers blotted out thoughts of death and got back to wrapping.

"Look, the bleeding's stopped. We're off the front line. Now we just get through the night."

Chalmers hoped Baker could regain some strength . . . somehow.

"First light, Paul. We'll get an ambulance back to a real medic. I promise."

Too tired now even to talk, Baker just nodded. His eyes sagged.

THE STATION. 0520 HOURS

The sun will be up soon, Chalmers thought, persuading himself that he could see a pink line of dim promise in the east. He didn't know how much longer Baker could last. *I won't leave him here,* he thought, as tears streamed down his muddy face. Unable to bear the prospect of losing his best friend, he gagged in anguish.

He didn't want to be left here either, not after what he'd seen happen to men who had died in the trenches.

Chalmers saw that Baker's eyes had opened again, this time wide with fear.

"Try to sleep. It's the best escape. Don't worry, I've got your back."

"John, promise me you'll keep 'em outta my fleabag tonight."

"You bet," said Chalmers as he pulled the bedroll covers over his friend's shoulders and head. "Almost time. We'll head out for the ambulance real soon."

Baker was shaking. From cold or shock, Chalmers couldn't tell which.

Chalmers added his own fleabag to the one covering Baker. He knew sleep would be a merciful escape, but he was afraid to close his eyes.

Everyone in the trenches knew the stories. Rats, millions of them, so large and powerful they could eat a wounded, defenseless man. They usually went for the ears, eyes, and lips first, then ate their way into the rest of the soft tissue. Usually, the victim was dead before the feast began. But not always.

೪

Contemplating his and Baker's death in battle was frightening enough, but the idea of being a half-eaten anonymous corpse destined for an unmarked grave was worse for Chalmers. To minimize the chances of dying as an unknown, all American soldiers wore two dog tags—one to remove from a fallen comrade as the official death record, and the other to remain with the body for identification until burial.

Chalmers clutched his tags tighter, as if pressing them together precluded their untimely separation later. Still and all, his spirit was crushed by the weight of what he knew were his bad decisions and foolish actions. He could taste the bile of raw fear coming from his knotted gut.

So he closed his eyes, just for a moment, just to shutter the burning fatigue, just to blacken further his vision of this godless night.

4

THE STATION. 0620 HOURS

A sudden increase in the already heavy fusillade shook Chalmers from what had started as reverie but had transitioned into sleep. Along the way, dawn had finally managed to lightly infiltrate fear's dark encampment.

The firefight now under way complicated his plan to get Baker, and himself, to an ambulance. He still intended to move out as soon as possible, but right now he knew he'd better take his position on the fire bay, because it sounded to him like the Krauts were about to start their final assault.

He knew the strategy. Meet them head-on. Contain them or force them to retreat.

Before grabbing his Lebel rifle, Chalmers reached in his rucksack and took out his last piece of *rooti*, trench slang for bread. Actually, there was almost a totally separate language for wartime life in the trenches, and the French, Brits, and Yanks all spoke it.

He checked on Baker, who was rolled up in his fleabag with his back to Chalmers. Baker seemed to be resting comfortably. *Good, he managed to grab a few winks, too.*

Chalmers tugged on his pal's shoulder and whispered roughly. "Pssst, Paul, I've got to leave for a while. You need to eat something."

Baker rustled, slid down a bit, and rolled over toward Chalmers.

He didn't say anything, so Chalmers jostled him again.

"Paul . . . wake up. Talk to me."

But Baker still didn't answer, so Chalmers pulled back the top flap of the bedroll. Skin afire with burning gooseflesh, he recoiled from the macabre sight.

Baker's face was a nightmare—his lips chewed off, his teeth fully exposed. His head was a bloody hunk of grated flesh. His features had been stripped away, raggedly, almost as if they'd been sheared off by shrapnel.

What had been his ears, nose, and eyes were now open portals to his brainless, ransacked skull.

Horrified, Chalmers slid backward, and his friend's body did, too. The sudden movement flushed a pack of rats from Baker's cannibalized innards. Some pulled forth his entrails as they fled from his splayed mouth.

Chalmers vomited. Too repulsed even to scream, he lurched backward farther, lost his balance, and tumbled into the deep trench they'd climbed from last night.

He landed in a sea of squealing rats busy devouring other corpses, and like a tidal wave they flowed over him, too. He screamed and flailed wildly when they began to bite him. He tried to stand, but the vibrating, blood-slick duckboards gave him no purchase. He batted at the ravaging horde and felt his hold on sanity start to slip.

But the boardwalk was undulating not, as Chalmers thought, from the weight and cresting wave of rats scurrying forward for more cadavers.

The duckboards rattled from the pounding wave of infantrymen now running down the line as they readied for the early morning trek into no-man's-land.

Chalmers vaguely heard the French soldiers echoing the command mantra of General Henri Philippe Pétain as he rallied his troops to stop the German advance. One of the soldiers reached down and pulled Chalmers to his feet.

Conscripted into the formation, he stumbled along with them.

"*Ils ne passeront pas!*" they shouted. They shall not pass!

Just like rats, the Krauts were on the move, he determined—surprised that he could still form rational thoughts. He concentrated on the words, desperate to keep his mind away from the ghastly image of Baker imprinted there. Anything, anything to get away from the rats.

Then there were more words.

"Git yur bloody arse a-bumping, Yank," said the big Brit who shoved an Enfield rifle in Chalmers's one good hand. "Slap on yur Rosalie, lad, it's Uncle Charlie to hop the bags and stunt the fookin' box heads."

"What?"

Rosalie, a woman's name, thought Chalmers hazily. *My wife? No, my wife is Margaret. Rosalie? Rosalie is a . . . bayonet.* And then, in an instant, he was back from his fugue state, jarred into reality by the feel of the troops who shoved past him.

"Get your ass in gear, Yank," the British soldier said more clearly, "and fix bayonets. We've been ordered to go over the top and charge the Germans."

Slogging forward, Chalmers clamped the rifle barrel in his left armpit and used his single serviceable hand to attach the bayonet he'd pulled from his waist belt. He couldn't do it. The Enfield would not accept the Lebel's bayonet, and Chalmers's old rifle was now buried somewhere beneath the red mud and feeding-frenzied rats where his best friend had died.

He dropped the Rosalie and was swept deeper into the advancing column, moving forward largely by virtue of being squeezed in tightly with men whose compressed shoulders supported him better than his own legs could at the moment. His mobility, he knew, was virtually naught, weakened from the mind-numbing shock of Baker having been eaten alive while he slept. Then shock turned into something else.

Guilt. Soul-damning guilt. It was the most painful thing he'd ever experienced.

He tried to scream out the demon, but he had no voice. So he soldiered on, shuffling down the zigzag trenches and finally entering the main channel that led to the perpendicular front-line trench just ahead. With his mind now more in the moment and his physical resolve returning, he fanned out and on command jumped up onto the edge of no-man's-land.

Ahead of him were strands of barbed wire, land mines, mortar bursts, machine gun slugs and, as he'd see, the first of two white clouds he would encounter moments from now.

Crouching, Chalmers prepared to charge into no-man's-land, across the field of death.

He was ready for its embrace now.

5

THE CHARGE. 0640 HOURS

"*Avancez la ligne, avancez la ligne.*" Even if Chalmers hadn't spoken French he would have understood the phrase. He and the other weary soldiers began their stoic assault, even though they knew it was suicide.

Chalmers ran, splattered with chunks of flying mud and bloody viscera from the dismembering mortar blasts striking around him. Comrades fell to his left and right.

The first strand of razor wire he hit sliced into his calves and thighs. Two rounds from a 7.92mm Spandau machine gun, called the Devil's Paintbrush by the Germans, hit Chalmers in the side and passed completely through his body. The hot lead cauterized the wounds even as the slugs tore into him.

The third round hit Chalmers in the head.

His helmet deflected the bullet, but the impact knocked him off his feet. He fell sideways into a water-logged mortar hole. He no longer heard the battlefield noises around him. The crash of mortars and zing of bullets were drowned out by the ringing in his head.

He was still in the throes of emotional anguish, but he now experienced more physical pain than he'd thought possible. The combined agony brought with it a surprising thought: *I'm still alive.*

Chalmers struggled to stand, determined to continue the charge as he stumbled in with the second advancing column. Those men, too, thousands of them, began to drop in front of him. He wondered why, then he realized.

A swirling white cloud settled on them, one that rained not water but death.

Gas. The worst kind—Diphosgene. Spewing from artillery canisters that he saw shattering on impact. He'd been briefed on this poison, which formed hydrochloric acid the instant it mixed in agonizing unison with the moisture of its victim's eyes, mouth, and lungs.

All around him men clawed at their faces. Some had bloody, empty sockets from which they'd torn their scalding eyes. His own eyes started to burn, first with disbelief at what he saw and then with searing pain as the diphosgene cloud engulfed him, too.

His last sight was the walking dead around him coughing up their blistered innards. He began to cough—sure he'd breathed his last.

❧

He heard a deep, pulsing bass rumble. A large motor? One of the new-fangled war machines . . . a tank?

Suddenly, a solid white wall appeared in front of him, followed by a flash of crystal luminescence that burst forth from what he took to be an open door or a ship's portal. Through blurred eyes, Chalmers saw a strange figure emerge, not a soldier but a mysterious swirling apparition that seemed to flow forward and reach out for him.

As the peculiar mass advanced, Chalmers watched it morph into a form he believed he recognized, though he could not account for who it was or why he could have a sense of knowing such a stranger—especially at a godforsaken place like this.

His eyes still full of scalding pain, Chalmers managed to identify the unmistakable shape of slender white hands suddenly touching him, and he felt their gentle strength when they lifted him and carried him across the door's threshold. Struggling to keep his clouded mind working, Chalmers knew he was inside something, somewhere, but all he could see was a white void.

An odd form of blindness?

Inside his head he saw a kaleidoscopic swirl of strange symbols that somehow *spoke* to him in what he believed were comforting words. He knew he was being told something important, but he wasn't sure what it meant because what was left of his battle-rattled brain had begun to shut down. The stranger's form, too, began to evaporate.

A merciful form of death?

And then Chalmers, spiraling even deeper into anaphylactic shock and physical trauma from his fatal injuries, felt himself released from conscious life.

6

Chalmers had no idea how much time had passed, but he knew he was breathing, and he calculated he was alive thanks to a Good Samaritan field medic who must've worked a true miracle. Opening his eyes, he found they no longer burned, but they were unfocused. He blinked them into service and noted he was still surrounded by whiteness. He was both intrigued and frightened by it.

Where am I? . . . Still in that misty netherworld?

He stretched out his good arm and realized what it was when he touched cool cloth—a sheet curtain around a hospital bed he could now tell he occupied. When the curtain suddenly parted, he saw a nurse in fresh starched whites come to his side.

She smiled, noting how much he'd improved, and how handsome this American looked since the orderly had washed his strong angular face, trimmed his thick locks, and given him a shave. He had sandy brown hair and dark, penetrating eyes—the kind, she thought, that take in everything, even now in his condition. He was tall and had an athletic build, and though broken and bed-ridden at the moment, she sensed his aura of intelligence and strength. After what she could tell he'd been through, she knew him to be a lucky man . . . or, more likely, one whose path in life he was fated to walk.

"Why, hello," she said in a friendly brogue. "'Tis happy I am to see you with us today."

He tried to reply, but his scarred lungs and raw throat wouldn't cooperate.

"Shh," she said. "Give it a bit. We can talk when you're feeling better."

He coughed and swallowed as he watched her remove the white cotton gloves that encased her slender hands. The nurse eyed the cast on his left arm appraisingly as she took his pulse on his other wrist. Her touch felt like heaven.

She inspected the bandage that covered his right side from the bottom of his rib cage to his waist. She then placed her left hand across his forehead and her right hand over his heart. It was clearly a purposeful, yet at the same time unusual, medical gesture, he thought.

"Well, now, the fever's gone, and your heart and pulse are strong, so how do ya feel this beautiful day in London?"

Clearing his throat he rasped, "Uh, tired . . . confused."

"And you're lucky to feel it. You've had a lovely ferry ride across the channel and should be rested from yur week's nap here. You've been in something of a coma, a merciful one," she said cheerfully. "Take this. You almost lost it the hard way."

He held out his hand.

"Other one's still aboot your neck, Private Chalmers," she said as she gently placed an aluminum dog tag in his palm. "You were a bit . . . detached, for a while. I'll put this one back on the chain, if you'd like."

"Thank you, Miss . . . Gretchen," he said, squinting at the name tag on her uniform, "for your kindness and care. My wife and family . . . do they know I'm here?"

"That they do, Private. I had administration pull your regimental records and send a telegram. You'll likely have an answer from them sooner then you'll think. In the meantime, are you perhaps a wee bit hungry?"

"Yes. Definitely. For some meat . . . maybe a London broil?" He licked his dried, cracked lips just thinking of the taste.

"Ah, there's a'course the beef ration. But I can git ye some lamb and something to read afterward."

"Sounds fine."

She cranked up his bed and plumped the pillows behind his shoulders before leaving. As she walked away, he marveled at her beauty. She reminded him of Margaret.

He wanted to go home—to kiss his wife, embrace his mother, talk with his father, return to academia, and resume his charmed life in the Oyster Bay mansion.

"Please, Lord, see me home quickly and safely, guide me to my wife and family," said Chalmers, praying, truly asking for God's intercession, for the first time in his life. But he knew life would never be the same, not without Paul Baker.

He surveyed the cast. He was even luckier than he'd thought. He might not lose that arm after all.

~

Gretchen returned with a large tray bearing two stainless-steel plate covers.

"Ye've gotten a fair spread here," she said with a radiant smile. "Braised chops from the hospital galley. An answer to your prayer to see your home again, compliments of the regimental administrative officer. And a response to your question from someone who knows why you didn't die in the same gas attack that killed over eight thousand others in a matter of minutes." She smiled, touched his shoulder, and seemed to glide away.

He wondered how she knew he'd prayed about going home.

But that didn't matter right now—his first hot meal in many weeks did. Chalmers lifted the cover. The aroma made his mouth water. Despite his wounds and his strained throat, he made short work of the food. After his time in the trenches with meager rations, it tasted divine.

His hunger sated, he lifted the second cover and found some very interesting items. His discharge papers, his travel orders, and a telegram from Mrs. Margaret Chalmers were clipped to a steamship ticket home to New York. He would be leaving the London infirmary soon and, it appeared, the war as well. He clutched the envelope, wanting to open it immediately but hesitating. Better to savor it. *I'll save it for last.*

A Bible was stacked with the paperwork that signaled his release from hell. He quickly read through the documents, joyous that he was truly headed home.

He set the Bible to one side as he opened his wife's telegram:

"I LOVE YOU STOP HURRY HOME STOP"

Tears filled his eyes. He put his good hand up to wipe them and felt the bandages that swathed his head.

Taking a deep breath, he felt his brow tighten and wrinkle.

He was *very* lucky to be alive.

Then why did he not feel safe?

7

MERCY HOSPITAL. MARCH 15, 1916

Chalmers was going home. An attendant had gotten him ready to leave first thing this morning, and now his nurse, Fetchin' Gretchen as she'd called herself, and whose last name someone had told him was Wellman, had stopped in to say good-bye.

"Thank you. For everything, Nurse Wellman," he said from his gurney in the hallway. "I'll never forget your care and kindness."

"Go home to yur family, Private Chalmers. Whatever your troubles still may be, know that you'll always travel safely with God. I can see His grace and goodwill shine on you."

His hand was pulled from hers when the orderly rolled his bed toward the front door where trucks would take him and other wounded servicemen to the docks. Craning his neck to catch a final glimpse, he saw her smile and then step back, seeming to disappear into the bright sunlight streaming through one of the beveled-glass windows.

SOUTHAMPTON PORT, DOCKING BERTH. LATER

A crewman guided the gurney down Pier 15 and up the inclined ramp to the ship's foredeck. Topside, Chalmers observed other wounded men being moved below to wardroom infirmaries shared with one or more bunkmates. He had his wife's telegram in his pocket, already worn from rereading it, his shaving kit tucked under one arm for good hygiene, and Nurse Gretchen's Bible under the other arm for good luck.

He knew he would need a lot more than that to get back to being the man he'd once been.

"Here you go, Private," said the crewman, rolling Chalmers into a wardroom, "home for the next week." The stout mate muscled Chalmers into his bunk.

"Thanks."

"All part of the friendly service, Yank."

Chalmers gave a weak smile and nodded.

"That's yur roomie, out cold with morphine. You can introduce yur-selves when he comes round," said the crewman, pushing the gurney into the hallway.

Even with a roommate, Chalmers suddenly felt alone. He heard the steam whistle bellow above and felt the twin propellers churn thunderously in the depths as the massive cruise liner inched away from her mooring.

Very glad the coast of England was receding in the distance, Chalmers was determined to go on with his life and put the past behind him.

But though he'd survived Verdun, he had a premonition that more trouble loomed ahead of him. Though he'd never mentioned it to anyone, not even his wife, Chalmers was a bit superstitious. Perhaps even more than a bit.

⮝

He had felt a strong twinge of it this morning when he had seen the name HMHS *Galactic* on the stern of the British-registered troop transport and hospital ship taking him to America. *Galactic* seemed an odd name for a seagoing vessel, he'd thought. It was larger than the war. Larger than the ocean or Earth, even. The ship, much of it painted in a shade of white sel-dom used on such vessels, projected an unseen though to him an unmis-takable aura, and this perceived radiance reminded him somehow of the strange white light he'd seen on the battlefield.

The second twinge of his je ne sais quoi uncertainty came soon after the roommate opened his eyes and slowly focused on Chalmers.

"Hey, there," Chalmers said, relieved to see signs of life from the oppo-site bunk. "I'm Jonathan Chalmers. From New York. I was with the 407th in Verdun." He raised his sling. "Grounded and sent home with a busted wing and some holes in my feathers."

"Nice to meet ya, Chalmers," the young man said with a labored voice. A faint grin tweaked the corner of his dry lips. "Name's Baykur. Pauley Baykur. Legs shot to shit near some sour Kraut village whose name I can't even pronounce."

Chalmers could hardly believe it. Baykur? Pauley Baykur? As pain and guilt for his best friend's death crashed through him, the man in the bed across from him kept talking. "So, we're in this together, huh? I mean the room and everything that goes with it . . . sharing pills, gauze, and a bed-pan. We New Yorkers gotta stick together, ya know."

Chalmers searched for the strength to reply. "Pauley Baykur?"

"Yeah. Whatsa matter there, pal? You look like you've seen a ghost."

"Maybe. After Verdun, I expect to be seeing ghosts for a while . . . maybe forever."

"Got that right," Baykur said.

Chalmers stared openly at the man across from him, amazed at how much he looked like a younger Paul Baker. He'd even suffered the same massive leg injuries as his old friend. He drew a sharp breath and forced himself to deal with this moment.

"Sorry. Guess I'm somewhat distracted. Bad memories, you know."

"Yeah, Johnnie boy, got a few myself. Some of 'em are horrible. I mean, can you believe it, one day I saw two rats chewing on a dead guy."

As strange as it was to have his best friend's doppelgänger in the next bed, it was His Majesty's Hospital Ship HMHS *Galactic* that really had Chalmers playing mind games with himself. The only reason Chalmers knew the real story behind the *Galactic* was that his father was the attorney and financial adviser for the founders of the White Star Line, the shipbuilding firm that produced the Olympic-class vessels *Nomadic, Olympic, Britannic,* and the legendary, ill-fated flagship the RMS *Titanic.*

"Know anything about ships, Baykur?"

"They either float or sink," the guy said in a flat tone but with a smirked grin.

Chalmers snorted a breathy half chuckle. He appreciated the kid's wry comeback.

⌘

Jonathan knew that after the *Titanic* went down in 1912, the White Star Line had purchased the *Theka Pente,* a Greek luxury liner whose design and nautical specifications were similar to the Olympic-class vessels. White Star had refitted the *Theka Pente,* christened after the Greek word for "fifteen," and renamed her HMHS *Galactic.*

And here she was, "the Fifteenth," sailing from Pier 15 on the fifteenth of March. *Beware the ides of March,* his jittery mind warned him.

Maybe he was crazy after his near-death experiences, but the name felt like a bad omen. He knew it was a foolish thought. Chalmers tried to shake it off.

⌘

"Mortar, rifle, or machine gun?" asked Baykur, nodding toward Chalmers's sling.

"Mortars. Only tore up my arm. Same blast chopped off the legs of my best friend. It's just weird. My buddy looked and sounded like you. Even had the same name. He's dead. I don't know what happened to his body.

His passing is probably my worst memory of the war. And I've got a bunch."

"Sorry about your friend. At least you missed the gas, though, huh?"

"No. But it didn't kill me. I don't know why. I'm not really sure what happened to me in no-man's-land. Don't know if I'll ever figure it out."

"What a fuckin' nightmare . . . all of it," said Baykur, as he shifted his weight. He popped another painkiller and took a sip of water. Then he caressed his bandaged legs. "Doctor said they might get gangrene. May have to cut 'em off here on the ship. Hope he's wrong. Hope I don't have to go ashore in a wheelchair—be in it for the rest of my busted life, all because of a damn recruitment poster in Manhattan."

Chalmers winced. "So . . . Uncle Sam's finger beckoned to you, too?"

His roommate grunted. "More like the SOB *gave* me the finger."

"Baykur, you know what the convergence of coincidence is?"

"Nah, and I don't care. Back home I was a plumber. All I know is that without legs I'm shit outta luck now for earning a living." He sighed. "And out of energy. Feelin' kinda . . . dizzy . . ." His head contoured into the pillow.

Chalmers raised his head from his own pillow and glanced toward Baykur.

"Hey, Baykur, about coincidence. What are the odds on two New Yorkers meeting like this?"

Baykur didn't respond. He'd sunk into another morphine stupor.

He hoped Pauley Baykur could sleep in peace. Chalmers doubted *he* could. He wondered if he'd ever escape the nightmares he'd already started to have.

ౠ

The bass pulse of the engines reminded Chalmers of the remarkable sound he'd heard in no-man's-land. He had thought constantly about how badly he'd been wounded there, replayed over and again the bizarre incident with the light, especially the unknown figure that had emerged from the mysterious door.

However he had inexplicably been revived, he was now certain he'd nonetheless departed the living world that day, spending some amount of time somewhere ethereal . . . with someone unearthly.

The more he had analyzed all of this while in the hospital, the more convinced he was that he had seen and learned extraordinary things during his moment of death. He felt that all of it had to do with existence and reality, the past and the future, or God knows what else. But his recollections were as vague as the netherworld he had visited.

He knew there was more to know. "And I want to go back for it," he whispered.

ᴛᴏ

He knew that yogis and spiritualists could summon a meditative state that let them voyage mentally away from their bodies. The feat required a special mind-set that Chalmers had years ago discovered through reading, and research could be *scientifically* cultivated, usually with the assistance of particular rhythms and frequencies of sound.

The mind-set was a self-hypnotic state based not on any tenuous mystical trance, but on an empirical phenomenon called the binaural beat. It was something Chalmers had studied and gained some proficiency with as a student back at Columbia. His father had also used the technique, even coaching his son on the use of mediation to temper the migraines that plagued Chalmers after he had suffered a serious head injury as a youngster.

The binaural beat was a gamma brain-wave state, or a frequency, like a radio station. And it tuned itself in when different sound patterns were heard separately within each ear. Or when simultaneous mental mantras were chanted in opposing lobes of the brain.

The brain, as Chalmers knew, adjusted to the discordance to avoid being distracted by it. This new beat became the gamma-wave compromise between both cranial spheres.

Chalmers had found that the resulting cerebral plateau, the gamma beat, aided concentration and enabled him to absorb vast quantities of information in a very short period of time. He'd used it extensively to study, particularly to read books—which he could digest at the speed required to turn the pages . . . surfaces that Chalmers did not see as being full of *lines* with *words* but covered in *symbols* that flashed with *light*.

The gamma zone also blocked out distractions, something he figured he'd need to get through this ocean voyage. And maybe he could figure out what the heck he was doing here, on this ship, with the image of his dead best friend in the next bed, snoring in a drugged delirium.

He wanted to be in a similar place, to enter a self-induced cerebral space necessary for the deeper contemplation and the problem-solving capacity he required to face his strange life in the present.

Inhaling deeply and slowly, Chalmers closed his eyes and focused on the asynchronous throbbing of the ship's twin screws. The vessel's pulsing sound and vibrating tempo were accompanied by alternating shades of black, gray, and white strobes that flashed inside his head. His body swayed gently, as though rocked by the sea's same hands that cradled the ship's hull . . . but he knew it was not the rippling ocean that moved him.

It was the *Galactic*'s mechanical mantra that had lulled him into the desired realm of gamma consciousness. But this time he sensed it was more than his mind that had assumed an enhanced cerebral plateau.

He was sure his body was somehow also moving in a disjoined direction, into some different compartment of the ship . . . into a new *dimension* within the *Galactic*.

8

Intellectually aware that his physical body was still under the bedsheet—for he could *see* it as he moved upward and away from himself—Chalmers nonetheless was aware he had begun to float down a tubular passage. He moved in what seemed like slow motion and light speed at the same time.

Though there were more questions about how all of this could *really* be happening, he did not want the sensation, whether real or surreal, to stop.

Ahead he saw the end of the tunnel and a round hatch from whose edges radiated a liquid stream of crystalline light. *Like in no-man's-land,* he thought. Now, hovering in front of it, he could tell that the hatch itself was composed of light, and at its center was a swirling motion—a beckoning maelstrom. Chalmers wanted to cross that threshold again, this time while alive, which he damn well hoped he still was at this point. But there was no handle. *How do I get in?*

Ever the analyst, his mind raced with other questions.

If he'd been dead when he entered this door the first time and found life on the other side, would he now as a living, though trance-induced, individual return to the ranks of the dead if he crossed over again?

Curiosity's compulsion overpowered the caution of his fear, and he took an aerial step into the light. His lungs felt the shock of taking in a breath of textured light, and then it was as if his body exploded *into* and merged *with* that unearthly candescence.

He exhaled. His escaping breath turned him inside out, reconstituted his body . . . but in another realm beyond where any of his binaural moments had ever taken him before. The color of his clothing, his hair, and even his skin had turned celestial white. He touched his left forearm. Completely healed, not even a scar. *How can this be?*

He couldn't tell if this was in his imagination or a new reality, or a coma into which he'd permanently lapsed because of a binaural beat gone bad . . . or maybe a profound psychosis, a kind of schizophrenia he feared might grip him because of the emotional trauma he'd sustained in the war.

Accustomed now to the brightness, Chalmers looked as far as he could into the white mist that filled what appeared to be a room containing a dozen shadowy somethings—maybe storage cabinets or sofas or other types of furniture. These whatevers formed a semicircle around an imposing vertical spire perched atop some kind of elevated platform. Maybe it was a stage. The spire, Chalmers assessed from his vantage point, could be crystal or even ice.

He seemed to recognize the setting, even with its unworldly touches. It was as if he were back in academia, though unlike any earthly classroom he'd ever seen. Chalmers glanced at his father's watch. The hands were spinning wildly, then they vanished—followed by the numerals, disappearing one after the other, counterclockwise.

This was truly a *timeless dominion,* as he'd decided to call the place.

He suddenly witnessed a form materializing from an inestimable distance across the room's cloudy ambience. Was this apparition the same thing he had seen before on the German killing field? He'd know soon enough. It was apparently heading toward him, increasing in size as it advanced.

Fear, uncertainty, curiosity, excitement, disbelief—all of it gripped him at once.

The shape floated toward Chalmers, changing into a man, though not exactly a man, but definitely the most exotic-looking individual Chalmers had ever seen.

The approaching entity was tall, almost translucent, and swept through with light, as though he were clothed in it. Though much closer now, the strange being was still blurred by the pearl white mist that enshrouded him. Or that formed him. Nor was Chalmers sure whether *he* should correctly be called *it.*

Despite the entity's appearance, Chalmers felt its tranquillity and was reassured by the profound peace in its deep-set, oblong eyes—which were, Chalmers thought, *heavenly blue.* And those eyes, other than the detached black stool seat floating in air beside him, were the only colors Chalmers saw in this white dreamworld.

The entity was directly in front of, and towered over, Chalmers, who was now certain this was *not* the person, being, alien creature, angel, or whatever

Chalmers thought he had seen in the killing field. Nor was this about death. If anything, Chalmers's intuition said this moment was about learning. He also realized what he believed the individual *did,* and therefore what he *was. This does remind me of a seminar setting,* he thought again, *and this mystery form does have the bearing of a professor, imprimatur, or even a university dean.*

As he tried to think how to address his distinguished visitor, a deep voice reverberated inside Chalmers's head. The entity had no mouth, and hence Chalmers saw no lips moving in concert with the words he heard, so he figured this was telepathic communication—a concept he'd studied but never truly believed could be performed. What he was hearing however, could not have been clearer or more astounding.

ᴋᴀ

~You think this is a classroom, and so it is. It is part of a larger locale called the Tutorium. You have thought this space to be a timeless dominion, and truly it is. I am the Headmaster, and Samaritan students will soon arrive for their lesson. This SUNDE syllabus is for them, and the enlightening moment that follows will be orchestrated by Ga'Lawed. His will must be done, and his expectations are mine to fulfill . . . as are the burdens you shall come to know.~

This Headmaster may not have had a mouth, but Chalmers's entire jaw dropped. And the electrified amperage of his spine shot a million kilowatts through his already goosefleshed skin.

A willowy arm, to which was attached three long, slender fingers, rose from beneath the malleable glass robe covering whatever the Headmaster's body must have looked like. He pointed to the floating stool next to Chalmers.

~Take a position there,~ he intoned inside Chalmers's head. *~You are what I call a Chalmerian. You can speak your mind later. Listen now, for I have much to tell you.~*

9

THE TUTORIUM. TIMELESS DOMINION

Chalmers didn't exactly feel he'd *listened* to anything, though he'd clearly *heard* something about an important individual called Ga'Lawed. Everything had crackled through his brain like an electric arc, and he was confused by much of it.

He believed, however, that in a blink of his own eyes a moment ago Chalmers had *absorbed* the Headmaster's lengthy revelation—to include the fact that this dominion measured time differently than Chalmers. He now knew that in the nanosecond it took for the Headmaster to blink his eyes, millions of years would have passed on Earth.

Chalmers also knew from the instantaneous tutorial—and accepted the otherwise unimaginable facts presented to him—that Earth at present *did not yet exist*. According to the Headmaster, neither Chalmers's home planet nor the universe and galaxy in which it revolved, much less the greater cosmos, could even begin to form until Ga'Lawed initiated an event called SUNDE. The beginning of time?

It had first registered in Chalmers's mind as Sunday, but the Headmaster had clarified his point. Chalmers's math and physics enabled him to comprehend the conceptual sense of what he'd learned thus far from this alien imprimatur, but from a practical, emotional, even spiritual standpoint, he was still stupefied by what was happening—still unsure whether he was in a dreamscape world or a nightmarish insane asylum.

He was certain the Headmaster's telepathic *words* had been a scroll of bizarre symbols îíìîfî⁎⁎δ⌐—⊛—⌐δ⁎⁎Vʌʌʋʋ that Chalmers nonetheless had understood as spoken English. How? He couldn't imagine, but they had confirmed what Chalmers had suspected. He had died on the battlefield and been pulled into another dimension where one of the Samaritans— the Prime one, in fact, as the Headmaster had called him—had restored his life. The restoration was done for a profound reason, and as the Headmaster had explained, Chalmers would spend the rest of his life processing and dealing with this new information, even though he might not remember *what, when, where,* or *why* he had originally come to possess such knowledge.

He already felt uncertain about what he was *supposed* to know right now.

When he read H. G. Wells's *The Time Machine,* Chalmers had been entertained by its science-fiction premise, but to *hear* the Headmaster also explain that Chalmers had been brought to the moment in which time as Chalmers knew it was about *to begin . . . yet again, as another new day of eternity*—well, that was difficult to comprehend, even if all this Tutorium business were really a reality. However, it was more frightening for him to believe the alternative . . . that everything happening simply meant he'd gone crazy.

But he had repeatedly pinched his whitened skin and rubbed his totally healed arm. *By God, this is* not *a dream,* he silently vowed. *I* am here *in this white moment.*

Suddenly, more telepathic symbols flashed, and his cerebral ear translated the new information. *~Again you are right, Chalmerian. Ga'Lawed commanded that you be here.~* Before Chalmers could think of asking specific information about Ga'Lawed, the Headmaster turned away to watch what Chalmers, too, could see in the distant mist—the emergence of more swirling forms.

Must be the Samaritans, Chalmers thought, still unsure exactly what they were. He was suddenly mindful that perhaps this misty realm might be Satan's own habitat, thus making Lucifer the supreme master in this place.

~Both right and wrong this time, Chalmerian. The Samaritans have arrived, but neither they nor this moment bear a satanic nature. Quite the contrary,~ scrolled the Headmaster as he wafted toward the crystal spire surrounded by the semicircle of *whatevers* Chalmers had noticed when he first walked—*transported,* he reassessed—into this place.

Still seated on his floating stool, Chalmers watched the twelve thundercloud forms morph into an array of exotic shapes. Now their incarnations included colors, none of which Chalmers had ever seen back in his real world . . . which he now feared he would never see again.

The Samaritans were beginning to look similar to the Headmaster, though each one was distinctly different. They flowed to the semicircular *whatevers,* which Chalmers now realized were settees, their classroom seats.

At the same time, the Headmaster glided to the crystal spire, which Chalmers, thinking all along he'd been in an academic setting, clearly

recognized as a podium, the most intricately etched glass lectern and
most radiant, beautiful thing he'd ever seen.

~Students, pay attention. We must begin promptly if we are to end at the
beginning of SUNDE.~

Starting up a new day's eternity—SUNDE. Apparently acronyms exist
even in this world, Chalmers thought, recalling what the Headmaster's
mind-burst briefing had revealed earlier. And Chalmers figured something
else was about to happen, perhaps about SUNDE, when he saw the Headmaster look at the Samaritan who'd just occupied the first settee nearest the
podium.

~Won, your position is prime, so you may initiate,~ Chalmers heard the
Headmaster's symbols say.

Chalmers felt an odd sensation. I know this . . . person, this Won. Then
it hit him with the same impact as the mortars and the Devil's Paintbrush
in the killing field. This Won, if that is its name, Chalmers thought, was
the it—the force, the Good Samaritan, or whatever—that had pulled him
into the light.

Chalmers noticed that the first Samaritan glanced at the one in the
next settee, the second in the row of twelve. Chalmers saw a different set
of telepathic, talking symbols speak to him in eavesdrop fashion as the
two Samaritans shared thoughts.

~Tu, my friend, I've got a feeling this is going to be the same old lecture,~
beamed Won to his colleague.

~Could be different this time, Won. Some days they are, you know,~
replied Tu.

~Yes. New destinations, new challenges are always welcomed.~

Chalmers wondered if he should communicate with Won and Tu. But
a second later, he knew that probably wouldn't happen because suddenly
a diamond bell jar materialized over each settee and filled with glistening
pearl mist. Inside, the Samaritans were bathed in blue lightning flashes.
Then, like a choreographed procedure whose movements were rehearsed
many times, Chalmers watched the students place their left hand across
their foreheads and their right hand across their hearts in perfect unison.

He sensed that an important milestone had arrived—time for the
Headmaster to commence the lecture. Excited by what he believed was
coming, Chalmers leaned forward, intent on catching every nuance of the
pending presentation.

In the process, he slipped off the stool.

ᙏ

The Headmaster's symbolized thoughts blurred inside Chalmers's mind, and the telepathic words became sloughed syllables. Chalmers watched his vision of the Tutorium vanish in a blink. He was back in the white cylinder hallway outside the classroom.

Having first come here in war, his last thoughts in this disembodied, binaural-entranced moment were centrifuged from the ghastly memories of war.

He imagined himself as a German artillery round being fired through a long rifled barrel—or perhaps a torpedo in a launch tube.

But he wasn't being fired *out*.

As he already knew—because he'd been told before time ever began—Chalmers and the HMHS *Galactic* were about to be fired *on*.

10

"Feuer eins, Feuer zwei,"—"Fire one, fire two," ordered *Kapitänleutnant* Walther Schwieger, commander of the U-20 Submarine called *Sea Cobra*. The forward compartment torpedo man slammed his palm against two red launch buttons. Schwieger grinned fiendishly as he heard the twin *paah-woossh* that signaled the *Cobra's* propellered fangs had lashed out.

This "U-Boat" was the same steel serpent that had struck the RMS *Lusitania* just over a year ago. A staunch German patriot, Schwieger was proud of his attack on the luxury liner. It had killed almost twelve hundred passengers, including one hundred and twenty-four Americans, and had been one of the factors in President Wilson's decision to declare war on Germany.

Schwieger watched through the *Cobra's* periscope as the torpedo's frothing bubbles tracked toward the *Galactic's* starboard side. He'd spotted the *Galactic's* signature profile of a cruise liner, with four funnels and two masts, as she'd left the English Channel and headed for open water earlier this afternoon.

The *Cobra* had slithered after its prey for the past several hours. Now, with the orange slice of sun slipping below the watery horizon and the ship settling in for a night of blacked-out running, the *Cobra's* strike was seconds away from lighting up the sky with a fiery explosion.

Schwieger checked his watch and mentally counted.

Vier, drei, zwei – Four, three, two . . .

"Chalmers. Chalmers! Wake up—you're having a bad dream. And clam up, you're caterwauling enough to raise the dead."

Chalmers's eyes flared open. His head came up from the pillow. He felt as grayish-white as the sweat-soaked sheet tangled around him. He wasn't quite sure where he was, but he remembered the guy in the next bed.

"Baykur? Oh, sorry. Flashbacks. Or something. Do you need some . . . uh, more what, morphine?"

"Yeah, I can always use a dose. But I think you need one, too, pal. You're delirious."

"No, I'm . . . I was . . . dreaming—well, maybe I *am* delirious."

It had seemed to him that he'd been someplace real only a second ago, and now he shuddered with the prescient fear that in just another second he'd be somewhere else—engulfed in black smoke, then something else even darker.

And in a burst of fire and fury, he was.

Eine – One . . .

The initial blast knocked both men from their bunks and filled the room with thick smoke and acrid fumes. Though he didn't yet know what had triggered the first one, Chalmers felt the massive explosion in the coal-fed boiler, correctly assessing that this secondary jolt had probably split the *Galactic*'s hull.

Seconds later, Chalmers heard a raw rumble of tearing metal and felt a shudder from the ship's core. His room flooded with razor-cold water as the *Galactic* broke in half.

Chalmers may not have known where he'd been earlier in his foggy reverie, but he damn well knew where he was now. He choked on the black smoke and salt water that competed for space in his panicked lungs as cresting water flushed the remaining air from the wardroom ceiling.

Chalmers had to find air *now*, but he wanted to save his bunkmate at the same time. He'd had already lost one Baker and didn't intend to lose this one. Suddenly, he felt Baykur's arms wrap around his waist. He knew the plummeting wreckage would drag him and Baykur to their death in a few seconds if he couldn't find a way out of the room. Kicking for what he hoped was the surface, Chalmers cleared the outer hull just as a cabin section cleaved downward like a guillotine.

He swam upward, bumping into one, then another corpse. Suddenly there were hundreds of them, free falling like mangled ghosts to the depth of their briny graves. They were packed so tightly now that Chalmers had to push them away from him with his right hand while towing Baykur upward with his painfully wounded left arm.

But his pain was overshadowed by fear, panic, and delirium—the three transitional stages he knew preceded unconsciousness . . . then death.

In what he calculated were his last seconds, he saw again what he feared most for himself and certainly for Baykur. Rats. A school of swimming rats, gnawing at the viscera of the torn bodies. How, underwater like this?

In the final second of his life, he reached the surface, purged his burning lungs and refilled them with sweet night air. Then he pulled Baykur to the surface, hoping he, too, was still alive.

"Baykur . . . Baykur!"

"Shaul . . . mers," Baykur gasped, spitting water and sucking in air as his arms flayed about in the frigid night, "help me."

"I've got you now," sputtered Chalmers. With Baykur in tow, Chalmers headed for a floating mattress. He pushed Baykur onto it, then heaved himself up into the night air. Both men hung on for dear life, shivering with cold and praying for the dawn to bring light and a rescue ship.

Lifeboats were lowered, and *Galactic* survivors, as Chalmers could now see, were being picked up, but there were far fewer of them than right after the explosion and sinking. By the time rescue boats were close to them, the mattress supporting Chalmers and Baykur had become totally waterlogged. Even as rescue was in sight, it sank.

Chalmers fought to keep his and Baykur's head above water while the lifeboat crews pulled other passengers to safety. With his scarred lungs, he couldn't shout to be heard over the waves and screams of other survivors.

Chalmers felt a ray of hope when one boat finally spotted him. Its paddles splashed in the waves as oarsmen rowed toward him and Baykur, and then there was another splash when Baykur abruptly pushed away from Chalmers's arms.

He went under but resurfaced a few feet or so away. Baykur's eyes were wide in alarm. His mouth was open in a silent, horrified scream.

"Pauley, what in tha hell are you doing?"

Chalmers used his last ounce of strength to swim to Baykur, whose eyelids surrendered to the moment as he slowly rolled sideways and flipped upside down. Chalmers kicked backward and gasped for the breath that disbelief had just sucked from his lungs. He would've screamed, but revulsion choked his throat.

Baykur's broken legs were gone. A jagged portion of his pelvic bone and some distended bowels were all that remained of his lower body. Chalmers was frozen more by fear than the icy water.

A split second later, another splash occurred as a large gray fin broke the surface. Chalmers watched, terrified, as the spiked mouth of the monstrous shark took the remaining half of its prey. One savage gulp and Pauley Baykur was gone.

The fin circled out, turned, and headed straight for Chalmers, who again started to swim for his life—this time trying to calculate the distance between the advancing fin and the rowing lifeboat.

It was too close to call, and he was too tired to care.

So he just closed his eyes, relaxed, and let the cold dark Atlantic cover his head.

11

Chalmers opened his eyes as he dropped deeper beneath the waves. He saw the water-blurred faces of anxious men in the lifeboat directly above him. Some looked down at him, others pointed toward the distance. One rescuer pushed a long oar down toward Chalmers, and another motioned for him to grab it and be pulled to the surface.

But nothing mattered anymore, so he just let himself drift down toward what he hoped would be a merciful release from life's living hell. Maybe he'd make it back to the Tutorium, suddenly thinking it might be an academic heaven. Perfect place for an intellectual like him.

With that last thought, his rational mind had partially reengaged, and as always he was naturally curious, even to the end, so Chalmers turned his head slowly in the icy water to look for what those above him could see. Through the salty blue veil of his chilled mind he could've sworn he saw a submarine.

A second later he saw what it really was—a great white shark the size of a submarine. Having eaten Baykur in two bites, it was now blood hungry for Chalmers, who again was in the grip of hypoxia and numbed to the approaching slaughter.

He glanced back up at the boat. The dawning sun was bathing his would-be rescuers with heavenly light and had turned their faces and clothing into brilliant white reflections. Chalmers recognized them.

They were Good Samaritans. He wanted to rejoin them in class.

When last he was there, the Headmaster was about to commence the lecture. *I want to hear everything this time,* Chalmers thought. And with a massive effort he reached slowly for the oar handle.

And there he was—pulled up and onto his same black floating stool seat where he again leaned forward to catch every nuance of the Headmaster's presentation.

But instead of the Headmaster's melodious mind-voice, Chalmers heard a very real and raw *ack-ack-ack*. It jolted him backward. When he turned in the lifeboat's hard flat seat, he saw that a submarine had surfaced fifty yards astern, confirming his earlier speculation that the *Galactic* had been torpedoed.

He already had proof that this moment was bad, and it looked like it was about to get even worse.

Schwieger had uncoiled the *Cobra* atop the waves and started to tidy up his loose ends. The captain's methods were cruel and efficient. Chalmers watched as German crewmen, firing deck-mounted 12.7mm Maxim machine guns, systematically ripped through the line of defenseless lifeboats headed back toward their mother ship.

Chalmers tried further to reactivate his sharp analytic mind, sought to make sense of what he witnessed as fiery hail thudded into the dories and hapless men screamed in agony. Shredded wood and severed flesh exploded from what could no longer be thought of as lifeboats. But he was sitting there, still half dazed, when his turn came. He never felt the slugs that hit him, but he saw their effect as puffs of smoke wisped from his body, which he noticed had suddenly become white and spongy.

Perhaps he had slipped through the tunnel's liquid lighted door again. He'd prayed he could. Or perhaps Death had come for him once more, and this time its grip would hold.

He heard a thunderclap and saw flames shoot skyward. Something had just happened to the U-boat, but he wasn't sure what. He tried to concentrate, make further assessments of his circumstance and his physical condition.

But he felt nothing. Not the heat from the fire. Not pain from his wounds. He slumped forward in the rowboat's seat, his body soaked in blood from the man who'd been sitting next to him.

He thought it was strange that he didn't tremble with fear from knowing what had just happened, or, for that matter, that he didn't at least shiver in the dawn's cold mist rising from the sea.

Instead, Chalmers felt something else.

It burned through him like a meteor in the night sky.

12

THE TUTORIUM. TIMELESS DOMINION

He had once more been divorced from his own time and space—returned to this unworldly classroom by virtue of his own will or summoned by higher powers. Had Ga'Lawed, whoever that was, arranged this again?

Vowing this time not to fall from his stool, and seeming as though he'd picked up where he had left off earlier, Chalmers watched the Head-master remove a large pear-shaped Crystal from inside the lectern. The Headmaster held the Crystal aloft, and it began to glow brightly, emitting a deep, pulsing hum. Then he placed it on top of the lectern, whereupon it sank back into the liquid glass podium. As if the podium had been loaded, an even brighter galaxy of lucent rays burst forth.

~*Learn now the syllabus of the Tabula,*~ the Headmaster projected.

Chalmers noticed the Samaritans' bodies twitch slightly. He watched their slender hands, one held over their foreheads, the other over their hearts, assume a crystalline brilliance before bursting into white liquid fire.

So the Crystal was called a Tabula. *And this is the process,* Chalmers thought, *as their minds and hearts, the tabula rasa of their souls, are filled with learning's light.*

Blue lightning arced inside the diamond bell jars. The hum from the Crystal rose to a crescendo, melding with a haunting chorus of alien sound that sent frightening, yet scintillating, shivers through Chalmers's own soul. Even through the electrifying choral cannonade he again heard the Head-master's thoughts.

~*Samaritans, as you do every day, embrace Ga'Lawed's Holy Trinity of language, math, and sentience.*~

Sentience, Chalmers thought. The ability to feel, perceive, be conscious, or have subjective experiences. He wondered if he was lucid enough to know whether he was conscious or comatose. Either way, he continued to listen.

The Headmaster explained that Ga'Lawed, the ultimate thinker and visionary, was a force for both constancy and change. He made all natural and spiritual laws and issued commands. He created and defined the process of evolution as a gradual, layered passage from simple to complex— and then back again, with day and night alternating as cycles of respective eternity.

Good Lord, he thought, *God is not only real—he has a name . . . Savantis Ga'Lawed. Does he also have, a what . . . a house or an office somewhere near the Tutorium? Does he ever make an appearance here as a guest lecturer?* He knew it was all too insane to be true, and he feared he was insane for believing, for taking on faith that what he was seeing and hearing was truly evidence of divinity.

But if everything here *is* real and true, Chalmers thought, it means that *all* knowledge is relearned by the Samaritans each dawn of a new eternal day. What do they do with it? Surely they must eventually leave the Tutorium and, if so, where do they go, how do they get there given the size of Eternity, which is about to do what, start up again with this SUNDE thing? Can they just step through liquid light doors and show up anywhere? His mind was spinning like a galactic dervish, generating countless questions.

Suddenly, the Headmaster looked at Chalmers and cast two small light beams, one from each oblong eye, which focused for a split second as a blue dot in the center of Chalmers's forehead. Jolted slightly from the impact, Chalmers saw only blackness, not the buzzing brightness or the talking symbols as before. And this time he had a massive headache for a few moments, after which he was fine.

Though too early to know their specific facts, Chalmers knew he'd just been infused with another burst of concentrated answers, more potent than the one he'd received previously.

ᚺ

Even as Chalmers's direct data dump occurred, the Headmaster had continued to address his class.

~Ga'Lawed has always known everything. Even so, my Samaritan acolytes, you must understand that he still makes mistakes, and you must never forget the severity of vengeance he imposes on those who violate his goodwill.~

While not an agnostic, Chalmers had never held traditional religious views about God, though he believed there was a supreme order in the cosmos and that only a supreme being could have created it. For Chalmers,

God now had a name and, as he surmised, might have a form, a face, even physically occupy a place like the Headmaster here in the Tutorium.

It was staggering. This newfound spiritual knowledge pierced Chalmers to his core. The purpose of his life, though, as explained by the Headmaster, had been done in elliptical fashion even though Chalmers had asked for specific details. He found himself quaking with the uncertainty of what would happen next . . . to include his life after death.

More than that, he suddenly felt as though he were dripping wet and shaking with cold. Chalmers had more questions to ask, but he felt himself losing connectivity with the Tutorium.

He realized his mind was rewinding into its normal frame.

He felt his body again assailed physically by outside forces.

13

Chalmers heard human voices and felt the ministering hands of others who rubbed him down as they tried to bring warmth into his shaking body. He opened his eyes and saw that the luminescent Tutorium was gone. The Atlantic's icy wetness was back in his body, even if his body, he'd now determined, had been moved to someplace new.

Chalmers blinked, trying to make out the concerned faces of these new strangers who surrounded him. He felt the rough scratch of wool blankets they'd draped over him and realized a cup was pressed to his lips. He struggled against it for a moment, then surrendered to the liquid's intent.

"Drink up! That's a good mate," said the burly Irishman who supported Chalmers's head, ruthlessly pouring tea down his gullet.

Chalmers choked, then swallowed. The hot brew was a welcome relief from the cold water that'd nearly taken him.

Other orderlies moved about the room tending to the rest of the survivors.

"Where . . . am I?" asked a dazed Chalmers, rubbing his eyes to resuscitate his vision and hoping to refocus his mind in the process.

"HMHS *Angelic*. We pulled ye outta the drink early this morning, lad, seconds away from yur being breakfast for the biggest shark I've seen during me thirty years at sea. Then we all had even more drama and tragedy when the Krauts come acalling the second time."

"The submarine . . . lifeboats . . ." He concentrated and made the connections. The memories were slowly coming back to him.

"Yup. That sub torpedoed yur arse off the *Galactic* from below, then tried to finish ya from above when the Kraut bastards surfaced to shoot you like fish in a barrel."

He clutched the stranger's forearm. "How many survivors?"

"Twelve of ya, with you the last, what's all that made it off the *Galactic*. The *Angelic* here was steaming 'bout eight hours behind yur ship. We're headed for New York ourselves, so ye'll be making it home just like scheduled."

"The Germans. They were killing everybody, survivors and rescuers . . ."

"Rest easy on that. The Fritzies ain't on any kind of schedule anymore, neither killing nor traveling."

"What do you mean?"

A broad smile spread across the Irishman's rosy face. "Well, the *Angelic*'s got an eighty-eight-mil cannon topside. Deck crew put a round down that captain's throat and right out his Nazi ass. Sent his U-boot to the bottom, we did."

"Thank you . . . and the gun crew, too. I'm Chalmers. Jonathan Chalmers."

"We got that off your tags, right enough. Want some more tea, lad?"

Chalmers waved the cup away. He wanted information more than anything else. "Can you tell me your name?"

"Paulson. I'm the galley's baker. Just filling in here while we git you new folks dried off and squared away."

A Baker? No, not again. Chalmers felt disbelief at yet another convergence of coincidence. *Will I ever be free?* A red tide of memories swept over him, and he lay there motionless, trapped in the guilt-ridden prison of his mind.

"Mate?" Paulson shook him. "Lad, are you all right? Hope you're not drifting into that same state you were in when we got you outta the water and into the dory."

"What . . . I'm sorry, what?" Chalmers shook off his temporary shutdown. "What was I doing?"

"You were having convulsions and delusions at the same time. Plus you was damn near froze to death. I gotta tell you, what I saw while you was in the dory . . . what happened there . . . it was frothin' unbelievable."

Chalmers swallowed, then tried to put his worries into words. "What was wrong with me? Was I losing it . . . my mind, I mean?"

"Hmm, thought I'd lost mine when I saw you turn snow white at one point, like all the blood and life was sucked out of ya. Even your hair and clothes, they was blanched out. Quite a right shocker for me, I can tell you. And you were making strange sounds, like you were a-talking, only it weren't like no language I'd ever heard afore."

"What did I say?" Chalmers's hand absentmindedly stroked his chest, now covered in a fresh dry shirt someone had slipped on before he'd regained his wits.

"How do I know? It weren't human speech, is all I can tell ya. And then, lad, well, I was seated right behind ya, and I'll never forget what I seen next."

"What? Tell me everything, please."

"When Fritz started choppin' us apart, the bullets somehow missed me. Lucky I was for sure. But the bosun, he's the one what saved you and was sittin' right next to you . . . he was hit several times and killed dead. You was hit, too, but . . ."

"Yes? Go on."

Paulson took a balled-up shirt from the nightstand and unfurled it. "Yours. Leastwise what's left of it."

Chalmers stared at the shredded, blood-splattered fabric, and then his confused eyes searched Paulson's ruddy face.

"You took a ton of lead and was jerkin' like a Saint Vitus dancer. Covered in blood, you was, but turned out it was all from the bosun and the other poor bloke next to ya." He placed the shirt back on the nightstand. "Now here you are. Whole and strong."

Chalmers's face was slack. His eyes begged for an answer.

"Don't ask me how, Mr. Chalmers, but the lead passed plum through yur body. Seen it I did with me own eyes. Then there was this," Paulson said as he handed Chalmers a Bible. "It was floatn' next to you when we snatched you outta the jaws of that seagoing meat grinder."

Chalmers grabbed it and clutched it to his chest. "Thank you, Paulson, for saving it. It's a special gift from a special woman. An angel, I now believe . . . really."

"Lad, you've no idea how special it must be. I reached into the water and grabbed it with me own hand. Can't imagine how it remained next to you in the waves during the night, much less how it kept from sinking."

"That does seem rather remarkable."

"Sir, that ain't even the half of it."

"How so?"

"They do say the Lord works in strange ways. What was strange aboot this Bible were the fact that when it come outta the water it was . . . well, it was *bone dry*."

"Really?" He was aware his heart had begun to beat faster. It seemed that his night of visions and miracles wasn't all the crazed nightmare of a dying man.

He clutched the book more tightly.

"Thank you, Paulson. For everything. And especially for this."

"Yur entirely welcome. Good luck to ye," said Paulson, as he stepped through the bulkhead door and disappeared.

ↄ

Chalmers felt for the Bible at his side and placed it upright on his chest so he could see it clearly. It had opened in the middle. Chalmers read the first line: *Proverbs 1:1—The Beginning of Knowledge.*

"Knowledge," he said softly. It was what he'd been promised by the Headmaster and what he'd received in the Tutorium. He would read this for its knowledge, too, but in the right order.

He flipped to the first page and read the line: *Genesis 1:1—The History of Creation.* His eyes went to the sentence, "And the Spirit of God was hovering over the face of the waters." He slowly closed the book.

It was enough for now. Another crewman had told Chalmers he'd soon be moved to a cabin where he could eat and take a nap. There he'd absorb every word of the Bible, which he knew would only take a few minutes at the rate he could read.

He still wanted to hear the rest of the professor's lecture, but Chalmers had a strange sense that such a divine tutorial would take an eternity to play out.

14

SUNDE—BEGINNING OF TIME

The Headmaster noted when the human, on cue, had again vanished from the Tutorium, and he knew that in his time realm it would take only a sectic, or about one trillionth of an Earth second in Tutorium time, for the Chalmerian to be returned to his previous, proper place.

In that interim, the Headmaster had finished preparing the Samaritans for SUNDE.

He'd reiterated to Won, Tu, Tha-Ree, Vor, Fieva, and the remainder of the twelve emissaries that their assignment was to help ensure that Nobility was instilled in the hearts and minds of the inhabitants in the galaxies, universes, and specific worlds to which the Samaritans were to be assigned today.

~You may assume appropriate forms, interbreed, and spawn a cadre of disciples,~ he informed them, ~and they in turn will assume the shape and souls of the evolving inhabitants where you minister your missions. Use your spawnlings to assist you, but never directly cause accelerated development that otherwise will destabilize normal, evolutionary development in your assigned arena.~

Still standing at the glass podium, the Headmaster released the Crystal Tabula he'd held throughout the lecture, and it floated in front of him. He extended his arms, palms facing toward his Samaritans. The large floating Crystal silently exploded, and a smaller pear-shaped Crystal appeared over each bell jar. An instant later the jars dematerialized in a final flash of blue lightning as the reclined settees tilted up.

Removing their hands from over their foreheads and hearts, each Samaritan grasped a Crystal and pressed it *into* his chest, whereupon their bodies burst into dazzling light and they all vanished—instantly reappearing in a lesser chamber adjacent to the Tutorium where, as the Headmaster had instructed, they assembled in front of a blue door shaped like an oblong eye.

~*The Crystal Tabula embedded within you,*~ the Headmaster reminded them, ~*is a membrane of compressed light that assimilates all sights, all sounds, all that is extant and extemporal in the realm to which you carry it. Trust in the faith of your knowledge that you will know when to relinquish it to the one you select as the noble guardian.*~

Then the Headmaster did something unprecedented—the most dramatic departure from all the previous yesterdays in which he'd begun a new-dawn service for his Ga'Lawed. He had an exclusive, closed mental moment with a single Samaritan.

~*Won, you are Prime, as your rank so indicates. And unique, as this new day for you will prove. I will inform you how different your mission is to be, and how perilous it will be if you consent to the altered undertaking I propose.*~

The Headmaster added that he could not force Won to take such action, but he hoped his Prime Samaritan would consider it since so much was at stake today.

Won nodded as he mentalated his response. ~*Sir, as always I obey Ga'Lawed and perform my service through your direct guidance. His commands, and your presentation of them, are mine to follow.*~

~*As I trusted you would respond,*~ replied the Headmaster.

ﻪ

Trying to remain dispassionate as he listened to his new mission parameters, Won was nonetheless shocked to hear that today would be one in which Ga'Lawed made a mistake—allowing a deserving world, according to the Headmaster, to be destroyed because its own inhabitants failed to establish global harmony through Noble actions. Even more shocking, his Headmaster was suggesting that Won might intervene in that world, though he was not slated by Ga'Lawed to do so.

~*Won, should you agree to this new destination, you will discover the beings that evolve there will think they are alone in the cosmos. But their core instinct will tell them they came from an all-knowing savant they will choose to call God. They will look to the sky in search of Him and some will believe they have found His son, immaculately conceived on the face of their own world. Ga'Lawed so informed me of this earlier.*~

~*That individual,*~ continued the Headmaster, ~*will be revered as the Lord, Ga'Lawed incarnate. His task will be to put his Father's notion of Nobility into the hearts and minds of that world's inhabitants, but he will be only partially successful at first, then fail altogether.*~

Won gently nodded his comprehension.

~An academician in the planet's eventual so-called modern times, whom you will soon encounter, should you agree to go in the new direction I outline, has two different tasks with which I have already imbued him. One is to safeguard the Crystal Tabula you carry and are obliged to relinquish at some point. And the other is to use its power to resurrect a fallen world where Nobility will have its final chance to shine.~

The Headmaster then explained that both he and Won might incur Ga'Lawed's wrath for meddling in an experimental locale that the Headmaster knew Ga'Lawed had reserved for Himself.

~As you tutored, sometimes he makes mistakes,~ Won replied.

~Indeed, and in those instances we serve him best by correcting what we know he will regret later.~ The Headmaster then nodded for Won to make a vital last-sectic decision as the Prime Samaritan joined the others.

෩

~Won, what mission site did you get?~ Tu inquired as his friend materialized.

Won reached into the cloudy mass of his chest and extruded his Crystal. His own blue, oblong eyes lightning-flashed with excitement.

~As I've just decided, I sojourn to a galaxy to be called the Milky Way. I already have a contact there whom I will encounter on a galactic field of battle. It is someone the Headmaster labels a Chalmerian, a human being that is to evolve on a little blue orb that very shortly will be called Earth.~

Not fully understanding, Tu nonetheless was pleased and comforted by Won's serene mental tone, and he wished his friend Ga'Lawed's speed.

On a nodded command from their Headmaster, the Samaritans stepped through the door and into the blinding light and infinite power of Ga'Lawed's self-ignited dawn.

They were instantly swept across an endless cosmos and into their respective venues, where they began another new eternal workday.

15

TIME AND SPACE—FIRST SECTIC

From the gaseous burst of burning light within which he now journeyed, Won discerned a white spiral galaxy forming just ahead. He mind-jotted his observations.

~One accretion disk of compacted energy and matter just started fusing hydrogen, what the Headmaster described as one of Ga'Lawed's cosmic elements. The disk has now ignited into a burning star and has already spun some surrounding nebulae into gravitating planets, one of which just congealed and has turned blue. I am ready to begin my service there.~

He had positioned himself in a locale called High Stasis, a vantage point from which he and other Samaritans at their mission sites could best observe everything in their respective dominions. He noted that time, as it would soon be officially measured on this little blue world, had undergone more than four billion years' worth of geological and biological changes.

~Evolutionary mutations are this planet's unrelenting force of constancy. This world is still mostly hydrogen and oxygen, mixed as a formless sea of blue liquid.

~Single cell organisms now slither from this world's wetness. They enlarge, process information, become sentient, stand erect, and migrate across continental terra firma as anthropoid primates.

~Asteroids continue to decimate the planet's emerging species, even the largest creatures. But new plants and animals rebound almost instantaneously.

~Primates become bipedal, form groups and acculturate. And now they are using bone, wood and stone tools.~

He realized that the last evolutionary development was his signal.

It was time for *Homo sapiens*, as the Headmaster had indicated the first earthlings would be called, to have some guidance, some Noble socialization. Won knew his first good deed for them must be seminal. *~In* *the totality of this world's eventual history, this moment must be the most historic,~* he noted.

He knew exactly what to do.

~The very force of solar inception, its birth by fire, is my inspiration. And so I will give as the first offering to these beings a burning motivation to learn and to grow.~

Won knew that to make his presentation he'd have to leave High Stasis and set foot on Earth, where, as he planned, fire would be not mankind's discovery but its offering.

Won could tell he startled the first beings he approached—not by carrying a burning branch from a natural, lightning-struck flame into a Neanderthal campsite but because he instructed clan members in the use of flint to strike a spark and build their own campfire. He startled more people later by introducing the lever, wheel, a glass magnifying lens, and many other gifts of discovery presented by a goodwill Wonderer who dropped in every several hundred Earth years to visit one civilization after another.

And in less time than it had taken Won to mentally note *fire, wheel,* and the other thoughts, a million years of precivilization and all of modern history—as measured by earthlings—had constructed itself.

ᴊᴀ

And in the same Won moment, Jonathan S. Chalmers had awakened to the ministering hands of the *Angelic* rescuers who had just fished him from the Atlantic's cold clutch of death. Warmed by blankets and tea, he had been taken to a private room.

Alone in his cabin, he looked forward on this special night to reflecting on what he now thought he understood better about the meaning of life, as well as everything else he believed he would soon learn from reading the Good Book given to him as a special gift.

✦16✦

Blinking his eyes back into normal focus, Chalmers closed Nurse Gretchen's Bible, holding it against his chest as he remained stretched out on his bunk. It had taken Chalmers only a few minutes to scan every page, reading and retaining everything he saw—not as printed letters but as strobing light that crackled electrostatically in his brain while locking his eyes into a strange visual trance.

It was the way he had always read.

Even as a youngster, Chalmers had constantly flipped through books in his father's library, digesting huge amounts of information impossible for a normal six-year-old to commit to memory, much less to comprehend. His father had certainly noticed that phenomenon, as well as other of his son's amazing intellectual skills, and he discussed them one day as they walked along the beach near their Long Island home.

"The way you tear through books, my boy," his father had said with pride, "and a moment ago calculated the number of stones in that old lighthouse over there is a result of something called savantism. It's a remarkable gift with which you've been blessed."

"Dad, I don't count numbers, I hear them." He had tried to explain to his father the way he was able to calculate how many of *anything,* even leaves on a tree or gallons of water in a pond, there were simply by looking at something for a few seconds.

"Numbers are like music notes when Momma plays her piano," he'd said. "They spin in circles and make humming sounds inside my head. They always . . . I don't know, they just somehow *tell* me the right answer."

He had started to cry, telling his dad he was afraid he was insane—a fear he'd developed after hearing some of his teachers talk about savantism and autism, words the boy knew described a medical condition of crazy, dysfunctional people.

"Son, autism is a problem some children have . . . but you don't. The word 'savant' simply means a person possessing superior abilities in multiple, often unrelated subjects. Somebody brilliant. A true genius. That's the kind of savant you are."

"Oh. I thought there was something wrong with me."

"No, son, there's something very right with you."

"Will I get smarter as I grow up?"

"Yes, indeed . . . and I believe in my heart it's for a very important reason."

ఆ

Though reassured by his father's words at the time, Chalmers had always been concerned about what he'd later learned as an adult while continuing his research into savant syndrome. Apart from its characteristic compulsive behavior to put everything in an orderly fashion, he had been alarmed to discover savantism was one of the "psychotic spectrum disorder" conditions, which included schizophrenia—a severe mental illness whose symptoms were hearing internal voices, seeing visions, and thinking that other people read your mind, control your thoughts, or plot secret conspiracies.

Chalmers was confident he did not have the more dysfunctional problems associated with autistic savantism, but he knew that factors accounting for the onset of regular savantism were genetic predisposition and accidents or illnesses that damaged the left side of the brain.

Having never forgotten the severe head blow he suffered when he was only four years old, he wondered if that accounted for his advanced intellectual skills . . . as well as the schizophrenia that he feared now afflicted him.

ఆ

Chalmers sat up, placed the Bible on the small shelf next to his bunk, and surveyed all four heavily riveted steel walls in the cabin. He checked out the framed schematic of the ship's below-decks compartments. *Number of rivets in here times number of compartments . . . probably around a hundred thousand,* he calculated almost instantly—*maybe another ninety thousand topside, to include the stacks.*

Chalmers had always craved order, perhaps even more than knowledge, although as he'd become an adult, he realized that order came from knowledge. *Just as cosmic order came from the Tutorium and Ga'Lawed's syllabus of knowledge,* Chalmers reflected, trying to push aside his lingering worries that his mind was draped with a schizophrenic shroud.

Seeking additional comfort, he glanced again at Nurse Gretchen's Bible. "Every page mirrors the Tutorium curriculum," he said softly, "matching the knowledge, order, and divine origins of life." He wanted to believe, had to believe, that there was something divine, perhaps even as a purpose, about his unusual life. Mostly, he was desperate to feel solace in the certainty that he was not crazy.

ᔥ

Chalmers undressed, flipped off the light, and lay back on his bunk. Listening to the deep rumble of the *Angelic*'s engines, he knew he'd never be able to explain his incredible journey to his family—or to *anyone*—and he didn't imagine he'd even try in any event.

What he wanted now, what he hoped and was even prepared to pray for, was that God, whether called Ga'Lawed or any other name, would grant him peaceful dreams instead of his usual nightmares about no-man's-land.

He closed his eyes and counted rivets.

❖ **17** ❖

Chalmers was yanked from his troubled sleep by a thunderous explosion and flash of light. Beyond the riveted bulkhead, a raging squall clapped thunder and, as Chalmers imagined, sought to shatter the *Angelic*'s hull with pounding whitecaps. Lightning bolts made every oval portal, as he could see from inside, wink like an alien eye peering in on powerless passengers.

Earlier, the ship's steward had brought Chalmers some food, clean towels, and a sleeping tablet from the medic. And now, his eyes and mind groggy with desperation's need for continued sleep, Chalmers pulled the covers over his head.

❧

He immediately experienced another lightning flash. This time it was blue arcs of crackling current which, as he could see through the cloud-white sheet surrounding him, had dispersed when the bell jars covering the Tutorium's twelve settees suddenly dematerialized and the Samaritans pulled the floating Crystals into their chests.

Rising from the fourth and fifth settees, Vor and Fieva mentally motioned for Chalmers to join them. When he did, they all instantly dissolved and reintegrated with him in front of an oblong portal—*an eye,* Chalmers thought, beyond which he saw a powerful force. *More of the storm . . .* but one beyond human comprehension.

Chalmers felt himself not tossed, as in the sea's tempestuous storm, but sucked into a maelstrom's nightmare. As he'd been positioned between Vor and Fieva in the Tutorium's ready room for SUNDE's departure, so too was he flanked by them now, spewing forth as instant energy in all directions at once—yet somehow still side by side. *How odd,* Chalmers thought, *the instant creation of time also appears to unfold in a surrealistic, slow-motion fashion.*

❧

Though Vor was not mentalating directly to Chalmers, he nonetheless could tell what was on the Samaritan's mind. *~Familiarity breeds contempt.~* He wasn't sure why, but Chalmers believed Vor intended to carry out an alternative course of action, something violently different from a Samaritan's standard GoodWill mission.

Vor's true essence flowed from the depth of his anger and impatience, sentiments now unmistakable to Chalmers. He watched as Vor's fury erupted like a solar flare, as he became the embodiment of contemptuousness bred from eternal familiarity.

Suddenly SUNDE's moment of creation ended. And as Chalmers calculated—not from his father's watch, whose hands were still missing, but from the fact that Vor mentalated it—another day had begun.

Still not understanding how or why he was here in a place called High Stasis, Chalmers witnessed what Vor also monitored—cosmic forces compacting a gaseous mass, followed by galactic gravity crushing it into a blazing orb. In a Samaritan sectic, Chalmers observed the cauldron of magma cool, crack, and rotate in space as a new planet. And though he couldn't seem to follow him, Chalmers watched Vor descend from High Stasis, taking a position on this new world's highest escarpment.

⮌

Chalmers could hear Vor mind-jotting his thoughts.

~A desolate planet of black obsidian, newly birthed and mine to nurture . . . again. But not by Ga'Lawed's dictate. This time it will be my way and by my hand only.~

Chalmers saw Vor's tentacle arm stretch forward, the long finger of his slender hand pointing to the ground. And he overheard another mentalation.

~In every yesterday I have always touched dead landscape and turned black crust into a pastiche of universal color, watched as the force of life arced from my fingertip and charged the mantle's core with GoodWill and noble purpose. But not today.~

Chalmers noted that Vor's finger had brushed against a jagged shard of obsidian, its razor edge slicing open the Samaritan's celestial skin. The gash unleashed a white nimbus that turned gray, then stormy black, roiling in a wave against the shore. Black droplets cascaded down the steep escarpment, descending to the lowest possible level of this new world.

~The dark solitude of a breeding pool,~ he heard Vor whisper mentally.

In disbelief and horror, Chalmers watched a putrid, undulating glob of what he assessed as infection bubble up from a crevice and slime its way over the obsidian landscape, each sharp encounter slicing away a piece of material, each excised portion in turn self-generating into a new creature of indiscernible though hideous form.

Chalmers saw them immediately as what they were—newborns—and his instinct said they would be hungry and impatient to feed. He could no longer see Vor, but that didn't matter. What did was getting as far away as possible from this terrifying place.

And in the next sectic he was. He didn't know where it was, but he knew he'd been escorted there by Fieva, who, throughout the explosive dawn, Chalmers had seen nearby in the gaseous mist, as though waiting to be alone with him.

Now closer to Fieva, Chalmers could tell his essence was pure and bright. He also shared Fieva's High Stasis view of the eye-blink creation of another world, to include this time the evolutionary appearance of good and noble beings. And again Chalmers was left in High Stasis when Fieva descended to inculcate his new-world charges. But he noted something about Fieva that was at odds with the enjoinder given to all Samaritans about their mission sites. ~Never cause accelerated development that otherwise will interfere with normal evolution.~

Chalmers could see that down below, Fieva was flying like a bat out of influential hell and promoting hastened technology. It made sense when he overheard Fieva mind-jotting elements of a recent back-channel mentalation with the Headmaster.

The Fiverians, as Fieva's planetary inhabitants were called, were threatened by an approaching enemy against whom they were defenseless. The Headmaster had authorized Fieva to intercede in whatever way was necessary to enable the Fiverians to flee their doomed world and colonize elsewhere in the deep reaches of space.

Caught in what he both feared and hoped would forever be the accelerated pace of time in this eternal day, Chalmers continued to watch from High Stasis as space travel technology advanced. Sectics later, an exploratory flotilla was launched. Fieva pulled him aside just as nine white-hot balls of light, propelled by pure ionized energy, streaked through the yellow atmosphere and disappeared into deep space.

~In a blink they will be at the first convoluted portal,~ Fieva informed him, ~and faster than that, Chalmerian, I will be on my way to another assignment.~

Fieva's abrupt departure startled Chalmers, and frightened him since he was now alone in deep space. He had no idea what to do next but hoped he could find his own portal back to the ship on which he wanted to continue his travel.

ta

Chalmers turned and saw something that caught his still half-closed eyes. It was another faintly illuminated oblong eye. *The portal. The way home?*

He reached for it but found he was entangled in a white shroud. Struggling to free himself and stave off the panic he felt building, Chalmers slammed his hand against something hard. Metal. *With a bumpy surface?*

Pulling his hand back, he noticed his father's watch, its hour, minute, and second hands glowing in the dark unknown. Only it wasn't unknown, not anymore, because as he pulled back the sheet under which he'd slept so soundly last night and felt again the stubble of rivets on the bulkhead, he knew he was back in the *Angelic's* safe embrace.

And the faint eye? It was the porthole in his cabin, filled now with a brighter, though very pale blue light. Outside he heard familiar sounds . . . the engines and horns of tugs muscling the HMHS *Angelic* into her New York pier.

His eyes shot to the wristwatch. "The hands," he whispered with an incredulous tone. Back, after all this time. *Unbelievable . . . and yet, maybe not,* he thought.

He noticed the time. Six o'clock. Dawn.

"The start of a new day," he said, swinging his legs onto the floor.

ta

Reaching for his shirt and pants, he detected a putrid smell. *Fishy, polluted water under the pier? Or the stench of something heinous, horrid?* He gasped and recoiled from the sensation of having his arm suddenly clutched by a creature he saw as a black glob of protoplasm hovering in the cabin's dim light. *Vor,* his mind shouted.

He lurched back, took a deep breath . . . and felt his racing heart begin to slow when he realized what had brushed against his arm—a damp, dark-colored towel hanging from a wall hook.

"Oh, Lord," he whispered, then prayed that everything he'd seen during the long stormy night had only been a nightmare, rather than proof of the schizophrenic paranoia he now, more than ever, feared had taken hold of him like a mental demon . . . or a ravenous, alien creature that was coming for him.

Part II

MORNING

18

His seminar finished for the day, the Headmaster had closed down the Tutorium. He knew the Samaritans had been properly dispersed as part of Ga'Lawed's dawning light that had just formed the cosmos, where the rich diversity of life slated to evolve on selected planets today was well under way this morning.

Unprecedented events, however, had occurred in the Headmaster's Tutorium, including his detecting Vor's inexplicable mental attitude of impatience and intransigence.

He had sensed that Vor planned to violate today's routine GoodWill mission . . . to pursue an independent plan harming not only those closest to him—either Tha'Ree or Fieva—but also altering Ga'Lawed's intent for an experimental-life-form world called Earth.

In deciding to intervene against Vor, the Headmaster had further complicated his superior's plan by countermanding Won's preordained mission instead redirecting him to Earth at the last sectic. The Headmaster knew his actions had placed Won and himself in danger of suffering Ga'Lawed's vengeful wrath. He'd also jeopardized Fieva, authorizing him to accelerate the otherwise regulated evolution on the Fiverian world.

As if all that were not bad enough, the Headmaster—knowing Ga'Lawed would send his own divine incarnation to Earth—had manipulated his Prime Samaritan into selecting a natural being, a Chalmerian, to be Earth's Noble champion.

In the process and against all protocols, the Headmaster had dislocated the Chalmerian from his own time, bringing him to the Tutorium where he'd subconsciously conditioned the earthling's binaural mind to play a critical role, along with Won's support, of course, in a galactic conspiracy meant to ensure Earth prevailed long enough for Ga'Lawed's concept of Nobility to take root.

There was one additional thing that weighed heavily on the Headmaster's mind.

As the Prime Samaritan, Won was eligible after today's mission for Ascension, a crucial evolutionary moment slated to occur at a unique place in this particular cosmos.

As the Headmaster knew firsthand, that place was the Iris Portal, the event horizon for what lies beyond the overlapping folds of Eternity.

Not able to recall where he'd come from in his last transition, the Headmaster was nonetheless aware he had journeyed through the portal to get here in order to begin this assignment at the Tutorium.

The Headmaster would not be relocating for a long time, but he knew that very soon, by day's end, Ascension would take Won into the unknown.

19

From his leather chair angled toward the library's stone fireplace, Jonathan Chalmers scanned the great room of his family's home in Oyster Bay. The house was empty. His father, mother, and wife were gone. He was mindful, but not saddened, knowing that it was ten years ago today they had died in an airliner crash.

He was to have been with them on that vacation trip, but couldn't go because of a last-minute meeting of department heads at Columbia University. He had encouraged them to take the trip without him.

His demeanor a model of dispassion and analytical acuity, he noted that the great room's beamed ceiling was reflected in the glass doors of the oak bookcases surrounding him. On the shelves were thousands of leather-bound volumes.

His father, and grandfather before him, had spent hours here reading and reflecting on history, politics, business, and countless other topics. Chalmers had been in here for several hours today, and as he stood up to cross the room he figured he'd gone through more books in that time than either his dad or granddad had managed to read in an average year—and they'd both been voracious readers . . . just not as fast as he was.

Chalmers stopped in front of an ornately framed mirror and studied his face.

He saw more than the reflection of a fifty-year-old man who looked half that age. *Understandable,* he thought, *no longer able to register guilt and sadness after a decade.* But he remembered that he'd not felt what he believed should have been devastating shock on learning of the accident. Nor had there been lengthy sadness in its aftermath.

There had been only an imperative to restore order to his newly changed world.

And he had adjusted very quickly . . . too quickly, it seemed to him.

He figured his unnatural detachment from the tragic loss of his loved ones, and other stoic behavior he'd demonstrated since returning from the war, was a result of the emotional stress he had gone through in no-man's-land, not to mention the incident with the Tutorium. Real or imagined, the revelations he'd experienced there had left him with confused, conflicted notions about his future and a vague, troubled concern about life in America . . . and the world. He knew he possessed certain knowledge about something important and was frustrated that in spite of his best efforts he could not recall it.

It was partially for those reasons, and his own preoccupation with academia, that he'd not warmed all those years ago to his wife's wishes to start a family. Chalmers had been content to share his and Margaret's lives with his parents in the mansion, which was located only a short train ride to Manhattan and the Columbia campus where he had conducted his classes every day since returning from the war.

He had never discussed any of this with anyone, including the psychiatrist who had counseled him for a few sessions about his fear of being schizophrenic. The shrink pronounced him normal, though excessively focused on the acquisition of knowledge.

Chalmers wondered what the shrink would think now, knowing that after that last session he had taken an indefinite leave of absence from Columbia and enrolled in Harvard, where after only one year he'd picked up another PhD, this one in statistical mathematics. He had then leased a small house near Cornell University, in Ithaca, upstate New York, and in record time earned yet another doctorate, this time in philosophical epistemology and astrophysics. Now back at Columbia, he taught only postgraduate courses, leaving him maximum time to continue his own research into binaural existentialism.

❧

Spiritually awakened by his Atlantic crossing after the war, Chalmers had attended church a few times with his wife and mother in the first months of being home. But those services felt pointless in view of what he believed had been his own true encounter with God, or at least his disciples. Hence he remained as religiously nontraditional as before he had enlisted in the army.

After the tragic crash, Chalmers arranged a funeral service largely to provide an opportunity for his parents' and Margaret's friends to express their grief and condolences. He had no faith that a mortal, fallible man of the cloth could provide any spiritual comfort to him.

However, he had material comfort and financial security. As the only child, Chalmers had inherited not only the family's historic home but also his father's entire estate—including stocks, bonds, investment properties, and other assets.

ᛒ

Still standing in front of the mirror, Chalmers touched his face, tilting it side to side to study the texture of his skin as it caught varying angles of light. No wrinkles or blemishes. He really did look, as well as feel, like he was twenty-five. *If I'm aging at all, it's in slow motion.*

"Oscar Wilde," he said softly, whereupon he walked to one of the bookcases and pulled out a rare volume of the author's only published novel. He considered *The Picture of Dorian Gray* to be a classic work of Gothic horror fiction with a strong Faustian theme, and had enjoyed reading it years ago. He scanned through it again in less than a minute.

My God, could I be like Dorian Gray? he wondered, who had sold his soul to remain ageless, but whose youthful portrait that hung in the attic evolved further into a hideous visage every time Dorian committed another of the heinous crimes to which he had become pathologically addicted. He wondered if his unworldly journey to the Tutorium—where he had been pulled back to a period before time had even begun—could somehow account for his otherwise inexplicable appearance.

He looked to his own portrait hanging on the wall, painted when he was still a teenage student, for signs it had turned into a wrinkled, gray-haired fifty-year-old. *No changes . . . unless those cracks in the oil canvas near my eyes are really crow's feet. My eyes . . . did one of them just wink at me?*

Still holding the novel, he noticed its publication date—1890, the year he was born. *A convergence of coincidence?* He thought of mentally computing the odds that there was any conceivable relevance among the date, the book, and the otherwise preposterous notion that he was *not* aging.

There was no empirical evidence for making such a calculation, so he immediately sought to distance himself, as he always did, from the latent forces of schizophrenia and paranoia when he felt them team up in his mind.

At the same time, he figured that if this slow or nonaging trend continued, he would eventually have to account for why he looked so young when everyone who knew him was obviously getting older.

A bridge to be crossed only when and if it must, he thought as he closed the library's massive carved doors behind him. But as he proceeded down the hall, he knew it was difficult to close certain partitions.

And Chalmers knew it was impossible to walk away from the other black secret . . . the symbolized voices in his head that told him evil lurked behind *all* of his doors.

⟡20⟡

Chalmers had given up on the graduate faculty lounge, where debate about recent passage of the Lend-Lease Act among professors had caused more of a stir than suited him. Tossing his folded newspaper on the couch, he walked briskly to the door.

"Congress has given Roosevelt the authority to sell, transfer, or lease war goods to the government of any Allied country," Chalmers said as he stood with his hand on the doorknob while continuing to face his seated colleagues, all of whom had either steaming coffee cups or smoldering pipes in their hands. "It's a waste of time to discuss America's neutrality policy, gentlemen. We don't have one anymore . . . nor should we."

Stepping through the opened door, he turned again toward them. "Check the *Times* article. Brits sank the *Bismarck* two days ago. Germany and Japan are only going to increase aggression throughout Europe and the Pacific. Mark my words. Nine months from now we'll be in the middle of the Second World War."

He closed the door and headed down the hall toward the privacy of his office where the clarity of his own thoughts would not be blurred by the hazy logic of others.

For months, Dr. Jonathan S. Chalmers had thought about the Volterra theory and Malthusian doctrine, combining them in a new analytic paradigm that he believed better addressed the complex political, economic, and military issues that threatened world stability.

As he had recently lectured his students, "An Italian mathematician and physicist named Vito Volterra created a nonlinear, differential equation to describe the fluctuating balance of prey and predator populations." Noting some blank stares, Chalmers had added, "For math students not also versed in anthropology, that means Volterra turned Darwin's survival of the fittest into a graphed matrix. Which means that when the prey increases, so do the predators, and the predator population continues to expand until the quarry itself diminishes. Conversely, when the predators starve away, their food source begins to increase."

One of his students raised a hand.

"Yes."

"I guess it would follow, then, Dr. Chalmers, that these two populations always fluctuate out of phase with each other, because reproduction cycles mean that one group continues to flourish even as the other subsides."

"Yes. Excellent. And the notion is conceptually compatible with Thomas R. Malthus, an eighteenth-century British political economist who theorized that mankind will eventually outstrip man's ability to supply the necessities of life, thus causing his own downfall."

Chalmers further explained that with more predators entering a worldwide war, and with the disruptive nature of conflict knocking the prey's production of goods and services out of balance, the only logical conclusion to draw was that the world could easily destroy itself in a short period of time.

What Chalmers did not share with his students was his belief that planetary destruction in a more total sense would result from such galactic forces as meteor strikes or even, as his Tutorium-influenced mind allowed him to envision, predatory alien forces for which Earth would serve as a breadbasket should they ever invade.

Chalmers had other notions—in fact, a compulsion, he realized—that he'd chosen to avoid discussing with anyone, and they involved building not just bunkers to store war matériel or shelters for protecting groups of people, but also designing a much larger safe haven—a self-sustaining production center into which entire cities, perhaps even a nation, could be sequestered while waiting for a predatory force to exhaust itself.

He was already writing a paper on the subject—"The Chalmerian Gambit: Hibernatory Defense Tactics." He wasn't thinking about publishing it as a book, because somewhere in the back of his worried mind about a second world war soon to hit full stride, and a third one that he calculated would follow it, he imagined he'd simply disseminate his report to the government or military officials in need of a long-term self-defense primer.

In the short term, he had an appointment with Dr. Steadman, a neurologist at New York's finest diagnostic hospital. Chalmers felt it was time to find out what besides machine gun thoughts were firing in his brain and causing severe migraine headaches.

‍‌‍⁌

A few weeks later, he had a pile of medical reports spread across his office desk.

One of the tests had revealed a significant anomaly with Chalmers's corpus callosum, the band of tissue that connects the left and right cerebral hemispheres and permits normal concept functionality in a healthy brain.

"This X-ray," Steadman had said to Chalmers recently, "indicates that your corpus callosum is dangerously enlarged and discolored, which I initially thought was due to residual bleeding from your concussion. Falling from a balcony and landing headfirst on a stone patio . . . hell of an accident for a four-year-old, John. Amazing you didn't fracture your skull. Probably should have ended your life, or at least dramatically altered it."

Maybe it did . . . in unimaginable ways, Chalmers thought.

"Yes," he said. "I remember going over the rail but not the crash landing. Cried with a headache for several days, though. The family internist told my parents it was a miracle I'd survived at all but that I'd be fine after some rest."

"He was correct. I've subsequently determined the connective tissue between your cerebral hemispheres is four times denser than the average person's. That's why it looks like this on the X-ray."

"And that's bad?"

"No, I don't think so, but it probably accounts for how your brain processes information and why you're so damn smart."

As for the headaches, Steadman said they might stem merely from Chalmers's brain being tired from the nonstop academic stress he'd been under while researching, writing, and defending two additional PhD dissertations the past few years. He'd given Chalmers pain medication and advised him to slow down his academic pace.

‍‌‍⁌

After again reviewing and personally researching his own medical files, Chalmers tossed the reports and pill bottles into the trash. He prescribed his own treatment.

Leaning back in his chair, Chalmers concentrated on inducing a binaural mind-set. He'd used it only sparingly since the Atlantic crossing, and never again to attempt to return to the Tutorium. He didn't believe that was possible now in any event.

He figured he'd need only a few thoughtful minutes to knock out something as simple as a benign migraine.

21

Chalmers raced up the steps and into the student center, where rows of chairs, most of them already occupied by professors and students, faced a twelve-inch viewing screen protruding bug-eyed fashion from what appeared to be a strange version of a family room radio.

"Ah, Dr. Chalmers," a man said, motioning to the empty seat next to his.

"Dr. Mackelton," replied Chalmers, nodding his head as he sat down. "Glad to see the history department's well represented for this event."

"And I'm pleased to see someone is here from physics. You think this contraption will actually work, John?"

There were only a few hundred television sets in the state of New York and fewer than seven thousand in the entire country. Here, on a first-come-first-seated basis, everyone was drawn as much to the novelty of the machine as for the dramatic content of the planned broadcast. With the now-packed audience anxious for the program to begin, Chalmers provided his colleague with a quick history lesson—presented in his usual pedantic way.

"Mack, your contraption is a model TRK-12 televiewer, or television as it's called by some. The Radio Corporation of America invented it. And another group, the National Broadcasting Company, or NBC for short, televised a news program on RCA's televiewer that was on display in the World of Tomorrow theme pavilion at the '39 World's Fair. Last year NBC conducted the first official network television broadcast on New York's WNBC station." He was satisfied he'd covered the subject.

Before Mackelton could even think *how* to respond, another individual standing in front of the audience—who'd just checked his watch—cleared his throat loudly and said, "Uh, may I have your attention please . . . it's time."

The room fell silent. The test pattern screen blipped twice and was replaced with the WNBC Channel 1 logo, a microphone surrounded by transmission lightning bolts. Then came the distinctive accompanying sound *bing-bong-bing*—the three-tone chime long used on NBC radio shows.

The screen stage was set and everyone leaned forward. A man's face appeared.

↩

"Good evening, everybody," said the familiar voice of Lowell Thomas. A world-renowned traveler, author, and radio broadcaster, Thomas was now the host of NBC's *Esso Television Reporter* news program.

"We have some new details, some terrible facts, and unprecedented motion pictures about the December seventh sneak attack on Pearl Harbor. As you see here, Japanese torpedo planes and light bombers damaged or destroyed twelve U.S. warships, including the USS *Arizona,* destroyed one hundred eighty-eight aircraft, and killed two thousand four hundred and three American servicemen and sixty-eight civilians."

The pictures were grainy, but the visual impact was clear and powerful. Audience viewers stared at the screen with horror and disbelief as burned bodies floated in the flaming, oil-slicked water, and black smoke billowed from the shredded metal of once invincible warships.

Watching footage of wounded servicemen being carried on litters, Mackelton's lips moved in silent prayer that they would survive long enough to reach infirmaries. With memories of no-man's-land on display in his mind even as he watched another war's ghastly imagery on the screen, Chalmers's mouth was a tight line of stoic resolve, for he believed no amount of prayer would change the inevitable—that the final death toll would continue to rise in the coming days . . . and the coming wars of the future.

↩

"Hours after the raid on Pearl Harbor," Thomas continued, "Japanese bombers destroyed most of the American air force stationed at Clark Field in the Philippines, and Japanese ground forces stormed ashore in Malaya. Caught unprepared and now considerably weakened, America has been abruptly brought into the Second World War. Our nation and its citizens face grave and perilous times. We will bring you more information as it becomes available. May God protect us."

And then Lowell Thomas closed with his standard refrain: "So long until tomorrow." The WNBC logo reappeared followed by the *bing-bong-bing* chime.

"Heaven help us, John," said a distraught Mackelton. "It's worse even than the newspaper and radio reports. You were right about neutrality. It'll be war now for sure. What do you think will happen next?"

Chalmers paused, looking at his colleague and through him at the same time.

"Yes, war for sure," he almost whispered. "For now . . . and forever, I'm afraid."

⊱

A fast, avid reader of books on every topic imaginable, especially world history and anything having to do with the U.S. military, Chalmers was disturbed by his knowledge that the army had steadily shrunk in size and strength since the end of World War I, which he recalled with irony had been billed at the time as "the war to end all wars." For him, the conflict's even more preposterous title was "the Great War." While he was aware that many took for granted that the Treaty of Versailles between the Allies and Germany had restored world peace in 1919, Chalmers believed the world had only become more complex since then, with new political events generating pressures for new regional wars, which of course he was convinced inevitably would lead to a new global war.

Chalmers believed nations were caught in the dilemma of repeating history's mistakes because of mankind's failure to heed history's lessons.

And just now, watching the NBC news program on Pearl Harbor, his fears about a world trapped in the whipsaw forces of the Volterra theory and Malthusian doctrine hammered home his concern that his homeland was once again in jeopardy—as any prey is to all predators.

Even though he knew that U.S. military capabilities had been undergoing a revitalization for the past few years, even as the nation maintained a policy of neutrality, Chalmers had been concerned that the pace and extent of war-fighting upgrades were inadequate given America's probable support of Great Britain's ongoing battle with Germany. He had been somewhat encouraged last year when President Roosevelt signed into law the first peacetime selective service draft in U.S. history.

In Chalmers's mind it was academic, even irrelevant, whether it was Germany or, just now, Japan's aggression that had forcefully shoved America into war.

All that mattered to him was that a second world war was under way.

⊱

Though at fifty-one he was well beyond the draft age, Chalmers nonetheless lined up the next day in the campus gymnasium with Columbia students complying with mandatory registration for military conscription. Based on his youthful appearance, the draft board officials didn't hesitate for a moment to believe Chalmers when he told them he was born in 1916, and that he was twenty-five years old.

The next day, after Chalmers had time to alter the 1890 date on his birth certificate and other documents he thought he'd need to pass chronological muster, he enlisted at the army recruitment center in Manhattan— where he'd seen the original *Uncle Sam Wants You* poster that had landed him in no-man's-land a quarter century ago.

"I'm volunteering for an infantry billet," he told the sergeant behind the desk. "Pacific or European theaters, I don't care."

The burly, seasoned sergeant took a casual glance at Chalmers's documents, including his latest Cornell, but *not* the far earlier, Columbia school records.

"See you got a lot of education, mister. Want to put in for an officer rank?"

Chalmers shook his head.

The sergeant shrugged with indifference and handed him a pen.

22

General William "Wild Bill" Donovan sat in the Oval Office anteroom. He had an eleven o'clock appointment with President Roosevelt, and it was always best to be early for a session with the commander in chief. Especially when the country was at war.

"General Donovan," said the receptionist, "you may go in now, sir."

Donovan nodded, put down the newspaper he'd been reading, and stepped into the most powerful office in the world. Given the surroundings and the company, he kept his posture ramrod straight as he walked to the desk and snapped a smart salute.

"Good morning, Mr. President."

"Good morning, General. Take a seat." Roosevelt nodded toward a leather armchair. He rolled his wheelchair around to be closer to Donovan.

"Bill, I wish the circumstances for your visit were better. I'd relish the luxury of time to reminisce about our days together at Columbia, but . . . frankly, what I have to tell you this morning is difficult and unpleasant."

Donovan remained at attention, even though seated.

"One of the smartest things I did the past couple of years while this goddamned war's been looming on the horizon was to send you all over Europe as my 'information-gathering' emissary."

"And I deeply appreciate your confidence, sir, in naming me as your COI."

"It was a bold-ass move, for sure. Not everyone in town was keen on my decision to create a national coordinator of information . . . much less to make you the first overall chief of United States Intelligence."

"Yes, sir, I can—"

"Too bad all the crap you call intelligence gathered by the army, navy, FBI, State Department, and every other spook shop didn't spare Pearl Harbor from that disastrous sneak attack."

"Mr. President, if that's what you've called me in to discuss, I can only say—"

"Holster it, General. I summoned you here for another reason, to tell you something in person."

Roosevelt rolled his chair back behind his desk.

"General Donovan, you've been relieved of your COI command, but you're not relieved of duty. I've read your comprehensive memo on creating a . . . what did you call it? The OSS—a Strategic Services outfit meant to operate behind enemy lines?"

"Yes, sir. Espionage, propaganda, subversion, counterintelligence, and selected covert paramilitary activities designed to break the Axis fighting spirit and its back—all under one civilian agency reporting directly to you, sir . . . providing *you* . . . the Oval Office, with a deniability option that falls in the gray area between diplomacy and official U.S. military action."

The president had removed his glasses to clean the lenses. He perched them back on his nose and studied the general.

"Even the idea of such an organization would make the pinstripes at State and the War Department brass roar like caged lions being castrated."

"Yes, sir, I know."

"Fine. I'm naming you OSS director. I mean, you are unemployed now, after all," ended Roosevelt with a wink.

Donovan's disbelief prevented him from speaking.

"No more days of infamy, General. Remember, war does not determine who is right, only who is left when the shooting's over."

Donovan nodded, his square jaw locked in firm agreement.

The president picked up some papers and casually waved toward the door.

"Now get outta here, Bill, and make the OSS into whatever you choose. Try for something that will make Europe envious . . . and the Japs and Krauts shit their pants."

23

The bugler's raspy, annoying notes sounded reveille, and Chalmers's eyes saluted the wake-up call. Wincing as his blistered feet hit the hard floor, he somehow made his aching toes wiggle into his stinking boots, and he felt his bruise-battered body stumble into the faint dawn's light for another exhausting day.

He joined "Hud" Huddleston, a fellow New Yorker he'd met on the train ride down to this boot camp, and the other haggard infantry grunts in the mess line.

"Ah, more sumptuous GI cuisine," said Chalmers, surveying the long table.

"Yeah. Tin canteen of blistering coffee, a scoop of cold, runny scrambled eggs, and my favorite . . . lukewarm SOS."

Chalmers managed a smile. He actually liked SOS, the chipped beef on toast, whose more popular GI moniker was shit on a shingle.

"Hey, Chalmers," said Huddleston, "trade you my eggs for your coffee."

"How 'bout I trade you my entire breakfast for a plane ticket outta here."

"Break up and break out. PT field on the double," bellowed the sergeant.

Everyone ran to the parade ground for physical training. The dreaded early morning calisthenics jump-started the day, literally, for every other grueling activity that followed. And the days had become weeks—six, in fact, which Chalmers found hard to believe.

ᛣ

Obstacle course, calisthenics, hand combat, bayonet drills, and endless platoon tactics had turned Chalmers into a hardened, combat-ready solider— as similar training had done twenty-five years ago when he'd prepared for Verdun's trenches. Amazed by how well he had been holding up, he could only assume that the pre-time transportation to the Tutorium somehow accounted for his strength and endurance at this age. Even so, tonight's drill would be a challenge.

୨

It was hot and drizzling. Covered in mud and mosquitoes, Chalmers belly-crawled under a tangled grid of barbed wire. While he was concerned about keeping his rifle dry and clean, Chalmers was more worried about the live tracer rounds from a .50-cal. machine gun painting red lines of death barely twelve inches above his head.

He'd already been shot in the head during the first Great War and preferred that it not happen again, especially here in training.

He made it through the course and was slogging his way back to camp with the other recruits when he heard a jeep pull alongside. He turned and squinted at the DI master sergeant who shined a flashlight in his face.

"Private Chalmers, that you?"

"Yes, Sergeant."

"Then get in," ordered the drill instructor brusquely, "and don't say a word to anybody." He gunned the jeep, its wheels spinning for a moment in the muddy roadbed until they made traction. Chalmers sensed urgency as the DI steered past the marching column.

"Yo, John," said Huddleston as he saw Chalmers go by, "youse gotta chauffeur now, you lousy Lawn Guyland rich prick." He flashed a toothy white grin and snapped a middle-finger salute. Chalmers knew he would be in the barracks long before Hud and the rest of the hapless privates would waddle in for the night.

Why did I get picked up? He answered his own question. *Who cares? Maybe I'll get a few extra minutes of sleep tonight.*

୨

Back in camp, the muddy jeep slid to a stop and the DI motioned for Chalmers to get out. "Get cleaned up. Packed up," he said. "Everything in one duffel bag and be back in this jeep in five minutes, solider."

Chalmers had learned a great deal in the weeks here, in particular that it never paid to question an order from a drill instructor. So, five minutes later he was back. *But for what?* he wondered, as the DI drove off again into the darkness.

୨

After a short, rough ride, Chalmers heard a pulsing sound traveling through the ground fog of the Mississippi bayou night. The DI switched off the lights and continued on. *What in the hell is this all about?*

The dull pulsing sound grew in intensity and conjured thoughts from a long time ago. Chalmers saw dim lights in the distance and he felt that now the jeep was on a much smoother surface. *That's the sound of an engine. A plane engine.* "Sarge, are we on a landing strip?"

The sergeant didn't respond.

Chalmers could now see that it *was* a plane, a Douglas C-47 Skytrain.

The jeep stopped between the port wing and rear stabilizer, directly in front of the open door and extended foldout steps.

"C'mon, Sarge, what gives . . . ?"

"I don't know who you are, Private, and I don't wanna know. Just get outta this donkey, get in that buzzard's belly, and don't say nuthin' to nobody. Got it?"

Chalmers nodded, slid out of the seat, and grabbed his gear as the jeep turned sharply and accelerated into the darkness. In the same moment, the prop blast increased and the plane had begun to taxi even as Chalmers mounted the steps.

Thinking *Why the rush?* and with no idea where or why he was going, he stepped through the hatch. A uniformed solider, barely visible in the dim light, retracted the steps and closed the door. He turned to face Chalmers, who saw the glint of a silver eagle on his collar. He was a full bird colonel, and Chalmers snapped an immediate salute.

"Sir. Private Jonathan S. Chalmers . . . reporting for . . . for duty, sir?"

"Sit down and buckle in, trooper. Try to grab a few winks. Somebody wants to see you first thing in the morning."

24

WASHINGTON, D.C. JUNE 13, 1942

Chalmers was so tired he slept through the Skytrain's buffeting four-hour flight. His chin bounced off his chest when the wheels double-thumped onto the runway at Bolling Field. As the plane taxied, Chalmers noted that a river paralleled the tarmac strip.

"Ummm, where are we?" he asked, yawning and only half awake as he heard the engines throttle down and saw the colonel approach him from the cockpit.

"Sorry, sir, I mean good morning. May I ask where we are . . . sir?"

"We're *here*, Private. There's a car and driver waiting for you." He returned to the flight deck. Obviously dismissed, Chalmers grabbed his bag, exited the C-47, and immediately crawled into the backseat of the black Lincoln Zephyr.

An army corporal was at the wheel. *Top-brass travel accommodations. Why me? And where am I?* Chalmers wondered as the Zephyr sped through the pale dawn light. He noted he was still alongside the river and seemed to be in a city—*somewhere.*

When the corporal veered away from the river and onto a broader street, Chalmers saw military vehicles and a mix of civilian and armed forces personnel on the sidewalks. A moment later he passed classic architectural buildings. He recognized them at once. The nation's capital, which was very busy this morning coordinating America's rapid mobilization into the Second World War.

"I'll be damned. That was the Potomac. And this is Washington," he muttered aloud. It was a long way from boot camp. He knew nobody in the Washington hierarchy, so he again wondered why everyone was in such a big-ass hurry to get him here. What was waiting for him at the end of this unlikely journey? Whatever the outcome might be, daybreak's soft glow signaled to Chalmers that at least *this* day had begun.

≈

"This is it," said the corporal, braking to a stop. "Go through the main door, straight to the duty desk. Give them your name. They're expecting you."

Chalmers exited the car, leaned down toward the driver's open window. "Thanks . . . I guess. Incidentally, where exactly am I? What's the name of this building?"

"You're *here*," replied the corporal as he drove off.

"Here," as Chalmers saw on the sign, was 2430 E Street NW. It was an imposing granite edifice, one of several that he was about to learn formed a special area called the E Street complex located a few blocks from the White House. Even though it was Saturday, Chalmers knew in these busy times it was just another typical workday, as evidenced by the hustle and bustle around this place.

≈

"Follow me and keep your eyes straight ahead," said the orderly assigned to escort Chalmers, who was marched down a long corridor and into an outer office.

"You may go in, Private," said the orderly as he opened the inner door.

Stepping across the threshold and coming face-to-face with what he immediately sensed was a turning point in his future, Chalmers saw General William J. Donovan.

The general pointed to a chair. "Take a seat, Private. We've much to discuss."

"Yes, sir, General," said Chalmers, feeling uncharacteristically awkward in the general's presence.

Donovan rose and sat on the corner of his ornate oak desk. He picked up a pencil, studied it for a moment, then looked into Chalmers's eyes.

"Chalmers, I know you . . . remember you. Columbia University, class of oh seven, I believe. I was in my first year of law school, and you were around eighteen or so . . . the youngest and smartest PhD candidate in the school's history, I recall."

"Correct, sir. And Franklin Roosevelt was one of your classmates, *I* recall."

"Chalmers, I knew your father and subsequently learned that after completing your dissertation in record time and becoming head of the math department you volunteered for duty in War One. Good Lord, man, you even beat me over there and got more shot up than I did."

Chalmers was worried that his age deception at enlistment had caught up with him and he was in serious trouble. He simply nodded.

"Sorry about what happened after you returned . . . your family trag-edy, the plane crash and all."

Chalmers nodded again.

"Seems like in the ensuing years you've picked up, what . . . two or three additional doctorate degrees, *and* you've enlisted in the army again—as a private?"

"That, too, is correct, sir."

His brow wrinkled with perplexity, Donovan stood and returned to his desk chair.

"Chalmers, I can understand that at age fifty-one you've got enough gumption to lie about it because you want to fight for your country . . . but I'll be damned if I can comprehend how you manage to look like the twenty-five years you claim to be."

"It's a long, complicated story, sir."

"And so is how I know about you and why I sent for you."

"How much trouble am I in for lying to the draft board?"

Donovan chuckled. "It will be our secret, Jonathan . . . one of many. The first one is that America has a new, powerful spy outfit called the Office of Strategic Services or OSS, which the president signs into effect today. I'm in charge of it, and the first thing I'll do is create a second organization within the OSS—the Office of Strategic Assessments. OSA will be this country's first national think tank, a place where wild ideas become cutting-edge actions."

Chalmers nodded. "Sounds like Sun Tzu. He wrote that strategy with-out tactics is the slowest route to victory. Tactics without strategy is the noise before defeat."

"Jonathan, I need you. I need every bit of superior brain power I can round up. I won't cut you any more slack for being a former classmate than Roosevelt cuts me. You're going to work harder for me and make more of a contribution in winning this goddamned war than you'll ever imagine. Even if you're not in the trenches this time."

"I always give it my best, sir."

"And you will start by taking the train to your beautiful home in Oys-ter Bay. Breathe some Long Island Sound air and pick up whatever you need to set up quarters in a brownstone we have for you near here. I want you back in exactly seven days."

"Yes, sir. I can handle that."

"But there'll be a couple of other new adjustments you will have to deal with."

"Sir?"

"While you're back *vacationing* in your mansion, you'll be visited by a member of a special group. It's called the Committee. I belong to it, and so do some prominent men you already know, or will soon enough. You'll recognize your visitor immediately. Not everything he says will make sense to you, any more than it makes sense to us, but pay attention to what he tells you . . . especially the part about strict compartmentation and something call the K-RED. You and I will talk more about this in the future."

Chalmers nodded. "You said a *couple* of adjustments."

"Yes. A week from now you will be Major Chalmers, and the new chief analyst for the OSA."

The Committee talk had intrigued Chalmers. The promotion stunned him.

"And Jonathan, you're starting more than a new future for yourself. You'll be safeguarding that of your nation."

25

Senior officers from the War Department were assembled in a high-ceilinged conference room. They had been summoned here by General Donovan, seated at the head of a large conference table, to hear a special briefing.

Looking like the Headmaster he'd been at his graduate physics classes at both Columbia and Cornell, Major *and* Dr. Chalmers stood behind an oak podium adjacent to his boss. Wild Bill Donovan nodded to Chalmers. Time to begin.

"Sir, I have a theoretical model of what will have happened in the Pacific five months from now, the first anniversary of Pearl Harbor. Based on what I'll call for now causative extrapolation, I can show you the various Axis geopolitical and military events affecting American strategic force-planning in Europe, as well."

"This is a projection the major has worked out over several weeks of intense analysis," Donovan told the others.

"Yes, sir. Together with staged-entry, U.S. industrial capability, and Allied participation," Chalmers continued, "and, of course, allowing for constant course corrections along the way, this is how the war will play out in both theaters."

Chalmers pulled on a white cord. Cloth tarps hanging like blank tapestries on all four of the large walls of the briefing room suddenly fell free. Uncovered, the chalkboard walls revealed a strange artistic graph involving numbers, letters, and peculiar symbols. It was visually stunning.

Heads turned in all directions, syncopated with a chorus of murmurs.

"This is a Cartesian, hybrid architecture that analytically links the Malthusian doctrine and Volterra theory, and it graphs out America's mathematically calculated odds for producing the logistic means to sustain ourselves while surviving as Allied prey against the Axis predators."

"And for those of us, Major, who aren't math savants or philosophical theorists?" asked Donovan. "Can you put it into simple English?"

"Yes, sir. The chart shows how our logistical planning will proceed in accordance with the degree to which industrial output of war matériel will increase each quarter of the calendar year."

"You mean as new production plants come on line," said Donovan.

"And as workers gain experience, increasing output through faster skills," said another general.

"Exactly, sirs," replied Chalmers. "And this time line," he continued, pointing to a massive chart, "addresses specific battlefield engagements and the extent of our projected losses in both theaters. Within the risk-versus-gain parameters, there is a high likelihood for our ultimate victory. Indeed, I believe this model's predictive efficacy speaks for itself."

Donovan and a few others nodded as if they agreed.

Most everyone else, however, looked at Chalmers like he was crazy.

"Major Chalmers," said General Edwards, one of the non-nodders, "let me get this straight. You've looked at our entire war plan over a several-week period and abruptly scrabbled together this . . . this, what do you call it, a . . ."

"A Jacobian matrix, sir. When everyone stands up from the table, I will connect the various charts on the four walls with strings crisscrossing the room. That will give three-dimensionality to the quantum physics formulas."

"Strings?" Edwards said emphatically. He cut Chalmers out of his line of sight as abruptly as if he'd used a knife and turned all his attention on Donavan. "General, with all due respect, I'm sure your Major Chalmers here is a brilliant man, but all I see on these walls is scribbling that looks like Chinese ideographs and Egyptian hieroglyphics. Only less legible. Which, since I can't read either language, is saying something. What the hell am I supposed to do with this kind of information?"

"General," replied Donovan, "*my* major, Dr. Chalmers, is undoubtedly the only person in this room, indeed in the War Department and the entire U.S. government, who fully understands this. But I believe in him. And his scribbles. And his astounding organizational and managerial skills. He will see to it that all of us know how to exploit his brilliance. I'll make sure you get the memos."

And later, Donovan convinced the president as well. As commander in chief, FDR ordered the plan into action.

In the end, everyone who watched Chalmers's prognostications pan out in the following months and years agreed he'd been right.

They just weren't sure how he'd gotten there.

But among the relatively few people in Washington political and military circles who actually knew Dr. Chalmers, his name was spoken with the same awe and reverence afforded to America's other undisputed genius, Dr. Albert Einstein.

The two men were, in fact, well acquainted and had engaged in numerous brainstorming sessions while collaborating on a range of mathematic problems.

In casual discourse one day, Einstein had mentioned that his birth certificate did not list a middle name. When asked by Chalmers if that meant Einstein did not have a middle name, the frizzy-haired physicist flashed his trademark wry smile and said, "*Ja, mein freund*—yah my friend, of course I have von, but it is somezing of *ein geheimnis*."

"Now you've got me interested, Herr Doktor. What's so secret about it?"

"De zecret is not about a name," Einstein replied. "It is about my life. Vhat really interests me, Jonathan, is vhether God had any choice in za creation of ze vorld und the human forms, especially mine, that evolved here . . . or vere sent here."

Chalmers nodded, aware Einstein had drifted into a more serious discussion. "I definitely understand the conundrum inherent in that philosophical issue."

Einstein had then explained that he felt there were two ways to view life—as if nothing about it is a miracle, or to live as if everything is a miracle.

Chalmers had said he took that answer to mean it would be a miracle if he ever learned his friend's middle name.

Einstein had chuckled. "Jonathan, I vill tell you za middle initial. It is *W* . . . and in the miracle zhat is your own life you vill come to understand vhat it means von day."

"Why not just tell me now?"

"Because you vill most appreciate the power of W vhen you personally discover its benefit to you."

Chalmers grinned. "Brilliant semantic dodge, Doctor, but still a nonanswer."

Einstein's eyes twinkled. "Trust in za personal friends you vill make in life, Johathan, especially those vith a W in zheir names. Some vill have special talents, knowledge or hold positions of power that vill be critical as you navigate a unique path that life has selected for you to journey."

"So I take that to mean—"

"Take it on good faith that life, especially yours my dear friend, is a miracle."

26

From his lofty perch, Won could see and hear everything happening on Earth. And every event, every conversation on the planet was instantly absorbed by the Crystal Tabula, a cosmic white hole embedded within Won's celestial chest.

He wanted to meet, ideally exceed, all of his Headmaster's expectations for this GoodWill mission. Thus far there had been about as many setbacks as advances in the promotion of Nobility.

~*Every civilization here,*~ he mentally reviewed, ~*has some kind of folkloric or mythological wonder worker—a sorcerer, shaman, wizard, or witch. These and other names related to the dual notions of magic and mystical fire are linguistically traced to a single root word . . . my word,* fyermun.~

It was the first concept and the first word Won had communicated to *Homo erectus* after demonstrating to a cave dweller how to spark flint rocks and make a pile of tender twigs burst into flame. Won called him Sháfyer. Won had returned many times, occasionally to morph and breed with the advancing humans, whose progressive journey he had never steered . . . but given occasional course-altering directions.

~*I have put my seed and my creed into numerous representatives from many civilizations, but most fail to last the course toward Nobility,*~ he reflected, disappointed that an early civilized group, the Egyptians, had also ultimately faltered. His galactic DNA had coursed through bloodlines that produced the likes of Ramesses and Tutankhamen. But the high nobility of Egypt burned less brightly through its brief historical flame. He saw the same thing happen with the Roman and Greek empires.

~*I am encouraged by the region called China. A few of my spawned progenitors there have managed to inculcate the race with a sense of order and mental tranquillity. I find that cause for hope.*~

Won was particularly impressed with a group of his spawnlings who had gathered as freethinkers and free-willed individuals in a place called

America. Though he had not planned it or influenced it, Won nonetheless found it to be an amusing convergence of coincidence that every one of his interbreedings during this period of Earth history had produced an offspring whose human-side parent had chosen to give a name with a *W* in it. It rather pleased him, actually.

~I see their passion for freedom, a resolve to fight for their own national values, and an abiding belief in their God. They now call themselves a nation—America . . . the land of freedom seekers and a home for brave souls. It has an encouraging Noble ring, but unfortunately in this last sectic they have already been at war with the rest of the world twice.~

He had identified one among many of these self-proclaimed Americans who was special.

If the pure human called Chalmers was to be the noble paladin for resolving destabilizing events already unfolding on Earth, Won realized he might have to take additional unauthorized measures if he intended to assist the Chalmerian in handling catastrophic events headed *toward* Earth.

That would mean more than merely marshalling the forces of his W-monikered spawnlings . . . it would entail Won coming down to Earth again from High Stasis.

27

Moving from one building to another, Chalmers packed boxes and sorted through memories at the same time. Five years . . . 1942–1947. So quick. So much history, he thought.

Japanese forces had gotten closer to the U.S. mainland than just the Hawaiian Islands. They had invaded the Aleutians and occupied part of Alaska, dropped bombs during air raids on the state of Oregon, and their submarines attacked along the coast of California. Chalmers had convinced the White House to make the press spike news of attacks in the continental United States, arguing that it would have demoralized or even incited panic among the citizenry.

America struck back on Japan with Doolittle's Raid on Tokyo and the Battle of Midway, among others; and against Germany it was Eisenhower's arrival in London followed by the first American air attacks on Berlin and the U.S. invasion of North Africa. All in the first year.

Chalmers assessed the targets and calculated the odds, especially for the OSS missions. Donovan gave the green light for sabotage, rescues, propaganda—even assassinations. American forces stormed through the Solomon Islands, reclaimed Palermo from the Germans, and destroyed the Japanese fleet at Truk Lagoon.

Then came the turning point of the war in Europe—D-Day and the hard-fought victory two years ago. And only three months later a terrifying event that resulted from Chalmers's comments to Truman on how to save U.S. lives by ending the war abruptly. Chalmers's calculations had been compelling. Two atomic bombs on two Japanese cities—a quarter million men, women, and children vaporized instantly or dead later from crushing injuries, burns, and effects of radiation. Enough to force Japan's surrender.

More than enough to cause two men a lifetime of postwar anguish. One was Albert Einstein, the physicist who served as the architect for designing nuclear weapons; the other was his friend Jonathan Chalmers, the mathematician who served up the statistically-justified notion of using such weapons.

꒰ꩌ

Finally, it was all over.

Chalmers had witnessed the end of another war and been promoted to full colonel along the way. And he had been with a "peace-time" civilian intelligence organization, the Central Intelligence Group, during its first two directors. Now he served a third one, Rear Admiral Roscoe H. Hillenkoetter, USN, who'd just taken command of the newly named Central Intelligence Agency, an outfit that was yet to define what its organizational role was to be in the post–World War II era and the "new-world order" that was rapidly emerging.

A bittersweet moment, Chalmers thought, unpacking official files and personal memorabilia he'd moved this morning from E Street into his new digs near the reflecting pool. For him this day truly signaled the end of the OSS and marked the beginning of the Central Intelligence Agency, whose CIA initials Chalmers and the rest of the world would soon equate with the most powerful, mysterious and perhaps feared organization in the world.

꒰ꩌ

As Chalmers also knew, the CIA, which was exempted from normal restrictions and accountably procedures regarding use of federal funds, was already conducting clandestine business—forming what some thought were unholy alliances and engaging in covert propaganda designed to influence political events in selected postwar nations.

Chalmers had recommended that the CIA co-opt the chief of Hitler's army intelligence, General Reinhard Gehlen, and use him, along with his former Nazi agents, to form the backbone of the Agency's longer-term penetration of America's emerging new enemy—the Russians. Chalmers had also been involved in strategic planning for the CIA's Project Paperclip, which altered identity records on Nazi technicians and then illegally imported German rocket scientists, including Dr. Wernher von Braun, safely into the country through U.S. immigration. When von Braun later ushered in the U.S. space program, Chalmers was enthralled with the unfolding exploration of the cosmos and proud he'd had a hand with enabling it to happen.

꒰ꩌ

Tomorrow, he would receive his honorable discharge from the army and become a civilian, though he was certain that his life at the CIA would always draw him into the country's most challenging problems, where he was likely to have all the pressure of warfare but without the support of a battalion of uniformed troops. Information, he figured, would be his weapon from now on.

Nobody knew better than he what a powerful weapon it could be.

But today was for unpacking, and he had the services of a strong back and, as he appreciated, an equally strong mind to help him do it.

He had specifically requested that Lieutenant Joseph Anderson be detailed to assist him with the pack out. A country boy from Kansas, Joe Anderson was tall and strong and sported unruly red hair atop a head packed with a brain to match his brawn. Because Chalmers knew Anderson's outstanding reputation and had read through his file, he'd also arranged for the lieutenant to be his special assistant in this new assignment. He was drawn to Anderson's sense of duty, loyalty, math background, and insights into the knotty problems that were Chalmers's duty to deal with. Besides that, Chalmers felt sorry for Joe's circumstances.

ﾅ

"Lieutenant," Chalmers had said when he first met Anderson, "you have to question your timing, don't you think? You've just graduated from West Point. Now you're starting a military career, but you just missed the second, and most massive, world war ever conducted."

"Can't change fate, sir, so I guess there's a lot of catching up to do, what with all these battlefield commanders ahead of me in the promotion pipeline."

Chalmers knew that combat, though it was terrible for soldiers to endure, was the ultimate testing ground for all the training they'd received. While he would never have wanted an experience like Verdun again, Chalmers was surprised to find that he felt regret, or maybe it was guilt, about having missed the shooting action this time around. Perhaps Anderson felt the same.

ﾅ

Anderson opened a box and pulled out a framed photo. "Who are these guys?"

"Me and a New Yorker named Huddleston. We went through basic together."

"You were both so young . . . and gee, come to think of it, *you* still look like this, sir," Anderson said, studying his boss's face.

Chalmers wanted to change *that* subject. "War eats up a lot of years, piles on loss and sadness," Chalmers said, taking the photo from the lieutenant. "Hud was killed on D-Day. I was pulled out of our unit, or I would've been there with him."

"Sorry, sir . . . hey, I imagine you're really proud of this." Anderson had unwrapped another photo. It showed Chalmers and Donovan standing between the U.S. and OSS flag standards in Wild Bill's office.

"You knew General Donovan well, sir?"

"Yes. Sometimes I wish he had let me get into the real fray."

"But everyone around here says you enabled us to win the war faster than a fresh battalion on the front lines. And they say that your work saved lives, lots of them."

"I imagine it felt like an eternity for those doing the fighting."

Joe wrinkled his brow. "How'd you do what people say you did . . . quantify the random variables of potential resources and weigh those against equally unknown variables?"

"The best way we could, every day, one day at a time."

"But what about unanticipated tactical losses and strategic delays from waging war in two different theaters and on many fronts? Did you use some kind of grid matrix?"

"Grids, maps, flashcards, pieces of string . . . anything that worked. Donovan and the brass," Chalmers continued, "tasked me with designing a plan to fight a war that used strategic approaches and systematic advances, but they also wanted a flexible plan that included improvised tactics and risk taking. Plus, they expected contingency plans for managing chaos. For that I drew on the work of Poincaré and other ergodic theorists I'd studied. Nothing ever goes as planned in a war zone. So I had to allow for constant and unpredictable changes to my calculations."

"Heisenberg's uncertainty principle?"

"You're right. I employed a matrix of differential equations and other recursive math with interpolation functions. But I relied on the boots on the ground to carry things out. I was merely the planner. They won the war."

"What else did General Donovan want from you, sir?"

"To quantify the percentage of likely victory over the shortest possible period of time in combat. He was willing to bet everything on one roll of the dice . . . he just wanted me to determine the odds for throwing a seven."

Chalmers glanced out the window for a moment. He wondered what lurked out there in the distance—or maybe he was looking for an image to replace the vision in his head of the war's terrible cost. One dead soldier after another, American and foreign, their numbers piled up into mountains of corpses—from trenches long ago in Verdun to beaches at Normandy, from iron concussion bombs on Germany to atomic ones on Japan.

"Joe, I'm afraid that a large part of my analytical projections strongly influenced Truman's fateful decision about how to end the war quickly. The filmed images of the aftermath still disturb me every time I think of them."

"I realize some of your history is painful. Thanks for sharing your memories, sir."

"Just five years, Joe. Just doing what had to be done."

"One of my instructors at the Academy said that all things considered, he figured it went relatively quickly for a world war."

"Yes, an efficient war," Chalmers said acidly, "but costly. Final worldwide tally's likely to be well over fifty million dead. And already international political realignments are fanning this conflict's dying embers. I don't think we'll see that lasting peace everybody wants. With religious, cultural, and ethnic differences as combustible hatreds to fuel the new fire, I figure trouble's ahead."

Chalmers looked out the window again. And up, toward the clouded sky.

"The question is, just what shape that trouble will take."

28

Ken Atler looked at his watch, a procedural habit when navigating, but he was not out for a joyride today, not here alongside the lower slopes of treacherous Mount Rainier—a broad area of operations, or AO, as someone in the military would call it. He checked his compass, changed heading a few degrees, but maintained surveillance on the terrain fifteen hundred feet below.

Three years ago, Major Kenneth Atler banked his American P-51 Mustang and fired his .50-cal wing guns broadside into a German Messerschmitt. *Wreckage on the ground,* Atler had noted on his flyby that afternoon through the Rhine Valley countryside.

Today however, as a Search and Rescue civilian volunteer, Atler piloted his Beech Bonanza 35, looking for other ground wreckage, a U.S. military plane from Fairchild Air Force Base in nearby Spokane.

"It was on a routine training flight," a base officer had briefed Atler earlier, just prior to preflighting his Beech. "Pilot missed his last scheduled comm check. Never sent a Mayday. We triangulated his previous transmissions and calculate he must've gone down somewhere on the southeastern side of Rainier last evening. Sure appreciate your volunteering to fly SAR for us, sir."

A strong glint of light suddenly caught Atler's eye, a pilot's eye trained to recognize and recall exact details.

"Fairchild tower, this is Bonanza three five niner Whiskey. How copy? Over."

"Bonanza niner Whiskey, Fairchild has you, Lima Charlie. Go your squawk."

Atler's transmission had nothing to do with what he'd spotted on the ground. He reported what he'd just observed in the sky above the glacial peaks of Rainier: *nine white-hot dots of light traveling at speeds and maneuvering at angles impossible for normal aircraft.*

"It's ... well, by God's grace I've never seen anything like this."

"Bonanza niner Whiskey stand by. Fairchild also tracking abnormal radar blips in your AO."

"Copy that, Fairchild. Glad to hear I'm not going crazy up here."

"Niner Whiskey, you are instructed to steer southwest immediately and are cleared for straight-in approach to Fairchild. Taxi to Base Ops and tie-down."

"Niner Whiskey. Roger that last squawk, Fairchild. What's going on?"

"Proceed to Base. Fairchild Tower, over and out."

໒ཀ

An hour later, Atler reported to the Flight Operations Center where the Base Security duty officer thanked him for assisting in the search and for cooperating in this new development. Atler inquired about the radar sighting but again got no answers.

"I've sent a preliminary report about your sightings to appropriate military channels in Washington, D.C.," said the duty officer. "But I still need an official, written statement. You can dictate if you'd like, sir, and I'll type it up for your signature."

"Sure. No way I'll ever forget what I saw." He pulled out a pack of Camels. "Can I smoke in here?" he asked and lit one when the duty officer nodded his head.

"There were nine disk-shaped objects moving ... *flying,* in a chain formation on a heading of approximately one hundred forty degrees. Altitude of around twelve to fourteen thousand feet. These craft, or unidentifiable flying objects, I guess you could call 'em, were bright as the sun. And moving at tremendous speed. Real eye-catcher, though, was the maneuvers," he said, waving his hands to simulate the motion, and in the process leaving contrails from the smoking cigarette pinched between his fingers.

"All of 'em made erratic, abrupt turns that were just impossible to do with any kind of conventional aircraft. The entire formation turned on a dime, scattered, then regrouped several times. It was all ... just incredible."

໒ཀ

The duty officer jotted notes and scribbled *flying disks, u-f-o* as a shorthand reminder. And later, when the Associated Press picked up the rest of the story, Atler was credited with the first widely reported sighting of a phenomenon which, from then on, had its own, universally recognized abbreviation—UFO.

A short while later, others saw the white dots, though they had no idea what to call them. Nor did the observers have a clue about what they were.

SALT LAKE CITY. 1000 HOURS

"Damn, did you see that?" the roofer shouted to his shingle-nailing partner.

"See what? Whaddya talking about?"

"That white line, like lightning, that just shot all the way across the sky."

"No, but I see you got the box of nails there next to your leg. Pass 'em over here."

PHOENIX. 1008 HOURS

"Never seen anything like that before. What do you think it was?" the uniformed station attendant asked as he pumped gas into the well-to-do couple's brand-new '47 Buick convertible.

"Don't know," the male driver said, "but it was certainly strange, like saucers without any cups."

"Like a pearl string," said his wife, stroking the strand around her neck, "but one of them broke off."

"Something made a sharp turn for sure. Headed due east," said the attendant.

"Maybe it was an airplane and the wing or something came off," the wife added.

"It was too fast, too high to be a plane. There's something eerie about it, though," said her husband. "I'll call the authorities when I get to the office."

"Yes, sir," said the attendant, holding out his hand, "that'd be good. It'll also be three twenty-five for the fill-up."

ROSWELL, NEW MEXICO. 1010 HOURS

All this way safely. And now a disaster. His mind raced even faster than he plummeted, yet he was in mental control even though his craft was spinning in physical chaos from an inexplicable failure in the hull.

He was more than an extraordinary pilot and navigator. The leader of the Fiverian flotilla, he possessed unequaled knowledge of math and science, certainly by this piddling planet's standards. Even so, the strange hand at the helm of this crippled ship could not stop what was about to happen.

He sent a last communiqué to others in the formation: ξϖξ ρωυэ ζэ ηγεκ.

Also a husband and father, he cast his faceted, yellow-green eyes on his mate and two adult offspring on board with him. He spoke his final words to them.

Breathing deeply from the cabin's yellow atmosphere, he pushed back into his contoured salon and mouthed a silent 0φ ξφιτ as the arid land raced up to brake him.

An instant later, the Fiverian entity known as Kul'da-Zak slammed into the dead-end surface of an alien world.

29

"Today's intel summary, Dr. Chalmers," said Lieutenant Anderson, folders in his hand.

Chalmers took the red folder. "I assume you've already read everything, as usual."

"Yes, sir. Even the newspapers. There's a boatload of stories about the strange lights out west. UFOs, they're being called. Disks, saucers, too. Anything to them, you think?" Anderson dropped the *Washington Post* on Chalmers's desk along with the other files.

"Tell me, Joe, you ever read Thomas Hardy?"

"Any connection to Laurel and Hardy?"

Chalmers glared. "Hardy was an English novelist and poet."

Anderson looked puzzled. "And he wrote sonnets about strange saucers?"

"No, but among other things, he said that while much is too strange to be believed, nothing is too strange to have happened. Trust me," he said while glancing at the window, "I know in my heart the truth of Hardy's words." Chalmers picked up the paper and read the article in a few seconds. "Be interesting, wouldn't it, if there was something real in these reports . . . something that would really shake us up?"

"Or maybe apart. I like ordinary things to stay ordinary."

"People can't learn if things don't change. Mysteries. Challenges. Even threats. All of them are opportunities to learn, which is one of life's greatest joys, if not its main purpose." Chalmers opened two folders and began to read them at the same time.

Lieutenant Anderson waited a moment to see if the great man, whose eyes were now strangely glazed over, would have any more words of wisdom. But when Dr. Chalmers failed to look up, his young assistant retreated.

Finishing all the folders less than a minute later, Chalmers returned his attention to the window, where sunlight sparkled against the dusty panes, their refracted impurities shooting tiny meteors of light rays onto Chalmers's desk.

ҌӨ

He drifted into a memory, recalling what his father had told him that night on the beach when they had observed the annual Perseids meteor shower.

"It's a burning rainstorm from deep space. There are scientists called astrophysicists," his dad had explained, "who believe all living things on this planet came from cellular life carried on meteors just like the ones we're watching."

Meteors. Celestial fire. Alien life from outer space. Chalmers had never forgotten that night. He glanced again at the secret folders and tried to imagine what he could learn from interstellar aliens.

And then, like a flashing meteor that was gone just as quickly, another memory streaked through his mind—something the Headmaster had told him about the future . . . or maybe something he'd seen in a nightmarish dream. He wasn't sure what it all meant.

But he believed there was something on the horizon for which he had to prepare.

And an unknown premonition that caused him to feel fear.

30

Mack Brazel coaxed his tired Ford pickup across the arid desolation that comprised his ranch located some seventy-five miles northwest of Roswell. A .30-30 Winchester for taking out coyotes and a 12-gauge Remington to deal with tick-infested jackrabbits hung on the rack across the back window.

"Pancho, there's less out here today than the nuthin' that's normally out here, boy," Brazel said. He scratched the flop-eared hound panting in the seat next to him.

Pancho's keen nose suddenly quivered, his hackles bristled, and he let out a deep, rumbling growl. The big dog then lowered his head and uncharacteristically whimpered.

"Easy, boy. You see something out there? Shit fire," whispered Brazel, spotting what the dog had been sensing. He braked, got out of the truck, but Pancho, always by his side, would not leave the front seat. He growled and cowered at the same time.

Suddenly Brazel's own hackles bristled. *Something was in the air.*

He walked toward what he'd spotted from the truck.

There was strange debris scattered over the rugged landscape. *Weird shiny stuff, like metal, but light and oddly soft. And that smell.*

He had read those wild-eyed UFO "flying disk" stories, and he was starting to wonder if there was a connection. He saw something under a piece of twisted material.

"Holy hell!" He was momentarily paralyzed with fear. Then his sense of survival kicked in. He pivoted and ran for the truck, completely unaware he'd vaulted over a buzzing rattlesnake in the process. Brazel cranked the Ford, spun a cloud of dirt, and sped home, where he immediately called his friend George Wilcox, the local sheriff in Roswell.

"George, I never seen nuthin' like this in my life," he said, phone in one hand and a whiskey glass, with nervously rattling ice, in the other.

An hour later, Sheriff Wilcox accompanied Brazel back to the site.

"Good God a'mighty, Mack, I've never laid eyes on anything like this either. It's even more unbelievable than what you described on the phone. Some are busted up pretty much. Hard to tell how many, maybe four all together, I'd say. But one looks intact."

Brazel was wide-eyed. "I hope it's dead. Looks dead, don't it?"

"Sure enough. But I wouldn't get any closer. Let's get back pronto. I gotta make some phone calls."

Later, the sheriff contacted Colonel William Blanchard, the commander at the U.S. Army air base in Roswell, who immediately sent two senior officers to investigate.

Major Jesse Marcel, chief intelligence officer, and Sheridan Cavitt, head of the Roswell Army Counterintelligence Corps, were on the scene within hours. The trained professionals walked through the scattered debris, manually inspecting random pieces.

"Major. Over here," said Cavitt. "You have to see—"

"Son of a bitch!" said Major Marcel, who'd just walked over to join Cavitt.

They stood in silent shock, staring at the mangled, foul-smelling remains partially visible under a portion of the craft, vehicle, or whatever the hell they were observing.

"I, uh, I don't know what to think," said Cavitt. "But it's for damn sure scary."

"Well, I'd say this is about to become the defining moment of our careers," said the major, who'd collected his wits. "We've got to get some of this debris back to base."

"What about the other stuff . . . the remains? Do we take any body parts with us?"

"Negative. I wouldn't touch the tissue. Might be poisonous, contaminated, who knows what. You've got the camera, Cavitt. Snap some shots. This is going to be one helluva story in the papers tomorrow."

"You're right about the defining moment," Cavitt said, "but I don't know what kind of story this'll turn out to be."

"What do you mean?"

"I mean that someone other than a journalist may write the copy. And I bet the readers will be on a very short list."

"You're too paranoid for your own good, Cavitt."

"Maybe. Betcha I'm right, though."

↜

They delivered the debris samples to a seldom-used base hangar. Marcel and Cavitt then briefed Colonel Blanchard.

"Give me a written report ASAP," Colonel Blanchard said. "I'll send it to Washington. Assemble Security and Flight Ops. We'll need a ground team to pick up the rest of the debris and everything else. I'm talking a full scrub. And let me know when those photos are developed. One copy. One copy only. My desk first and nowhere else. We need to coordinate carefully what's going to happen next."

ROSWELL ARMY AIR FIELD. JUNE 20, DAWN

The C-82 Flying Boxcar departed at first light, transporting some of the structural debris from the craft to Wright Field near Dayton, Ohio—home of the USAAF's aeronautical research labs.

"Engineers at Wright," Colonel Blanchard told Marcel and Cavitt, "will have to figure out what made that thing fly . . . if they can. We'll hang on to whatever those things are that did the flying. I'm sure top brass back east will be telling us what do with 'em."

"The cadavers are beginning to decompose even faster, sir," said Colonel Marcel, "so we've covered them with tarps and put down some big blocks of ice. As a precaution, I quarantined the area. And I'm controlling the flow of information tightly."

"I've drafted a press report, just in case, sir, although I doubt we should be making a public statement at this time," added Cavitt. "I agree with Colonel Marcel about the need to contain this story to the extent possible."

"This is the military," said Colonel Blanchard. "Orders and shit all roll downhill. Ranks around here higher than mine and yours have already decided to make a comment, especially after that rancher and sheriff went public. Those two will stir up more damned dust than a whirlwind. It's our job to damp it down."

"How?" Cavitt asked.

"Make it the most boring bureaucratic BS in the history of the military. If that doesn't work, we'll just zip our lips entirely . . . along with everyone else's."

ﹸ

Later in the morning, a front-page article in the *Roswell Daily Record* ran an official press report filed by the intelligence office of the 509th Bombardment Group at Roswell Army Air Field. It was about the crash of a strange craft. *A so-called flying saucer.*

Cavitt had done his best to craft language designed to downplay events otherwise described in the press statement. Unfortunately, his vague references to "carting away the wreckage and debris remains" were only accentuated and validated by related stories drawn from interviews of Mack Brazel and Sheriff Wilcox. The civilians added colorful and dramatic detail to the story with their sensational references to "alien forms, strange bodies, and monsters from the sky."

"Everything I saw out there made my skin crawl," Brazel was reported to have said. "It looked like hell had belched out its ugliest demons," another journalist said the sheriff had told him. Rumors spread around town like tumbleweeds in prop wash.

ﹸ

That afternoon, the base was hit with a flurry of encrypted messages from Washington. Some brass in the War Department had also begun to accelerate the spin to a high velocity, and they'd made their own sharp turn in the process.

Colonel Blanchard was relieved of his command.

Soldiers in battle dress and sporting dark glasses set up roadblocks and checked local citizens' documents, while some entered taverns and other public gathering places to disperse anyone congregating there. The rationale by the military for its unusual activity reportedly alternated between looking for AWOL servicemen and warning residents to go home and stay there until toxic fumes from an aviation fuel spill on base had dissipated in the wind.

Marcel and Cavitt were ordered to have private talks with Brazel and Sheriff Wilcox. Topics of discussion included possible annexation of Brazel's ranch by the U.S. government and tax proceedings possibly to be brought against the sheriff by the Bureau of Internal Revenue. Other military and civilian officials noted personal information and took photos of Brazel and Wilcox's closest family members in the area. After that Mack and the sheriff suddenly became unavailable for further comments.

ROSWELL. JUNE 21

The *Roswell Daily Record* ran an "updated" USAAF press release. It was issued by Brigadier General Roger M. Ramey, commander of the Eighth Air Force.

"An examination by the army," the general said, "revealed last night that the mysterious objects found on a New Mexico ranch came from a harmless high-altitude weather balloon and not a grounded flying disk as erroneously misreported earlier."

Nobody in Roswell bought it for a minute.

They were, as Chalmers had accurately predicted, simply too intimidated by the military's heavy-handed tactics to say anything in public.

And as he also calculated, the UFO issue would soon be too hot for the military itself to handle. New containment protocols would be forthcoming in the form of new administrative changes already set to take place in the U.S. government.

31

Abruptly, the Roswell case was closed, at least publicly as far as the government was concerned. Even so, the brand-new United States Air Force —set to be signed into law next month as part of the National Security Act of 1947—would continue to play what some called a "co-conspirator" role in a broader government cover-up of the Roswell incident.

During this period of government restructuring, a new Roswell case was opened. The dead life-forms and the exotic craft that brought them to Earth were handed over to another government agency. The Roswell incident, some Washington brass thought, was a better administrative fit for the CIA—like a clandestine glove on a deceptive hand.

"Dr. Chalmers," said Lieutenant Anderson, "skipper needs to see you immediately."

"On my way," said Chalmers, closing the Roswell file he'd been working on the past several days. With each new development, the file had thickened with more copies of encrypted messages and new memos about national security concerns stemming from the dramatic event. Chalmers had written many of those messages and memos.

The CIA director, Admiral Hillenkoetter, treated this issue like a brush fire. According to him, it had to be stamped out quickly. By lighting backfires if necessary.

Chalmers entered his office.

"I've got an interesting update for you," the admiral said. "Less than an hour ago, the president flew out of Andrews. His plane was barely airborne when base radar at Andrews, and over at National Airport as well, picked up eight UFOs. Two F-94 jet interceptors have just been scrambled from New Castle AFB in Delaware to investigate. These flying whatevers, the whole Roswell incident . . . it's starting to get complicated."

"As I indicated to you from the beginning, Mr. Director."

"Yes, I know. On your recommendation, I've put some containment measures into effect. Incidentally, I liked what you said earlier about applying intelligent, centralized control to the problem. Personalized pressure, too. That's been ordered as well."

"Yes, sir, a good decision on your part."

The director stood, walked to a window.

"There's a car outside that will take you to Andrews. A military plane will ferry you to Ohio and New Mexico." He turned back to face Chalmers. "Get everything from both bases. Every piece of debris, every shred of their remains. Then go to Camp McLeary. Unravel all of this before Hoover and his G-men get further involved or the counterintel knuckleheads at Army Air bollix up everything beyond repair. Hoover undoubtedly will try to dump this off on us in any event. SOB'll try to make us look bad. We, and I'm talking *you* here, have to manage the public's panic."

Hillenkoetter stepped toward Chalmers. "And after that . . ."

"Sir?"

"After that, I don't have the slightest idea where you're headed . . . or where this issue will take any of us, for that matter."

Chalmers nodded. "Understood. And as far as how I handle collateral events . . . ?"

"Any way you choose. Just keep me informed, John. You can roll around like a loose cannon. Fire wildly port and starboard. Just don't put one through my deck, Dr. Chalmers."

32

A gray C-47, the military's main cargo hauler, screeched like a parrot. Smoke plumed from its tires as the plane settled to the tarmac after its circuitous odyssey.

"Tie down at Flight Ops, or taxi straight to the hangar, sir?" asked the pilot.

"Straight *into* the hangar, Captain. Ground crew will close the doors behind us," Chalmers said. "You and the copilot will disembark, exit the hangar, walk to Flight Ops, and report to security for out-brief protocols."

"Wilco," said the pilot, continuing down the taxiway. Moments later his plane's wheels were chocked and he'd shut down the engines.

"Thanks for the steady, safe flight," said Chalmers. "We'll take it from here."

Walking away from the secured hangar, the captain asked, "Dr. Chalmers, where exactly *is* here? It's not on the CAA maps or military charts."

"*Here* . . . is where your mission ends," Chalmers said.

He knew more about this location than could have been revealed to the flight crew. A decade ago, the War Department purchased two of Virginia's Civil War–era cities lock, stock, and barrel. Thousands of people had to resettle after the sale. Churches, post offices, cemeteries, lodges, businesses, farms, and homes were simply left behind—a lifetime of family histories overtaken by weeds as thousands of acres were claimed by Uncle Sam. The cities' names were quietly expunged from official records.

Chalmers figured that these neighboring towns had been essentially conscripted, like troops drafted to serve a greater national cause, like soldiers who sacrificed their personal identities for a while, if not their lives forever. These towns, he believed, had been sacrificed so other U.S. cities might survive in a different kind of battle—a third world war whose prospects for global Armageddon were unavoidable, according to his analytical calculations.

The area now had a fence built around it and a landing strip on it. It also had a new name attached to it. Camp McLeary: the U.S. Navy Training and Distribution Center. Among its other uses, the camp was home base for the navy's Construction Battalions, the Seabees.

With thousands of tons of building materials and construction equipment, but only a skeleton crew on site, the location was perfect for Chalmers. *Plenty of room for what we need and privacy for the passengers in the C-47.*

ᵗᵃ

"Be *extremely* careful," Chalmers said as he monitored Seabees manually pulling the four crates from the fuselage to the doorway where a forklift waited to unload them. The crates were specially constructed for special cargo, and they, too, had been drafted into a different kind of service. Built from one-inch-thick wood planking reinforced with metal straps, each rectangular box was twenty feet long by three feet wide.

The sides were stenciled: D A N G E R HEXPLO—USN-ORD MARK 14 ET.

"Sailor," Chalmers asked, "what does the writing stand for?"

"Sir, that's a U.S. Naval Submarine Ordnance shipping container for a Mark 14 Electric Torpedo. A mean seabitch with six hundred pounds of high explosives that'll rip through a steel hull three inches thick. We sent a shitload of Jap and German ships to the deep and dead with those torpedoes. They get stored in New Mexico for the dry heat. McLeary is a humid hellhole in the summer, sir. What are we gonna do with 'em here?"

"Not to worry, sailor, the crates don't contain torpedoes or any other ordnance."

"Then what are we doing with the boxes?"

"Makeshift coffins. Only thing big enough to hold the bodies."

"Bodies?" replied the young sailor, who of course was clueless about any of this. He was just following orders today, tending to the arrival of a special flight. He stared at Chalmers, who as a civilian was always something of a puzzle to anyone in a military service uniform. Suddenly, he got it. "Aw, you're just shittin' me. Right, sir?"

"Yes, just fooling with you," Chalmers said. "A little joke."

"No torpedoes inside, no danger. We can use the forklift, right?"

"Yes. But carefully. Lack of explosives does not mean that we know the cargo's safe, so I'd handle those plywood boxes *very* gently if I were you.

Put them in a cool place, somewhere in the back. We wouldn't want any trouble. Right?"

The sailor got the message. He handled the crates like they were cartons of eggs.

33

A two-week, twenty-four/seven research blitz behind him, Chalmers was back in headquarters and had a slightly better handle on alien wreckage and remains. He'd hand-carried a report this morning from Camp McLeary and delivered it to his boss.

"What's this classification?" Admiral Hillenkoetter asked. "'Eyes Only'? Nobody here knows what it means. My own aide, Lieutenant Anderson, who was your former aide before I reassigned him, gave this thing to me, then told me he wasn't sure I was cleared to read it. Who the hell's Joe working for? Me or you?"

Standing to the side, Joe Anderson looked like a deer caught in the headlights.

Chalmers knew that look. Panic, held in check only by a sense of duty.

"Sorry, sir," Chalmers said. "You once told me it was a foul wind that ripped a good sail. I've been battered by such wind for two weeks. The classification is just a way of keeping the sails trimmed." He knew exactly how to steer the admiral.

Hillenkoetter sighed. "My sailor's gut is full of gas and I'm going to break wind like a high-pressure squall. Tell me something that calms this bureaucratic sea."

"Sir, the eyes only classification header means that you are the only one who's supposed to see this preliminary report. Lieutenant Anderson here was merely looking out for your security interests. You can, of course, subsequently send this information to whoever you choose. After all, you are the director and the president's chief intelligence adviser."

"And there's damned few eyes that'll see this report. This classification is official. Effective today. See to it, Lieutenant," said Hillenkoetter, nodding toward the door.

Saluting, Anderson turned and closed the door behind him.

The admiral cleared his throat. "Let's get down to the nut-cutting facts."

"Sir, you said you wanted the highest clearance precedent on the investigation, and you were right. If word of this leaks further, there'll be more people running for cover underground in peacetime than scrambled into shelters during the London air raids. They won't even know what they're running from. And neither will we, at least not until more forensics are completed."

"How many already know about the crash? Tens, maybe hundreds of thousands who've read about it in the newspapers? How are we supposed to keep a lid on this?"

"There's a way to handle the psychological aspects of such disruptive news."

"Easy for you to say, John. It'll be my nuts that get cut if the public goes crazy. How're you going to bottle this up when the genie's already busted out?"

"We don't even bother to put the genie back, we just redirect him . . . or misdirect everyone who thinks they see him. Our ploy will be the same one discovered by Poe's fictional detective, Auguste Dupin, who determined that the infamous 'purloined letter' was never found because it had been hidden in plain sight. Similarly, true stories about the aliens appearing in print and media news outlets will be the hypodermic to administer our deceptive serum. It's just counterintuition . . . a visually induced binaural if you will. In addition, I have some specific ideas about how to expand the bogus notion that all this centers around weather balloons. There is in fact an aspect of Project Mogul's high-altitude balloon-platform surveillance of the Soviets that can be refined into a more salient paradigm shift in the psychodynamics of public perception."

The admiral took a deep breath. "Bill Donovan told me there would be times when I wouldn't know exactly what you were saying."

"Yes, sir, Mr. Director. If you're ready, we can run though some key points now," said Chalmers, motioning toward the red-striped folder on the admiral's desk.

"Too much to read this morning," said Hillenkoetter, pushing the top secret report aside. "Just tell me what I want to know. Such as, what do these . . . aliens . . . look like? How does their ship, vessel, or whatever work? What are they doing here, and how many more of them are there, and where in the hell are they holed up? I mean, the pilot who first saw the UFOs reported there were nine, and we've got one. Even I can do the math. And so can the radar screens at Andrews that spotted eight UFOs last month."

His angst-driven sail now full, the admiral opened the report and flipped through some pages. "And where are my goddamned pictures? I was supposed to get pictures."

All Chalmers could do was nod in agreement. He didn't know nearly enough yet. But he was confident he'd piece together more as time passed.

"There are no clear photos of the alien remains, sir. We took hundreds, but none would develop. We finally just gave up. Their bodies gave off an infrarange luminescence, a sulfur-yellow aura that clouded any photographic image. We're working on something called a magnetic pulse resonance system that may solve the problem."

"Okay, stay on the photo business. For now, just describe them to me."

34

Chalmers sketched as he continued briefing the admiral.

"Think composite, Admiral. Visualize a gigantic *Limax maximus* in the form of a *Macropus rufus* with the elongated crainiofacial composition of a *Gymnothorax maderensis*. It is a multimorphological creature and not from Earth. I'm calling it an extraterrestrial entity."

"Toss the Latin overboard, okay?"

"I'll try. Think of it as a huge garden slug standing erect like a kangaroo with muscular bipedal legs, and a long spear-tipped tail. The head and face resemble a moray eel with a large bifurcated cranial lobe covered in thick scales and a wide, thin mouth that when open reveals rows of razor-sharp, sharklike teeth."

"Is it dangerous?"

"It is not a herbivore, Admiral. I wouldn't sit down to dinner with it."

His eyebrows raised, the admiral studied the sketch Chalmers had just finished.

"This extraterrestrial, or ET as I suggest we call it, has elongated openings on the neck and side of the head that could be gills, ears, nostrils . . . we don't know. Protruded rhizoids on the back of the skull could be antennae, radar . . . or antlers . . . we don't know."

"How big is this thing?"

"Standing fully upright, the aliens are probably eight feet tall and dragging another six feet of tail. They weigh around five hundred pounds."

"But some of the eyewitness reports of the cadavers described them as three to four feet tall."

"Except for one, they were badly mangled, with some of the pieces appearing to be shorter-bodied entities. The one buried deepest under the rubble was intact and indicative of their full size," Chalmers said, adding that such a mistaken identity of the size would come in handy when he factored the Project Mogul angle into the propaganda deception ploy.

The director nodded. "Okay then, back to the description."

"They have two protruding eyestalks tipped with diamond-faceted, triangular-shaped sensors that could provide a three-hundred-and-sixty-degree range of vision. Based on lens composition of the pupil, the creature probably sees in the stereoscopic, infrared-to-ultraviolet realm."

"You mentioned standing upright . . . they walk like us, then?"

"Yes, sir. The ET has a muscular torso with four upper extremities. The two long ones—arms, I suppose—have a cluster of claw-tipped squid tentacles at the end. These extensors apparently serve as hands and provide extraordinary phalangeal dexterity."

"Which helped them built that space schooner."

"Yes, sir, although space capsule might be a better term. The ET's two shorter arms are equipped with crablike pincers and located in midtorso. Probably function as food conveyers to the mouth."

"Damn thing sounds as ugly as that old fart senator from Alabama."

"Same kind of feet, too, Mr. Director. Our creature has splayed macro-stabilizers with sharp talons, very much like the anisodactyl feet of avians . . . birds," he said, noting the admiral's confused look again. "That means there are three toes and a rear ankle spur. In fact, the creature itself is built like a compact *Tyrannosaurus rex*."

"So it's scaly, like an alligator, maybe?"

"On the contrary. Body's covered with soft clam-shaped feathers, but the exodermis is soft, pliable, and slimy like the covering of a giant garden slug. There's a possibility the covering is simply a form of protective clothing . . . maybe a uniform . . . we don't know yet. The medical team has completed only a partial autopsy on the three dismembered bodies. The intact cadaver is in a separate holding area. It's hard to describe the inside of these creatures, other than to say it reminds me of a truck radiator."

"Unbelievable. It's just all too bizarre to believe."

"They are *very* intelligent, sir. The propulsion system of their craft is unfathomable, as are the materials from which it's constructed. Preliminary analysis suggests there is a possibility that the exterior of the ship consists of . . . well, perhaps a form of compressed gas, hardened or congealed by some kind of ionization process . . . we don't know. One thing is quite evident. These beings are superior to us as a neurosentient species. However, what remains unclear is why they've come, what their intention is—and if, whether, or when more of them will return."

"What happens next, John?"

"We'll continue the autopsies and search for all the cerebrocortical, biologic, and other anatomical or anthropomorphic discoveries we can make. For the moment the cadavers are secure enough in the refrigerated locker at the airfield, but we are moving them soon to a new facility. Part of the craft is still at the aeronautic research facility in Dayton, which is better equipped, for now, to carry out the preliminary reverse engineering."

"But everything will be under our exclusive control. Sooner rather than later?"

"Yes, sir, we'll continue to airlift everything to the naval facility at Camp McLeary since it has a restricted airfield. Then all of it will be transferred to a separate Agency compound already under construction. There are markings inside the craft, and linguists are working on a translation. A permanent reverse-engineering task force is being assembled to tackle the ship's mechanics."

"Good. Very good."

"Sir, this will take organization, investigation, and compartmentation on an unprecedented scale. And it will take years, maybe decades."

"If anyone can pull it off, it will be you. But as for the security strategy—"

"Manageable. Social control will be a multilayered cover-up of exquisite transparency. But frankly, I am just as concerned about all the rest that's coming."

Hillenkoetter nodded in agreement. "Yeah, me, too. We know more about the dangerous realities of our geopolitical world than this . . . otherworldly business. And I'm afraid we're headed for World War Three—when earthmen are probably more likely to destroy our country than these, what . . . spacemen?"

"Yes, sir, only thing the press has right so far is its name: cold war. The ice storm before the hellfire of atomic conflict. My real concern is not that it will be a war with earthmen *or* spacemen. Rather, it's that in the race to prepare for both it'll come down to a toss-up between good luck and bad will."

ʬ

Chalmers knew the staggering amount of inferential data made his analytical task on the UFO issue difficult beyond any imaginable complexity.

But hadn't he already encapsulated all of World War II into a giant wall graph? Could he perform a similar miracle again?

"Admiral, our postwar scientific technology is about to expand exponentially. There are some prototype computational machines that'll store information and process facts and figures with dizzying speed. They will soon revolutionize how this agency analyzes events and identifies trends. It's all in here."

Chalmers handed the director a second top secret folder.

"That's the outline for how we'll handle all the changes coming our way. A blueprint for dealing with everything from Roswell to the cold war ... perhaps beyond."

Hillenkoetter scanned the folder, noting Chalmers's plans for the CIA's Office of Strategic Assessments.

The OSA would direct the Agency's ultraclassified Division K Task Force. Division K, and everything else logistically classified in the CIA, was to be located in a new facility currently under construction in the deep pine woods of Tidewater, Virginia.

The facility was called the Covert Staging Compound, or CSC.

One CSC warehouse was designated as Building W01, and it would contain all of the secrets Division K had on Roswell.

Division K, or DivKay as Chalmers called it, had two forensic analysis projects, code names CRYPTOS and CONUNDRUM. He had chosen the names for both projects.

"*Cryptos*, least in part comes from the Greek word κρυπτsός."

"Sorry Dr. Chalmers, that truly sounds like Greek to me."

"Oh, right, sir. It's pronounced like that because ... well, it's Greek. But if you—"

"Please. Just the translation. Sometime soon."

"Yes, of course. The written version, especially in English is with a K, and specifically means hidden. But since the construction project will also deal with hidden messages and encoded information, the file name *CRYPTOS* more appropriately reflects the cryptographic protocols required to safeguard the project's written documents."

Hillenkoetter nodded. "That does seem to make it perfect for what's being planned down the pike for civil defense against a Soviet attack."

"Glad you agree. And *Conundrum* is particularly well suited for the UFO extraterrestrial investigation. It means a question or problem that has only a conjectural answer, and ironically, sir, its etymology, or its linguistic history as a word, is a total mystery."

"I like it. All of it. You're ready to set sail, then," Hillenkoetter said.

35

CIA DIRECTOR'S OFFICE. WINTER, 1947

Swamped with Division K priorities, Chalmers was also on the planning committee for design and construction of a unified CIA headquarters complex set for groundbreaking several years from now. In the interim, he'd continue to divide his time among Agency components located around the former OSS and CIG buildings on E Street.

He also shuttled from Andrews Air Force Base to the CIA's new CSC facility in Virginia's Tidewater Peninsula area, where he routinely bunked for days at a time in the BOQ, or base officers' quarters.

Today, he was updating the director.

"Reconfiguration at CSC is ahead of schedule. We've also made a fascinating discovery that might prove important later. It's detailed in the tabbed addendum of your sitrep," said Chalmers, handing the admiral the project's weekly situation report.

"A cave?" questioned the admiral, seeing the contents page.

"A huge cavern system, sir. Seabees located it during seismic testing when they started on the basement project at Building W01 a few days ago. My plan in any event was to get everything off the ground level and out of sight. But now we intend to create a second level in addition to the regular basement. A cover construction, if you will, for an even deeper-cover substructure."

The admiral indicated his agreement.

"More important, as you'll see in Tab One, I have the DivKay Task Force setup. Everyone's a pioneer in their field. Security's already issued them special designated K-RED clearances."

Everything about the project was complex, and the tasks in front of Chalmers were numerous. He felt exhausted merely at the thought of it all—assess the prospects for war with the USSR, then design an analytical matrix for the strategic and tactical prosecution of a global nuclear war; provide stewardship for the scientific, reverse engineering of the Roswell spacecraft; and structure a public disinformation campaign about the UFO incident. But that wasn't all.

He believed the most incredible part of the project would be directing his team's biomedical research on the extraterrestrial cadavers he'd personally delivered to the CSC storage facility recently. That's why Chalmers had left Washington and returned to Building W01, where he'd watched more of the continuing autopsy process.

CSC. 0200 HOURS

A marine corporal had just made a routine swing past the remaining torpedo crate that still held the intact alien body. He saw something unusual.

After another long day, Chalmers was finally asleep in his BOQ. It'd taken several rings before he found the light switch so he could locate the phone. He glanced at the clock.

"No, it's all right, Corporal, you're supposed to call me, regardless of the hour. Describe the yellow slime, if you can." Chalmers listened intently. "I'll be right over." Minutes later Chalmers was in his base car, speeding through the wooded night to take a stool sample of some banana-mush excrement dripping from the cadaver's crate.

Based on what the marine had told him, Chalmers knew the leaking crate was the one containing the alien whose body had been least damaged in the crash. It had not yet been autopsied. The other three bodies were in a hastily constructed medical forensics lab in another part of the building. Even with refrigeration in the building, the corpses were continuing to decompose, but he knew the others weren't dripping yellow goo.

ᴋᴀ

Chalmers stopped in front of W01, checked in at the duty post, and went straight to the back of the building.

"Okay, thanks, Corporal, you can leave now," Chalmers told the marine who was cleared only to make a routine visual check of the building but had no idea what was in the long crates. After donning the rubber suit and filtration mask, Chalmers opened the hinged lid.

"Good Lord," he blurted into the mask.

He knew immediately what the yellow sludge was, and he took the logical course of action. Plans were modified and enhanced—followed by a full-court press to assemble not only an entirely new DivKay team but also a special facility for everything that he figured would happen next.

Chalmers knew that in the military, C3 meant command, control, and communications. The three C's he wanted were cryogenics, computers, and construction. He wanted the best in the business. He went after them bright and early the next morning in his office where he met with Lieutenant Commander Lee Beckner, a navy engineer who'd been given a K-RED clearance and assigned as Chalmers's special assistant and liaison to the Seabees.

At five ten and one hundred seventy pounds, Beckner had the look and build of a middleweight boxer, including a slightly bent nose from a bar fight. His sun-bleached hair matched a rugged, tanned complexion from years of outdoor construction work. Chalmers had been impressed with Beckner's intelligence when they'd first met at Camp McLeary, and he'd quickly come to appreciate Beckner's demeanor—a mix of hard-working substance and a friendly, easygoing style.

Beckner was astounded when he'd first learned details about Roswell, and still couldn't believe he was working for Dr. Chalmers. But now, after what his boss had just told him—the sudden turn of events—Beckner could not imagine the impact of what the DivKay team was about to try.

৯৯

"Construction is easy," Chalmers told Beckner. "Your Seabees are already working on the regular basement. I want them digging the elevator shaft within the hour, and I expect the second level in the cavern to be operational ASAP."

"Yes, sir. And the people you had in mind for the special C3 requirements?"

"Names and phone numbers," said Chalmers, pulling a slip of paper from his pocket. He handed it to Beckner. "Make the calls, transfer them to my office. We've just had the most incredible thing imaginable drop in our lap . . . and there's no time to waste."

36

Though Won continued monitoring Earth for other Noble prospects, in the last sectic of his time he had devoted most of his omnipresent attention to the land called America and a human being known as Chalmers. Believing Chalmers was the right Noble leader, Won was pleased he'd managed to surround the Chalmerian with supporters who would come into his life at the right time—a well-tuned convergence of coincidence involving men who all had Won's *W* in their names, and at least a bit of Samaritan DNA in their heart and soul.

Won was also pleased he had managed to perform relatively well up to now, given the extemporaneous nature of this GoodWill mission, starting as it did with the last-minute change of plans by the Headmaster. And having just made a cosmic, mental connection with the Tutorium, Won had learned some new and important information of direct consequence to him.

He appreciated the Headmaster communicating with him about his upcoming eligibility for Ascension, though he was still uncertain what Ascension meant for a Samaritan.

~What goes around, comes around, Won, for a circled shape is the truest,~ the Headmaster had responded when asked for clarification on the Ascension.

From the Headmaster's other thoughts, Won knew that Vor, as a result of his ignoble actions, had been pulled from the Samaritan roster and cast by Ga'Lawed into the Meg'etheral—a far dominion, according to the Headmaster—*~where good and evil each takes its appointed place.~*

The Meg'etheral's description raised more questions in Won's mind than it provided answers. The place did not sound good, and Won hoped Ga'Lawed would not send him there for his transgressions on this assignment.

Though he was glad to have finally communicated with his Headmaster,

Won was now as worried about his fate as he was determined in his commitment to Chalmers and the earthman's homeland of America.

Won knew that in his next few sectics everything on the planet below
would accelerate, even by human time frame, in complexity and consequence. It was already happening with the arrival of the Fiverians, driven
from their own world because of Vor's treachery on another one.

He thought about the circle.

The truest shape, but not always connected at a positive point, he reasoned.

Part III

MIDDAY

37

It had been three years since Chalmers, now sixty but still appearing to be only in his midthirties, looked into the torpedo crate and discovered the three circular objects. Covered in yellow placental slime, the round eggs that had emerged postmortem from the alien cadaver had changed everything for Chalmers. Especially his plans for CRYPTOS and CONUNDRUM.

He walked quickly from the parking lot to the front door of Building W01. Wearing only a light jacket, he felt the morning's chill bite, but he knew that in the second subterranean level of W01, where he was headed, it was below freezing. Even below zero. *Two hundred and thirty-eight degrees Fahrenheit below zero.*

"Morning, sir," said U.S. Marine Sergeant Evans, saluting as Dr. Chalmers flashed his badge. "Go ahead. I'll buzz you, sir."

"Thank you, Sergeant," Chalmers said as he walked through the turnstile and toward a plain wooden door.

Hearing the *click,* Chalmers opened the electric door and entered an empty vestibule leading to the double-wide aluminum door of a large freight elevator.

He inserted his badge into a wall slot, and the door swished open. He stepped in.

Seconds later he'd plunged deep into a truly alien world.

"Locked at Level II. Zero eight fifteen hours," he said into the intercom.

"Copy you on L-II, sir," the sergeant said, checking his control panel lights.

Chalmers was more than three hundred feet below the surface and now standing by the handrail of a massive scaffold that supported a number of modular structures. They were elevated offices connected by a gangway balcony that overlooked an enormous cavern—its five-hundred-million-year-old floor strewn with mushrooming formations, its towering ceiling chandeliered with spectacular stalactites.

The geologic outcroppings cast eerie shadows from mercury-vapor arc lamps, their green illumination quickly absorbed by the endless black beyond.

In the open area beneath the scaffolding were a large welded steel vault, several storage buildings, and a pair of stainless-steel cylinders the size of grain silos. The cylinders were covered in frost, just as Chalmers knew they were supposed to be, and they dispersed a continuous vapor cloud.

Still standing on the balcony, Chalmers stared into the black abyss beyond the lamplit perimeter. He refused to be frightened by what it represented.

ka

Concerned that the control panel topside had not shown Dr. Chalmers access to his balcony office, the marine guard called his name over the intercom.

"Yes, Sergeant Evans, I'm still on the walkway. Just paused to admire the view and lost track of time. Sorry for the delay. I'm heading in to my office now."

He found his assistant, Lieutenant Commander Lee Beckner, in a small reception room.

"Morning, sir," said Beckner, who was always early and who Chalmers thought would forever be a bachelor since Beckner's work, like Chalmers's, left little time for a social life. Neither man seemed to care.

"Is everyone here?"

"Yes, sir, in the conference room, on their second cup of coffee."

ka

Five men in white lab coats sat around a table. Four held PhD degrees in their respective fields of technology, and one was a biosystems physiologist—a diagnostic physician specializing in internal organ functionality. They were Chalmers's unit chiefs for his DivKay Task Force.

Serious professionals, they neither expected nor exchanged pleasantries.

"Sam, how long to bring number one out of cryogenesis?" Chalmers asked.

"From minus two thirty-eight to laboratory ambient should take, on the safe side, about ten days," said Dr. Sam Conlen, professor emeritus of the Massachusetts Institute of Technology. Chalmers already regarded Conlen as the father of helium liquefiers, the process required to achieve extreme subfreezing temperatures required for long-term preservation of biologic matter. He was the one Chalmers had contacted first when the eggs needed to be placed in frozen stasis.

"Ten days it is, then," Chalmers said as he turned toward two others at the table.

"How's the language training going?"

Their heads swiveled back and forth, uncertain who should go first.

Maculey started. "The soft-service directional protocols, which I'm now calling the software, have been recalibrated." His connected-at-the-hip partner, Elmond, continued: "And I've incorporated experimental transistors to replace vacuum tubes in the hardwired grid. We've accelerated processing speed with the modifications."

Chalmers nodded at both men. "So ADAM's speech is more articulate and he can think faster, thanks to the combination of some new software, and what perhaps should be called in parallel syntax, some new hardware. Excellent work, gentlemen."

ɞ

ADAM was an All-Source Data Analysis Matrix machine, a revolutionary piece of equipment designed and built for the CIA by pioneering partners—Dr. Raul Maculey and Dr. A. J. Elmond. Chalmers had met them both during the war. They'd been central in some of his analytical projects for General Donovan.

Both of them electrical engineers, Maculey and Elmond had built a data-processing machine called the ENIAC, which the military used for weather prediction, random-number studies, wind-tunnel design, thermal ignition, and . . . to perform calculations for building the hydrogen bomb.

Through their own company, Maculey and Elmond had patented various commercial calculating machines and a data processor that used magnetic tape to store information. Remington Rand Corporation bought the men's first machine, refining it into a UNIVersal Automatic Computer, or UNIVAC.

"No pun intended, John," said Maculey, "but Elmond and I can't stay down here on ice with you forever. Technology's roaring through the private sector like a freight train and there's a ton of money to be made."

"But don't worry," Elmond said. "With the training program we've set up for DivKay's young technicians, it's safe to say no commercial company or government agency will ever possess in-house programmers or computers like the CIA."

"Nor a requirement to use them as the Agency does," Chalmers said stoically.

꙳

The other two men at the table were Dr. Stanley Edington and Dr. James Warner, men whom Chalmers had known professionally and personally for many years.

Professor emeritus at the Colorado School of Mines, Stan Edington was the country's foremost geophysicist, and he had written the definitive books on stratigraphy, structural geography, and mineralogy. Chalmers had assigned him on day one to assist Beckner and the Seabees with building the deep elevator shaft into this cavern.

Jim Warner had earned his MD in internal medicine from Harvard, post-doctoral fellowships in anatomy from Johns Hopkins, and a PhD in research chemistry from Stanford University. Chalmers knew Jim was without peer when it came to dealing with mechanical, physical, and biochemical functions of living organisms. He had placed Jim in charge of the autopsies still being performed on three of the alien cadavers.

꙳

"Dr. Chalmers, we all appreciate the enormity of your responsibility— sorting out the *whether or when* our country gets attacked by Soviets or spacemen. But I don't envy you dealing with all the ramifications of both."

"Thanks, Jim, but I couldn't do this without all of you. Especially what we're about to attempt."

Skepticism colored Warner's face. "Yes, *that*. Based on our *very* suppositional forensics of the sulfuric placenta, you still believe these creatures breathed that gas mixture where they came from?"

"Yes. I calculated the odds of likelihood," Chalmers said.

"And so now you want to thaw out one of the eggs, hatch the damn thing, incubate it, then nurture it in a sulfur-dioxide atmosphere . . . all because you *think* it can live on that?"

"That would be correct, Dr. Warner," said Chalmers. "Call it an empirical experiment in exogenous extemporaneity . . . or call it what it is: throwing a plate of pasta against the wall to see what sticks."

Everyone grinned . . . except Warner.

"Listen, John, nobody could be more excited about examining an outer space alien than me," Warner said, "but it goes back to what I said about dealing with ramifications. This is a huge, unknown step."

Chalmers clenched his jaw. "I know more about the dangerous unknown steps we, and the country, are taking than any of you. As I said, I can't do it without you, but if you're committed to DivKay's overall mission, you'll do what I am asking."

The table was silent.

"You want to hatch that egg and see what happens? Count me in," said Edington.

Maculey and Elmond glanced at Warner, then nodded their agreement, too.

"Okay, John, you win," Warner said. "I'm in."

Chalmers stood.

"Let's unplug the freezer and fire up ADAM. We've got an egg to poach."

38

As director of the Agency's Division K Task Force, and owing to the strict compartmented nature of information held in his K-RED clearance, Chalmers himself briefed the new director, Allen W. Dulles, on the CRYPTOS and CONUNDRUM projects.

Chalmers planned to save one issue till the end, certain that Dulles would be shocked by the information.

"Let's talk about your operation," Dulles said almost as soon as they'd shaken hands.

"Sir, for our planning purposes, the National Security Act not only authorized this Agency six years ago, it also sanctioned the creation of the National Security Resources Board."

"And I've been in favor of the board. If used correctly, it will provide important command and control for civil defense planning."

"NSRB does more than that. Inherent in the board's charter is a cover opportunity for denial and deception operations having to do with both of the DivKay initiatives."

"Break that down for me, Chalmers."

"Mr. Director, the CRYPTOS project prepares us for two different kinds of nuclear war—a shorter-term, though unlikely conflict . . . and a longer, almost certain one."

"Which means . . ."

"That the Soviets have nuclear weapons and strategic delivery systems, and they're our number one enemy . . . for now. My analysis, however, is that their economy is fatally flawed, sustained solely by limited exports, and will collapse within decades. It is doubtful we will ever go to war with them, but we nonetheless must have an offensive and a defensive contingency for a surprise attack . . . and as a political bargaining tool."

"Yes. The reason for the CIA's creation . . . no more Pearl Harbors. But you said two different kinds of war."

"The Chinese, sir. I believe they'll be our most dangerous adversary in the future."

"Chinese support for Pyongyang, combined with Soviet aid," said Dulles, "has made the conflict in Korea these past three years more challenging. But I think we're close to negotiating a cease-fire with the North Koreans. Would you agree?"

"The two opposing Korean governments may still be willing to fight to the death, but their respective patrons—the People's Republic of China and the Soviet Union on the one hand, and the U.S. and UN on the other—are not."

Dulles nodded.

"Even after the eventual settlement," Chalmers continued, "the emerging, modern world will continue to deal with the consequences of a divided Korea, especially a militarily strong, economically weak, and unpredictable North Korea under a Chinese puppeteer's control."

"I'd be interested in your take on the rest of Asia."

"Sir, I think this same scenario will play out in other areas of Southeast Asia like Vietnam, Cambodia, and the Philippines. Taiwan will always be a political tinderbox because China wants to annex it. Believe me, China will continue to stir the Pacific Rim pot. And one day it will boil over on us."

"But China does not have atomic weapons."

"Not yet, sir. And it is for that reason that we have plenty of Russia's atomic borscht in our soup bowl to last for a few decades. It's definitely our first priority."

"And that brings us back to the civil defense aspect of the NSRB."

"Yes it does, Mr. Director, the public, overt part of civil defense. While I believe we can expect to avoid war with the Soviets, we nonetheless must have plans for waging and surviving war with them. Most Americans are fearful about that."

"The press already refers to the new era as a cold war," Dulles said.

"I think it's more of a political war of brinksmanship," Chalmers said, "with rapid technological advances on both sides producing a bipoliticized world dominated by two superpowers. There'll undoubtedly be tension and some dangerous moments along the way, but I don't think things will get out of hand anytime soon."

"From your lips to God's ears. And I hope those trigger-happy ass-holes at Defense can be made to believe that before it's too late. I keep re-calling that line from Oscar Wilde . . . how just thinking about something is the beginning of making it happen. If we keep talking about war, plan-ning for war . . . it could all become a self-fulfilling prophecy, huh?"

"We can't afford to stick our heads in the sand," said Chalmers, who then quickly explained that another important NSRB plan was the Conti-nuity of Government initiative. "As you may already know, sir," Chalmers added, "COG involves excavation and construction of a massive bunker inside Mount Weather in West Virginia."

"Gives a new meaning to underground government, I'd say."

"It does. We're already excavating salt domes in other states where federal records will be stored and strategic reserves of petroleum can be stockpiled."

"Hmmm, so something'll be left after most everything else's been de-stroyed," said Dulles cynically. "We're all like a bunch of ostrich heads digging bomb shelters in our backyards. Even worse are those duck-and-cover safety awareness films being shown in schools. It's as though folks are telling the government to go ahead and wage war—we've all made plans to cope with the inconvenience of mushroom clouds. Damn stupid . . . as if ducking under a desk or digging a hole in your backyard will make it possible to survive a nuke."

"We're living in strange times for sure," said Chalmers.

"It's unthinkable," Dulles said, his angst meter in the red zone, "that we must psychologically prepare our citizens to live with the constant threat of a nuclear war. Good God, it is social brainwashing stemming from the insanity of confrontational politics."

Bingo. Dulles had provided the perfect segue that Chalmers had steered him toward from the outset.

39

"Sir, your comment brings us to the second element of CRYPTOS—the national psyche, the paranoia about nuclear war, and the rush to build shelters. All of which will in fact serve as the cover for a more comprehensive, covert civil defense shelter project."

Chalmers handed Dulles another red-striped report. "These are some of my preliminary thoughts on a long-term project called the SSI."

"SSI?"

"The Strategic Survival Initiative, Mr. Director. It surpasses anything currently conceived in the COG plan. The underpinning, quite literally, of the SSI is a covert activity code-named Black Spade. I suggest you read this summary, and then we can reconvene later to discuss details about it."

Chalmers noticed Dulles glance at the wall clock. He figured the director had another meeting soon, so there wasn't much time left to cover the remaining issue.

"Sir, your report contains key points on the CONUNDRUM project: status of the alien spacecraft; the counterpropaganda effort to minimize UFO hysteria by co-opting the phenomenology of UFO sightings; and the bioforensic study of the extraterrestrial cadavers. The alien craft is still an engineering enigma, but its propulsion system is what my people call a plasmalectric, an ion-charged turbine. It's our theory that this engine runs off the harvested neutrons from ambient space light and cosmic, electrical energy from the big bang. Figuring out even this much about the ship's been a reach, and I don't know if we'll ever be able to reverse-engineer it completely."

"Keep me posted on your progress. As for that term, big bang, I'm not sure—"

"It's a new theory, sir. Postulates the cosmos was formed from a singular explosion of compressed matter. A nuclear blast whose scale astrophysicists say is beyond comprehension. Religious members of the scientific community call it a divine moment, the birth of creation . . . the dawn of time."

"All that's beyond my comprehension, too. UFO engine probably is as well."

"According to my experts, the engine may operate like the scrubbing filters that enable air to be rebreathed and re-oxygenated in a closed environment, like a submarine. My computations assign a high probability that the turbine regenerates and enhances its own source of fuel as it draws from, then blends with, cosmic light particles. I believe it's a perpetual motion machine able to accelerate to the speed of its fuel supply—the speed of light."

"Good Lord. But even at that velocity the distances are so great. It would still—"

"Yes, sir, it'd take millions, even billions of years for alien life to travel across our galaxy, not to mention across the galactic cosmos. That's where Einstein comes into play."

"Ah, his theory of relativity. I know a few things, at least. It's a shortcut link between time and space, right?"

"Yes, sir. The time-space continuum. It's the emerging new astrophysical data about collapsed stars, the so-called black holes in the universe's dark matter. There is a brilliant young astrophysics student named Stern doing some amazing graduate research on this subject in New York. I may reach out to him at some point. He and others refer to these dark matter anomalies as wormholes—doorways that theoretically could enable space travelers, including us one day, to find shortcuts through a motor trip across the cosmos."

"Truly mind-boggling stuff. How can you, we . . . grasp the enormity of it?"

"Like anything else. We do what we have to, one step at a time. The public is dealing just fine with rumors of spaceships and alien life. The original crash site at Roswell, which you may not know was the old Air Force Flight Test Center, is now going by the enigmatic moniker of Area 51."

Chalmers explained that Area 51 was still an airfield complex, and it bordered the Nevada Test Site, the location of many of the Department of Energy's nuclear weapons tests. Everything in the NTS area was now ultra–top secret.

"John Q. Public still thinks we have aliens in there," Chalmers continued. "They're wrong, of course. The cadavers are someplace else."

Dulles tapped his pencil on the desk. "I want to stay on the aliens, but just a quick side question. What've you got at Area 51 right now?"

"Sir, Lockheed Martin Aeronautics is planning to use Area 51 for the test flight program on our U-2 high-altitude reconnaissance plane. Some of the fuselage and wing design is intended to lower the radar profile. It's a new aviation design concept called stealth technology. And the Agency's team at Lockheed got a few ideas from the UFO."

Dulles studied him. "You evidently know a lot about the U-2 program, then?"

"Yes, sir, of course. And I know that droves of people are watching Area 51 all the time hoping to see more UFOs. I believe some psychological stealth could be applied to the test flight program, with any sightings of the U-2 chalked up to a bunch of zanies looking for more little green men in spaceships. As it turned out, and based on my recommendation, we worked with our counterintelligence counterparts at Defense to arrange for little brown chimpanzees to be used in ejection-seat experiments. Most were killed in the high-altitude, high-speed jettison drills that were conveniently arranged over Area 51. We subsequently photographed them, decked out in custom silver flight suits and bubble helmets, splattered out on the ground, around which was scattered wreckage from some of the real failed weather balloons. Incident reports and all manner of other bureaucratic paperwork were backdated and are ready for public release should some of the relentless UFO sleuths turn up additional press-grabbing information on the actual crash at Roswell."

"Interesting. Anything else on the propaganda front?"

"Yes. From the outset the FBI has been involved in Roswell investigations, largely because the army CIC pressed for the Bureau's assistance. Hoover never really wanted to get mired in that particular kind of quicksand and he has steadily disengaged the Bureau . . . but in a sense the damage is already done, at least in terms of existing official FBI documents that, if they were ever obtained through public, legal pressure, would prove to be the smoking gun for the '47 event. Such an occurrence would not only incite major social discord, it would likely have a political effect on us as the mea culpa architect of the overall cover-up."

"And your strategy there is . . . ?"

"Based on Director Hoover's willingness to be mired in all kinds of *other* quicksand."

"What does that mean?"

"Turns out J. Edgar has been keeping personal secret records on thousands of politicians, entertainment industry folks, entrepreneurs, and anybody else he distrusts . . . and he's been doing it all the way back to when he came to the old Bureau of Investigation long before it became federalized. He's building a power base of potential extortion that I predict will keep him in control of the Bureau until the day he dies."

"And how does that constitute a strategy for your UFO containment propaganda?"

"Because of the file I have on Hoover, who, along with other reprehensible traits, is a hypocrite of high order. Rumors abound that Eddie is a homosexual and likes to cross-dress, and knowing now that we have that file on him, he has suddenly become agreeable to state that based on his own lengthy re-investigation of Bureau UFO files, he has ordered that all original photos, interviews, previous official DOJ documents, and every shred of forensic evidence obtained by the FBI will be declared bogus. In addition, the Bureau will officially stand down from all future discussions about Roswell, certainly including any mention of the cadavers."

Dulles loosened his tie, filled his glass, and offered the pitcher to Chalmers. At the same time he eyed Chalmers intently.

"Well, we certainly drifted far afield from the U-2, Dr. Chalmers. I know a great deal about our plane, too, and am aware generally of what you've just conveyed about the FBI. We share other knowledge as well, like the Committee—an organization Hoover and the Bureau have mistakenly referred to as Majestic 12, for the composition of its membership. Interesting group, huh?"

Chalmers was taken aback for a moment. "Well . . . yes, sir, I didn't realize—"

"We'll get back to Committee business, along with the aliens. Let me hear what else you know about the U-2."

"Yes, sir. The Dragon Lady, as our platform's already being called, will constitute a revolutionary aircraft, collecting multisensor photo, electro-optic, infrared, and radar imagery, as well as signals intelligence data. She'll transmit all of it to anywhere in the world, providing war planners with the latest real-time intelligence possible . . . exactly what we'll need to stay half a step ahead of war with the Soviets."

"Which means we can forget about the UFO watchers at Area 51," said Dulles. "The press will still have details about our plane before the first test flight . . . damn news mongers are better spies than we are."

"That's why we've developed the strategy of overt secrecy. We're going to make aliens so controversial, so conspiratorial that we will undercut the country's belief in them by our seeming openness."

᠊ᢙ

Feudal Japan's ninja warriors, who were believed to possess the art of invisibility, had inspired Chalmers's strategy. A ninja used misdirection to create stealth—stagecraft to trick the enemy into believing he had disappeared in broad daylight. In fact, he'd only twisted into an odd shape and blended with a tree, a rock, or shade being cast by something else. Chalmers knew it had worked historically for one band of unique warriors, and he was incorporating the concept throughout the still-evolving CIA.

᠊ᢙ

"Okay, I'm game. How do we make your overt secrecy happen?" asked Dulles.

"It's simple, really. With the flying saucer craze already sweeping America, it is inevitable Hollywood will see it as grist for the moviemaking mill. We'll just help the producers and screenwriters *get it right,* creatively speaking. I've already identified individuals in the film industry who'll respond cooperatively with our consultative briefings on story ideas. Through them we'll make what we're trying to hide so public no one can separate fact from fiction."

Dulles was impassive . . . then a slow grin painted his blank face. "Brilliant. Just brilliant. Make it happen, Chalmers."

"Affirmative, sir."

As Chalmers calculated, and helped orchestrate, the craze launched a spate of alien invasion movies, including *The Day the Earth Stood Still, When Worlds Collide,* and the riveting 1953 version of H. G. Wells's *The War of the Worlds.*

"We'll move openly on every other operational front as well," he told Dulles, "always making sure that CIA activities, especially the clandestine ones, are seen, reported, or rumored by others as something they *think* the Agency has done, rather than what the organization actually carried out."

There was no point, Chalmers believed, in trying to maintain true secrecy.

"Better to use the inherent weakness of secrecy as its strongest asset. As long as secrets can be safeguarded, we'll enjoy the dark bottom of the pail that contains them, but when the bottom invariably falls out, we'll simply make the mess on the floor appear to be something else."

Dulles's eyes narrowed. "I understand you had a mess, a yellow mess on the floor of Building W01 three years ago. What have you made that one look like?"

Chalmers was stunned that the director knew about the placenta discharge in the torpedo crate. Maybe he knew about the rest as well.

"How did you—"

"Know about the three eggs you placed into cryogenic hibernation? The same way I know about the Level II cavern basement and the combined research and storage facilities housed there. And it has nothing to do with getting a K-RED clearance. I had one of those before you did. You see, I'm one of the founding members of the Committee."

Chalmers stared silently at his boss.

"For now, tell me about the eggs, particularly the one you removed from its cryogenic habitat and have been incubating."

"Yes, sir."

"And sometime later, Jonathan, when the time's right, I'll tell you about the Committee."

40

Chalmers told Director Dulles that two eggs were still in their cryocooler cylinders, as was the alien cadaver that had extruded them in a postmortem delivery. The third egg was thawed, then placed in a sulfur-dioxide incubator. It had remained there for almost three years.

"During that time, my task force biophysiologist, Dr. James Warner, used every conceivable piece of technological hardware to determine if the egg pod was even alive. We probed it with X-ray, radar, sonar, galvanometer, electroencephalogram, electrocardiogram, and others—even combining EEG, EKG, and other machines to make new diagnostic equipment. It never decomposed, so we figured it was in some kind of dormant status . . . until six weeks ago."

"Then something changed?"

"Yes, the superficies, the external texture and color of the shell. It went from a dull greenish-gray to a reddish-brown mottle with spiderweb fissures. The EEG and EKG monitors lit up, a large crack opened, and more of the yellow sludge extruded. Moments later, the ugliest, most foul-smelling thing you've ever seen crawled out."

Dulles's eyes flared. "My God, that's incredible. And since then?"

"We moved the hatchling into a larger atmospheric chamber, a stainless-steel container inside the main welded-steel vault. We watched it through the viewing glass. We fed it anything we thought it might eat. It seemed to like roadkill venison, especially the hooves, bones, and antlers. In a week the alien being—the creature, really—doubled in size, then it doubled again a day later."

"Good Lord, that's amazing," said Dulles.

"A closed-circuit camera monitored the holding area constantly. Until two days ago. Suddenly, the control screen went blank. Dr. Warner and one of the technicians went down to the chamber floor to investigate."

"And what did they find?"

Chalmers paused, took a deep breath. "I don't know. They never came back. After some fifteen minutes or so, the marine guards went down to check. They found no trace of Warner and the tech—or the alien. Evidence suggests it effected an escape. It simply vanished, along with the two men."

"How could the . . . how did *it* get past the secured door?"

"It didn't go through the door, sir."

"Then through the glass viewing port? How'd it do that, given its size?"

"It ripped a hole in the stainless-steel inner chamber and then slashed open a huge gap in the steel-plated vault. I'm sure it killed Warner and the tech. Probably ate them."

"Good Lord, that's horrid beyond belief."

"Yes. And now, right now, sir . . ."

"Go on. What else?"

"Now it's loose somewhere in the deep, dark underground."

41

VIRGINIA CAVE—INWARD PASSAGE

The pitch-blackness of these strange surroundings represented no visual handicap to his multispectral eyes. He saw that his extensors had been ripped open when he'd clawed through the steel confines of his imprisonment, and he could see he'd left a blood trail to this point. It made him vulnerable, but there was nothing he could do about it now. His only option was to control the fear that gripped him and to plunge deeper into this rock corridor, where his instincts said he'd find safety.

δφγηφλ—*concentrate,* he thought. σ]ιχε—*think,* he implored himself.

But it was hard to do because his head pounded with pain and his gill slits flared wildly. At this point he wasn't even sure he knew *how* to think or *what* to think, and doubted he'd live long enough to figure it out. Meanwhile, his breath came in gasps as his body fought to adjust to the absence of sulfuric gas in this alien world's atmosphere.

Then came the first transitional moment, the reassuring awareness that he wasn't running away in desperation, but instead forward with determination, aided by a special strength provided by the βαφκιψυ in his body's remaining green blood. Though he couldn't account for his knowledge, he knew that βαφκιψυ was *ad'renal-oxulyte,* a chemical substance his glands produced during a crisis, like the fight-or-flight stress that clutched him now.

The entity suddenly felt a renewed imperative to hang on long enough for ζξϖωυκφ to take effect.

This strange being knew, perhaps from yet another deep-seated memory now surfacing as part of the next transitional moment, that ζξϖωυκφ was a biocerebral adaptation gene unique to his Fiverian species. He pressed onward, soon reaching a distance where he felt safe enough from his captors to rest and take stock of his situation.

As he surveyed this alien world he became increasingly aware of the genetic tools he possessed and the powerful advantage they afforded him.

He knew he was encoded to survive, even to flourish—which he'd done ever since his forced hatching into the barely sustainable, sulfur-tinted air of his former confinement. He focused his faceted eyes on a declivity of liquid and noted the gaseous aura wafting from it.

The liquid, he knew, as his rhizoidal sensors examined its content, consisted largely of the same universal chemical element that composed all the stars he now realized he'd traveled through during his mother's womb-wrapped journey to this place.

As even more data lights blinked on inside his head, he identified the liquid's main ingredient as ηψδρογεν, which he'd later learn this world's inhabitants called hydrogen. His instincts told him to bathe his wounded extensors in this ameliorative fluid. He did, noting with interest the foaming, tingling sensation that occurred. A moment later, he observed that his extensors were already healing. On impulse, he took the liquid into his mouth and felt the same peroxide sensation spread through his body.

Suddenly he felt his *or'ganel-ung* begin to process fully the oxygen and nitrogen his discerning tongue had tasted as it flicked into the black atmosphere of his newfound freedom. Many other sensations and recollections flowed from him as he ingested and inhaled more of the liquid and gas into his body. This world's chemical composition, he thought, was not merely elemental—for him it was miraculously *fundamental*.

He was healing and maturing, becoming holistically sound and fully sentient at the same time.

And then he surprised himself. He spoke into the darkness, which he knew surrounded him but through which he nonetheless could see. He suddenly realized the metaphorical significance of that incongruous contrast.

=φ αμ κλφαζαρ ατε οɜ καλδυζαμ= *I am Kaj'a-zar, son of Kul'da-Zak*, he said in a booming guttural growl that reverberated throughout the cavern. Those first words also echoed as a thunderous epiphany through his brain, shaking loose an avalanche of memories Kaj'a-zar could now recall from when he was only an egg in his mother's womb. Even then, the unborn son had sensed when his father was near him, and he had heard words spoken by his father. From those remembered words, Kaj'a-zar knew that before invaders drove his family from their world, his father was a physician, a scientist, and the leader of the last of his Fiverian kind.

More important for his present circumstance, Kaj'a-zar began to feel ξϖυ ηγεκ, the genetic absorption of his father's vast knowledge. *My father will live on through me,* he thought, now imbued with even more strength. *I will become myself as an extension of him, and I will find my place in this world. However long it takes.*

He felt a lonely pride in knowing that the Tyrannical Crown his father had intended for him to wear was in fact his ... if only, Kaj'a-zar reluctantly admitted, because he probably was the only Fiverian left alive.

And then Kaj'a-zar thought of something else, one particular thing he now remembered he'd also absorbed into his consciousness even before he was prematurely hatched. It was a name. *It was spoken by others also in the place of experimentation, a laboratory they called it, where the alien leader presided over my birth.*

=*Ch'al-murs,*= *Chalmers,* he rasped aloud. *A man, as I believe these aliens are called, who possesses power, prominence, and intelligence comparable to a Fiverian. Someone who brought me into this world, though painfully was it done.*

Kaj'a-zar resented what'd been done to him during captivity, although he admitted that without the experimentation he'd never have lived. Still and all, he felt the genetic distrust for this planet's inhabitants that his father had experienced when he first guided the flotilla into the blue planet's atmosphere.

If they feared Fiverians when we first came in peace, he thought, *under my Tyrannical reign they will know our savage power when they see us one day rule this world.*

If they are still around to witness it.

He had one last thought as he stood to continue his trek deeper into the cavern that he knew would be his retreat and his dark kingdom until he'd emerge later to claim the lighted world above.

=*Ch'al-murs,*= he repeated. *For you and yours I will come someday.*

42

During the alien's escape eighteen months ago, it had slaughtered and consumed two people. Not knowing how far into the cavern the creature had retreated, or if and when it might return, Chalmers and his assistant Lee Beckner had hastily constructed a temporary perimeter security system.

Chalmers had then called on his friend and CIA colleague, Dr. Richard Swanson, to design and install a permanent, more sophisticated system. Swanson, who'd been around the intelligence community block many times, was head of DSRA, the Division of Scientific Research and Applications. He'd been handpicked by General Donovan to design technological gadgets and gizmos used during the heyday of OSS operations behind enemy lines. Both Swanson and Chalmers had made the transition to the CIG and then CIA after the war and had been friends ever since.

*

"Dick, I can't tell you *why* I need special security at one of my project sites," Chalmers said that day when he'd called Swanson to his office a year and half ago, "and I'm going to require you sign a separate secrecy agreement before even showing you where it's to be installed."

"Secrecy agreement? Why? My clearances are as high as yours."

"Ever hear of something called K-RED?"

Swanson stared blankly. "So the hallway rumors are true." He shrugged. "Sure, John, whatever you say."

*

The next day, Swanson had flown to the CSC with Chalmers and Beckner, who escorted him into the rarefied subterranean air of Level II. With armed marines posted as security, Swanson installed a miniature radar-based DSRA motion detector that fed to a control monitor in Chalmers's office.

While an improvement over what he and Beckner had thrown together earlier, Chalmers was not satisfied with the jury-rigged nature of the new system either, and he added a few improvements of his own.

"C'mon, John, what the hell *is* this place?" Swanson took in the lighted cavern's vista. "What are those big cylinders? Is this where you are all those times I can never find you anywhere in the E Street complex?"

"Answers may come later. For now, I want you to go back to your lab and design a permanent motion detection system based on a steady stream of refracted light attached to a pulse activation switch."

"Something that will send an alert signal when a conveyance beam is broken?"

"Exactly. There's already some research in this arena. It's an emerging subscience of thermodynamic light amplification. Something Einstein posited as his principle of stimulated emission, or what he called putting atoms into an excited energy state."

"I read one of his articles on amplifying radiant light at a controlled frequency."

Chalmers patted his friend's shoulder. "Think of yourself as carrying on his work."

☙

Swanson had returned to his lab, resolved to fulfill Chalmers's tasking and determined to make whatever contribution possible to the work started by Einstein.

He designed exactly what Chalmers requested, and in the process the Agency's DSRA laboratory significantly advanced the development of the laser, an acronym drawn from *l*ight *a*mplification by *s*timulated *e*mission of *r*adiation.

☙

Today, eighteen months later, Swanson and his tech team were back in the cavern, hanging an updated laser beam that created a spiderweb of invisible monochromatic light around the Level II laboratory. He still didn't understand why Chalmers needed something this sophisticated to protect "a big ol' bat cave," as he now routinely called the place, but Swanson was pleased with his work and confident that nothing from this world could pass through without activating the alarm.

☙

Deep within the cavern and far removed from the cryogenic cylinder and its incubation pen, Kaj'a-zar continued to concentrate on surviving in the present, even as he planned for the future.

Kaj'a-zar thought continually about the man called Chalmers.

But something else was on his mind, too, and it was more important than how he intended to pay back Chalmers.

Kaj'a-zar was focused on the two remaining frozen eggs that held his sisters.

43

VIRGINIA CAVE—INWARD PASSAGE

His father's son in every sense, Kaj'a-zar was not only a technician and a warrior but also a born navigator. As he moved deeper into the cramped, twisting world that was now his to explore, he kept mental track of the place from which he had escaped.

Advancing in the darkness, he felt his body and mind reacting even faster to ζξϖωυκϕ, the adaptation gene that enabled him to remember his father's memories and comprehend all he needed to know about his Five-rian species.

Using his extraordinary strength, Kaj'a-zar clawed his way through lightless passages otherwise too narrow for his body. In the process, he discovered he could ζαρατε϶, or dramatically alter the natural shape of his body for short periods of time. Just another of the interesting, useful discoveries unfolding for him.

His rhizoidal sensors tweaked. There was something different in the atmospheric mix of nitrogen and oxygen that his *or'ganel-ung* was now adjusted to. This was more than satisfying respiration—this was ωυκ . . . a smell. And it came from the increased air flowing from a new crack in the sedimentary rock fissure through which he'd just wiggled.

There was something else, and it caused his multispectral eyes to adjust from the absence of light to its now faint presence. He clawed, twisted, morphed, and maneuvered his way upward toward it. In the process, he entered a new kind of open chamber, one with a grayish-blue ambient aura and leafy life-forms whose verdant appendages swayed in the increased flow of air he felt as he moved to the brightening light just ahead.

}{λδυζα)δσ —I am in another dominion, a new world, he thought.

Kaj'a-zar's sensors suddenly flared into an alert of multiple sensations, among them vibrating sounds emanating from a cluster of coiled creatures into which he had walked. They struck his legs, sending an exhilarating tingle of heat through his body. He pulled one free, studying it as it wrapped around his arm, alternating between flicking a forked tongue and striking him with more heat probes.

Having not eaten since he had fled the place of his experimentation, Kaj'a-zar saw these serpentine creatures as a source of {δευλφα, and he ate all the bountiful food his good fortune provided.

A few strides forward and he found the source of the light. It was amazing. He squatted in the jagged opening atop a high escarpment and absorbed the vista of green landscape and blue sky extending beyond.

}{λδυζα)δσ—*Very definitely another world* . . . a planetary surface that had an unmistakable physical element his long-range vision immediately telescoped onto.

It was a grid pattern of civilized construction . . . a small town. With planetary creatures.

And it was his next stop.

44

The destination was the NSF, the Naval Support Facility in Thurmont, Maryland. Or at least that's what CIA director Allen Dulles had told Chalmers when they'd boarded the UH-34 helicopter. Like everything about the Agency he headed, Dulles had lied to Chalmers about this trip in order to create a deception to hide a secret.

"Time to get away from the rat race for a while," Dulles had told him earlier. "We're going to Camp David. We'll meet with General Donovan and other old OSS hands, along with some political fast-trackers. You'll find it . . . enlightening."

"With all due respect, sir, this is a busy time. You have the upcoming trip to Cambodia to discuss the South East Asia Treaty Organization membership. Socializing at Camp David may not be—"

"We're not on a *social* visit, Dr. Chalmers. This is official business, a government anniversary. It's even listed as such on the calendar."

"Yes, of course, sir. A national day of remembrance for Pearl Harbor."

"Good, John. I'm glad to know you glance at the date occasionally. Since you never seem to sleep, I wondered how you kept track of time."

"Same as everybody. Near as I can tell, though, there's not enough to get all the work done. I just hate to waste a day."

"This will *not* be a waste," said Dulles. "We're going to reflect on where we've taken the CIA since the OSS years and speculate about the troubled world into which our Agency and our nation are headed."

After landing, Dulles and Chalmers entered Camp David's main building— a large log cabin lodge that served as VIP billets, conference room, and general headquarters for the other smaller rustic cabins that comprised the mountaintop retreat. After laying out his personal effects in his room, Chalmers freshened up.

He was not happy to be here. Today he'd hoped to finish his analytical paper on SEATO, a potentially powerful alliance formed last year among Australia, France, Great Britain, the United States, and others to prevent the spread of communism in Southeast Asia. He viewed SEATO with strategic favor, particularly because of the building tensions throughout the Asian region.

Chalmers knew that Eisenhower was already being pressured to commit American troops to a small rice-growing country called Vietnam, and Congress had passed a bill allowing mobilization of U.S. troops should China attack Taiwan. He knew this occurred against the backdrop of mounting tensions with the Soviets, who continued to test rockets, expand military forces, and rattle sabers throughout Eastern Europe.

As he'd feared, momentum was increasing for the next world war.

And for Chalmers, all of it demanded the CIA's attention, which meant his increasing overall analytical duties had to be carried out in addition to his specific CRYPTOS and CONUNDRUM projects. As he'd told Beckner only a few days ago, "We need more of everything—staff, space, money, and especially time."

"Well, boss, we know Eisenhower's just authorized money for the construction of a headquarters compound. That's bound to be good news for us, huh?"

"Could be. Especially if DivKay gets the new IBM computers I've requested."

෴

Chalmers entered the central room where Dulles and other distinguished men had already assembled. Drinks in hand, they were engaged in animated conversation.

"Gentlemen," announced General William Donovan in his commanding voice, "I see Dr. Chalmers has finally joined us."

Shaking with one hand and placing the other on Chalmers's shoulder, Donovan said warmly, "Damn good to see you again, John."

"You, too, sir. You're back in your legal element on Wall Street and doing well."

"Yes, back in New York where the focus is finance, not Washington bullshit."

Those assembled were a who's who of OSS legends and men Chalmers knew personally: General William J. Donovan, Allen W. Dulles, General Walter Bedell Smith, William J. Casey, William E. Colby, and Richard "Will" Helms.

There were some other younger politicos, whom Chalmers didn't know personally, only that they were touted as up-and-comers—Milton Wainright, Warren Winslow, Coleman Westfield, and Craig W. Weaver.

Taking the drink Donovan handed him after the introductions were over, Chalmers said, "Sir, have you noticed that everyone here has the letter *W* in his name?"

"So?"

"It's definitely a convergence of coincidence, and the twenty-third letter in the Latin alphabet. You may not know this, but in chemistry W is the symbol for tungsten, after its German name, wolfram, which is the hardest, longest-lasting metal with the highest melting point—3,422 degrees Celsius or 6,192 degrees Fahrenheit."

Donovan had been through this kind of thing with Chalmers before, and he knew exactly what to do. He took another drink from the waiter walking by and prepared to wait out Chalmers's encyclopedic discourse.

"And did you know, sir, that in Italy, *W*, which does not appear in the Italian alphabet, is a symbol that stands for *viva*, or long live?"

"No. But I know the longer you live the younger you continue to look. Remember my mentioning that the day you reported to my brand-new OSS office after I'd pulled you out of basic training? I also said then I'd tell you something one day."

It was Chalmers's turn to grab a passing drink. Apprehensive, he nodded.

"Umm, yes, seems like Director Dulles also has something he has intended to tell me for some time now."

"I'd still like to know your secret for maintaining a youthful appearance, and I will come back to that, but right now there's a bigger issue to discuss. It has to do with everyone here, including me and Allen. This is a close-knit fraternity of individuals . . . winners. Those who have *won*, I'd say, in their various battles or endeavors, and who share a Good Samaritan attitude—a common bond of patriotism, dedicated service to the country, goodwill toward man, and faith in God. Everyone here recognizes the extraordinary contributions you made during the war, John. We all have Committee clearances high enough to know about CRYPTOS and CONUNDRUM and your Division K Task Force."

"Yes . . . thank you, sir." *Where is this heading?* Chalmers wondered.

"John, we *are* the Committee, and we all believe that your greatest role in defense of our country's national security interests is yet to be played."

"And that it will involve the future of the country . . . indeed, the future of the world," Allen Dulles added, rejoining them.

Donovan placed his hand on Chalmers's shoulder. "John, something very . . . strange recently happened to everyone in this group, and it directly affects you."

He was about to explain, when they all heard a booming voice.

†ᴁ

"Attention, gentlemen," a marine said as he marched into the great room and planted himself in a ramrod-straight stance, "the president of the United States."

A second later, Dwight Eisenhower, known by the nickname "Ike" to his friends, powered into the room flanked by two other marines.

Chalmers had been introduced to the president once before but had spoken only briefly with him. He watched him now shaking hands with those in the room, addressing them as old friends.

"Bill, Allen, . . . Dr. Chalmers," Ike said as he reached the trio.

"Mr. President," they responded in unison.

"Mr. President," said Donovan, "we've given Dr. Chalmers a pre-brief but have been waiting for your arrival to . . . to articulate for him the main theme of this gathering."

"I'll come straight to the point, Dr. Chalmers."

The president, who had arranged today's gathering, explained that in the past several days everyone in this room, including him, had been visited by an individual who'd told everyone the same thing. Though a stranger to each of them, they'd all said later he was nonetheless someone they each seemed to know. This person simply appeared in their offices or homes, as if materializing from thin air.

"One minute I was alone in the Oval Office signing a document, and the next I looked up and he was standing at my desk. I've no damn idea how he got in the White House to begin with, and don't know how he got out. After talking to me for a moment, he just stepped through the door. And I do mean *through* a solid wood door, and vanished. Marine guard in the hall never saw him . . . come out."

"Happened to all of us, pretty much the same way," said Donovan, who could tell by the expression on Chalmers's face that even hearing this from the president of the United States made it hard to swallow.

"This visitor," said Ike, "gave us all the same message. That he was here to make sure we *won,* and that our strength in assisting you was our unity as a Committee. How the hell this character even knew there *was* a Committee came as another shock to me, until he explained that he had brought us together years ago and *ingrained us,* as he put it, to seek out each other and form a union of similar purpose." Ike looked at the others in the small group. "Turns out, Dr. Chalmers, that *you* are our purpose."

"Well, I must say," Chalmers said, "all of that seems strange indeed."

"That isn't the half of it," Ike said. "Not a person in this room can even describe what we think we remember this mysterious individual looked like."

"But we all said he reminded us of our fathers," said Donovan.

"So what do you make of this, Dr. Chalmers?" asked the president.

"Sir, it sounds like something someone even stranger than this individual, perhaps the same person, told me a very long time ago. I believed him then as I believe you now. I believe I am supposed to do something . . . special with my life. I just don't know what it is yet."

"In any event, I want you to have this . . . I believe you're *meant* to have it," Ike said, handing over a shiny box that the president's aide had just handed him. The strange container looked to be metal and about six inches square. "I'm the only person who got one. Everyone tells me you have a talent for deciphering the bizarre and the complex. White House security staff checked it out. No one knows what it's made of. It has no opening, no seams. If anybody can figure out how to get in, it's you and the technicians in the Agency laboratory. Good luck with it."

"Thank you, Mr. President," said Chalmers as he accepted the box.

৵

As he studied the box's strange texture, Chalmers thought he heard a deep hum and noted an even deeper pulsing sensation emanating from it. He felt an odd out-of-body confusion. Was the helicopter revving up its turbo engines outside?

A second later, he heard the bass beat of the rotors and felt the chopper slapping through the cold air of the return flight to Washington. He was dumbfounded. How had he gotten here? When, how, had the meeting ended?

Chalmers looked down and saw he was holding the box in his lap.

৵

The next day, Chalmers couldn't recall what he'd said to Dulles on the flight home. He hardly remembered the flight at all, much less any details about the trip to Camp David. It was as though the memory were erasing itself by the hour.

After taking the box to the lab for one of his technicians to evaluate,

Chalmers stopped by the director's office for a second. Both men said how restful it was to have gotten away from the grind for a day, and how enjoyable it was to visit with the OSS vets. There was some general sense that productive discussions were held about the CIA's role in the cold war with the Soviets and other issues of Chinese communism in Southeast Asia. Nothing was said about the box.

Chalmers took it on faith that in time he'd figure out how to open it . . . and would know what to do with its contents. He also knew the perfect place to store the box. On his next trip to CSC, Chalmers locked it away in Building W01, Level II, in cold storage with the CONUNDRUM project files.

His instincts told him that among all the CONUNDRUM secrets, this box was the most sensitive and that he'd soon have to include his staff in its investigation. Because he did not wish to explain its peculiar arrival, he'd have to fabricate a lie about its origin.

Chalmers knew the perfect deception.

He would simply tell his assistant, Lee Beckner, who had K-RED clearances, that the box had been found in the Roswell wreckage and had been set aside, until now.

Chalmers's analytical judgment was that eventually, when the mystery box was opened, he would have to create a more elaborate ploy to safeguard whatever was inside.

45

HIGH STASIS—TIMELESS

Won knew he was within GoodWill protocols on his decision to communicate directly with a group of earthlings who called themselves a Committee. After all, they were the offspring of spawnlings he'd produced in earlier generations and in other venues. ~*The convergence of circumstance,*~ he reflected, ~*truly an example of the circle's power.*~

However, having not consulted with the Headmaster on the Crystal Tabula, Won was concerned that he may have overstepped bounds in giving it to a Committee member, even if he was the leader of the Chalmerian's homeland. *The president.* Won liked the name . . . and the human it described. Knowing he was proscribed from giving the Crystal directly to any naturally evolved human slated to be the Noble champion, Won had still managed to accomplish getting the Crystal into the hands of the man called Chalmers.

Such was the intended nature of the cosmic theory about convergence of coincidence, he figured. *All will be well, provided everything ends well,* he hoped.

Yet some things were definitely out of harmony. Fieva's mission had failed, and though Won had not known the fifth-ranked Samaritan well, he hoped Fieva had not been cashiered the same way Vor apparently had been.

In any event, the Fiverians had fled the hostile invasion of their world by ignoble inhabitants cast by Vor's own hand. Voracians, the Headmaster had informed Won during a previous mentalation, were the invaders who destroyed Fivea's world. And now, as Won had witnessed from his celestial plateau, some of the Fiverians had wormholed their way to Won's benign blue orb, where they'd hoped to receive sanctuary from fellow hospitable Earth beings.

Pondering the status of his own GoodWill mission and assessing his prospects for success, Won worried even more than before that Ga'Lawed would find disfavor with what he and the Headmaster had done, with both of them suffering consequences for failure *or* success.

Either way, it was too late to change what was unfolding.

One Fiverian craft had crashed into Earth, and though Won had nothing to do with the subsequent convergence of coincidence, an alien life was roaming the planet below.

At the same time, the remaining eight craft circling the planet were causing great consternation everywhere they were spotted. Even worse, Won noted in his recorder, was that the remaining Fiverians now encountered military machines from Earth intent on intercepting and destroying them.

Won was surprised they did not simply leave. Perhaps they were trying to locate and rescue the Earthbound offspring of their deceased leader.

In any event, he thought it was clever that they were hiding in the most unknown part of Earth itself—the dark ocean depths.

46

Unadorned by moon or clouds, the night sky hung like a black tapestry profusely sprinkled with galactic glitter. It was a moment of incomparable beauty and the kind of quiet time at sea that Captain Hilton "Hill" Barlow would have enjoyed in any event, even if he wasn't standing midnight watch over his own ship.

"Any fresh coffee?" asked Barlow from his command chair on the flight bridge.

"Aye, sir," said the watch quartermaster as he refilled the captain's cup.

Short, paunchy, balding, and looking more like a banker than a brawler, Barlow nonetheless had a big man's command presence. He skippered the USS *Franklin D. Roosevelt,* a Midway class aircraft carrier with a complement of four thousand sailors and one hundred and thirty-seven planes. Known as the *Rosey* to her crew, the *FDR* had a proud reputation as a World War II fighting ship, and she was the first aircraft carrier to deploy Mark-3 nuclear weapons in the emerging new cold war.

Barlow knew about her other reputation as well.

During her deployments, the *Rosey* had logged UFO sightings and made many top secret reports to PACOM, the Pacific Command. Barlow's years at sea had proved that most voyages offered challenges, tragedies, and glimpses into the unknown.

"Holy shit," said the quartermaster. "Skipper . . . three o'clock starboard."

Swiveling hard to the right, Barlow immediately saw what the lieutenant was talking about. "What in the name of Neptune?" he said, staring at the expanse of chartreuse that glowed sharply beneath the black waves barely a stone's throw from his ship. A few seconds later, the yellow-greenish water boiled like haunted brew in a witch's cauldron.

"Helmsman, come twenty degrees to port. Give me Cat-see. I want radar, sonar, and any other available instrumentation on this. Stand by for general quarters, and get a cameraman."

A chorus of "Aye, aye, sir" rang from those on the bridge. An aide punched up CATCC, the carrier's air traffic control center, and handed the phone to the captain.

Watching the bubbling water turn even brighter, Barlow gasped when a large structure quickly rose from the incandescent foam. It was a spade-shaped craft, about the same size as the *FDR*. But unlike the *Rosey*, which rode the waves, this vessel now hovered some one hundred and fifty feet *above* them, on a level with Barlow's command center superstructure, the "island" tower that housed flight-deck operations.

"Gawd . . . what *is* that?" Barlow said, his eyes wide in amazement. But he kept the rest of his attention on his responsibilities to his ship. "Full hard to port; sound battle stations; CDC go One-RED status with standby scramble; get *T* and *Gs* to CNO . . . and I want HALUX sitreps to start *now*, FLASH precedent to CINCPACFLT!"

To anyone not in the navy, the acronym-rich vernacular would've sounded like gibberish, but to those on the bridge, Barlow's orders were crystal clear. The helmsman changed course; the combat direction center initiated the highest alert; time and map grid coordinates of the unfolding incident were sent to the chief of naval operations; and highest classified, code-word HALUX situation reports went straight to the commander in chief, Pacific Fleet, at Pearl Harbor.

In the time it took Barlow to bellow his commands, the UFO blazed like a reverse meteor into the night sky, its ascent bombarding the *Rosey* with vibrations that pulsed over her hull and temporarily sent instruments spinning.

His own ship returning to normal, Barlow watched the UFO hold a high position for a few moments, then zigzag across the horizon, where it again hovered low over the water but very far away.

"God almighty, Skipper," said the stunned quartermaster, "Cat-see radar had it at seventy-five thousand feet and doing twelve thousand miles per hour, to include the ninety-degree turns. Sir, that, well, that's impossible . . . isn't it, sir?"

"I've seen the lights . . . seen that kind of movement at other places before. Some of us on the *Rosey* have even seen UFO lights appear to dip below the horizon, possibly go into the water. But I gotta tell you guys . . . never have I seen anything like—"

Before he could finish, his voice was drowned out by a deep humming sound as the interior of the bridge, in fact the entire carrier, was bathed in a chartreuse hue as the UFO reappeared—this time just off the port side.

"All right, this big bastard's made a point of coming back, and I can't trust it's for any reason other than bad," Barlow said as he reached for one of several bridge phones at his console. He punched the intercom buttons for the flight deck control and launch operations room, and the CDC combat direction center.

"Red launch. Get six on wings, six more on standby for SCL," said Barlow, simultaneously flipping the switch that activated the alarm claxon and ship's open microphone. "Attention all hands, battle stations, battle stations. This is not, repeat, *not* a drill."

It took only a few minutes to get six A4D Skyhawk jet fighters airborne with another half dozen standing by for SCL, steam catapult launch. In that time the UFO zoomed away, returned, and was now positioned a mile or so away and holding an altitude of five thousand feet.

"Cat-see, I want direct comms with Wing Commander Thomas."

"Roger that, Skipper." The commo tech pushed a button. "Good to go, sir."

Barlow grabbed his mike. "Commander Thomas, how copy the bridge? Over."

"Fives across, Captain. Over," said Craig Thomas, the *FDR*'s most experienced combat ace and someone whom Barlow regarded as a surrogate son.

"Craig, get one of your boys in close, let whoever's at the helm of that shooting star know we mean business. You and the rest of the squadron fly flank and go burners if he books again. And roll your cameras."

"Roger, sir . . . I'll . . . ne . . . wit . . . meras . . ." and then there was nothing but static.

"Captain, Cat-see reported the UFO just shot across the formation," the quartermaster said.

"That fuckin' thing *fired* on my planes!?"

"No, sir, sorry, sir . . . it . . . uh, shot . . . I mean, accelerated . . . directly over the Skyhawks. The UFO is gone, sir."

Before Barlow could ask for details, his communications console sprang to life. There were three Mayday distress calls, as three of the Skyhawks suffered total engine and electrical failure after the UFO brushed by. Now they were losing altitude, fast.

ᛒ

A moment later, CATCC informed the bridge that radar had just lost three blips.

Barlow was stunned by the report but relieved when Commander Thomas came back on the air. Thomas was in the process of describing what had happened when he and CATCC simultaneously reported that the UFO was back again, about ten thousand feet directly above the remaining three Skyhawks.

"Craig, in your judgment did the UFO deliberately knock down our planes?"

"Unable to say for sure, sir. It could have been jet-wash turbulence . . . or an electronic weapons strike of some kind. Impossible to know. Over."

"Commander, my judgment says it *was* a deliberate, hostile action. So burn your ass up there and knock *his* ass—or whatever—outta the sky. Over." Barlow punched the console for CDC and ordered the combat center to launch the other six Skyhawks still idling on the flight deck.

Thomas and his two wingmen climbed straight up and fired their full load of Sidewinders, each one carrying a twenty-pound blast-fragmentation warhead triggered by an infrared proximity fuse. Aircraft aloft and carrier afloat—everyone held his breath . . .

But the missiles vaporized before striking the UFO. And a second later, so did the three Skyhawks, disappearing from the radar screen when they were disintegrated by lightning strikes that arced from the UFO like plasma sizzling out of a Tesla coil.

Barlow sat in stunned silence, consumed with soul-searing grief and guilt over the loss of his men. But an instant later, he sprang into retaliatory action, punching up the combat direction center.

"Bring back the second squadron, lock coordinates, sequence launch code X-ray triple sixer and cut loose a full battery of Regulus."

The SSM-N-8A Regulus cruise missile was essentially a modern, turbojet version of the World War II German V-1 Buzz Bomb rocket. A forerunner of the Tomahawk cruise missile that Barlow knew was on the drawing board, the Regulus was packing a three thousand-pound nuclear warhead. And right now he hoped it was on target to strike the UFO.

He twitched and squinted his eyes when suddenly his bridge and the *FDR* were again bathed in light. Not from the dull yellow-green emanating from the UFO, but now from a searing white flash as the night sky ignited from the Regulus's nuclear detonation.

"Sir, radar shows the UFO is moving slowly and erratically," said CATCC, "now it's coming down . . . out of control and coming down,

down . . . we *splashed* it, sir, we hit it and brought it down, Captain!" The command center erupted in cheers.

Barlow continued to look beyond the bridge window, focused on the distant glow of circular light in the burning ring of oxygen that was drawn back into the superheated periphery of the vacuum produced by the atomic blast. A few seconds later it was extinguished, and Barlow's mind returned to the immediacy of bridge command.

Barlow looked exactly as he felt. Like hell. "All right. Let's get search and recovery choppers out. See if we can find our pilots. Bring them home, one way or the other. And cable CNO and the CINC. Tell them that as of zero one fifty-five hours we've got six downed craft and six pilots MIA."

Moments later the *Rosey* received a return message.

It was *Eyes Only* for the captain.

❖ 47 ❖

PACIFIC OCEAN. TWO DAYS LATER

The coded cable Captain Barlow had received was a joint communiqué from the offices of the secretary of defense, SECDEF; secretary of the navy, SECNAV; and the commander in chief of the Pacific Fleet, CINCPACFLT: Immediate steam to Pearl Harbor PACOM. Full HALUX security containment protocols. Radio silence. You will be met during return transit for onboard advisory brief/debrief. SECNAV/CINCPAC chopper will squak 192.9 freq inbound with ID call sign High Visitors.

Even allowing for time to assemble the visitors, it was fewer than thirty-six hours later when a U.S. Navy Sikorsky helicopter from CINCPAC touched down on the *FDR*, some one hundred and fifteen nautical miles northeast of Honolulu. The VIPs were escorted to the small conference room adjoining the CATTC where they'd been greeted by Captain Barlow. The visitors included the SECNAV, Warren Winslow; CINCPAC, Fleet Admiral Kenneth W. Nelson; CIA director Allen W. Dulles; and Dr. Chalmers.

The political firepower of the group was intended to capture Barlow's attention, and it had, within seconds after the formal introductions were completed.

"Captain Barlow," said Secretary Winslow, "you performed superbly during the altercation with the UFO. However, our visit is to outline what you and your men will *not* talk about once you are ashore."

"Yes, sir, and I imagine some of the official reports will get lost in the piles of bureaucratic paperwork."

Winslow didn't like the captain's attitude.

"Captain Barlow, we will follow national security policies formulated by the president and the secretary of defense. In this case that means there will *be* no reports. No statements public or private by you or any of your crew . . .

none, period. Any breach of HALUX protocols will result in court-martial and military imprisonment."

He leaned forward and stared into Barlow's eyes. "Am I clear on this, Captain?"

"Yes, sir, Mr. Secretary, as clear as my recollection of the UFO and the loss of my six airmen that will forever remain in my memory . . . sir."

"Captain Barlow, I, too, regret the loss of your crew," Chalmers said. "But this truly is a matter of national security. I've made an exhaustive study of the UFO sightings. First of all, we believe eight craft are operating from various underwater bases around the world, but perhaps most specifically here in the Pacific basin. They're often reported in the Pacific Rim region, and they routinely fly over the western part of the U.S. mainland as well."

"Dr. Chalmers, I'd like to tell you that one of them is permanently based on the bottom of the Pacific right about now," said Barlow.

"In any event, you should know that UFO sightings in the U.S. began in the midforties with the first nuclear weapons testing at White Sands, New Mexico. Several distinct waves of sightings in the Pacific occurred after that."

"Yeah, I guess some of those are the ones in the *Rosey*'s old logs," said Barlow.

"Perhaps," Chalmers said with a shrug. "Regardless, all the sightings involved nuclear detonations . . . in Japan after Hiroshima and Nagasaki, and later dozens more throughout the South Pacific islands during hydrogen bomb tests."

"And I'd imagine in Nevada, too, during underground testing back home?"

"Right. Your predecessors posted an unusual number of sightings no doubt because this carrier was the first U.S. vessel equipped with nuclear weapons."

"You mean they were tracking us?" asked a somewhat astonished Barlow.

"Like sharks to the chum line." Chalmers quickly explained to Barlow that the U.S. Atomic Energy Commission had been created after World War II with a mission to foster and control the peacetime development of atomic science and technology. "The AEC later became part of the control element involving the Atmospheric Radiation Measurement, or ARM program," Chalmers added. "And from that program the rem unit was established. It measures and evaluates biological effects of radiation."

"What exactly is ARM?" Barlow asked.

"ARM monitors and records the amount of radiation extant in the atmosphere following weapons testing. I've compared ARM data before and after UFO sightings over all the detonation sites, and the results were amazing. The rem reading for atmospheric ionized radiation was zero after UFO flyovers."

"And that means what?"

"They fed off your radiation when they flew over this ship. The same way I believe their ionic pulse engines harvested ambient light in space during their transgalactic voyage. The eight known craft, perhaps seven now, are either storing up fuel for an onward voyage or they're establishing a permanent colony under Earth's seas."

"You mean I've just fed the bastards? After they took out my men?"

"Afraid so. You were kind of like a blue plate special for aliens."

Captain Barlow's face was blank and his jaw agape. Then he tried to pull it together. "I don't know what to say about this . . . any of this," he said.

"Nothing. You'll say nothing," said Secretary Winslow. "That's the whole point of this meeting."

Barlow sighed. "Nobody would believe me, anyway. But what happens now? What's being done about the—"

"There will be *no* further comments," said Winslow as he abruptly stood and walked from the briefing room.

48

Standing at the edge of the clearing, Chalmers and Beckner watched a crowd of dignitaries at a ceremony in the middle of a dense pine forest along the Potomac River. They were only a few miles from the White House. As Chalmers planned, a vital part of the CRYPTOS and CONUNDRUM projects would occur here in the deceptive shadows of broad daylight.

He had named it Operation Black Spade, for a covert tunnel project of extraordinary magnitude he would oversee. Digging it would be his race against time.

Lieutenant Commander Beckner, who'd formerly served as Chalmers's special assistant and liaison to the Seabees, had been instrumental in constructing the Level II facility beneath Building W01 at the CSC, which was the CIA's Covert Staging Compound in Tidewater, Virginia, and the site of Chalmers's extraterrestrial research lab.

Retired from the military, Beckner was now integrated into the CIA. As deputy chief of Chalmers's Division K Task Force, he was immersed in cold war politics, military confrontations, and alien intrigue, to include Black Spade.

"It officially begins," Beckner said as the marine color guard raised the flag.

"As now it must," said Chalmers. "I just hope we haven't started too late."

As President Eisenhower laid the cornerstone for the CIA's new headquarters compound, Chalmers looked at some of the senior Agency officials and former OSS operatives present. They included current director Allen W. Dulles, Richard M. Helms, Walter Bedell Smith, William Colby, and William Casey, to name a few. Only William Donovan was missing. He had died earlier in the year.

Construction would take two years. An exact time frame was important to Chalmers because it was from this location that he was going to oversee the most astounding part of CRYPTOS—the Black Spade construction project: a train track that would start in the new CIA basement and extend for fifteen hundred miles along *and below* the entire eastern seaboard.

ﻫ

"During the war," Chalmers told Beckner as he pointed across the trees surrounding them, "this parcel of land belonged to a wealthy gentleman who named his estate Langley, after his ancestral home in England. Union troops appropriated part of the Langley property and established two forts, Camp Griffin and Camp Pierpont, as forward observation posts and first lines of defense for the nation's capital."

"Interesting history," Beckner said. "Edington told me that while his crew was digging the foundation they found artifacts from those encampments."

"Excellent. Then the Agency's new roots in this land will be both metaphorical and literal." Having started the trend himself, Chalmers found it fitting that the headquarters compound, though physically located in McLean, took on the unofficial name of Langley.

ﻫ

Moments later, Chalmers and Beckner were joined at the construction site by two other Agency officers, Dr. Stan Edington and Dr. Richard Swanson. They all stood at the edge of a very large and deep pit that was still being scooped out by bulldozers and dragline cranes.

Dr. Edington, a specialist in structural geology, had helped Beckner and the Seabees design the elevator shaft in Building W01 that had punched into the deep cavern now used to hide the Level II laboratory.

Dr. Swanson, division chief of Scientific Research and Applications, personally designed DSRA's laser-based security system that Chalmers had ordered to be installed after the alien had escaped from the laboratory.

Both men were vital parts of the DivKay Task Force, the administrative epicenter for all of Chalmers's work. He would rely on them to implement Operation Black Spade.

ﻫ

"It's looking good," Edington said, pointing to the huge subbasement excavation pit of the main foundation for the seven-story headquarters building. "The minute the lower-level basement is under roof, we'll start the horizontal shaft."

"Most of the mining machinery DSRA engineered is already down there in parts," Swanson said. "The uncleared workers have no idea what the stuff is. Our guys will assemble it and the miners can start boring as soon as they're cordoned off from the rest of the main building's construction crew."

"What about the updated maps?" Edington asked.

"Our latest terrain software was on last week's orbital launch," Swanson said, "and Corona's reconnaissance satellites are already capturing remarkable stuff. The payload gets ejected every day in a parachute canister and one of our planes snatches it right out of the air."

"Amazing system," said Edington, "but seems like you rocket scientists could figure out how to get it down as some kind of telephone or radio signal, or something."

"Working on that right now, aren't we, John?" Swanson said.

Chalmers nodded. "First things first, though. Stan, don't worry, Dick's shop is printing maps as we speak. You'll have pinpoint survey capability."

"That's very good news," Edington replied.

"You and the crew may not be cutting a straight tunnel from headquarters to CSC," Swanson said, "but our satellite imagery will lay out the easiest path to dig."

Beckner added that the camera on Corona—officially designated as KH-1, or Keyhole—produced images with resolution in the area of twenty-five to forty feet. It was a far cry from the impressive standard that some of Chalmers's math formulas would help create in only a few years, but it was cutting-edge space technology at the moment.

"I know the U-2's role is still important," Beckner said, "but I'll bet the KH-1 shoots more images of the Soviet Union in a single day of operation than the Dragon Lady will during a year."

"I agree with you, Lee," said Chalmers, "and I hope we're both right, because based on some of the combinatorial numbers I've been running, I'd say there's a virtual certainty that the Soviets will knock one of our U-2s out of the sky with a surface-to-air missile in the next eighteen to twenty-four months."

"Well, in the meantime I hope the Corona's safe up there," said Edington, "because I'll feel a helluva lot better about the subfracture connector once I've got some high-Earth shots of the lateral drainage features east of the Appalachian rift."

Using existing charts and much of his own field surveys, Edington was confident that the cavernous crack running southeast from the Appalachian foothills just west of Washington, D.C., was connected to the large fissure running beneath the Tidewater area of Virginia.

"I'll run some additional probability numbers for you, Stan," Chalmers said, "but I'm already sure the substrata rent you're hoping for is there. Seems like most geologists believe it runs due south and fans into Florida's alluvial karst basin."

"Karst is a bad thing for us," Edington said. "It's unstable topography marked by sinkholes, caves, and underground drainages. Caves are okay, certainly on this project, but I don't want to be dealing with aggregate water on this dig, especially as we get closer to CSC."

Chalmers added that he'd just filled the latest generation of ADAM, the Agency's main information processor, to the electronic brim with every East Coast map and chart available from the Department of the Interior's U.S. Geological Survey.

"Scientists at the USGS know a thing or two about karst. They've studied landscape, natural resources, and the natural hazards that threaten the country, and in the process collected tons of useful data on caves and mountains. I've already analyzed enough of Virginia's geography, geology, and hydrology to assign a ninety percent certainty for connectivity between the headquarters and CSC compounds. Once the tunnel is in, laying track and operating the world's first totally underground train will be a straightforward process."

While Langley was being connected to CSC via a high-speed subterranean rail, a separate spur line was going in. Chalmers designed it so that Washington officials would have direct transportation to the Mount Weather bunker, site of the "government-in-exile" contingency plan should there be nuclear war or another national calamity.

Together these represented only one phase of Operation Black Spade.

There was more . . . much more. Chalmers had already presented a staggering plan, the Strategic Survival Initiative, to CIA director Dulles several years ago. Dulles in turn had briefed only a few senior policy makers who held the appropriate access levels to know about the SSI.

Fortunately, they not only had a K-RED security clearance, they also had a *W* in their names. Even better, they were members of the Committee.

And while none of them fully understood why they felt such a strong bond with Chalmers, they nonetheless were predisposed to give him all the support he needed.

49

RURAL VIRGINIA. JUNE 1960

Night afforded him some protection. So did his ability to change colors like a chameleon and to elongate and flatten his shape—stealth traits all Fiverians possessed.

His greatest asset was his remarkable intelligence, which he felt had evolved to even higher levels during his time in the caves. It was an intellectual adaptability that'd serve him well into the future, his intuition whispered.

Even so, Kaj'a-zar realized it was always a risk when he came to the surface on these foraging missions. And he'd lost track of how many times he'd done it since his escape from the man Chalmers. But compared to the gains, especially the acquisition of new knowledge, he knew there were no risks too great to take.

Kaj'a-zar recalled his father once saying it was vital for a leader to survive first, and after that to ensure the fitness and survival of others. To do that he needed materials, lots of different materials. First, he had to understand how the things he'd find were used on this earthen place. Only then could he modify them for his purposes, for his long-range plan.

And the scope of Kaj'a-zar's plan, as his father had imagined for him, was more than comprehensive. It was ϑλφζαρατε—*historically cosmic.*

Kaj'a-zar had advanced his earthen learning curve enormously during one of his earlier forays into a small town like the one he entered tonight. There he'd observed what he later discovered was called a television, which was displaying images on a siliconized screen inside a container referred to as a double-wide. *Apparently an alien habitat,* he'd calculated, peering through a window that night.

Indeed, the vision screen heads described many things, and those observing the screen made many comments. And through comparative extrapolations from the mental databank provided by his father's own genetic download, Kaj'a-zar had been able to decipher a huge amount of new information from his timely surveillance.

ΦαμΞϑ ατεφαλ—*These creatures are a combination of genius and stupidity.*

On this outing, he'd wriggled from a small crack in the cave system that connected all the way back to his point of original confinement. He'd been moving through the long rock fissure in a northerly direction, according to some at Langley and the CSC who'd made an effort to track him.

But those who knew of his escape had no idea where he was now.

Neither did Kaj'a-zar. Only to note that after exiting the cave he saw the lights of a small community down in the valley. He'd seen such lighted profiles before and each time located items of use.

=Πα τεω ɘφαλ= *May the hunt be good,* he growled as he bounded down the mountainside. It didn't take long to find a supply prospect. His faceted sight focused on a structure, a building, as he'd figured out it was called, where many television units and all manner of other electronic equipment were displayed.

So far, he was safe. But he'd definitely been noticed during other scavenger missions. Some resulted in dramatic confrontations with earthen creatures either in the habitation centers he plundered or in the very cave system where he normally took refuge and where certain humans seemed intent on exploring.

A number of times Kaj'a-zar had been forced to exhibit the extent to which he was the fittest of all when it came to survival. Tonight, in the alley where he'd effortlessly pulled the heavy metal door from its hinges, was one of those times.

A deputy county sheriff and his rookie partner cruised behind the building on a routine patrol. They were speechless when their lights shined on the intruder, his greenish-yellow eyes reflecting the flashlight beam like a laser as he leaped toward the patrol car.

🜰

The next morning, a trash truck driver discovered the patrol car. Its roof had been torn off, he'd noted when he called the police station, as if sheared by a rescue crew's jaws of life.

When other cops arrived and checked out the cruiser's bloody interior, all they found were the rookie's pants, still cinched around the lower abdomen and dismembered legs. His upper body was gone.

There was no sign whatsoever of the deputy sheriff, except for his blood pool.

They concluded he'd been snatched, along with some items from the store, by some mysterious force or entity their report listed as the *jaws of death*.

✦50✦

VIRGINIA CAVE—INWARD PASSAGE

Kaj'a-zar had learned much during his forays to the surface, and he'd accumulated many materials his innate technical knowledge told him would be useful. Having assembled them in a perfect location, he was now returning to the original place of his confinement and experimentation.

He knew he would soon be close to the human, the Chalmers who had forcibly birthed him.

Maneuvering through the tight passages, his mind continued to fill with his father's knowledge and memories—as provided by his mother's natal encoding.

ατελψ‥ħ ϖιεδ‿ωηιχ η◦↗-φλε—*My parents and their fellow travelers came to this planet in order to escape, provide warning, and seek assistance. My family was separated from the others. Ultimately, all of them came to be viewed by this planet's inhabitants as hostile. Some were killed by militants. My remaining clan members live in seven ships beneath the sea of this cruel blue planet, from which they will again have to flee.*

Through their process of mento-synchronicity, the subaquatic Fiverian colonists knew that one of their brethren had survived the crash and roamed somewhere on land. Kaj'a-zar knew they'd been searching but were unable to locate him because his bioaura had changed once his body adapted to the oxygen he now breathed. Kaj'a-zar sensed time was running out for his fellow Fiverians and they'd soon have to leave without him.

Though he had command of his incredible faculties, Kaj'a-zar wondered if he had sustained some cerebral damage from the crude hatching procedures engineered by Chalmers. He would continue to assess that prospect. Meanwhile, he could still do what all Fiverians were able to do—improvise, modify, and adapt in order to survive, undergoing rapid physiological changes in the process.

If not insane, he was certainly mad—angry-mad about everything that had gone wrong on his world and most definitely on this one. Knowing the dangers he faced trying to survive on this alien planet, Kaj'a-zar had summoned from his father's genetic construct the physical traits of a primitive hunter from his faraway world.

Acidic drool dripped from Kaj'a-zar's trihinged mandible full of sharp, jagged teeth. His long prehensile tail had now sprouted a poisonous barb, and the powerful squidlike fingers on his long hands were tipped with retractable talons.

Kaj'a-zar was more than a hungry hunter trying to stay alive. He was a cold-blooded killer with a long-term plan for the future. And his immediate course of action had brought him back to the large cavern where he sensed Chalmers could be found.

=*Ch'al-murs,*= he growled. In addition to his broader goals, there was still an obligation to repay the human for what he'd done to Kaj'a-zar.

Stepping from the darkness into the outer ring of halogen-green light, Kaj'a-zar noticed that his body was covered in strange red dots. A quick sweep of his spectral eyes revealed several devices in rock cracks that emitted the infrared rays now striking him.

Not a weapon, an alert sensor, he correctly assessed.

Even had it been a weapon, it could not have repulsed him, for such was his determination to return to the cold steel vault in which he had once been contained.

With hardly a break in stride, he tore into it with greater ease than he'd originally ripped out of it.

There were humans inside, dressed in bulky white suits and helmets, performing the same experiments that had been conducted on him. Chalmers was not among them. And in a surprised second, the scientists were no longer among themselves, at least not in whole parts. Kaj'a-zar shredded them with instant fury.

Recorded on a security camera and reviewed later by Chalmers and others, Kaj'a-zar left behind a visual calling card—consuming his slaughtered prey and spitting out the victims' bloody shoes like olive pits. With a blood-soaked talon he scribed some marks on the wall: ηακψυ.

He surveyed the vault's wreckage and saw what he'd come for.

}ψ κινδ ωιλλ σομεδαψ τη ωορλδ—*I or my kind will someday rule this world,* he thought as he'd gently lifted and cradled the two eggs.

The last camera frame showed the alien leave through the jagged hole he'd ripped open to gain entry.

ᴀ

Moments later, Kaj'a-zar disappeared into the dark cavern, carrying with him not just the eggs but also a specific plan. It was to take his sisters to the hatchery he'd prepared, and after overseeing their birth and maturity, to take them as his breeding mates.

51

Chalmers and Beckner had been at headquarters yesterday when the tragedy occurred at CSC. They'd flown down first thing this morning, even though the same weather front that had prevented them from traveling last evening was still strong enough to have made their flight today extremely rough.

Beckner had made a sobering observation about consequences for the Agency's CRYPTOS and CONUNDRUM projects if something happened to Chalmers.

Chalmers said it would certainly be faster, more comfortable and, he allowed, safer to travel to CSC once the underground rail service was complete. In the meantime, he'd said, "I'll just make sure I stay alive."

That prompted Beckner to make a casual reference about his boss's obvious state of health and fitness. He had known Chalmers for some time and estimated, based on his World War II service, that he was at least forty-five years old. "What's your secret, John?" he'd said. "You look younger than I do, for Pete's sake."

Chalmers casually dismissed the topic, but his age, or lack of showing it, was a secret even he didn't fully understand. Though he was now seventy-five, he could attribute his minimal show of aging only to the Tutorium incident, that strange moment in time—or perhaps timelessness. He knew there would come a time when the issue of his appearance relative to his actual age would be impossible to explain. So far everyone assumed he was born around 1920. He had almost no friends, and the only one who would have known he was born in 1890 was his former boss and onetime classmate at Columbia. And Bill Donovan was now dead.

But death was what he and Beckner now had to deal with.

They reviewed the lab's security tape in the office on the scaffolding above the cryogenic vault where the murders had occurred. Beckner was

nervous about the alien returning today, but Chalmers was insistent that
the creature would not return after having taken the eggs. Besides, this was
the only facility rated for K-RED discussions.

ฅ

Near the point of throwing up after he'd watched the tape, Beckner said he
couldn't fathom something so powerful and dangerous yet so obviously
intelligent. He wondered where the other aliens were, where *this* ugly bastard was hiding, what his wall writing meant, what the creature would do
with the eggs, and what he and Chalmers would do without their two remaining biophysiologists to study them.

Chalmers noted there were no longer any eggs to study, but he did take
his deputy's point.

"It was tragic and disruptive enough to lose Dr. Warner the first time
around," Chalmers said, "but this is even worse. I think there is still compelling reason to study the alien, if only through reviewing this tape." He
drummed his fingers on the desk. "Quite a few K-RED clearances for
CRYPTOS, but only a few people have a need-to-know about the CONUN-
DRUM file. I know of someone in New York who might be a perfect re-
placement. I'll get to work on reeling him in."

Beckner was surprised by how pragmatic and unemotional Chalmers
seemed to be about the horrifying event. It was a trend he'd noticed in
Chalmers over the last year or so. Perhaps the man was finally feeling the
stress and strain of his work all these years?

Mindful that he was being scrutinized by Beckner, Chalmers had his
own detached thoughts about this latest tragedy.

They, too, were pragmatic—but not without emotion.

Whether it was schizophrenia, paranoia, the Headmaster, or one of the
Samaritans, Chalmers was hearing voices in his head again. Maybe it was
merely dreamed chatter from a night's troubled slumber, words his memory
replayed during the day as a belief he was actually hearing them. Chalmers
didn't know and wasn't sure he could even differentiate between the two.

He decided it was less consequential how the voices spoke than what
they said.

And either way they told him the same thing.

Time was running out.

52

LONG ISLAND. SPRING 1966

Making one of his rare appearances away from Washington, CIA headquarters, or the CSC, Chalmers had gone to New York on Agency business—specifically to observe someone at a scientific conference. He was close to making a decision about this person and wanted to be sure before inviting him to a behind-closed-doors tour at Langley.

Something else was there, too, and he was overdue in giving it his personal attention.

While in Manhattan, Chalmers visited his home in Oyster Bay. He couldn't believe how long it had been since he was last here, and he couldn't be more grateful that the estate manager, who had been part of the Chalmers family for decades, was still there, along with a full-time housekeeper and gardener, caring for the property as if it were their own.

In some ways now it was, he reasoned.

The Agency had become his home . . . and his mistress.

He owned a beautiful town house near headquarters, and he was provided permanent VIP guest quarters at the CSC. But more often than not he slept—the few hours a night he allowed himself or believed he needed—on a small bunk in one of his offices. The rest of the time he did what his friend Albert Einstein did . . . take quick naps.

His timing for this visit was perfect. The estate manager, Mr. Albertson—who had known Chalmers for a very long time and would definitely have recognized the "master's" inexplicable chronological appearance—was away for the day. As it was, the housekeeper who also served as a cook had not worked in the home long enough to have met master Chalmers before.

Chalmers felt her eyeing him while he ate the meal she'd prepared.

She has to see there's something odd about me.

He had chosen to eat in the large kitchen, avoiding the formal dining room adjacent to the library. Though it was his favorite room in the house, Chalmers did not want to set foot in the study, fearful he'd see that his oil portrait had become the picture of Dorian Gray. His intellect told him that was preposterous, but his paranoia, buttressed by the fear of schizo-phrenia again rattling his nerves, told him to stay out.

When he'd finished his food, Chalmers inspected the remainder of the house and took a quick walk around the manicured grounds. He was both reluctant and eager to leave. A cab dropped him at the local train station, where he caught the commuter into Penn Station. A few hours later, back in Washington, he took another cab straight to Langley.

His office couch would serve him well tonight.

It was in a dark, quiet, and safe place . . . he hoped.

Part IV

EARLY AFTERNOON

53

Early in his administration, President Kennedy had pledged that America would put a man on the moon by the end of the decade. And here it was, eight years later, and Chalmers had just watched a live television broadcast of Neil Armstrong stepping off the bottom rung of the Apollo's Lunar Lander.

Chalmers and the CIA hadn't pledged to put America, or at least a selected portion of it, under the earth by the end of the millennium. But with support from successive administrations and power brokers from the Committee, Chalmers and the Agency had pushed forward the Strategic Survival Initiative. Far exceeding the Continuity of Government plan for handling a cold war crisis, Chalmers's SSI provided for "continued existence of the nation" by building a reserve USA—the underground safe haven of Appalachia. Or, as he'd taken to calling it, the Underground States of America.

Even with his planner's eye on tomorrow, Chalmers continued to assess how past and present events would invariably shape the very future he was trying to safeguard.

Today he was in his office jotting down notes:

- Chinese & French alternating atomic/hydrogen bomb tests monthly basis.
- U.S. Minuteman ICBM entered service to combat existing Soviet ICBMs.
- United Kingdom: member of so-called *nuclear club*; others to include India, Pakistan, Israel, Iran, & North Korea . . . more to join.
- War scenario brief for president: emphasize LBJ that U.S. defense systems able to stop only 20–35% of a Soviet ICBM attack.

- War protests/rioting & looting shake foundation of patriotism & nat'l cohesion. Will American psyche rally in a 3rd World War like the 2nd?
- Can country can handle arbitrary selection process to enter subground Citations when SSI balloon goes up? How to contain mass civil hysteria?

It was only a small list of troublesome issues that characterized the decade.

For the moment, Chalmers was over his concern about schizophrenia and the paranoia he had experienced in the aftermath of his Tutorium incident. Visitations with the Headmaster and what he hoped had only been nightmares about some of the Samaritans may have been behind him for the moment, but Chalmers had new fears now. And they were that the path ahead of him was paved with impossible challenges.

ᴉᴀ

He was still working on the list when his deputy walked in.

"Did you watch the landing?" Beckner asked. "And how about Armstrong's statement? Somebody must have written it for him, don't you think?"

"Small step for man, giant leap for mankind . . . a thoughtful phrase carefully chosen for the history it'll forever represent. But mere words can't begin to express what he did . . . or for that matter what *we're* doing."

"Outer space, inner space. Even if we had words, the public couldn't hear them."

"Exactly. The truth about what faces our nation would scare the population even more than the homogenized version we've been feeding them."

Beckner noted the chaotic mess in his boss's office. Stacks of files and mounds of books, which he noted Chalmers was reading at the rate of some fifty pages a minute even while talking. "What're you doing here, cramming for the next PhD?"

"Organizing thoughts for a speech. Sit down and I'll bounce some things off you. I'm trying to put issues related to the SSI in an unclassified historical perspective for some young analysts I'll be addressing later in the week."

Beckner moved books off one of the extra chairs.

"Technological developments during the sixties," Chalmers said, "particularly the space race with the Soviet Union, have compounded some of my math projections on sequential phase-in. Especially for industrial up-grades to SSI's mining, construction, and communication elements."

"How in the world do you go about quantifying the prospects for wag-ing, and then surviving, World War III with the Soviets? I know you did it for the last war, but we're talking nuclear holocaust here. This time the scale's going to be off the chart."

"I'm still sticking with my calculations that we'll win the cold war. It's the longer-range conflict and ultimate showdown with the Chinese that I'm worried about."

"You've designed the most thorough survival plan possible."

"We'll see. I still have to sort through the instability derivative of com-plexity." He caught Beckner's look. "You know, the tangle of political and social issues here at home and abroad that skew my new math for quanti-fying and measuring the rest of technology's changing variables. The SSI project aside, the ancillary issues having to do with the rate, scope, and directional change of modernization are precisely what our intel analysts need to consider, regardless of what topics they're following."

"It's an overwhelming amount of data, John, and impossible to sort out now, I guess, without computer technology."

Chalmers nodded in agreement. He was a total convert to computer sci-ence, and under his DivKay stewardship, the Agency had replaced ADAM with cutting-edge scientific computers designed by Seymour Cray's Con-trol Data Corporation.

"Even so, I'd swear you still think faster than the new Crays. You've correctly analyzed most everything that's unfolded during the sixties. I imagine you've already got a clear sense of where the nation's headed in the seventies."

"What our nation has been through these past ten years has definitely realigned its path to the future. I want to get the essence of the decade in this speech, before some historical revisionists either rewrite it or just misinterpret it."

"Why not begin your presentation with the U-2 incident? Didn't the Russkies shooting down Powers escalate the cold war and push all of us closer to Armageddon?"

"Yes, but that same year we launched the first Polaris submarine missile and deployed the Atlas and Titan intercontinental ballistic missiles. In po-litical poker, America's ICBM ploy was a check-raise move on the Soviets' hand. I remember that tension between Washington and the Kremlin increased dramatically following our support for the Cuban exiles and the Bay of Pigs invasion to topple Fidel Castro. In some ways we're still paying for Kennedy's political embarrassment when our ragtag army was defeated in three days."

ᵺ

Beckner had heard rumors about what his boss had done during the Cuban missile crisis—that Chalmers was one of the senior analysts who'd briefed the president on the Agency's photo intelligence that identified Soviet nuclear missile installations on the island.

"I provided Kennedy and Secretary of Defense McNamara with probability ratios for outcomes of the administration's possible strategies for dealing with Soviet premier Khrushchev. The president took my recommendations."

"I'd say Moscow's decision to withdraw peacefully from Cuba beat the hell outta the alternative," Beckner said.

Chalmers looked toward the bookcase and a photo of him in the Oval Office with Kennedy. "There are many who believe his assassination was a Cuban-orchestrated plot."

Tilting his head, Beckner glanced at one of Chalmers's open files on terrorism. It was about the Palestinian Arab Sirhan Sirhan, who had gunned down Senator Robert F. Kennedy after he'd won the California presidential primary.

"I take it you believe 'terrorism' is a word we'll soon become more familiar with?"

"I'm afraid so. Which brings us to *those* files," said Chalmers, nodding to the pile next to his deputy. "They need to be taken down to Data Processing and added to all the other CRYPTOS and CONUNDRUM info that Swanson's DSRA geeks are programming into DivKay's newest Cray 1000. They're pulling Sunday duty, too."

"On my way now," said Beckner, standing to leave. "Oh, almost forgot," he said at the door, "what did you decide about going to CSC tomorrow?"

"Let's grab a cup of coffee in the cafeteria and hop the zero seven hundred shuttle. You can take the last train back tomorrow evening. You'll be home in time for dinner with your new wife, and since you spent your weekend here with me, stay home and rest on Tuesday."

"Thanks. What about you?"

"Think I'll stay over a day or two and take another crack at the mystery box."

"Perfect. See you in the morning then . . . and by the way," said Beckner over his shoulder as he stepped into the hall, "thanks for sharing all that history with me."

"Let's hope somebody learns something from it for a change," Chalmers said as added more books and file folders to his simultaneous-reading marathon.

✦ 54 ✦

From the coffee shop, Chalmers and Beckner walked to a freight elevator in a side corridor off the main floor. When their car reached bottom, Chalmers hit Stop and inserted a red key in the control panel. The back wall of the elevator compartment slid open to reveal a neon-lit cavern. They stepped out, the false wall closed, and the elevator automatically returned to service.

"I don't think I'll ever get used to this," said Beckner, surveying the silver fuselage of what looked like a torpedo tube with oblong windows. The shiny cylinder was positioned next to the concrete platform upon which they were standing, along with other DivKay personnel.

"SpadeLiner Express," Chalmers said, his open hand making a sweeping gesture of pride for the most exclusive and unique railroad ever built.

"All aboard," said Beckner.

The train's three-rail track ran inside a one-hundred-and-fifty-mile tunnel that had been excavated over the last ten years through a geologic fault line that connected a series of caves in the Appalachian Mountains of southern Virginia. Overseen by Chalmers, it had been completed on time and within budget, and it was now part of his and Beckner's daily one-hour commute between Langley and the CSC Level II laboratory.

ﬁ

The moment they had departed, Chalmers began to unpack his briefcase.

"We're behind the Japanese in public-rail transportation," he said, already reading two books at once while also tutoring Beckner on Japan's Tokaido Shinkansen—the first passenger train capable of traveling at 125 mph.

"But we're kicking ass in the undercover world of secret subways," said Beckner as the SpadeLiner rocketed to 150 mph in the time it took him to open the press clippings booklet that contained national and international news articles prepared each day by the Agency's Media Affairs staff.

ﬁ

"Uh-oh, look's like Jack's back," said Beckner moments later, spotting a story related to a series of atrocities that he and Chalmers believed was the handiwork of "Jack the Ripper"—their nickname for the alien that had escaped years ago from CSC.

Closing his own books, Chalmers peered over his glasses at Beckner.

Still finding it hard to believe the creature had been roaming underground for some sixteen years now, Chalmers was at least grateful that Jack had thus far not run up a greater death toll and generated nationwide front-page publicity in the process—though he had been periodically spotted by spelunkers, who described him as everything from a prehistoric dinosaur to the "abominable caveman." Others believed that some kind of creature was responsible for the disappearance of several explorers who over the years had entered a variety of East Coast caves but never returned.

Chalmers was sure Jack accounted for all such vanishings, even those in small towns located in mountain valleys, and no bodies were ever found because he assumed the extraterrestrial had eaten them. But as Chalmers had anticipated, stories about an "Appalachian cavern creature" became like Bigfoot and the Loch Ness Monster—mythic sightings that no serious researcher ever believed.

ka

"Where and how's he struck this time?" Chalmers asked.

"Just another sighting," Beckner said. "A gigantic ground bat, according to an electrician. He'd been installing lights in a recently expanded walking path through a small tourist cave in northern Pennsylvania."

"Interesting. Jack's still moving northward. Still underground, which validates our contention about macroconnectivity of the Appalachian fault," Chalmers said. "In fact, we've tracked press stories of Jack's movements just like a surveillance team would use an Agency Trak beacon to monitor a suspect."

"Or like medical science is now experimenting with putting dye in a patient's bloodstream to find the location of dangerous arterial blockages."

"Ah, an even better analogy," Chalmers said.

"Then that'd make the Appalachians like a giant living entity, with its cavernous fissures similar to a circulatory system."

"Very impressive, Lee. I have to admit I'd never thought of it that way. Oh, did you know that these mountains were formed during the Cenozoic era? It was an angry time, topographically. Uplifted streams and rivers cut downward into the bedrock, carving canyons across rock layers and geologic structures. Fortunately for our purposes, the countless caves and caverns along a common fault line will enable us to realize the totality of SSI and Black Spade."

"Mmm-hmm, I've actually been in some of the caves, the tourist types," Beckner said, hoping he hadn't rolled his eyes *too* much during yet another of his boss's frequent pedantic lectures. "Like Luray and Skyline caverns here in Virginia, Seneca in West Virginia, and Howe in New York. Never imagined I'd have this kind of interest in them now."

"Who could've? In tomorrow's post-apocalyptic world, those will be the names of American cities belowground—the Citations—each with manufacturing plants, aquaculture farms, hospitals, living quarters, military stockades . . . anything and everything currently available in any city in any state."

"John, you've done a great job with Cryptos and Conundrum, and your personal stewardship of DivKay has produced results that surpass anything we'd expected."

"But . . . I sense a *but* is coming."

"No, not at all . . . well, maybe, yes."

Beckner explained that the scope of what was coming next made him question if the sheer logistics of building the Underground States of Appalachia were perhaps beyond Chalmers's vision. His greatest concern was the time frame.

"Connecting headquarters to the CSC with this rail line is one thing. But an undertaking as gigantic as the SSI? How can we do that in the time you calculate is available? And how in the hell do we keep that kind of construction a secret?"

These were good questions.

❖ 55 ❖

"If the Egyptians built the pyramids without power tools, we can build a national safe haven along the eastern seaboard. We already have a hundred and fifty miles and two substations," Chalmers told Beckner, "and we've kept a tight wrap on all of our projects so far."

"I've never doubted your imagination or determination, John. But as we continue to build, we'll have to use more non-Agency workers. That's my security concern."

As with everything he did, Chalmers had calculated all the angles and had planned contingencies for the sharp sides.

"Lee, look at how they handled the Hoover Dam project. Six construction firms created a consortium that ultimately won the competitive bid contract. The Interior Department gave incentive bonuses for speed and efficiency yet fined that company for each day construction overran the assigned schedule. It worked. The dam and hydroelectric plant were completed two years ahead of schedule."

According to Chalmers, the Hoover Dam's bonus-versus-fine caveat was like a reverse risk-versus-gain factor that'd always applied to CIA operations. Hence, by applying a similar, albeit modified, dual-purpose incentive to Black Spade contractors, Chalmers assured not only that work on the initial SpadeLiner excavation came in on time but also that no one spilled any classified beans about it. As Chalmers ironically noted, it turned out that private companies were able to do a better job than government agencies of maintaining secrecy among their workforce.

"The fear of some CEO canceling bonus checks or docking pay," Chalmers said, "was a powerful incentive for forcing private sector employees to be discreet. Better than the wrist slap, negative performance report imposed by Uncle Sam on his bureaucrats."

⚸

But there was something Chalmers did not tell his deputy. About the burden of guilt he carried whenever hard tasks required him to make hard decisions, or to use his intelligence and persuasion to make an analytical argument that resulted in someone else taking a hard action on his behalf. He'd done that with Truman and the result was Japan's immediate surrender after the horrific death toll from two atomic bombs.

In a similar vein and while he was still at Columbia University, Chalmers had prepared a statistical analysis of the Great Depression's impact on the economy. Invited to the White House to brief Hoover, Chalmers had planted the idea that led the president to deport about a million Mexican immigrant workers to free up jobs for unemployed Americans. After the war, Chalmers did essentially the same kind of study for Truman, who also had deported more than two million illegal immigrants in order to create jobs for returning servicemen. Even Eisenhower, who'd always supported Chalmers, had gotten in the act by authorizing Operation Wetback, another huge roundup of Hispanic workers who earlier had entered the country "officially" as part of the Bracero guest worker program.

That trend continued, but with a twist. President Nixon, who earlier as Eisenhower's VP had admired Chalmers, now sought his analytical advice on global political issues, especially China's emergence as a world power. Anticommunist to the core, Nixon agreed with Chalmers's analytically driven contention that China would eventually be the world's dominant power and represent the greatest military threat to America. Briefed on and supportive of Chalmers's SSI project, Nixon decided after one of Chalmers's visits to the Oval Office that it was best to communicate openly with the very enemy he was determined to neutralize, if not in fact defeat. His open door policy with China was merely a front to shut out the Chinese, especially in what Nixon worried would be the domino effect certain to occur in the wake of America's disastrous quagmire and departure from Vietnam.

Now, a current administration's policies once again included rounding up illegal aliens. Only this time it was carried out very quietly, with those apprehended given the opportunity to remain in the States, where they would work on a series of underground storage facilities for oil reserves, mothballed government equipment, hazardous waste, and other bogus items. In exchange for signing nondisclosure forms and agreeing to work five-year stints, they would not only be paid top wages but also receive citizenship.

Chalmers simply chose not to think about the fact that when these workers completed their assignments most would get Uncle Sam's boot rather than the promised hand. Based on his previous success with open deception and covert propaganda, he was confident that those deportees who complained about what had happened would be regarded as disgruntled people looking to file frivolous lawsuits against a federal government that was already, as Chalmers had planned, very adept at stonewalling and misdirecting. It was also a government that with subtlety and sophistication was rapidly building a power base in what some had already labeled the military-industrial complex.

Good, bad, or indifferent in the long term, for Chalmers all of these developments meant that he had the infrastructure and support necessary here, in the short term and probably from one administration to the next, to push forward all phases of CRYPTOS and CONUNDRUM. And even with manageable news glitches now and again, it would all remain an open secret.

ю

Though almost at their destination, Beckner was still pressing his boss about leaks and related security issues. To reassure Beckner further, Chalmers said that when revelations about mysterious excavations and attendant press stories about "underground Area 51s" in Virginia and elsewhere did inevitably appear, such news would be discounted as yet another urban legend dealing with government conspiracy.

"Fact and fiction," Chalmers added, "are often hard to tell apart, and sometimes, for propaganda purposes, they can be interchangeable."

ю

There was one fact for sure. Chalmers played a major hand in theoretical design for much of the Black Spade technology engineered and built by Dr. Richard Swanson. Chalmers was equally innovative with other scientific disciplines used in his DivKay's overall mission management of the CRYPTOS and CONUNDRUM projects.

In the end, Chalmers also tried to make sure that CIA technology, whether borrowed from the private sector and modified, or created from scratch in DSRA, was "technologically repatriated" and made available for public use once the Agency's classified application of such technology was finished. He figured that reinforced the burgeoning military-industrial complex and hence worked to his and the CIA's benefit.

Chalmers and Swanson finally developed a method for magno-optically penetrating the yellow light aura emanating from the alien bodies stored at CSC. The digitized photographs they produced led to the medical industry's breakthrough with MRI, magnetic resonance imaging. And what would eventually emerge as the Landsat commercial mapping satellite, the 3-D seismology techniques used by petroleum-drilling companies, and the GPS employed by the U.S. military and commercial sector were all outgrowths of CIA "overhead collection platform" technologies pioneered during the early cold war years. In addition, much of the commercial sector's use of laser science came from advances Dick Swanson made over Einstein's original invention of laser light.

Two things Chalmers did extend with his mathematical formulas were the life span and speed-efficiency quotient of the cutting tool used on the Black Spade boring machine built by Dr. Stan Edington. Later Edington provided assistance to English and French engineers and the thirteen thousand European mine workers who in eight years constructed thirty miles of tunnels under the English Channel, connecting London and Paris by high-speed passenger and freight train service.

ഛ

And in the span of one time-compressed hour today, the SpadeLiner delivered its passengers to the CSC substation. After a full day of work here, everyone would return to Washington. Everyone except Chalmers.

During the course of his day in the Level II forensic lab, an otherwise routine procedure was changed by a random event . . . another convergence of coincidence.

The result was an accidental discovery of profound consequence.

56

Every day since 1955, when President Eisenhower gave him the metal box at Camp David, Chalmers and his DivKay staff—believing it was discovered in the UFO wreckage—had tried to penetrate its seamless construction and discover the mystery within. Chalmers tried on the box everything he'd used on the alien egg, but nothing, including the latest laser technology, had been able to peer inside or even dent the exterior.

This morning a technician had removed the box from its lead-lined storage bin and placed it on a stainless-steel workbench. Chalmers expected today's exploratory efforts to continue past midnight.

He and other staffers were scribbling physics formulas on a large wall-mounted chalkboard. Nearby were three televisions sets. As he worked and talked with his colleagues, Chalmers simultaneously listened to the evening network newscasts.

Extremely interested in the space program, he of course was watching everything CBS and Walter Cronkite had to say about the lunar landing and the Apollo crew's return. ABC and NBC were following regular news issues as well. Chalmers expected NBC's *Huntley-Brinkley Report* to update the U.S. troop withdrawal from Vietnam and Nixon's new Asia policy.

Chalk scratching against the green board as he worked the differential equation, Chalmers also differentiated from among the TV channels, noting that NBC's commercial break was using a nostalgia theme from the network's bygone years of radio and early television. The familiar *bing-bong-bing* instantly took him back to Columbia University and the first televised news footage of the destruction at Pearl Harbor.

He didn't have a chance to finish that memory, or the math formula.

᠊ᠣ

Suddenly, a rumbling hum filled the laboratory. Everyone looked around as it steadily grew in intensity.

"Okay, that's interesting," said Chalmers. "Pete, kill the TVs and hit the tape recorder."

"On it," said P. J. Peterson, the senior lab technician who everyone called Pete.

In the next instant, a thin, bright stream of light flashed from the box, then returned to the same unknown location from which it had mysteriously radiated. Left behind, and suspended between the floor and ceiling, was a tiny starlike dot of spinning energy that immediately began to diffuse. A faint cloud quickly filled the room, and from within its mist appeared strange symbols—in numbers too great to count and with shapes too alien to describe. The wiggling string shadows danced to the box's eerie vibrations.

Mesmerized like everyone else, Chalmers still knew he had to take action.

He engaged the ultraviolet MRI scanner, hoping it would capture this imagery.

"Somebody grab a camera and start snapping regular photos," shouted Chalmers above the increasing tempo of the bass hum. In an instant, the volume exploded into an eardrum-crushing, pressure-pounding pulse that forced everyone to cup hands over their ears.

No one heard Pete's scream as the Kodak exploded in his hand, but everyone saw the Cray computer, televisions, tape recorder, and anything electrical spew out sparks, while everything made of glass shattered into silicon dust. With bulbs blown to smithereens, the room was dark save for the odd celestial light coming from the cloud.

Two other brave technicians moved to secure the box but were stopped in their tracks. Their cotton lab coats flapped as though they faced a fierce wind, and the white fabric became solar-bright, along with everything else, as an incredible beam of torch-white light began to radiate in a throbbing rhythm from the top four corners of the box.

Everyone donned dark, protective glasses and hard hats with clear pull-down Plexiglas shields—safety gear always at arm's length on any workbench.

The floating symbols and the pulsing light seem to be syncopated, Chalmers thought, even as his mind raced to take measures to safeguard his staff. To him it seemed like they were communicating . . . and building to a climax of some kind.

Abruptly, the mist and its floating symbols were sucked back into the box; the sound stopped and the room plunged into total darkness.

"Pete, you okay? Everyone accounted for?"

There was a nervous chorus of positive replies.

"Good. Can somebody find the emergency power switch?"

When the lights came on, Chalmers saw that the box was gone, but what remained was that which had been inside of it: a clear crystal about the size of a pineapple and shaped like a pear. The soft glow it emitted was interesting to him, but not nearly as much as his observation that the crystal, in defiance of gravity, floated some three inches above the steel table where the box had been.

Further visual analysis was supplanted by the disbelief of what Chalmers saw in front of him, for he was stunned by the realization that he knew what this thing was . . . and where it had come from.

"The Crystal Tabula," he whispered, his mind flashing scenes from the Tutorium.

ᚺ

Chalmers did not return to Langley the next day.

Using tongs, he moved the Crystal to another location, where it continued to hover. In addition to laser optically measuring the circumference of the Crystal as part of his initial forensic investigations of its properties, Chalmers also discovered later that wherever it was placed, the Crystal always floated over the surface at 3.14159 inches—pi's universal value.

Chalmers knew there were countless additional math formulas to work, and he accepted that for him everything was even more complicated and amazing than before. It was this way, one of the inner voices told him, because CRYPTOS and CONUNDRUM had just become one.

And as he also now believed, his race against time had just accelerated—fueled by more of his still undefined, though ominous, sense of what lurked around future's corner. Now focused almost exclusively on the Crystal, Chalmers's weeks, months and even years raced ahead.

❖❖ 57 ❖❖

Called by security and told his guest would soon arrive, Chalmers had walked from his office to the lobby, where he'd personally meet Dr. Walton Stern.

Head of the Astrophysics Department at Cornell University, Stern had recently won the nonfiction Pulitzer Prize for *Mankind's Cosmic Origin and His Search for Extraterrestrial Life*. The book was not his only claim to fame.

Stern was an internationally acclaimed astronomer and had popularized science for America's television audience while also promoting SETI, the Search for Extraterrestrial Intelligence. He had also established astrobiology as a legitimate scientific discipline that combined astronomy, biology, and geology.

But what intrigued Chalmers was the fact that Stern also helped create another scientific discipline: exobiology, the theoretical, physiological study of alien organisms and life-forms—microscopic, cellular material found in meteorites that struck Earth and were recovered for investigation. Chalmers believed that Stern's knowledge and suitability for what he had in mind exceeded that of Jim Warner and the other two DivKay biophysicists who'd been slaughtered and devoured by the alien.

Chalmers and Stern had far more in common than being native New Yorkers with doctorates from Cornell. Chalmers wanted to strengthen the bond of their other mutual interests by opening for Stern an entirely new cosmic door—the front door to Langley and the basement door to the CRYPTOS CONUNDRUM.

It had started with an official call from the CIA to Stern's office at Cornell.

Stern was intrigued by Chalmers's tantalizing telephone invitation to visit the CIA for the purposes of "discussing a matter of national security whose problematic origins are cosmic in nature." As arranged, Stern was met this morning at his home near the Cornell campus by two credential-carrying CIA security officers, driven to the airport in Ithaca, and escorted to Washington on an Agency plane.

Now flanked by the officers, Stern walked across the lobby. Dressed in his trademark sport coat, vest, and bow tie, Stern had the dimpled, square chin of his grandparents' Germanic ancestry and even a quaint trace of their accent. Like the stars he viewed through a telescope, his blue eyes twinkled behind the silver-rimmed spectacles set forward on his strong, straight nose. A mane of professorial-gray hair receded from his prominent forehead, and neatly trimmed gray eyebrows matched the groomed quality of his salt-and-pepper goatee.

Very much a dashing, impressive figure, Dr. Walton Stern headed toward the security desk where Jonathan Chalmers stood with a visitor badge in his hand.

ᴋᴏ

"Welcome to the Agency, Dr. Stern. I've looked forward to our meeting."

"I wouldn't have missed the opportunity, Dr. Chalmers." Stern pinned on the badge he'd been given after the men exchanged handshakes.

"As you can see, we have our own galaxy of stars," Chalmers said, pointing to the memorial wall commemorating fallen CIA officers. "Each one chiseled in the marble represents an Agency officer killed while performing secret service for our nation. Individuals who even in death must remain anonymous."

Stern scanned it carefully. "Yes, a secret universe in which all of you work."

Chalmers was not surprised by his guest's respectful tone. It tracked with all the other things he knew about Stern's personality, which was part of the overall evaluation the security office had completed while conducting the man's background investigation.

He had a visitor badge for today, but his host was about to give Stern a ticket for more than a tour of the lobby.

"I'm glad you brought the overnight bag," Chalmers said, nodding toward the leather valise one of Stern's escorts held.

"Your request that I bring one only added to the mystery of this visit."

"Let's walk around. I'll show you a few things of interest on the main floor here and then I'll treat you to lunch in the cafeteria before we get down to the serious business."

"Secret recipes, John . . . if I can be so informal?"

"It's the only way we cook here, Walt."

"Good. I'm hungry. And what do I have to look forward to after we eat?"

"I'll take you down to the lowest-level of the several basements."

"And what's down there?" Stern asked, grinning with anticipation.

"The train," Chalmers said with a wry smile.

"And where will it take us?"

"On the ride of your life, Walt, traveling on a special pass called K-RED that will stop at cosmic stations you and I could never have imagined. That is assuming you want to ride with me today and work with me for the rest of your life."

58

From his executive suite on the top floor, Chalmers had a commanding view of the forest that surrounded the compound. He was not only adjacent to the director's office, he also had a chauffeur and used the private elevator from the underground executive parking garage to the seventh floor—the CIA's senior management command center. Chalmers had been moved upstairs years ago and afforded the other perquisites of power thanks to his friend and longtime colleague and former director, William Colby.

An OSS operative in World War II, Colby had worked his way up Agency ranks. Among his duties he'd been the CIA's senior man in Saigon during the Vietnam War, where he ran the Phoenix program. Colby's covert mission there, which Chalmers helped design and for which he provided analytical support, was directed against the Viet Cong insurgency and involved infiltration and disruption of the enemy's infrastructure, and capture and assassination of its leadership.

Colby served as CIA director in both the Nixon and Ford administrations. When he'd been replaced as Agency head two years ago by George H. W. Bush, one of Colby's parting, public comments had been, "The CIA owns everyone of any significance in the major media." Initially, Chalmers wished Colby had not made that revelation, but he subsequently decided it added to the perception of absolute power everyone believed the Agency actually possessed.

In Chalmers's mind, using power was like betting in a poker game. Sometimes you showed the weak cards you'd bluffed with, other times you revealed the strong cards with which you'd won the pot. Doubt and misdirection were the hallmarks of how he played his own hand in the clandestine game of CRYPTOS and CONUNDRUM, which for him was winner-take-all stakes.

Today, as he stood at his office windows taking his pulse and breathing deeply, he was grateful for his reflection. He finally looked like he was in his early sixties rather than someone eighty-eight years old. And he was still as fit as someone half his age, a condition he attributed at least in part to his exercise regime, the second phase of which he was now ready to continue.

Amazed by how fast and far his life had unfolded, he was surprised that no one, not even Colby and Bill Casey who'd known him from OSS days, had yet become suspicious of his apparent age discrepancy. It was another of the secrets in his world he didn't want to be blown.

Though he'd been standing in front of the floor-to-ceiling windows, he had not been looking out. He looked within and ahead, assessing events and calculating mathematically how they would affect overall planning for the Strategic Survival Initiative.

He turned, walked across his large office, and reassumed his position facing a bank of television sets tuned to news and documentary channels. There he continued his contemplative process while simultaneously engaged in a rigorous aerobic program of running in place, isometrics, and stretching. He never wasted time.

⌖

Due to technical problems, a nuclear-powered Soviet satellite had recently fallen from orbit and disintegrated, scattering radioactive debris over parts of northern Canada. Later, in an unrelated event, the USSR conducted a nuclear test in eastern Kazakhstan. UFO sightings were immediately reported in both areas.

There had been two more reports of missing cavers in recent weeks in New York State, and some gruesome slayings. Even common theft in scattered towns along the mountain range was being attributed to what the press called the "Appalachian Monster."

Chalmers preferred his nickname for the marauding alien—Jack the Ripper.

Having lived with the UFOs for so many years, Chalmers found himself becoming complacent about their relatively benign presence, except for Jack. Ironic. It was how he'd conditioned the public to feel about little green men from outer space through his covert manipulation of the entertainment industry.

He was more worried about the terrorists and illegal aliens than extraterrestrial aliens. Chalmers saw Jack as a single creature belowground that

killed occasionally to eat and stay alive. The other two groups were spreading like cancer.

੮ੰ

Beckner stopped by to deliver left-over copies of finished intelligence reports that had previously been disseminated to the White House, State
Department, and Pentagon. Their control numbers, on file in Chalmers's
office, had to be checked off prior to being shredded.

"PLO guerrillas kill Israelis on a bus traveling along the Tel Aviv–
Haifa highway; Israel invades south Lebanon and hits PLO bases; Italian
politician Aldo Moro gets kidnapped and murdered by Red Brigades terrorists. Outdated atrocities already replaced by new ones. There's no end
to it," Beckner said as he dropped the reports in the shred basket.

"Including the latest trend in freelance terrorism," Chalmers said.
"You're aware that our operations officers are closing in on Carlos."

"Yeah, the Jackal. Bold move attacking OPEC headquarters in Vienna,
and now this Venezuelan mercenary is offering his services to the Pales-
tinians as a bomber and assassin. Who would ever have imagined all this
chaos?"

"Terrorists everywhere are making their political and ideological intent
clear. They'll kill even more people and destroy entire nations if they manage to get their hands on nukes, or just some nuclear material or chemicals
they can disperse with conventional explosives. Frankly, this is my greatest
concern."

"It's already complicated and going to get worse, I guess," said Beckner.

"Yes. Simple solution: locate the bastards and kill them. We've done it
before."

Taken aback by Chalmers's ruthless tone, Beckner changed the subject.
"What's your answer for that?" he asked, nodding toward a pile of research
files that included press articles and intelligence reports about Moscow-
backed Afghan armed forces that had seized power in Kabul, killed the
president, and installed a Soviet puppet. "There's bound to be a full-
blown Soviet invasion, don't you think?"

"Yes, and a guerrilla movement followed by a protracted insurgent
war. Our best response, the solution, is to equip the Afghans so they can
kill the Soviet bastards. I trust the war in Afghanistan will do more damage to the USSR than Vietnam did to us."

Beckner was not surprised by what Chalmers said because he agreed
with his boss . . . in principle. What Beckner noted, however, was the

detached, even cruel, tone to his voice. He had always seen Chalmers as an aloof individual with quirks and self-centered righteousness—negative off-sets to the man's incomparable brilliance and patriotism. But in his mind there was something as mysterious about Dr. Chalmers as there was about the CRYPTOS and CONUNDRUM projects over which he presided.

Though there was professional friendliness between them as colleagues, Beckner didn't feel he and Chalmers had become genuine friends over the years. Not because Beckner wouldn't have enjoyed a more personal rela-tionship, but because he felt Jonathan Chalmers never let anybody get that close.

Beckner wanted to change that. With him and his wife, Janice, ex-pecting their first grandchild, he realized how much family mattered, and he was glad he'd not missed the opportunity for having one in spite of the insane work schedule he'd shared with his boss for the last thirty-one years.

He hoped Chalmers wasn't sacrificing his personal life trying to safe-guard others.

However, even as he worried about Chalmers's life, Beckner was shocked when Chalmers threatened his.

59

Now working, at least on occasion with Dr. Stern who had begun "consulting" frequently with Chalmers, Beckner had found it as difficult to get beyond the friendly colleague stage with an astronomer as with a mathematician.

What is it with really smart guys? he wondered as he plowed through a stack of papers on his desk.

He'd already missed dinner with his wife, and at this rate he wouldn't be home until after Janice had gone to bed. She'd been remarkably tolerant of his long days, largely, he knew, because Chalmers was taking on even more DivKay managerial duties in order for Beckner to have additional time at home. Beckner appreciated that.

In fact, he believed he'd made a major breakthrough with Chalmers who, while sending his deputy to Ithaca recently for a meeting with Stern, had also asked Beckner to make a quick stop at Oyster Bay to drop off some administrative paperwork to Mr. Albertson.

Chalmers had subsequently told Beckner that he and Janice should feel free to go up whenever they liked and spend a weekend in the Long Island home—"Provided you have any free time," Chalmers had added flatly, though Beckner chose to take it as a joke.

The invitation had surprised Beckner, who took that, too, as an example of the warmth and thoughtfulness he wanted to believe was actually present in Chalmers's heart, rather than the likelihood that Chalmers just wanted to let the property's caretaker staff know that the "master" had someone keeping closer tabs on them.

Either way, it didn't matter. He and Janice had taken up Chalmers's weekend offer. The tradition, wealth, and prestige that filled the mansion only added to Beckner's amazement of the man he worked for. So intelligent, capable, and accomplished, he thought, yet so isolated by his brilliance and powerful position in an agency whose mandate for secrecy and manipulation did more than simply suit Chalmers's temperament. As near as Beckner could tell, over the long course of Chalmers's career, his boss had instituted many of Langley's secret, manipulative practices.

And now, during his last stay at the mansion, Beckner had seen something in the library that he simply could not understand.

Owing to the Agency's compartmentation and need-to-know mind-set, he had not shared what he'd discovered with anyone, including Janice. She had been in the presence of her husband's boss—and, as she thought, gracious host—only a few times. While she found him intellectually eccentric and opinionated, she also found him pleasant and even charming in a pedantic, professorial way.

Beckner thought she'd find *him* crazy if he told her what he'd seen.

He did not know when or how he would bring it up, but he knew that when it came to Chalmers, a new page had just been added to the CRYPTOS CONUNDRUM.

60

Chalmers had just finished an encrypted phone call with his CET, the Crystal Exploitation Team, down at CSC. He'd provided them with new light resonance computations yesterday and wanted to know how the experiment had turned out.

Negative results, like the various probes conducted every day since the Crystal inexplicably sprang to life eleven years ago.

Following that event, Chalmers had taken a bold step and held the Crystal in his hands. If he relaxed his grip the Crystal immediately began to hover above his palms. It was cold, but not enough to be uncomfortable. Exposure to a heat lamp didn't warm it, and when he placed a tongue thermometer next to the Crystal, the mercury exploded through the bottom. The CET later determined that the Crystal's temperature was absolute zero. And wherever Chalmers or anyone placed it, the Crystal continued to float at Π distance above the surface. At least that ruled out the possibility it would be damaged if ever it were dropped accidentally.

Its incomparable clarity permitted him to see through it, almost as if he had nothing in front of his eyes. But when he pointed a beam of light into it, the beam would not pass through, although Chalmers could see the beam disappearing into what seemed to be the Crystal's depth. Not wanting to damage the Crystal but compelled to explore it further, he eventually fired a ruby laser into it. No red ray, or refracted elements of one, emerged.

From the second he'd seen it floating free from its dematerialized seamless box, he knew what the Crystal was. A repository of all knowledge—at least that's what the Headmaster had said, or *thought* into his head at the Tutorium. He believed in the depth of his soul that he had been in a timeless place and that a cosmic entity had explained more than Chalmers could ever have comprehended, even with his intellect.

Though Chalmers had come away from his out-of-body experience with a renewed belief in a supreme being—in fact, a dozen or more of them—he still struggled with how his personal puzzle piece fit into the cosmic picture. Unbelievable things had happened to him and undeniable events were occurring on Earth.

And in his mind a vague notion—conveyed as strange symbols his brain had somehow translated while he was in the Tutorium and that now remained as a lingering thought—said that unspeakable things were yet to come.

That notion and the symbolized voices he periodically heard still haunted him.

Years ago, he had almost gone crazy trying to sort out fact from nightmarish fiction, and even now he was torn between certainty and doubt. He knew for sure that he could never tell anyone that he understood what the Crystal was without explaining *why* he had that knowledge.

He couldn't do that. Not without being sent to an asylum.

His only alternative was to prod, probe, and persuade the Crystal to self-activate again, and in the process reveal its own secrets. Chalmers would keep trying, but he could use some help.

ﯓ

Dr. Stern had seen the Crystal but had not been able to devote much time to assisting the CET. He'd spent more time with the APT, the Alien Pathology Team which worked on issues of greater professional and personal interest to him, and even then his time on target had consisted mostly of studying the vault videotape and observing autopsies on the cadavers.

He and Chalmers had become good friends.

Stern had recounted to Chalmers and Beckner his dual frustrations. One, he'd had several full-time jobs before learning of the wondrous CRYPTOS and CONUNDRUM projects, and regardless of how much he wanted to seclude himself at CSC and collaborate exclusively with his friend Chalmers, he simply could not do it. His second, and in some ways more frustrating, frustration was that while continuing to promote SETI within the astrophysics community, he had to keep his mouth shut about having firsthand knowledge of such intelligence. The same K-RED clearance that gave him a once-in-a-lifetime opportunity was denying him another one.

Chalmers hoped Stern was not a ticking bomb, his frustration fuse about to trigger an explosive revelation to the media.

ﯓ

The Strategic Survival Initiative continued to produce success and optimism for Chalmers. Under the SSI, Operation Black Spade had carved out hundreds of additional miles, and a second SpadeLiner was moving farther north through additional substations. According to Chalmers's plan, when completed these stations would become cities and take the name Citations.

The ultimate reality of CRYPTOS was getting closer by the year.

୧

There was now one particular, important thing Chalmers had to do.

With the discovery of the Crystal inside the box, and based on his confidence that he'd figure out how to access it—as well as extract the contents he believed he was meant to have—Chalmers knew he must design a plan for its long-term safekeeping . . . and it had to be a place that even those on his staff with K-RED clearances could not know about should Chalmers die or be killed before unlocking all the Crystal's secrets.

If the Crystal contained what his vague, dreamtime voices seemed to be telling him, Chalmers knew that only a blood heir—if or when he was ever to have one—would be the proper individual to take stewardship, and properly manage exploitation, of the Crystal.

More now than ever, Chalmers felt this celestial jewel was the single most valuable thing in the world.

61

LANGLEY. LATE OCTOBER 1978

An art magazine in his hand, Beckner stepped into Chalmers's office. "John, you ever hear of a sculptor named Brenton Crawford?"

Looking like he was embarrassed for having been caught wearing them, Chalmers quickly removed his reading glasses.

"Yes, he works with stone and metal. Likes to incorporate hidden messages within sculpted alphabetic letters. Stern has seen some of his work in Manhattan and called me about him not long ago. Why do you ask?"

"Oh, I just thought this story about his art cryptology was interesting," Beckner said as he handed the magazine to Chalmers, who read the four pages in half as many seconds.

"You're right. This is a detailed account. I'll pay more attention to him in the future, but I've got to finish the presentation right now."

態

"Don't forget about the lecture," Beckner said as he stuck his head in Chalmers's office again an hour later. "What's it this time, another CIA 101 class?"

"I'm about to head down now. I plan to explain intelligence collection and the analytical issues facing this crop of new career officers."

"Lighten up, boss. Tell them about the *real* facts behind all the outer space movies you finagled the studios into making."

"Don't think so," Chalmers muttered as he looked around his desk for the glasses.

His discussion today would not include CRYPTOS and CONUNDRUM because none of these recent hires had, or probably ever would hold, the K-RED clearance necessary to access such classified information.

態

With his focus on the cold war and the emerging new asymmetrical warfare called terrorism, Chalmers told the class that for years his analytical judgment had been that the cold war revolved less around the possibility of conflict and more from the reality of competition with the Soviets.

"Logic suggests that by simply outspending them we will win that war, probably sometime in the next decade. In the interim, my calculations indicate that terrorists will wage a far more aggressive, tactical war against us. But the real *strategic* danger is with the Chinese."

A woman raised her hand. "Dr. Chalmers."

He nodded toward her. "Yes."

"I can perhaps understand your downplaying the Berlin blockade, Cuban missile crisis, and other confrontations. But current Soviet incursions into Afghanistan could trigger an insurgent backlash. Don't you think that will further inflame already unstable relations throughout the Middle East and Southwest Asia? In view of our dependence on foreign petroleum reserves, could it not cause political and economic problems for us, and even pull America into the probable war there?"

Chalmers was impressed.

"The Soviet-Afghan imbroglio reflects the same paradigm of mathematical phenomenology that applies to the USSR-USA conflict," he said. "Either way, Moscow loses. Whether it's by economic attrition or loss of political will, Moscow's going to have to pull out. Meanwhile, we keep our eye on the terrorists and the Chinese."

"Have you co-opted Hegel's concept of dialectical phenomenology? Maybe augmented the ontological and metaphysical spirit behind the competitive phenomena with a Malthusian twist involving logical and mathematical calculations?"

"Why, yes indeed," Chalmers said with a warm smile, "that's exactly how I would have described my own thesis. You are quite perceptive."

That was Chalmers's kind of woman—brains and beauty. He intended to talk with her after class, but first he had to finish the presentation.

He concluded with overviews of key terrorist events, to include the assassination six years ago of Israeli athletes at the Munich Olympics, which he pointed to as the dawning act in an age of terror. Coupled with the threat of a nuclear-armed China, he believed America faced an ominous future.

"China's status as an international political pariah will change virtually overnight. At present, it has more than nine hundred million citizens, and orbiting satellites, deliverable nuclear weapons, and a technological industrial capability that will soon explode into the international commercial arena. It's becoming the superpower that will fill the vacuum left by the Soviets. And it'll be a far more fit and determined competitor for us in the continuing global race. All of it will define your role in this Agency . . . to serve as America's first line of defense."

The audience applauded, but Chalmers had eyes for only one member of it.

↩

As the auditorium emptied, he noticed that the woman seemed slow to exit.

He increased his stride as he weaved through the crowd, and upon reaching the bank of exit doors he was delighted to find her apparently waiting for him.

With her high heels she was almost as tall as he was. Long shapely legs supported a lean body clothed in a knee-length gray skirt and a navy jacket over a white silk blouse. The top two buttons were open and revealed that while she was thin, her breasts were ample.

As his eyes traveled up, they came into contact with hers. They were dark, as was her hair pulled back in a ponytail. She had a classic, contoured face with high cheekbones, a perfectly sculpted nose, and full lips adorned with a blush of pink gloss. Small pearl earrings matched the stringed ones around her elegant neck.

Somewhere in her early to midthirties, he figured, her overall appearance was that of a consummate professional and a stunningly beautiful woman rolled into one.

Occasionally, Chalmers had dated a few of the many attractive Agency women who found him handsome, intelligent, and "prominently positioned" on the seventh-floor home for CIA senior managers. With little free time and even less interest in idle dinner conversation, he had seldom dated the same one twice.

He could tell this woman was different, and he hadn't even introduced himself yet.

She stepped toward him. "My name's Paula Baker." She offered her hand. "I'm a cryptologist and have just been assigned to DSRA. Do you have a moment? Perhaps now, for a quick coffee?"

That name. He gathered his wits, scattered as they'd just been by another convergence of coincidence he felt take hold and shake him. *Why that name?*

↩

Chalmers had selected a quiet corner of the massive CIA cafeteria, where unusually good coffee and even better food was always attributed to secret recipes known only to Agency chefs.

"How long have you been with the Agency, Paula?"

"Nine months, or thirty-seven weeks, to be exact. And you, Dr. Chalmers?"

"A long time. To be exact. And it's Jonathan, or even John, if you'd like, okay?"

She smiled softly and nodded.

"Cryptography is a discipline of mathematics concerned with encryption and access control to secure information," he said. "What's your educational background?"

"I went from South Jersey High to Princeton on a smart-kid scholarship, then compressed undergrad classes and a doctorate in math and philosophy into a six-year fast track to intellectual irrelevancy." She slowly ran her finger around the lip of her coffee cup as she pondered her next statement. "I couldn't see being an out-of-touch college professor, so I launched into a corporate stint in the greedy world of New York bankers." She took another sip. "But I couldn't identify with the shallowness of most rich people, so I signed on for a code-breaking tour with the *second* best intelligence agency, NSA"—she returned the cup to the table—"from where I was recruited here with an offer I couldn't refuse."

"Well, it couldn't have been for more money."

"No, I was offered a chance to work for the *first* best intelligence agency and its Division of Scientific Research Applications. And as I've learned more in recent months about Langley's legendary Dr. Chalmers, perhaps eventually to collaborate with him . . . with *you,* John."

"And this is a career plan you've mapped out, Paula?"

"No, not believing in René Descartes as I do. He said, and I believe, that except for our thoughts, there is nothing absolutely in our power."

"He also said everything is self-evident."

She smiled again. And nodded. Then she glanced at her watch.

"Thank you for taking the time to talk with me. I'd love to continue, but I've got another training session."

"The pleasure was mine, Paula. I, too, wish we—"

"Then let's pick this up over a glass of wine, perhaps Friday evening if you're free? I live in Old Town. A classic Alexandria brownstone." She scribbled on a napkin and pushed it toward him. "My number."

"Nice penmanship," he said. "I'll call you."

62

"Second page, orange tab," Beckner said, sliding the folder across Chalmers's desk. "Tabulations from the latest Atmospheric Radiation Measurement tests at the Columbia River complex, as well as eyewitness accounts of the UFOs spotted there."

"The Hanford Site," said Chalmers. "Largest plutonium processing complex in the world and responsible for tens of thousands of weapons in our nuclear arsenal."

"And still plagued with accidental leaks of radioactive cooling water and steam."

"And the tallies?" Chalmers asked.

"Rem count is back to zero, like always. Sightings were the same, like the other locations. Seven again. Everyone interviewed who saw them had high-plus credibility."

"Lee, this is the seventh major leak at different sites around the world in the last three years. I'll run another combinatoric, but it will just assign the same low-random probability and high-cause modality as always."

"Jack's relatives are somehow causing the accidents just so they can harvest the radiation?"

"Makes sense. They would have feasted on this fallout as well as the others."

As Chalmers knew, this spate of sightings began in 1976, when the reactor core of East Germany's Lubmin nuclear power plant nearly melted down due to the apparent failure of safety systems during a fire. Five similar events subsequently took place around the world, to include the Kozloduy power plant in Bulgaria and the Tokaimura complex in Japan. Chalmers was now worried about the Three Mile Island power plant in Pennsylvania, and planned to recommend safety checks and perhaps enhanced security around the perimeter. A meltdown there, he calculated, would constitute the worst accident in U.S. nuclear-reactor history.

"I do believe the alien craft have been, and still are, harvesting radiation from the atmosphere," said Chalmers, "and my analytical judgment tells me they'll eventually have enough power to move away from Earth—or to move against Earth. Either way, my gut instinct tells me it's getting close to showtime."

꡸

"Something else?" Chalmers asked when Beckner continued to sit in silence.

"Uh, yes," he said, showing his discomfort. "If you have some . . . a few extra minutes . . . I have a personal issue I'd like to discuss."

Chalmers leaned back in the imposing leather desk chair. "Go ahead."

"It's about Long Island. Janice and I enjoyed the comfort of your beautiful home and—"

"The point, Lee."

"A question first, then the point. Did you get your PhD from Columbia and serve in the Second World War? Of course, I know the answer is yes."

Chalmers was impassive.

"Assuming you got your doctorate at an early age, given your IQ, and if you went into the army right after Pearl Harbor, say age twenty-one, that'd make you around sixty years old now, even though you look, as I and others have said before, considerably younger than that."

Chalmers's face remained blank, his eyes boring into Beckner's.

"While I was exploring your incredible library, something caught my eye."

His face suddenly ashen, Chalmers leaned forward. "The painting."

Caught off guard, Beckner seemed confused. "Painting? . . . Uh, there were some beautiful ones, yes, but that's not what I'm talking about. This is," he said, pulling a large manila envelope from his briefcase.

It was Chalmers's turn to look confused, though relieved—at least for a second.

"I found these on one of the shelves," Beckner said as he removed two leather-bound volumes. "One is your university yearbook, the other a small scrapbook with various photos, including you in military uniform, plus other odds and ends that look like they were assembled by a relative, probably your mother, I'd say."

Chalmers took a deep breath. "And that brings us to the point, doesn't it, Lee."

"Definitely. We're talking about *two* yearbooks, *two* PhDs from Columbia, and *two* goddamn world wars, John. You'd apparently already been teaching several years before volunteering for Verdun in 1915. And if the photos of you weren't enough evidence, here's your birth certificate . . . 1890. John, how can you be eighty-eight years old and look, sound, move, and act like someone half that age? I guess the point is just how in the hell can that be, my mysterious friend . . . if indeed we *are* friends?"

"Your lack of knowledge about my life doesn't diminish my friendship for you, Lee, nor should it lessen whatever regard you have for me, I hope."

Beckner was pleasantly surprised by that comment . . . but alarmed by the next one.

"I will tell you this, though. You are opening doors that lead to rooms where even I don't like to go. You have to forget this business in my library—literally. And you'd better do it metaphorically, too . . . from a personal security standpoint."

Beckner was sure that meant there'd be no more invitations for weekends in Long Island, but he could tell something else was implied. He didn't like it. It scared him.

"I wasn't snooping in your personal business. And if, as I sense, there could be dangerous reprisals for what I've done . . . well, look, I recognize the kind of power you have in this Agency. Most people around here think you are some kind of secret director. You control the biggest budget and have total backing from whoever actually sits in the director's office, as well as the Oval Office, it seems. I don't doubt for a minute that you could arrange for me to be transferred, so to speak, because of your displeasure about what I innocently, and with no malintent whatsoever, discovered while a guest in your home."

"Lee, you've been at my side for a long time, and I want you to be with me as we face the truly troubling, probably catastrophic times ahead. Secrecy will be paramount in all we face . . . professionally and personally. When it comes to the CRYPTOS CONUNDRUM and our future, you will be my friend and ally. But don't ever forget . . . you will *always* be more expendable than me."

63

OLD ALEX'S INN. FRIDAY, 1920 HOURS

Entering the tavern, Chalmers noted his reflection in the beveled-glass inset of the oak door. He liked his outfit—tan slacks, dark blue blazer, and a white, open-collar shirt. He hoped Paula would like the rest—hazel eyes, some interest-factor wrinkles on a taut, angular face, and lightly grayed temples in his thick brown hair.

He didn't look fifty-eight, which everyone assumed he was, but he didn't look thirty either, which was how old he'd judged her to be. He hoped that apparent disparity, and certainly their true age difference, wouldn't matter to her. In either case, he knew he was lying to Paula even as he sought to develop a true, honest relationship with her.

Physically, Chalmers had an everyman appearance. But he had what someone once described as a handsome stature. He radiated confidence and power—products of his amazing intellect.

A CIA intelligence analyst, he was a war planner, not a war fighter, not a derring-do clandestine operative. He was not dashing in looks or dazzling in demeanor like James Bond, but he was a thousand times smarter. In any event, Chalmers, not Bond, was the one meeting the beautiful and brilliant Paula Baker for dinner.

He'd arrived several minutes early to be there before Paula, but he saw she was already seated in a candlelit booth tucked away in a corner.

Feeling nervous excitement as he approached her, he noted that her dark hair, in a ponytail at their first meeting, was now up in a French bun, which showcased the classic lines of her tanned Mediterranean face. A faint dust of rouge highlighted her cheekbones, as the red gloss did for her full lips, and dangling black bobbles adorned her lovely ears. She wore an elegant gray suit with a pale pink sweater whose V-neck exposed a black necklace, its intricate design lost to his otherwise keen eyes, which were, in this case, focused on her cleavage.

Elegant, beautiful . . . desirable, he thought, arriving at the table. In its center was a bottle of Merlot and two sparkling clean glasses.

�

"Hello, John," said Paula as she gestured with her hand for him to join her. "You struck me as a red wine drinker, so I took the liberty . . ."

"A proper analytical deduction, Paula, and easily verifiable," he said with a smile as he slid in across from her. They shook hands. "It's nice to see you again."

"You, too. I've been looking forward to this."

"So have I." He motioned toward the bottle. "Ready?"

"Anytime you are."

He filled their glasses. "That's a very nice outfit. You look lovely to-night."

She smiled demurely. "Thank you. And you look very handsome."

He raised his glass, casting his gaze from her eyes to her sweater and back to her eyes again. "To your . . . enchanting *necklace,*" he said with a wry smile that popped into a full grin and a chuckle.

She clinked her glass against his. "And to your discerning eye, Dr. Chalmers."

ᴀ

Between bites of their dinner and wine from a second bottle, the couple discussed history, math, science, philosophy, international events, and language. Though the meal was wonderful, it was less delicious for them than the conversation and companionship.

"'To think a thing is to cause it to begin to be.' Oscar Wilde . . . my favorite quote," Paula said. "What's yours?"

"Don't know. I haven't written it yet."

They laughed.

ᴀ

With a deft move, she pulled out the hairpin, tilted her head back, and gave it a gentle shake. Free from bunned restraint, her shiny dark curls tumbled to her shoulders. "Whew, I needed some head room. The Merlot's starting to buzz around in there."

The maneuver was so natural but so seductive that it almost took away his breath. He couldn't believe the transition. She was even more beautiful and desirable than before.

"I really like your name. Paula Baker. It has a special significance in my life."

"Oh? The same as a former girlfriend?"

"Several people with variations of your name. All guys. Some classmates in college, some buddies in the war. But all of them lost to me through the twists and turns of life . . . and the deadly ravages of war. I've never understood the coincidence of it all."

"That sounds so sad. I'm sorry for your losses."

Chalmers poured more wine, changed the subject, and the evening continued.

ॐ

"I heard someone at work say you knew Albert Einstein," Paula said.

"Yes. From my academic days at Columbia."

"What a thrill that must have been. What was he like?"

"What most impressed me about him was the relatively simple way he thought about decidedly complex issues. He had a quiet faith in the ability of the human mind to understand the workings of nature, and he was very much a romantic at heart. He told me that anyone who studied physics simply had to believe, as he did, that the distinction between past, present, and future was merely an illusion. And he genuinely believed love transcended all three realms of time."

"And do you believe that, the part about love?"

"Yes. I was in love once. We were married, but I lost her, too, along with my parents in a plane crash."

"Oh, John. I'm so sorry. I—"

"It's okay. That was a *very* long time ago."

Now Paula poured more wine, changed the subject, and the evening continued.

ॐ

"I've been reading about astral projection," she said. "Fascinating stuff. Deals with out-of-body experiences that supposedly can be initiated either awake or through lucid dreaming . . . or even deep meditation. It's rooted intellectually in Theosophy."

"And you believe in its philosophical, metaphysical doctrine, that all religions form part of a spiritual hierarchy meant to help humanity achieve perfection?"

Paula nodded. "Yes, with each religion having a portion of the truth." She studied him. "What are your religious beliefs, John? Catholic, Baptist . . . or maybe agnostic?"

"I believe in the divine architecture of everything and that God drew the plans. Beyond that, my views are . . . unorthodox. However, I think life should be a journey filled with learning and enlightenment that leads toward a noble purpose."

"I would love to know what you believe your purpose is."

Glancing at his watch and scanning the now empty tavern, Chalmers said, "Paula, we seem to have lost track of the time."

"Oh, my gosh, have we ever. I feel bad for our poor waiter," she said, seeing that he sat patiently at the bar.

Chalmers signaled and he came like a flash, bill in hand.

"Well, I *have* to know what your purpose is, John," she said, laying her hand across his, "and we never got around to dessert, you realize."

"The analytical deduction is clear, then," he said, placing his other hand over hers. "We track down some more time and a new place where we continue this. We'll start with dessert, and of course I want to know what your purpose is as well."

"It's a date," she said.

She took his arm as they walked to the front door, which the maître d' unlocked and opened for them.

Outside, the quiet streets glistened with midnight's dew.

"I'm parked down there," she said, slanting her head to the right.

"I'll walk with you," he said, offering his arm again. She took it.

"I think it's always good to go in the right direction," Paula said as she opened her purse and removed her car keys.

Gently taking them from her hand, he unlocked and opened the door.

"I really enjoyed this evening, Paula, and I will call you very soon."

They embraced and kissed tenderly. She slid in and lowered the window.

"I loved our evening, John," she said, starting the engine. "Don't get lost on the way home, Dr. Chalmers . . . and try not to lose another Baker."

Part V

LATE AFTERNOON

64

McLEAN, VIRGINIA. EARLY JANUARY 1979

After his very unsettling conversation with Chalmers a number of weeks ago, Beckner had said he needed a couple of days off to regroup his thoughts now that the secret age issue and implied threat about him safeguarding it had suddenly brought his professional, if not personal, future into doubt. He was only slightly reassured when Chalmers then told him how much he valued the friendship and how important it was for Beckner to continue as his deputy.

Not wanting to inflame a dangerous side of Dr. Jonathan Chalmers that Beckner had seen that day, he nonetheless didn't want to appear totally cowed in front of the man. There'd be no way whatsoever to work things out between them unless Beckner could reestablish his individual identity vis-à-vis his boss.

"You're asking me to overlook a lot, John. To act like none of this happened?"

"All I want you to *act* like is that everything we're doing together for this Agency and for our country matters more than how we feel about each other. The nation . . . the entire planet is a ticking time bomb. So take your two days, go wherever you choose, but get over the emotion of the moment, and when you're back, get on with your work. If you can't do that, then don't bother to come back at all. I *will* replace you."

Beckner left feeling like he had just received another implied threat.

"Didn't need two days," he told Chalmers the next morning, realizing his career and his life were better served by staying as close to Dr. Chalmers as possible. "Decision was easy. I just ran the numbers the same way you always do, and everything added up analytically. Bingo . . . the right decision."

Chalmers sat back in his chair, an odd expression on his face. "Bingo . . ."

Beckner realized his boss probably had no idea what that meant. "Uh, yeah, it's a board game with—"

"Numbers that complete a game sequence . . . or chords that comprise a tune."

Beckner now had the puzzled look.

"Lee, call Peterson. Tell him I'll be on this afternoon's SpadeLiner. I want the entire CET assembled and ready for a twenty-four/seven surge. And have Pete bring in another laser probe as well as a television camera."

"You mean one of the new video recorders, like a Panasonic home camera?"

"No. A commercial-grade, live-broadcast camera, like for NBC news. And while you're at it, find a copy of an old NBC radio program from '47, the Lowell Thomas evening news. I'd like to take that, and whatever is required to play it, with me down to CSC."

"On it," Beckner said, not knowing what in the hell any of this was about but excited by the sense that Chalmers, as was often the case, had just been seized with another of his brilliant ideas.

"Oh, and Lee," Chalmers said, catching Beckner on his way out, "nice to have you back on board . . . my friend." —

ہ

Pleased that his deputy was exhibiting his former positive attitude about work, Chalmers gave him even more of it to do so he had more time to spend with Paula.

He cared for her deeply and could tell she shared his sense that theirs was a relationship with purpose and promise for the future.

"I'm not much for looking in the rearview mirror," she had said on another date when Chalmers turned the conversation to her past. "I've always felt it was more important to stay focused on the road ahead."

Chalmers had the same general orientation, but for different reasons. "I've always sped ahead in an effort to keep from being rear-ended by the past, and looked ahead to avoid being blindsided by the future."

"I certainly have dated other men," Paula said, "and I'll admit I was looking for a soul mate and a father figure. No one was ever smart enough to suit me."

Chalmers described his emotional state of mind after the death of his wife and parents, admitting that felt a greater loss about his life-long friend Paul Baker than he did about Margaret. "I was too young when we married. Plenty smart, just not about sharing life with someone."

"When did the accident happen?"

"A very long time ago . . . in more emotional and physical ways than one," he said, not wanting to go through the age issue with her like he'd just done with Beckner.

"After that, I simply never had time or interest or the fateful convergence of coincidence to find someone who . . . who *spoke* to my emotional silence. Until now."

༆

Continuing to date and talk, their initial friendship and mutual attraction had grown into a common view about how they wanted to live and to share a future together. And that meant marriage, which he realized included the prospect of raising children.

And that meant an honest discussion about his age—not only with Paula but also with his deputy, whose support *and* friendship Chalmers realized he needed now more than ever. He owed them an explanation. It just couldn't involve any revelations about the Tutorium incident, which in his mind would only complicate questions about his age by adding new ones about his sanity.

Chalmers gave them a blended tale of fact and misdirection about the head injury he had sustained from falling off a balcony as a child. It had affected his corpus callosum in a medically miraculous way, he'd explained, not only increasing his IQ but extending his life span as well.

༆

"The specialist who years ago treated my migraines discovered the abnormality and believed it had benefited me from the standpoint of intellectual growth," Chalmers had told them, "and it was only later, when he and I both noticed the slowness of my outward aging, that he surmised the fall had also triggered a change in my brain chemistry, which in turn somehow affected what he called the pituitary gland's chronology trigger."

"So your physical growth was normal," Beckner had said, "but the . . . uh—"

"—but the calibration factor of normal degeneration associated with the passage of time was slowed down," Paula had said as she gently caressed her husband's cheek. "I always told you I found older men attractive, and I hit the jackpot with you, my dear."

As Chalmers further recounted, his physician planned to conduct additional studies on his patient's remarkable anti-aging syndrome and publish the findings in a medical journal—a revelation that Chalmers did not welcome. Citing concern about his professional privacy, Chalmers tried unsuccessfully to convince the doctor to abandon the plan. Feeling bad about some heated disagreements that followed, Chalmers said he was nonetheless relieved when his doctor suddenly died of a heart attack, thus taking all knowledge of Chalmers's condition to the grave.

For an instant Beckner had wondered if Chalmers somehow engineered the heart attack, but he quickly pushed from his mind the notion that his boss had killed the doctor.

"I don't know how long I will live," he'd told his wife and deputy, "but I don't want any more medical attention focused on me, nor do I want to be a freak story in the tabloids." Like the story he'd spun about his physician, Chalmers was confident his wife and Beckner would take his secret lie to their graves, too.

ᴙ

Later, Paula and Lee shared their own thoughts about what they'd learned.

"After all this time I'm still in awe of him," Beckner said, "but I've never felt truly close to John."

"Lee, I love him with all my heart and even I feel at arm's distance from his inner soul. Jonathan is as complex as he is brilliant . . . and always burdened with secrets."

"Well, yeah, the age issue. Sure revealed a side of him I'd never seen before."

"It's more than that. During the few hours a night he sleeps, I hear him mumble . . . strange things probably having to do with nightmares he's always had."

"I can't begin to imagine everything that must be in that man's head. The history he's lived through, the pressure he's under for all these projects."

"It's more than that, too. Based on bits and pieces of what he's told me, I think something happened to Jonathan a very long time ago. Something so strange and probably frightening that it left him wondering all these years if he . . ."

"If he what?"

"Lee, if I tell you it becomes *our* secret, like the one he shared with us, but I don't want you to think any less of him for knowing it."

"Never. I respect and love the guy too much."

"Whatever John experienced in his past has left him with demons and doubts. On top of the benign, superstitious nature he has, he's been professionally treated for schizophrenia and paranoia. He's always worried that being a savant carried with it personality disorders, but the other thing, the mysterious event that seems to give him additional insight about the future and drives him to prepare for it . . . well, that dark knowledge makes him fearful that he might also be insane."

"And you don't know what that event was?"

"No," she said softly. "But when he's ready, I believe he'll tell me."

ఠ

Chalmers's other concern about Paula was that he knew things, secrets having to do with the CRYPTOS and CONUNDRUM files, that would also have a bearing on her future and, by extension, the nature of his relationship with her.

He knew that soon he'd have to describe for her an amazing scene in his rearview mirror—one that accounted for much more than the true difference in their ages.

But first Chalmers had to arrange for Paula Baker to be issued a K-RED clearance and then see to it that she was reassigned to the Division K Task Force.

After that there was a short list of issues he had to brief her about. Knowing she enjoyed surprises, he figured that what he was about to drop in her lap would be the thrill of a lifetime.

The general topics were spaceships and thermonuclear war, while the specific agenda included a description of an alien creature *underneath* the earth and a projection for the end of life *on* Earth.

There was also unfinished business with the Crystal Tabula.

65

Armed with an eight-track recorder/player and the NBC radio tape Beckner had located, Chalmers had stepped off the SpadeLiner and gone straight to the Crystal Exploitation Team lab.

"CET is primed and ready, sir," Pete Peterson said. "We borrowed a camera from Channel Nine in Richmond. Are we making a soap opera about this chunk of glass?"

"No. Can you route a live television feed directly into the laser?" Chalmers asked.

Peterson shrugged. "It's theoretically possible, but—"

"Is it technically doable through the Vortax if I write a melded metrics program?" The Vortax-1000 was an ultra-high-speed computer that Agency designers, under Chalmers's supervision, had recently brought online. Its capabilities were vastly beyond those of the Cray computers.

"Never heard of such a program. What does it do?"

"It will harmonize the particle beam functionality of the two machines provided you can structurally align their transmission trajectories."

Peterson shrugged again. "Sounds interesting. But we've pumped laser, infrared, thermal, ultraviolet, and every photometric measurement technique known into the Crystal for years. Except for that first day, it just floats there. Is it supposed to come to life because of television?"

"No, but I think it will for radio," said Chalmers, who then recounted that the NBC chime had been playing a second before the Crystal had inexplicably "exploded" to life and almost destroyed the lab. He explained his "analytical gut feeling" that the instant the Crystal *heard* the activation chime, it would open up again—for whatever inexplicable reason the three tones served as an actuator—and spew out the strange signals and perhaps emit the powerful light as well.

"After you and I get the laser vision operable," Chalmers told Peterson, "we'll set up the regular video cameras to capture the symbols, which we can feed into the ganged Crays for linguistic analysis. Oh, and we'll also remove or tape up any glass in the lab so we don't have *that* disaster again."

"Okay, but your jury-rigged laser vision . . . when and how does it figure in?"

"Pete, if the Crystal responds like my analytical deduction predicts, you are going to fire the laser vision to a set distance within what I believe is the limitless depth of that chunk of glass. And when the television signal embedded in the laser transmission line is fed into that big monitor, I believe we will be able to see what's inside."

"And you think there's something *in* there to be seen?" Peterson asked.

"Yes. Now let's perform a simple task to get started," Chalmers said as he pushed the recorder's Play button.

The *bing-bong-bing* chime filled the air.

And seconds later, so did something else.

✦✦ 66 ✦✦

After the last *bing,* the Crystal had again spewed the symbolized mist but thankfully not the powerful blast of light as before. It had also again vacuumed the swirling squiggles moments after they appeared, but not before they had been recorded on still-frame and video cameras placed strategically around the lab. Now the Crystal emitted a ghostly aurora that spun around it in a tight three-foot orbit.

Though he'd not wanted to, Chalmers had to return to Langley the next day for a meeting with the director and president about pressing issues with the Soviets. Beckner had gone to CSC to oversee the CET.

Chalmers had returned today to get briefed on what Peterson and the Crystal Exploitation Team had accomplished.

ᕃ

Beckner met him as he stepped onto the platform.

"Thirty-seven minutes. Two hundred and ten miles per hour," Chalmers said.

"We'll outrun the Japanese and European surface trains pretty soon," Beckner said, taking his boss's small travel bag. "You'll get these other project briefs first," he said, handing over a thick folder. "That'll give Pete more time to prepare and then you can stay with the CET as long as you like."

Chalmers nodded his concurrence. He read the comprehensive folder in the fifty seconds it took for them to ride the escalator up through dozens of massive stalactites and to another chamber containing forensic labs and test sites.

"Excellent. Remarkable advances," Chalmers said, returning the folder to Beckner as they walked through the biometric-coded, cipher-locked security door, which swished open after a pale blue light scanned each of their faces. "I want to see the SpadeLiner's holographic route map and 3-D blueprints of the Citations."

ᕃ

The train was almost ready for its first full-speed, fifteen-hundred-mile run. Beckner was working on the addendum to Walt Stern's clearances so he could make the inaugural journey. In any event, the plan called for Stern to use the line for his trips between Ithaca and CSC as he continued to study the alien cadavers and assist Chalmers with the CET when he could.

The maiden run would take eight hours, stopping at each Citation only long enough to see the downtown center. Chalmers, Beckner, and other DivKay seniors would revisit the sites individually as building progressed. Over the next decade they would become major industrial, urban enclaves with housing, manufacturing, agricultural, medical, educational, and other city amenities.

As Chalmers had designed from the outset, the Citations were already staffed with government employees, caretakers from a highly compartmented section of the Federal Emergency Management Agency who thought their site was the only such facility. They believed—and correctly, except for the interconnected and massive national scale—that their mission was to coordinate responses to disasters that overwhelmed the resources of local and state authorities. FEMA had been officially unveiled last year by the president, whom Chalmers had never briefed on CRYPTOS, and certainly not CONUNDRUM, because the Committee had never given Jimmy Carter a K-RED clearance.

Chalmers knew that FEMA's actual performance on ground, so to speak, was already spotty and drew criticism. But as he calculated, as a belowground, undercover facility, FEMA would serve his deception requirements nicely. A long time from now, and in response to the future escalation of terrorism in the United States, Chalmers would use his personal influence in the White House to ensure that FEMA would become part of DHS, the Department of Homeland Security.

Finished with his CRYPTOS SpadeLiner brief, Chalmers was ready for CONUNDRUM and the CET.

ᔨᐯ

"Our makeshift laser vision worked like a charm," Peterson said. "As you can see, the monitor is still grainy, but if you tweak the Vortax I think you can clear it up, maybe even get it in color."

"Regardless of quality, the images are chilling," Beckner said. "It's the ultimate historical documentary."

"We have no way to . . . uh, control the . . . channels, Dr. Chalmers," one of the CET techs said, "so the time periods are all over the . . . calendar."

Chalmers leaned in to the monitor and slipped on his glasses. "Hmm, that's the Seine River . . . and that Gothic structure *there*," he said, pointing with a pencil, "which I'd say is late twelfth century, is the construction still under way for Notre-Dame Cathedral. Anybody toured Paris and seen it lately?"

"How can we be seeing this, sir?" the CET tech asked.

Before he could respond, the monitor blipped and a new image was discernible on the static-flickering screen.

"Looks like . . . cavemen stalking a woolly mastodon," Peterson said. "Well, we've just got a new name for our glass ball—the Time Crystal."

"Pete, I have to tell you I like it better than chunk of glass," Chalmers said.

"Whatever the name," Beckner said, "the question still stands: how can this be?"

Chalmers scratched a formula on the chalkboard: $P\mu = k\sqrt{\Sigma x^2} + \Sigma_k \binom{x}{k}$.

"It's based on Einstein's quantum physics and photoelectrics, with the values of x and k as variant amplitudes of radiant temperature. He proved wave-particle duality seventy-five years ago, establishing that all light and matter exhibit properties of both waves and of particles, each of which describes the behavior of quantum objects."

"Meaning what?" Beckner asked.

"It means Einstein observed that when intense light is focused on metals and minerals, some of their electrons are knocked loose and begin to flow, like a current in a circuit. A charged force moving freely but predictably through the transmission lines of time and space."

Beckner was blank-faced. "And . . ."

"And similarly, bioluminescence is the production and emission of light by a living organism—a plant, mammal, or reptile that generates a chemical reaction during which chemical energy is converted to light energy."

"Meaning that energy from any kind of living thing can also be measured like a current flowing through a circuit. Or radiating from a crystal," Peterson said.

"Exactly. I wrote the metrics program and melded Vortax's AIC2 linear correlation coefficient with search protocols based on Einstein's $E = h\nu$ for measuring wave-particle radiance."

"And the computer's artificial intelligence command and control axial modal slaved the laser beam to the camera signal," Pete said, "and is now recording whatever it *sees* as it randomly refracts through the crystal maze of time."

"Yes," Chalmers said, walking toward the huge computer, "and we've got to get the next three Vortax generations online as soon as possible. Otherwise we'll blow this model 1000 to smithereens."

"Why is that?" Beckner asked.

"Because this machine is in the process of committing circuit suicide," Peterson said, looking at digitized data being displayed on a separate bank of monitors.

"The Crystal is emanating electrons," Chalmers explained, "but it's also absorbing them . . . at a rate of one hundred to the hundredth power greater than a googol, which is 'impossible'—except the math is true."

As Peterson quickly explained, a googol was the mathematical term for the massive number ten to the hundredth, a sum derived by multiplying one million by one million fifteen times, then further multiplying that number by ten thousand.

Beckner was a structural engineer with a different comprehension of numbers, so he had no idea what googol meant. Chalmers put it in perspective for him.

"A googol is an amount equal to all the sand grains in all the deserts and beaches on Earth. But the Crystal's absorption capacity is so great it needs a new term—a gorgon, which is equal to all the grains of sand from ten billion Earths."

Beckner was wide-eyed.

"I believe our Time Crystal is literally a white hole, pulling reflected electrons and bioluminescence into its limitless clear core. It's absorbing and storing the radiant energy from every life force and inanimate object upon which the sun shines its powerful light, knocking loose the duality of energy waves and actual particles of living material."

This concept set Chalmers's mind reeling even faster, prompting him to recall what he'd learned in the Tutorium about the Crystal Tabula being a living membrane, assimilating through energetic osmosis the totality of everything in its designated realm.

☙

"Gentlemen, I don't know if you believe in a supreme being. But I do. And I truly believe this Crystal is a recording instrument of divine architecture . . . whether it was on the UFO or not," he added as part of his cover story about the Crystal's origin. "This is something we simply take on faith. This Crystal probably contains an electronically retrievable

image of everything that ever occurred anywhere on the planet throughout time on Earth."

"What do we do with it, John?" Beckner asked.

Looking at his CET staff, Chalmers said, "Our first job is to figure out
how to change channels so we can watch the entire series. And after that,"
he added with a twinkle in his eyes, "I've got something *really* interesting
in mind."

67

There had been several developments in the four years since Chalmers and the CET had reactivated the now-named Time Crystal. A new DivKay-engineered Vortax-3000 enabled Chalmers, Peterson, and other CET technicians not only to bring a sharper, color image to the monitor but also to bracket the depth of time into which they fired the laser-vision telemetric. Or as Chalmers had called it—changing the chronological channels.

To handle the storage and retrieval of gorgons of information to be downloaded from the Crystal, the Agency's hardware engineers piggy-backed on a Department of Defense research project to connect a number of different computer networks into a macronetwork that was being called the Internet. The result for CET was a hybrid laser-optic coil drive, which Chalmers labeled a "cyber Slinky," onto which an unprecedented amount of digital data could be loaded.

An auxiliary staff was now devoted exclusively to cataloging film clips from the Crystal's global documentary. Chalmers and the others had just seen some amazing footage that solved the first of history's many mysteries locked inside the Crystal. It was how the Egyptians transported, lifted, and positioned more than two million blocks, each weighing tens of tons, to build the pyramids.

"Collateral image forensics from Vortax," said a CET tech who worked at a separate console, "confirms that the pyramids were built not around 2500 BC as popularly believed . . . but eleven thousand years before Christ."

"A time frame when ice age lakes and rivers made that region exceptionally wet and not the desert it became much later," Beckner added.

"What we've just seen," Chalmers said, "means that during the Pleistocene epoch, when most *Homo sapiens* were barely beyond picking fleas off each other, a group of anomalous technocrats figured out how to build coffer dams, divert and systematically elevate a huge body of water, design and operate Panama Canal–type locks, use barges to move giant stones, and then build a megalithic structure _not_ on dry land and by hoisting massive weight upward, but with far more brilliant ease by lowering the weight downward in water. Which later was simply drained away."

Beckner was stunned. "And we saw how it happened. Like a movie." Chalmers was thoughtful. "Perhaps we've actually witnessed it, _just_ as it happened, or is still happening, at least inside that living Crystal."

"What are you talking about, John?" Beckner asked.

"That while looking into the Crystal, we've been standing on a threshold to the past. Theoretically, once we know more about what we're doing here, we . . ."

"We what?"

"We could reach into the Crystal and _feel_ the time, learn more from it," Chalmers said, "touch it somehow with a more substantive laser probe . . . perhaps even alter it."

"Boss, don't you think you've got enough on your plate already?"

Chalmers shrugged. "Right. Timing's probably bad." _And yet it's everything._ He couldn't let the notion go. He was sure the Crystal had direct application to the operations directorate—the Agency's "tactical arm" responsible for recruiting spies, stealing information, and conducting covert action abroad that enabled America at least to influence world history . . . and in some cases change it dramatically. What kind of change could be wrought if there were a way to go back in time? _What if I could send something . . . or someone, into the past?_ He knew it would be hard, given everything on his schedule, to find the time to develop such a fantastic notion into reality; and yet there was nothing _but_ fantastic notions, even phantasmagoric ones, in every aspect of his life, and it was already a reality that Chalmers seemed to be living longer than an average life span. Suddenly, he thought of someone he would approach, if . . . or when, he found a way to step across the Crystal's threshold. It was one of the CIA's most highly regarded paramilitary officers—a fearless individual with an extraordinary ability to improvise, modify and adapt to overcome any challenge confronting him . . . at least that's what the seventh floor hallway chatter said. His name was Grayson. And Chalmers intended to meet him. He remained pensive, silently vowing to explore further this time travel concept and to learn more about Mr. Rick Grayson.

Beckner had continued to stare at the immobile, blank-faced Chalmers. "John. Time, remember? We're a bit short on it at the moment."

"Oh, sorry, Lee. Yes. The images we've just seen validate many of the alternative theories concerning not only the great pyramids but also other megalithic sites around the world. These aren't structures from civilizations and cultures known to conventional history; they're much older remnants of unknown and advanced populations."

"Granted, it's all incredibly interesting . . . amazing," Beckner said.

Chalmers was still captive to his own thoughts. "Great knowledge has been lost over time. Where would we be today if it hadn't been?"

"It'd sure be a miraculous gift if we could rediscover it," said Beckner.

"It's imperative to safeguard it. Otherwise Black Spade and the SSI will have been pointless when the dark moment arrives," Chalmers said, not in response to Beckner at whom he was not even looking, but to himself, again thinking of new notions and another name, which he hoarsely whispered . . . "Crawford." Beckner and the others exchanged a puzzled look.

&

Trying to pull his boss back into the moment and move him along to the next briefing, Beckner literally took Chalmers by the arm. "John, we've other stops to make."

"Oh, yes. The Vortax-4000. That's important, too," Chalmers said, knowing that in the adjoining laboratory a laser was going to be used for more than looking into the Time Crystal's mindful eye.

If Chalmers's other DivKay researchers had carried out his computations properly, this time the Vortax and BK-PULSE would look directly into the mind itself.

68

A linear thinker and organizationally compartmented to a fault, as Paula often joked about her husband, Chalmers had closed his mind to the CET and now followed Beckner to another laboratory where he'd see the latest demonstration of his BK-PULSE project.

Using the Vortax's laser probe, BK-PULSE was a programmatic way to mechanically and involuntarily induce the binaural beat, or self-hypnotic mind-altering state that Chalmers had learned—if not genetically inherited—from his father. An Agency cryptonym, or operational code word, BK-PULSE operated from a mathematical paradigm Chalmers had created to meld neurolinguistics and psychotherapy.

"In the pulse variation of the binaural beat," Chalmers had explained to his staff when he'd first conceived the project a year ago, "we'll direct a sonic wave embedded in a low-intensity laser into one ear of a lab animal."

As Chalmers had already witnessed several times during early phase testing, his so-called blotter beam had entered one ear, then successfully exited the other ear, casting the expulsed light on a conical reception dish. His staff had been amazed by the experiment but had no comprehension of the mathematical computations Chalmers used to program the computer. Nor did they understand how the beam avoided frying the test animals' brains. Dr. Chalmers did, and he had explained the process.

"The remarkable fact about this light transfer," he said at the time, "is that when the laser pulses through the animal's brain, it blots every single neural emitter, absorbs every pixel of cerebral encoding, and degausses every electronic byte of memorial information from the synaptic recesses of the skull's hard drive."

"But you'll erase the self-survival program," Beckner had said.

"No. As I theorized before rewriting Vortax's graphical user index, the goal-directed syntax programmed into the GUI enables the blotter beam to focus on what I've termed synaptic selectivity. Think of it as sighting in a rifle scope, calculating the variables of distance, elevation, windage and velocity of the ammunition required to hit the target's x-ring."

Chalmers further explained that the brain has a chemical topography with a distinct chemical composition linked to specific neural functions. The Vortax pulse follows a computer map produced from a cerebral MRI scan. It does not disrupt the autonomic nervous system, or alter the brain's regulation of heart, lung, and other involuntary body maintenance.

"The animal's body will remain healthy, but its brain will be empty, stripped of the chemical formulas that empower it. It will be a tabula rasa awaiting reincarnation and reinscription. But the most amazing feature of this program," Chalmers said, "happens after the neuron-impregnated beam of DNA data exits the second ear."

Under Chalmers's direction, the sponged data matter from previous tests had been directed into the reception dish where BK-PULSE software assigned digital, semantic values. Those values were fed back into the Vortax-4000 as what Chalmers called the coefficient of cognizance, which meant the chemical formulas had been adjusted before beaming them back into the subject's gray matter. Chalmers chose from a range of designed results . . . linguistic, psychological, physical, or anything else he decided to program.

Beckner thought the whole thing bore an uncanny similarity to the old television series *Outer Limits,* whose opening narration had said, "We will control the horizontal. We will control the vertical. For the next hour, sit quietly and we will control all that you see and hear."

Owing to his increased penchant for deception, manipulation, and secrecy, Chalmers viewed what he was doing more in terms of a quotation from Voltaire: "Men use thought only to justify their injustice, and speech only to conceal their thoughts."

♤

Today, as Beckner and the research team were about to see, Chalmers's Vortax-4000 would manipulate a primitive database extracted from the primate brain of Mr. Tom Morrow.

Tommie, as he was affectionately called by the staff, was a chimpanzee whose recent testing had already produced results with interesting possibilities for the future. It was time for another test.

"Dr. Chalmers, sir. We're pleased you and Mr. Beckner could join us today," said Dr. Roselle, the task force chief giving the briefing. He handed

Chalmers a summary of recent work. "In the past few days, Tommie's brain has repeatedly been deleted and replenished in a variety of first-phase AAM experiments you designed."

Finishing the report before Roselle finished talking, Chalmers handed the folder to Beckner. "Lee informed me that some adjustments were made to the alternative adaptation modality."

"Yes, sir. Most of the AAMs were successful, but perhaps the most notable one was replacing Tommie's innate tendency to swing by his arms with an exclusive preference for walking."

"And the linguistic element?"

"It was a very successful first run at neurolingual programming, Dr. Chalmers. We eliminated his inherent high-pitched chimp screeches and coarse grunts. But of course Tommie's ability to articulate sophisticated phonemes is limited by the construct of his vocal cords, larynx, and the oral configuration of his teeth, tongue, and lips."

"Of course," Chalmers said. "We can do more in the program area of phonetic communication . . . or we could perform reconstructive oral surgery."

Chalmers eyed Roselle. "I assume you got the new cerebral program I wrote?"

"Yes, sir," said Roselle, waving his hand. "Marco, there, pumped it right in."

Technician Marco stepped forward. "Dr. Chalmers," he said with a nod. "Sir, first we restored the chimp's regular traits and then plugged in the new psychocerebral component for cognition and articulation."

"Show me," Chalmers said.

"This way, John," Beckner said, opening the door to a room with a single chair in the middle. A chimpanzee sat with one leg comfortably crossed over the other.

"*Go'dah mor-neeeg, doe'akta chamah,*" Tommie said as he stood and offered his hairy hand to Dr. Chalmers.

"Good morning, Mr. Morrow," said Chalmers, his own hand lost for a moment in the long, powerful grasp of Tommie's. "Are you ready to try something new today?"

"*Oh, oh, oh, yah'ess,*" said Tommie as he pulled his lips back in a broad, excited grin, bounced on his bowlegs, and slapped his head with both hands.

"Good. Please sit down and we'll get started."

Tommie did a back somersault into the seat. Chalmers smiled at him, then nodded his approval to Roselle, Marco, and the other technicians.

"Good Lord," Beckner said. "This is astounding. The medical possibilities. The social implications. Neurotechnology with limitless capabilities . . . and consequences. How do we use it . . . and how in God's name do we control it?"

Chalmers stepped even closer to Beckner, who'd been at his side the whole time. "Yes, profound operational utility. I can see how this might come in handy someday," he said softly.

69

LANGLEY. 1984

"Remind me again, John, when did your alien offspring run away from home?" Casey asked Chalmers, who already wished he had not committed so much time to this private lunch in the director's office. He was also increasingly restless with Casey's bulldog questions and inane agenda.

"Thirty years ago."

"You and Beckner call him Jack the Ripper."

Chalmers nodded.

"Some reason you never located the jackass during the past three decades?"

"Bill, exactly how would you suggest I find a space alien living in a cave system that runs the length of the Appalachian Mountains?"

"Offer the bastard a government job! That's what I want to do."

Chalmers stared at the director.

"No, really. I want you to rig up something with your big computer, write one of your laser beam programs, and we'll stick it on a geosync bird over the East Coast. Lock on his sulfur scent or other trackable indicators Stern should have discovered by now. What are we paying him for, anyway?"

"Stern's a very busy man. We don't compensate him for his time and expertise."

"Good. But I still want the alien. You zap him with your dream beam or whatever it's called. Turn him into a Republican and then I'll hand him over to Defense so the marines can make him into a mean, green fighting machine. Kick some Soviet ass."

"Don't you think you're in enough trouble already with Congress over our Central American program?"

Casey motioned for Chalmers to pass him the bread basket. "Then blotterize the Senate select committee and the goddamned reporters . . . get all the political bloodsuckers off my back . . . the president's, too."

"You shouldn't eat bread. What happened to the youth potion I prescribed?"

"I've been pissing lemonade for months and look ten years older than I did. You look even younger. I think *you're* a space alien."

Casey guffawed as he spread butter on his croissant . . . and his tie.

⤶

Age was not a joking matter for Chalmers. Except for Casey, Paula, and Beckner, everyone thought him to be in his midsixties. But at ninety-three years old, Chalmers was aware he could drop dead at any moment.

Under way for almost twenty-five years, Operation Black Spade was near its first major milestone. In view of what he saw as mounting pressures leading inexorably to a third world war, Chalmers felt his own imperative to complete the SSI by the end of his already long life.

In spite of his best efforts to control leaks about the project and to use Committee member support to cover up the increasing number of press allegations, there had always been periodic tabloid articles about "Ultra–Top Secret" facilities in remote areas of the Appalachians. They were just the kind of stories Chalmers had predicted about underground Area 51s. These included a prison and research center for the Roswell aliens, Bigfoot, and the Loch Ness Monster; a sanatorium where "brain-dead" JFK and RFK were maintained on life-support systems; a warehouse for history's mysteries such as Amelia Earhart's coffin and wreckage of her plane; storage for "mothballed" government equipment, records, and other materials; and fallout shelters for atomic war with the Soviets.

Many of these stories appeared in the *National Reveal,* a sensationalist tabloid that was funded by a New York "investor" who received financial backing and marching orders from Washington. The *Reveal* was one of Chalmers's many propaganda ploys designed to hide the truth about Black Spade in the plain sight of patently unbelievable, utterly dismissible headlines.

However, the more credible, mainstream press stories, especially in recent years, claimed that these mountain locations were construction sites for military weapons such as laser beams, robotic devices, aerial drones, and other space station technology linked to President Ronald W. Reagan's highly publicized Star Wars program—which Reagan and CIA director William J. Casey had labeled the Strategic Defense Initiative, or SDI.

Chalmers had recommended that overt name as a misdirection campaign for his, and the administration's, covert SSI project.

⤶

From OSS days throughout his CIA years, Chalmers always enjoyed strong relationships with Agency directors and certain presidents, especially Eisenhower. This was particularly true now. As Committee members with the letter *W* in their names, Casey and Reagan often followed Chalmers's lead not only about the Cryptos and Conundrum projects but also other political and military issues where his analytical evaluations supported their needs. In turn, they gave him unprecedented levels of backing, particularly in increased budgets from Congress in order to support Black Spade's spiraling costs.

Both New Yorkers and favorites of Donovan during the war, Chalmers and Casey were especially close, with each awarded the Bronze Star for meritorious achievement while in the Office of Strategic Services. Eccentrically brilliant in his own right and even more of a curmudgeon than Chalmers, Bill Casey was definitely aware of how much younger Chalmers looked these days, and he had become persistent in knowing his friend's fitness secret. Chalmers finally told him the same tale he'd spun for Lee Beckner and Paula. Knowing Casey as he did, Chalmers threw in one extra ingredient to spice up the lie and to deal with his atrocious bad breath at the same time.

"You bullshittin' me, John? Sixteen *concentrated* ounces a day? How do you get it all down without puckering up your lips and ass at the same time?" Casey had asked.

"No BS, Bill. Lemon concentrate. Four-ounce shots, every six hours. Dissolve a couple of peppermint candies in each glass first. I've been on the program all my life, and you can see the results."

ↄ

At Casey's first senior staff meeting in the director's conference room, he had made a statement about his views on the CIA's covert action policies.

"We'll know our disinformation program is complete when everything the American public believes is false." It had shocked his subordinates but brought a restrained smile to Chalmers's face.

Now, years later and in view of the spate of recent *New York Times* articles about the government and the CIA's "secret sanctuaries" scattered throughout the Appalachian Mountains, Chalmers was counting on Casey to add more muscle to his strong statement.

ↄ

The current problem was Robert Graham, an investigative journalist for the *Times*. He had been approached by a few of the disgruntled illegal immigrants who'd been co-opted during the Eisenhower administration to work underground in exchange for Green Card promises that were never kept. Most had subsequently been deported and told if they ever returned or spoke about their work they'd be arrested and thrown in jail. A few had now taken the risk of telling their stories to Graham, who had spent years piecing together other elements of their revelations, particularly government contracts issued to a consortium of companies involved in "excavation and tunneling" projects up and down the East Coast.

Along the way, Graham had run across the name of Jonathan Chalmers, a "senior government official" who seemed to be a thread of continuity throughout whatever mysterious activity the federal government and the CIA seemed to be up to, according to his sources. Using public real estate and tax records, Graham eventually tracked down Chalmers's residences in New York and Virginia.

Graham went to the Long Island property a few times but never found Chalmers there, nor got anything but vague, suspicion-enhancing responses from the estate manager to whom Graham directed questions about Mr. Chalmers. Graham had eventually showed up in Virginia and knocked late one evening on the front door of Chalmers's home in McLean. Paula answered and told Graham her husband was not at home, but neither she nor Chalmers would have any interest in talking to a journalist about anything.

With Paula expecting a year after their marriage in 1979, Chalmers had bought the elegant McLean home that was just minutes from headquarters. After Steven was born, Paula had returned to work part-time at Langley, armed with a K-RED security clearance and a position as executive assistant to Lee Beckner on the DivKay Task Force.

Sensing that the elusive Chalmers was somehow the key to his soon-to-be revealed blockbuster story about conspiracy and cover-up, Graham mounted his own surveillance on the McLean residence, observing Chalmers being picked up in the morning and driven to nearby Langley, and following Paula on a few occasions when she went shopping or took Steven to his private school.

꜀

It was Graham tailing his son that had finally prompted Chalmers to talk with Casey over lunch today. Finished with the meal, they had moved to some sofa chairs.

"So this is the same asshole I've already called the *Times* about before?"

Chalmers nodded.

"I made the editor a deal," Casey said with his usual coarse, growl.

"Told that fuckhead he could run the occasional front-pager blowing some of our projects, even an asset now and again, provided they spiked selected stories . . . especially Graham's."

"Well, now you know the editor's policy on Graham's brand of journalism."

"This has gone beyond the paper's publishing policy and any one writer," Casey spat. "Graham's crossed my line by intruding into your family life. *We* conduct surveillance. Neither this Agency, and for goddamned sure not the child of one of its senior officers, is going to be followed by some hack reporter."

Chalmers simply nodded again, content to let Casey head in the desired direction.

"I'll make a few calls. One to the chairman of the board of directors. So happens he also manages the trust fund of the wag who owns the paper. Always follow the fucking money . . . and then pinch it," Casey grumbled. "Only favorable thing I can say about this shit head Graham is that he's doing the right thing from an investigative standpoint . . . he just picked a bad topic to research, and in your case, my friend, the wrong onion to peel."

"And the other calls, Bill?"

"NYPD, IRS, and DOJ. By the time they get through launching their own investigations, subpoenas, audits, and court appearances with Graham, his ass will be in such a crack he won't have time to fuck with us."

"And the evidence for the charges you'll arrange to be brought against him?"

"Don't know. But whatever you decide will be fine," Casey said with a wink.

⊢⊣

Chalmers was too busy to deal with building a legal case and constructing forensic evidence that Agency lawyers could use to confront Graham—who, faced with a probable prison sentence, would undoubtedly have opted for the out-of-court-settlement option of simply dropping his investigative case.

Owing to a timely convergence of coincidence, Chalmers was spared further effort or worry about Graham when the reporter abruptly suffered a fatal heart attack.

✦70✦

Chalmers was at his desk scribbling notes, listening to several world news broadcasts and skimming through a couple of books at the same time when Beckner walked in.

"Bad news," he said, holding a piece of paper. "Memo to you from Jamesly. He's retiring at the end of the year. How do we find another linguist like him?"

Chalmers didn't look up. "We don't. After all these years and his own Vortax, the professor hasn't managed to translate any of the Crystal's symbolized mist. If I'd had the time, I would have done the job myself."

"He determined the floating symbols and the blood scrawl, the ηακψυ marks that Jack left on the lab wall, were totally unrelated. That seems odd considering you've always said the Crystal came from the UFO," Beckner said with a provocative tone, for some reason testing waters he knew he shouldn't. "Could the Crystal floaters be something else . . . *from* somewhere else?"

This time Chalmers looked up. "Forget the damn linguistics, Lee," he said sharply. "All you need to know is that I understand more about the Crystal than you or Jamesly or anybody else. We're watching a silent movie every time we're running the laser vision anyway."

ﺲ

Chalmers thought he knew what the Crystal hieroglyphs were, in any event. They reminded him of the mental symbols he'd seen in the Tutorium. When those same types of symbols first appeared in the lab, he and everyone else heard a powerful static sound that accompanied the blast of light.

Chalmers had later realized that was probably the sound of a gorgon-sized stream of phonemes coming from all the conversations throughout time, somehow recorded along with visions of all events on Earth. Knowing he'd never be able to replay even a nanopercent of the imagery, there was hardly any point worrying about the total of human words spoken over the past million years—especially if they were digitized representations of alien thought.

For that, Chalmers would need the Headmaster plus all twelve Samaritans, not just Jamesly as the translator.

ᕙ

"I've reprogrammed the Vortax," Chalmers said. "Picture's going to be sharper and with a zoom feature. I want you to get two of the best lip-readers you can find. It'll be a slow process, but we'll make transcripts of the most important visual time blurbs when we find them. As soon as I figure out how to dial in more contemporary channels, we can find current, usable intelligence instead of just solving history's mysteries."

"Yes, that'd be a major breakthrough, "Beckner said, relieved his boss had lost the sharp tone he'd used a moment ago and that was disturbingly familiar to the tone used back when Beckner had felt Chalmers had threatened him over the age issue. "What's your take, John, on why the Crystal has simply shut down a couple times recently?"

"Not sure yet. Fortunately, it continues to respond to the recorded chimes from the old radio program, but I don't like depending on a single source for emergency reactivation any more than I'd want to depend on NBC for real news."

"I see your point. The tape could break or wear out. The old recorder, too."

"That's why I want you to track down an old-fashioned xylophone, a kid's toy model . . . like the one Paul had," Chalmers said as his eyes glazed with a distant focus.

"Paul?"

"Hmm, yes. A pal I grew up with." Chalmers was reflective for another moment, then suddenly drew a quick sketch. "About this size and shape. With a little wooden mallet. You can probably find one in the antiques mall in Williamsburg."

ᕙ

After Beckner left, Chalmers thought again of another name that had been on his mind lately . . . Crawford. And another future issue with the Crystal that Chalmers continued to address—a critical one, the key for locating and unlocking a unique vault other than the one currently in the Level II laboratory at CSC.

This unique repository was in an even deeper part of the cavern, a place Chalmers had already selected for someday storing the Crystal until its custodial heir, his own son, Steven, would assume stewardship of the celestial jewel.

Involving an uncleared civilian named Crawford to assist Chalmers in creating a clue to where that vault was located, and leaving instructions on how to use the key to unlock the Crystal, would require creativity and finesse.

Chalmers knew he could do it.

And that it was time to take action.

71

Chalmers was in the cafeteria having coffee with Darwin Carlosi, director of the CIA's Fine Arts Commission. They watched bulldozers tear into the forested hill on the backside of the Original Headquarters Building, the OHB, which even as it was being designed in the mid-1950s included a provision for eventual expansion. That time had arrived.

Groundbreaking was under way for the New Headquarters Building, the NHB, which would share a large open courtyard with the contiguous OHB. Chalmers knew that Carlosi was responsible for coming up with an appropriate piece of artwork to be displayed in the courtyard.

Carlosi had previously heard of Brenton Crawford in a memo from Chalmers. He now listened to Chalmers's ideas on a sculpture that he believed the artist could be commissioned to create—something with the themes of intelligence gathering and problem solving. Beckner had prepared a background folder. After reviewing it, Carlosi agreed that Crawford had the right credentials.

Chalmers mentioned that his friend and renowned astronomer, Walt Stern, had some of Brenton Crawford's pieces and had offered to make a personal introduction. Carlosi suggested that Chalmers should be the one to reach out initially to Crawford.

Chalmers had called Crawford, who accepted his invitation to visit Langley and evaluate an "artistic opportunity." Enthusiastic about it, Crawford had immediately agreed to undertake the project and returned to his shop, where he laid out a design. It was submitted later and immediately accepted by Langley's NHB Planning Committee, which was chaired by Carlosi.

Crawford was back at headquarters today to discuss specifics with Chalmers.

"These aluminum columns" Crawford said as his finger traced the blueprint like a director's baton harmonizing an orchestra, "support this fifteen-foot-tall right-angled steel wall, which represents the point of a spear. Doesn't CIA use a symbol like that?"

"Yes. General Donovan's gold-on-black spearhead insignia for his Office of Strategic Services. We still use that OSS symbol today in our covert operations component. I'm impressed you know so much of our history."

"Yeah, I've put a lot of thought into this project."

"And I'm duly impressed. Please continue."

"Together, I see the columns and wall forming a metaphorical barrier— a bulwark of *intelligent*, first-line-of-defense protection that this Agency provides for all aspects of our national security. As this page shows, I'll cut thousands of alphabetic letters to form several coded messages that will represent CIA cryptology and the use of dead drops, one-time pads and other forms of ciphers your clandestine operatives use to pass or hide intelligence."

"You really have done your homework, Jim."

"Ah, it's just stuff anybody can learn from spy novels. But I'm something of a linguistics guy, especially the origins of words. I found that the Greek word *kruptos* means hidden or secret, and it also probably accounts for the word cryptography."

"A system of secret writing. Yes, you're probably right."

"I believe I am. I certainly think cryptographic protocols will become common place for safeguarding proprietary information in the banking, business and technology development world . . . just like your agency uses it now for classified information. I think computers will eventually take over everything, except artwork, I hope."

He and Chalmers exchanged smiles.

"In any event I have kind of created a new word, *Cryptos*, and it's what I will call my sculpture. Since *Cryptos* will contain a coded message I'm thinking about, my art work will also be a mystery, a puzzle for puzzle-workers and code-breakers to figure out. You know, a conundrum. Maybe someday someone will even learn something important from my work and my philosophical message."

Unbelievable convergence of coincidence, Chalmers thought.

"A fitting choice of words," he said.

"If your director will let me, I plan to issue a challenge at the *Cryptos* dedication ceremony for the workforce to break . . . well, *try* to break the code and my secret message. Fun, huh?"

"Indeed. And you've no idea how much I approve of your proposed name. The notion of someday breaking through the deceit of the encrypted message is more relevant than you can imagine." For a moment Chalmers's eyes focused elsewhere. "For someone to do something at some point in the future with my, uh, your mystery code is an elegant idea . . . with perhaps even a cosmic consequence," he added, suddenly snapping back from where he had mentally wandered and now looking directly at Crawford again.

"Well . . . I'm, uh, I am very glad you approve," said Crawford, who'd also been staring blankly at his host as he puzzled over what Chalmers had just said. "I've done some research on codes," he continued as he shuffled other pages of notes to regain his composure, "and I'm thinking about using a method developed by the sixteenth-century French cryptographer Blaise de Vigenère. I'll certainly welcome your thoughts on the code."

"The Vigenère cipher is based on the letters of a keyword," Chalmers said. "A polyalphabetic substitution where each letter in the plaintext is replaced by a letter some fixed number of positions farther down the alphabet. Simple but effective."

"I don't know what the variability ratio would be, but I imagine it'd make the code damn hard to puzzle through."

"Even a three-position shift over a twenty-six-letter base produces an algorithmic equation with almost limitless solutions," Chalmers said. "The French call it *le chiffre indéchiffrable*—the unbreakable cipher."

"We agree on it, then. What's needed now is something profound for the message itself. I've got some ideas, but I invite yours as well."

Another convergence of coincidence, Chalmers thought as a wry smile etched his face. "Oh, I believe we can make the Vigenère even more abstruse, and I definitely can contribute to the mystery message. Think of it as my secret for *you* to figure out."

"You're on, Dr. Chalmers," Crawford said with an enthusiastic grin.

You don't stand a chance, Chalmers thought as he flashed a mischievous one.

৯

Months later, Chalmers was at the ceremony when President Reagan and Director Casey officially broke ground for the NHB. The following year he watched Vice President George Herbert Walker Bush lay the cornerstone.

Partial occupancy began in 1988. The *Cryptos* sculpture was finished and the dedication ceremony took place on October 10, 1990. Chalmers listened that day from the back row as the new director, William Webster, had addressed the crowd.

"Today, this very talented artist has presented our Agency not only a beautiful, intriguing piece of art, but also a challenge to break the code within the enigmatic *Cryptos* sculpture. Only time will tell if its final message is ever revealed."

72

Chalmers was in the director's office and Casey was in a lather.

"Jack's pals are going to get us in the middle of a goddamned nuclear war rather than merely complicate this nuclear accident," Casey said.

"Bill, the Soviets don't believe we took out their MiGs," Chalmers said, handing him a report, "but it would be better for us if they did, certainly after this."

❧

Casey was bellowing about two related events and their possible repercussions.

The first one occurred two days ago, when the Soviet Union's Chernobyl nuclear power plant in Ukraine experienced an extreme spike in power output that caused a reactor to rupture, which sparked a series of explosions and sent a plume of radioactive fallout into the atmosphere. The second happened yesterday when Ukraine military radar operators reported seven blips streaking back and forth above the burning plant. Ground observers described them as smudges of intense light moving erratically.

In response to the presence of unidentified craft in Soviet airspace, the military launched ten MiG-29 fighter jets. What happened to them complicated everything.

All of the Soviets' intruder reports, and the incident that ensued, were picked up or confirmed by CIA field sources, as well as NSA listening sites—one of which recorded radio transmissions between the MiGs and the base tower when the pilots claimed they'd been fired on by UFOs.

❧

"Explain how this is good for us," Casey said. "Gorbachev's already been on the hot line claiming we had multiple spy planes and Department of Energy planes taking atmospheric readings. Accused us of taking preemptive shots at the MiGs when all they'd done was fly routine surveil-lance on otherwise unidentified aircraft."

"Preposterous. It's cold war politics. The Soviets have been tracking UFOs, real or imagined, for as long as we have, including the same seven that routinely pop in and out of the Black Sea."

"I know that," Casey said, "but neither *their* UFOs nor *ours* have ever fired on each other's military planes."

"Not true. The USS *Roosevelt* shot one down in 1958. And we believe Jack's sister ships, often reported in the Pacific as well as Atlantic, destroyed the USS *Thresher* a few years later in retaliation . . . or to harvest the sub's nuclear reactor."

"I thought that was an accident."

"So did everyone. You didn't have a K-RED back then, Bill."

"How do we know the submarine was attacked?"

"Same way we know the MiGs were struck, though this time it was obviously a warning shot, which is why all of them were able to land," Chalmers said.

"You're talking about the matching holes through their vertical stabi-lizers?"

"Yes, the lightning arcs that were reported to have come from the UFOs punched flawless round holes in the MiGs but avoided any serious structural damage. They were just trying to harvest nuclear fuel, not start nuclear war."

"What do you mean by 'flawless'?"

"*Perfectly* round, at least mathematically, like the Greek pi, a transcen-dental number that is the ratio of a circle's circumference to its diameter in Euclidean geometry. It's similar to the concept of numeric universality you find in the Fibonacci sequence, which—"

"Get to the point, John."

"Okay. Underwater photos revealed that *Thresher*'s hull had two holes, entry and exit wounds—both were 3.14159 inches in diameter. They were not cut or bored, at least not by any cutting, explosive, or other penetrat-ing force known to us. It's as if the steel plate simply dematerialized. And that's exactly what we see in these satellite photos taken of the MiG's tail assemblies."

"So how does any of this work for us when both sides are poised to push red launch buttons?"

"By now, Soviet scientists have discovered the remarkable nature of

those holes. You've already got the president selling the Star Wars scam.
Have Reagan call Gorbachev back and admit the UFOs are our latest generation stealth fighter planes. Or tell him they're *real* space aliens with
whom the United States has formed an alliance. Either way, it'll give Gorby
something else to think about when he looks at his red buttons."

"John, I actually like that idea . . . but you, my friend, are one crazy
son of a bitch."

73

PHILADELPHIA CITATION. 1987

Two hundred years ago, Independence Hall was filled with delegates to a convention where the country's Founding Fathers hammered out a Constitution and forged the American republic. Today, *under* the historic hall, workers and their equipment filled a huge cavern that Chalmers's SSI team had discovered when the Strategic Survival Initiative was implemented more than twenty-five years ago.

Operation Black Spade's bulldozers, hydrolytic shovels, jackhammers, cranes, and scaffolds supporting an army of DivKay delegates continued to forge a new republic—one that according to Chalmers's plan would wait in reserve for the day when thirteen underground bunkers would be all that was left of America's hope for a new future.

Like all East Coast states, Pennsylvania had an abundance of caves and caverns, and Chalmers was familiar with all of them, especially the largest— Laurel Caverns, which was located fifty miles south of Pittsburgh. It was originally the site for the SpadeLiner's Pennsylvania Citation, or city-station, even though it was far west of the train tunnel's northeastern path toward its ultimate destination in Ithaca, New York. Chalmers viewed it as a convergence of coincidence that one of his DivKay geologists had calculated from satellite photography and subsequent seismology testing that a large cavern system was directly below Philadelphia.

Black Spade workers ran twenty-four/seven at all Citations, as well as the Triple-T, or tunnel-track teams that ran independent projects to link the Citations.

Hank McGraw was the supervising engineer at the Philadelphia site. He reported any problems, from an engineering or security standpoint, through an encrypted radiophone to "somebody big" in Washington.

McGraw had recently made several such calls—some about expensive electronic equipment that had gone missing, others about workers who had disappeared. Unfortunately, part of one missing worker had been discovered in a passage leading to another part of the huge cavern system. There were already rumors about the "Appalachian Cave Monster," and though no one really believed the myth, the worker's remains had everyone spooked.

ᕮ

"Sure this will work?" McGraw asked.

"Oh, yeah, boss, this'll snatch up anybody's . . . or any*thing's* ass that tries to make off with another generator or solar panel," said Carlos, a work foreman with big biceps who'd just rigged a cargo net activated by a spring-loaded trip wire. "And even if they or it or whoever's been ripping off our stuff and dragging off our crew knocks out this section of lights first, then we'll hit 'em with reserve floods that'll activate same time the net does."

"Good work, Carlos," McGraw said, patting his foreman's back. "Word from uptown is that we, meaning you and me only, have got to handle this, keep it quiet from everybody else down here."

"*Correcto.* That is why I put the spare gear here, away from the main chamber and close to this side fissure."

McGraw looked around nervously. "Let's head back."

"You're the boss, *hombre,*" Carlos said.

ᕮ

They had taken only a few steps when the halogens went out, leaving just their helmet lanterns to light the small chamber. An instant later the net's spring release echoed with a loud *twang.*

"*Puta madre,*" Carlos said when the auxiliary floodlights snapped on to reveal a dark shape flailing in the swinging net. And another instant after that, the emergency lights began to flicker.

"What the fuck's going on here?" McGraw said. "What's in there?"

Just as the emergency lights failed completely, Carlos twisted a valve on a steel tank, struck the sparker, and the acetylene torch he'd picked up shot to fiery life. "*No se, pero lo quemo,*" he said, moving forward to burn whatever was trapped. "*Jesucristo,*" he shouted as another dark shape brushed by him on its way to the twisting net.

"Hank."

"Yeah, Carlos, I saw it," McGraw said, now catching only shadowy glimpses from his helmet light. "You okay?"

Carlos was too busy to answer.

"Eat *fuego,*" he bellowed as he waved the hissing torch at the dark bird-shaped *thing* the size of a Volkswagen Beetle that was trying to untangle the other *thing* just like it.

McGraw heard a raw screech, which he assumed came from whatever Carlos had torched. It was followed by a deep rasp, something between a hiss and a growl. In the dim light of the chamber he saw a third shadow— this one huge, moving across the ceiling and down the rock wall. "Carlos, another one's above you," he shouted.

McGraw stepped back, stumbled, and broke his helmet lantern. Lying on his stomach, he heard a cracking, ripping sound and felt warm wetness spray across his arms. He swabbed at it and felt the thick stickiness of what he knew was Carlos's blood.

Terrified, McGraw started to belly-crawl and then pushed up to his hands and knees as he scrambled to escape. Suddenly, he screamed in pain from the crushing pressure around his hips as he was lifted from the floor and hurled through the darkness.

ᕮ

Ten hours later, Beckner handed Chalmers a sitrep from the DivKay Coordination Center's watch officer at Langley who'd just taken a cipher call from Philly Citation.

Two more people were missing.

So far the search team had made only one discovery.

It was a large splatter of blood near the top of a high wall.

✦74✦

Although they possessed the adaptation genes that enabled them to recall their mother's memories and the ability to reshape their bodies temporarily, Kaj'a-zar's sisters were not genetically programmed to mature in size, function, or intellect as quickly as male Fiverians. Fortunately, like their brother, they healed quickly from injuries, so the one who had been burned had already recovered.

Still, Kaj'a-zar would have to care for both females considerably longer before he could take them as ψσ-σλδ, or breed stock to produce his own offspring. In the interim, he had to provide food, shelter, and specific education for them, even as he continued to educate himself about this alien world where he was stranded. And he knew from ζξϖωυκφ, his father's genetically inherited brain cells, that the keys to survival anytime or anyplace were knowledge and the power it provided.

During his many nocturnal trips into the population centers, he'd picked up some indigenous vocabulary from the vision screens, which he now knew were called Sony, Samsung, or sometimes Panasonic. He knew for certain the vision screens he'd seen inside the human's habitats were his best source for learning about this world, which he believed was called Earth, among many other names, such as USA and Hollywood.

Kaj'a-zar had explored the Appalachian caves and connecting fissures for years, establishing a number of small sanctuaries close to the ones he observed being constructed by a different category of humans who—as an apparently separate race from those who lived aboveground—worked and lived exclusively in the artificially lighted subterranean world. He observed and exploited these human underlings, or ψϖωϖδχ as they would have been called on Fiveria, just as he did with those who lived in larger enclaves above. He took technical equipment from both populations . . . and oftentimes ate them as well.

ใอ

One of his safe havens was this technical laboratory where he'd constructed a communications center to further his knowledge and to attempt
to contact the remaining Fiverian ships he hoped were still on or around
Earth. Using electronic items he'd taken from the humans, Kaj'a-zar had
assembled a bank of vision screens in a grotto he had found some time
ago. On a mountain peak above the grotto, he had positioned other glass
panels he'd taken after determining they captured energy from this planet's sun to produce the electrical force required to illuminate artificial
lights and power the various sound boxes and vision screens upon which
this planet's inhabitants were so dependent.

After much trial and error, he'd figured out the energy wires—or cables,
as he learned they were called in human language—and he now had
transmission power. But there was another kind of cable that he realized
was required to see talking heads on the vision screens, and he had not
yet figured out that part. He wasn't worried. This world's technology was
not sophisticated. Its crude power transmission system and unusual form
of communication may have slowed him, but he was a Fiverian . . . he would
prevail.

Although he no longer needed it, Kaj'a-zar had also constructed his
own biologic laboratory, like the one where the human Chalmers had ex-
perimented on his mother's eggs and subsequently hatched him under
torturously painful circumstances.

After escaping and later returning to that laboratory to reclaim the
eggs of his sisters, Kaj'a-zar had slaughtered two more humans and left a
blood-inscribed message on the wall for Chalmers: ηακψυ, a declaration
of spirit and intent, predicated on a Fiverian's creed that Kaj'a-zar would
find a way to pay back to the human in full measure what Chalmers had
done to Kaj'a-zar.

It would be life for a life, soul for a soul.

Whether he did it before he escaped this world or after he ruled it,
Kaj'a-zar would pick the time and the place to strike his obligatory blow.

75

As often as work permitted, Chalmers and his family spent weekends on Long Island. There today and looking like a vibrant, athletic man in his late sixties, Jonathan Chalmers quietly celebrated his one hundredth birthday. He sat in front of the same stone hearth in the library where, for almost two centuries, his father, grandfather, and great-grandfather had read, contemplated, and smoked pipes.

No longer to be seen, however, was the portrait of him as a teenager. Superstitious to begin with, and plagued off and on with schizophrenia and paranoia after the Tutorium incident, he'd never wanted to see it again after thinking it was his *Picture of Dorian Gray.* He'd ordered it to be removed and stored in the attic before he began returning several years ago with Paula and Steven for weekend retreats.

ка

"In case you go looking for Steven," Paula said, walking into the study, "he's down the street playing with a new friend. It's good there'll be another ten-year-old in the neighborhood when we come up for our getaways."

"Oh, thanks. I wondered why it was so quiet," Chalmers said over the stack of math and physics books piled in his lap.

Steven was brilliant and a great source of pride to his parents, though Paula was concerned that her husband spent too much time on the CRYPTOS CONUNDRUM and not nearly enough with Steven, who adored his father and hung on every word his dad said.

At five, the kid's IQ scores were exceptional. His parents had enrolled him in Washington's top-ranked private academy for uniquely gifted and talented youngsters. Steven loved going to the Smithsonian, especially the Air and Space Museum, where he'd seen the giant IMAX screen presentation of *To Fly!* a half dozen times. Fascinated with space, Steven relished his opportunities to visit periodically with his dad's famous friend, Dr.

Walton Stern who, as the surrogate uncle he had become, encouraged the youngster to become an astronaut.

ʖᴐ

"Better pack your briefcase, dear, they'll be landing soon," Paula said, entering the library. "I've already got your other bag ready."

Chalmers smiled and nodded. He stood and walked to his desk, continuing to read the books that he held in each hand.

Because of Chalmers's unique position, the Agency provided him with special administrative and personal support. In addition to being driven to and from Langley, Chalmers was ferried by private helicopter from headquarters to the backyard of his Oyster Bay estate. It made sense from a time-efficiency and personal-security standpoint.

When Black Spade was finished, Chalmers would make these periodic trips on the SpadeLiner, either being helicoptered from upstate New York's Citation to the mansion, or driven there in armored Agency security vehicles.

Chalmers still liked his work and believed it was as vital as it was unfinished. But he did truly love the serenity here on Long Island. He wished he could have spent more of his life here.

With time passing so quickly and his analytical judgment that the Armageddon of atomic war loomed ever larger, he could only wonder how many escapist moments he and everyone else had left.

McLEAN, VIRGINIA. APRIL 24

Chalmers and Steven were having breakfast at the kitchen island while Paula finished dressing in the bedroom. Chalmers had muted the sound on all but one of the four televisions that carried the morning news on NASA's long-awaited launch of the Hubble Space Telescope, or HST.

"We have liftoff of the Space Shuttle *Discovery* at eight thirty-three eastern standard time," said the announcer over the rumbling rocket and the huge burning clouds that spewed from the Kennedy Space Center launch pad. Steven was totally wide-eyed and gripped with emotion by the space flight.

"The HST's main goal," Chalmers told Steven, "is to establish what Dr. Stern calls a UDF, or an Ultra Deep Field image."

"Is Uncle Walt in charge of this mission?"

"He's the senior astronomer at the Space Center, which makes him in charge of the telescope and the UDF."

The UDF image, or celestial snapshot of time, as Chalmers had previously explained to Steven, was to be taken in a small region of far space located in a grid adjacent to the Orion constellation, which was one of the best-known and most conspicuous cluster of stars found along the night sky's celestial equator. Dr. Stern had randomly selected that constellation, popularly known as the Hunter, as a starting point for NASA's cosmic picture taking.

"Dad, tell me more about what the Hubble will see."

"First, it's focused on something called right ascension and declination. These are bearings, or celestial versions of longitude and latitude on Earth, that cover a telescopic lens area of three arcminutes square. Walt would tell you that's an astronomy term to describe a line of sight smaller than a grain of sand held at arm's length."

"That's pretty small, huh?"

"And very far away. Hubble will capture the deepest image of the universe ever taken. The pictures will allow Walt and his team to look back in time more than thirteen billion years . . . plus survey some ten thousand galaxies in the process. All of it will help us better understand how Earth and our solar system were formed."

"So, Dad, how long before the telescope sends back pictures, and do you think Uncle Walt will let us see 'em? It'd be awesome, wouldn't it, to be on the *Discovery* right now seeing everything firsthand?"

"Yes, it would, and I hope someday you'll see it for yourself, too. But for now, the only discovery needs to be the location of your shoes and pack. Mom's taking you to school, I'm leaving for the office, and we're both already late."

"I'm glad I got to watch this with you, Dad."

"Me, too, son," said Chalmers, hugging Steven, then walking out to the driveway where the Agency chauffeur waited.

Ꮗ

En route to Langley, Chalmers again thought about the convergent coincidence, as well as the irony of his and Stern's respective projects—one using a crystal ball, the other a glass lens, with both looking into the past in order to gain a clearer view of the present . . . and perhaps the future.

When the first UDF photos came back, Chalmers and Stern were faced with an entirely new aspect to the CRYPTOS CONUNDRUM, for Hubble's view of the Hunter provided more information than how Earth was formed.

The telescope's photographs rekindled vague thoughts in Chalmers's mind about his surreal visit to the Tutorium, which he still acknowledged might exist only as a nightmarish dream. In any event, looking into the deep-set cosmic eye of the Hunter, Chalmers had a strong though unclear sense that nuclear holocaust was the least of America's and planet Earth's concerns.

76

As Chalmers later learned, a team of eight spelunkers had gathered this morning to explore Endless Caverns, the state's largest tourist cave. They were professional cartographers from the National Speleological Society and seasoned cave sleuths from the nearby James Madison University Department of Geology.

The four NSS experts, led by Kirk Marshal, planned to reconnoiter and map new passages, some of which might eventually have lighted trails for *touries*, a spelunker's derisive term for tourists who casually sauntered through caves that'd already been explored by others. The three JMU students and their professor, Dr. Greg Chayson, would photograph stalactites, stalagmites, and other geologic formations.

ᐟᐠ

Already in more than one mile, the team had reached a point called the turnaround. It was where touries would head back to the surface. And the gift shop.

Instead, the team squeezed through a small keyhole-shaped opening and ventured down a rough passage that previous mapping teams had followed for an additional mile before hitting a narrow, dead-end chamber with a high wall. At the top was an unreachable ledge. Even more skilled as a mountaineer than a caver, Marshal intended to scale the wall, leading *his* team through another keyhole he felt existed on the rim above.

ᐟᐠ

"Belay on," said the NSS caver, who looked high up into a vertical fissure as he cinched the safety belay, a kernmantle climbing rope, around his waist. Marshal was tied to the "working end" of the rope and balanced on a toe-size ridge some one hundred feet above the cave floor.

"Climbing," shouted Marshal as he put his weight, and his life, in the belay line that connected his shoulder harness to the carabiner hooked to a steel-shank piton he'd just hammered into the escarpment. With the strength and fluidity of a gymnast, Marshal executed a series of palm presses and lay backs as he chimneyed himself up the remaining crack and onto the ledge.

"Belay off," Marshal yelled down. He unsnapped his harness and slithered into a small hole, the light from his helmet growing fainter as he moved deeper into yet another chamber in the aptly named Endless Caverns.

Marshal was gone for a while. Dr. Chayson and the others were nervous. Chayson was about to voice his concern when dim light again shone from the hole. Seconds later, Marshal's helmeted head poked through.

"Windows and shaft splits everywhere," he shouted. "I'll rig a top rope." A few minutes later, using a mechanical device called a Jumar for ascending a free-hanging rope, everyone crested the top ledge and shoehorned their bodies through the small hole.

ﾚﾑ

Marshal and Chayson were bringing up the rear. The others were just ahead. "Ever see a spelo like this?" asked Chayson, shining his light on a cluster of jagged stems and nodular tips that resembled marine coral. He snapped several pictures.

"Looks like standard cave coral, but I've never seen a variety with such sharp edges," said Marshal, already walking toward the team's lights and hearing their voices.

"Holy shit . . ." "My God, what *is* this . . . ?" "Dunno, but it's unfucking-believable," exclaimed some of the cavers who had enough wits to speak. The others stood silently, first in confusion, then with a spine-tingling fear that paralyzed them—and not with a sense of wonder about some unknown geological cave features, but with horror about the unknown structural features in this suddenly terrifying cave.

ﾚﾑ

"What's going on in here?" said Marshal as he and Chayson slipped sideways through a narrow crack and into an area with the other six cavers. They shined their lights in the direction the other team members pointed theirs.

"Gawd a'mighty," exclaimed Marshal, "How'd this . . . whatever *this* is . . . possibly get in here?"

"It's been fabricated. From regular commercial products, judging from the pile of junk over there," said Chayson, directing a larger hand lamp to a far corner of the huge chamber. Everyone looked at the pile of metal windowframes; thick slabs of broken glass, perhaps from storefront doors;

sections of garden hose, drainage pipe, and electrical conduit tubing; stripped-out bodies of refrigerators, microwaves, water heaters, and desk-top computers; commercial grade electrical cord; an assortment of propane and acetylene welding bottles; empty bags of ammonium sulfate nitrate fertilizer; and other stuff at the bottom of the huge trash pile.

"And from that . . . this," said Chayson, turning his light back to the structure in the middle of the high-ceilinged chamber, "looks like Fran-kenstein's laboratory."

There were a dozen custom-fashioned rectangular glass cases. Each re-sembled a five-hundred-gallon aquarium standing on end. At the top and bottom were innards from the appliances and computers, and their jury-rigged components seemed to provide a combination of heat and mixing movement for the gruel swirling around inside.

The twelve cases were arranged in a circle around two porcelain bath-tubs full of straw grass and what looked like pieces of broken plastic. Each tub was connected via a network of bizarre makeshift plumbing to the surrounding server cases.

The bathtubs were surrounded by sections of chain-link fence interlaced with electrical wire that fed into the same main junction box to which were attached all the other power cords serving the other strangely configured equipment. One main coaxial cable trailed away from the junction box and into the cave's continuing depth.

"Damn. What's that smell?" asked one of the JMU students.

"Whatever this green shit in here is," said Marshal, taking a closer look at the sludge swirling slowly inside one of the aquarium cases. Suddenly a large piece of material, something really nasty-looking, and for a second suggestive of a face, brushed the inside of the glass.

Everyone instantly recoiled. There was a moment of total silence, then a nervous chorus of "See that?" "Yeah." "What was it?" "Don't know, don't wanna find out."

"Renderings," said Chayson from his position on the other side of the chamber. "Chunks being cooked down from the leftovers of this second scrap heap . . . here."

Everyone walked over and stared in horror at the giant mound of bones and decaying carcasses. Cattle, deer, and household pets were among the recognized tangle of broken bones and stripped flesh. So, too, were the in-termittent human skulls that the cavers' helmet lights visually exhumed from the satanic grave site.

"Oh, good God . . . have mercy on man and beast alike," said one of the NSS cavers.

"And on us, too," said Marshal. "We have to get outta here—*now*."

"I say we follow the power cord," said Chayson as he snapped pictures of everything. "It's gotta connect to something and could be the quickest exit."

ఠ

The team began to track the cable even deeper into the cave, squeezing through another narrow crack at the rear of the chamber.

Jerry was the last man left, and as he prepared to wiggle out he felt something on his arm. When he looked down, his helmet light revealed a glob of slime that now burned into his skin. Another one splatted on his shoulder.

The disgusting drool came from above.

Looking up, and barely visible beyond the optimal range of his helmet light, Jerry saw two greenish-yellow slits.

77

CAVE. SAME TIME

Kaj'a-zar biometrically scanned his prey, whom he saw as a wavy thermal image.

Physically, he'd morphed into something that now resembled a bulky praying mantis rather than his original tyrannosaur–garden slug appearance. Kaj'a-zar could also flatten and elongate himself in order to better move through the narrow cave passages. Perhaps he'd revert to the dinosaur mode later, but for now his ability to hang upside down like an insect or a bat better served his purposes.

He released his grip on the high ceiling.

In the time it had taken Jerry to look back down to his stinging arm, the dim color slits above had flared into crimson red orbs—mad eyes that grew in frightening diameter after Kaj'a-zar launched his free-fall attack.

Jerry never had time to notice. A second later, his body exploded, ripped apart by the savage choreography of Kaj'a-zar's teeth, tail, and talons.

Farther down the cave, none of the others had yet missed Jerry.

The team was focused on a strange sound, and as the group ducked, one after the other, beneath a cluster of low-hanging stalactites, they saw a faint glow of wavy light just ahead. They approached cautiously.

Marshal rubbed the back of his hands. They were damp with humidity.

"Sounds like falling water," he said, leading the group around a sharp bend where they encountered a massive sheet of cascading water. "We're behind a waterfall."

"And look out beyond it, in the distance," said Chayson. "What's that strange, shadowy movement?"

"Hey, look at this," said a JMU student, pointing out that the coaxial they'd been following was jury-wired into another power line, which appeared to be a permanent installation. That line was further divided and branched off into some cracks above.

"Whoever built that slaughterhouse seems to have tapped into somebody else's power system," said Marshal as he moved forward, closer to the waterfall. As he advanced, his body was suddenly pockmarked by several red dots. "What the hell's this?" he said, instinctively trying to wipe them off.

"Laser beam security system," said Chayson, also stepping through the beams, "and it's drawing juice from this line leading up behind those clusters of cave coral."

"I'll be damned," said one of the NSS members. "There are cameras up there. Other than us, who could've ever stumbled on this place?"

"It's an early-warning system for them. Down there . . . out there, past this water," said Chayson as he found a small vantage point made by a jutting rock that partially diverted some of the waterfall.

One by one they all strained to take in the view.

ॐ

In a chamber that was easily five times larger than the largest domed sports facility in America, they saw cranes working on multistory buildings, trucks moving workers and equipment, liquid fire spritzing from dozens of welding and cutting torches, and people exiting an ultrasleek Washington Metro car that was running a *really* strange three-track subway route from where Chayson surmised was Northern Virginia.

Everyone was literally too stunned to make a comment. Chayson at least had the presence of mind to snap more pictures.

"Uh, Marshal, I think we lost Jerry," said one of the JMU students.

"Damn it," said Marshal, looking around quickly. "Okay, we all stay together, and we all go back to find him. Then we'll come back here and work our way down to that subway station."

They walked, sometimes crawled back, in silence. Marshal and Chayson exchanged a look, shared an unspoken thought. *We're being followed,* their eyes shouted.

As they retreated, returning ever nearer to the cadaver-strewn chamber, everyone's heart beat faster, and the shadows from their helmet lights made the otherwise beautiful cave formations appear like fiends from a monstrous world. The team walked single file down a long narrow corridor formed by tites and mites that had grown together to form flanking columns, a geologic construction that would've been spectacular under other circumstances.

～

Everyone's foreboding turned to pants-pissing fright when they heard Death whisper, then shout from the darkness behind the columns. Marshal's hackles bristled from a rasping hiss and deep, guttural growl of the unknown. Chayson and the others trembled when the hideous sounds were followed by abrupt shadowy movement in *front* of them and then seconds later as dark blurs *behind* them. They felt trapped in a circumference of death. The creature, for that's the only word Marshal could think of, moved with alarming speed as it crisscrossed their path, showcasing its murderous red eyes as it stitched through the ageless rock towers.

There was a scream as the last man in line suddenly disappeared.

Marshal pulled everyone together, their huddled helmet lights flashing in all directions like a strobe, which lacked only music to complete the disco demon's eviscerating dance. Like flocked birds in frightened flight, they spun in unison when seconds later the shredded remains of the JMU student taken from the back was flung from between columns and landed in front of the group.

"Move back," said Marshal in a rough whisper. But as the team backed down the narrows, the NSS caver who had been at the front was pulled away in a flash, his screams of agony echoing throughout the cave. A moment later, those remaining saw the victim's headless and dismembered carcass hurled out behind them.

Marshal was shaking so hard he could barely form words. "What . . . ever it . . . is'll kill us one at time . . . we can't stay here. We're gonna run together, so stay tight and follow me."

"Wait," said Chayson, whose fear-wobbled legs somehow provided enough strength for him to kneel down and remove the still-burning helmet lamp from the decapitated head that'd landed a few feet from him. "Running's good, but so's a diversion."

"Yeah, throw it thataway," Marshal said, pointing his finger so Chayson could see it, "and on my command we'll haul ass the other way."

Chayson hurled it, and as the tumbling helmet bounced its light off the ceiling, the cave floor rumbled with the sound of the unseen terror pursuing it.

"Now," Marshal whisper-shouted. Fueled by adrenaline and steered by fear, the five remaining cavers bolted and backtracked in record time to the original keyhole ledge.

ᛒ

"I'll go through first," said Marshal, squatting at the keyhole, "and rig a rappel line down the wall. There's only room on the ledge for two of us at a time."

Two cavers roped down to safety one after the other while Marshal ensured that the kernmantle did not fray against the sharp rock ledge.

"C'mon. Let's go," barked Marshal, calling for the last two, Chayson and a student, to squeeze out onto the ledge with him. The student pushed Dr. Chayson into the hole. Marshal snapped him on the rappel line and sent him down.

The remaining student never heard the creature but smelled its fetid stench behind him. He turned, and his helmet light showed just enough dim detail for the student to know he faced hell. Even so, he had the presence of mind to snap a flash picture. And for a split second, inches away from his face, the young man saw a white-hot satanic flash as Kaj'a-zar's teeth snarled and his crimson eyes burned with hatred.

The kid spun away as the monster lunged.

From the other side of the wall, Marshal saw the kid's hand stick the camera through the hole. He grabbed the wrist and pulled. But only the arm, bitten away from the elbow, came through the opening. Anticipating more resistance from the pull, Marshal lurched backward and tumbled off the ledge. Fortunately, he was already snapped into the rappel rope and he managed to stop his fall after a few feet.

Marshal was in the process of continuing down in a controlled rappel when he started going back up, pulled by a claw-tipped hand attached to a long and ugly black arm extruding through the keyhole and reeling in the rope.

ᛒ

"Ka'maw-n"—c'mon, was what the guttural hiss emanating from the keyhole sounded like to Marshal, who'd released the rope brake and begun to slide down faster, even as the rope accelerated upward.

"Go, go, go," shouted Chayson from below.

Marshal ran out of rope, the end slipping through his carabiner some twelve feet from the bottom. He shouted in pain as he hit hard and twisted both ankles badly.

"Hang on, we've got you," said Chayson as he and the other two cavers made an arm-carry gurney for Marshal.

The creature roared as he punched his way through the wall. Rock and dirt rained down on his escaping prey.

"Hurry," implored Marshal through clenched teeth.

"If we can get to the lighted section, we may have a chance," panted Chayson as he and the others hauled Marshal toward the surface.

Somehow they outdistanced the creature and made it to the surface, although it was not quite as they later remembered.

SAME AFTERNOON, 1630 HOURS

The exhausted, stunned, and disorientated cavers were met topside by two men in dark suits and sunglasses who escorted the four survivors to a helicopter.

"Where are we going?" asked Marshal.

"CSC," said one of the dark suits.

"What's that?" asked Chayson.

"The closest medical facility. You'll be treated by a specialist."

En route, a paramedic administered sedatives to the weary explorers, and he wrapped Marshal's ankles in pressure braces to minimize swelling. A short while later, the unconscious passengers were taken into another cave.

THAT EVENING, 1840 HOURS

The exhausted, stunned, and disorientated cavers were met topside by two men in Endless Caverns staff shirts who'd found the explorers wandering near the gift shop. Hearing that others were lost in the cave, the staffers had called the state police.

"We last saw them at a window divide, on a northeasterly traverse some three miles past the turnaround," said Marshal.

"It's a grave situation," said the trooper. "They've got to be found, and soon."

"Yes, otherwise they'll die . . . in profound blackness," Chayson said.

"I know the waiting is hard," the trooper said, "but an NSS search team is on its way. They'll bring out everybody alive and well. You'll see."

The trooper asked if there was anything else they could remember.

Chayson said that earlier he'd felt an unusual warmth inside his head and thought it was because a strange light had been shined into his left ear.

"Probably from my helmet lamp," Marshal said, "when you arm-carried me to the surface after wrapping my ankles." Chayson shrugged, then nodded in agreement.

78

Prints from the cavers' cameras were spread across the table.

"You can see that the extraterrestrial's physiognomy is different since we first reviewed the surveillance video of him breaking into the lab," said Stern.

Chalmers nodded. "Like everything else going on around us, even Jack is changing and moving with haste."

"We can't blotter-beam everybody who goes into these caves," Beckner said.

"Nor stop Jack from roaming underground," said Chalmers.

"Comparing the list of things reported stolen over the years from mountain valley towns and these photos of his makeshift laboratory," said Stern, "I am stunned by the intelligence and technological adaptability of a creature from whose perspective *this* world must truly be alien."

Chalmers nodded. "Jack's a remarkable species. He made his own hatchery."

"John, why didn't we send soldiers or our paramilitary teams after him?" Beckner asked. "You could've convinced Casey to do that."

"The director never wanted Jack harmed, only captured and turned into a weapon. But in calculating the risk-versus-gain quotient, and the tactical complexity of locating him underground, I never felt it was worth the effort."

"But to have had him, even for a while . . . all the experiments and tests," Stern said. "It would be an exobiologist's dream come true."

"If we caught Jack tomorrow, research would be focused on making a front-line marine out of him . . . all *three* of them now, given that he's probably hatched those eggs."

Stern nodded. "That we've had an extraterrestrial entity, even in a free-roaming status, has been a miracle for me, if only for the video footage and photos we've now got and can study in depth. But to have him in the laboratory . . . hell, even I would agree to the exploitation of his military potential. It'd be a good exchange for the other science applications we'd derive from studying him—especially communicating with him, which I believe is very possible." Chalmers indicated his agreement.

Beckner's head swiveled as he cast brow-furrowed glances at both men. "The military angle is unconscionable," he said, coming unglued. "I'm shocked . . . disappointed with you both. I don't think we should draft his alien ass into the army, but we better grab him while he's still relatively accessible. He's dangerous beyond description. What if he goes topside again, decides to eat a town full of people rather than steal from them?"

"I'm sure he relocated his base camp and the hatchlings the moment his location was compromised," Chalmers said. "I've thought a lot about Jack over the years. I believe he wants to stay underground . . . he's waiting, running out the clock until something new, whatever it is that's supposed to happen, finally occurs."

Beckner was troubled by his boss and Stern's emotional detachment. Maybe it was the nature of brainy, science types. Maybe he'd been involved with the CIA and the enigmatic, mercurial Dr. Chalmers for too long.

In any event, his personal situation had already made a big decision for him.

79

Won worried that he had not properly handled this GoodWill mission. And he knew that upon its completion today he was eligible for Ascension—a process whereby he would enter another realm of eternity's limitless dimensions.

That transition, whether it turned out to be Ga'Lawed's reward or punishment for Won's time on Earth, would take place at the Iris Portal. Ascension would occur in concert with the Hastening—an evolutionary moment in Earth history when global events reached a critical, if not prophetical, convergence of coincidence.

Everywhere he looked, Won saw negative forces mounting toward the perfect storm. They were the same kind of events he'd seen sectics ago when Earth had engaged in two world wars, but this time the forces were stronger, to include intensified versions of the seven deadly sins prejudicial to human spirituality. Moreover, this time a self-imposed global war of atomic potent would result in catastrophic physical damage to the planet as well.

But because of Vor's treachery, there was yet another force mounting. And Won knew that it would result in an altogether different kind of war—one that surpassed all other man-made threats and would completely destroy this planet as it had Fieva's.

Such was the power of untempered anger and wanton voraciousness.

Knowing there was nothing more to fear than the wrath of Ga'Lawed, which he potentially faced anyway, Won made another in what had already been a series of dramatic ad hoc decisions. And that was to visit the Chalmerian he was now committed to support as the champion for safeguarding the Crystal Tabula and ensuring that Nobility had a fighting chance to take root on Earth, regardless of what catastrophic events occurred there.

He had interacted with this Earth being once before, saving him from one of the global conflicts that would have ended his life prematurely. Faced with other instances of impending death, the earthman had even been spiritually summoned to the Tutorium by Ga'Lawed himself, and there received the Headmaster's briefing on what the Chalmerian's role on Earth was to be.

However, the magnitude of information and the intense nature of its transmission directly into the Chalmerian's limited mind had left the earthman, Won realized, with an incomplete picture of that role— which included fathering a son, whose subsequent sons would safeguard something important. Toward that vague end, Won believed, the earthman had indeed performed admirably.

But now it was time for Won to leave High Stasis, reunite with the human called Chalmers, and convey to him the precise information he needed to understand the full magnitude of danger confronting him and his world.

Like Won, the human too had a mission to complete. And not unlike a Samaritan, Won figured that Chalmers's ultimate fate probably also rested in Divine hands.

80

McLEAN, VIRGINIA. APRIL 1, 1991 – 0315 HOURS

Chalmers awoke from the brief and troubled sleep that usually marked his night's rest. He listened to Paula's rhythmic breathing for a moment and then detected a deep pulsing sound from across the expansive bedroom. Lifting his head from the pillow, he saw a pearl mist seeping through the center pane of a large bay window. He had seen this kind of mist before.

Now he saw symbols—not within the mist, which was backdropped by moonlight, but inside his head. They spoke to him, just as they'd done at the Tutorium. Then it had been the Headmaster's voice . . . now it was someone else's. Still, it was strangely familiar.

~*Chalmers, I come to you again.*~

The one in no-man's-land . . . the killing field, Chalmers thought.

~*Yes, I am the Won to tell you there is to be another killing field.*~

A mixture of intrigue and fear prompted him to stand. Stepping toward the window, Chalmers watched the mist compact into a ghostly mannequin whose cloudy content spun like a tornado funnel filmed in slow but powerful motion. The apparition's blue, oblong eyes peered peacefully into Chalmers's soul while its long arms reached toward his body.

Chalmers wanted to step back but found himself unable to move.

Transfixed, he felt a gentle pressure as the white, slender-fingered hands took positions over his heart and forehead. Chalmers felt chilled and warmed at the same time. He felt the awe and apprehension of the new knowledge that filled him like an August night's sky showering lighted droplets of Perseid meteors. This knowledge included strange multidimensional images that flashed within his mind, and at the same time in front of his eyes, to reveal the future he had partially glimpsed in the Tutorium before time's clock had ever begun to tick.

Shapes, sounds, colors—a pastiche of everything physical and metaphysical . . . all of it depicting cycles of beautiful promise and ugly horror that swung together with the clock's pendulum. All of it an expansion of what Chalmers had experienced with the Headmaster, whose mentalations had caused Chalmers to doubt his own sanity even though they had provided the knowledge and motivation that defined most of his life.

Won's transcendent revelation was a powerful jolt for a mortal, and it caused Chalmers, whose intellectual faculties were exceptional, nonetheless to shiver in fear and stammer with confused questions about what he had just learned from the Samaritan.

↜

"Hon," Paula whispered into his ear while at the same time squeezing him tighter from the spoon position in which they normally slept.

Chalmers awoke to the pressure on his forehead and heart. He again shuddered with fear, then immediately became aware of Paula's arms around him and her slender hands resting on his head and chest. He took a deep breath and rolled over to face her.

He knew he was back in bed, but not sure how he'd gotten here. Nor when the misty alien had dematerialized.

"Hmmm, something wrong, honey?"

"You were talking in your sleep again. Bad dreams, darling?"

"Visions," he said hoarsely. He plumped up the pillow, elevating his head slightly so he could look at least initially toward the bay window, and then down into her eyes. "Feel like listening to me for a minute?"

She kissed him gently. "Of course. Is it about the dream?"

He inhaled deeply. "About the past. Where I went a long time ago and what I saw while I was there . . . and about the future, where we're all headed."

He pulled her into his arms, tears trickling from his eyes. "Oh, Paula, I hope you won't think I'm crazy."

Smiling tenderly, she caressed his wet cheeks. "Never. I've waited a long time to hear the story that's haunted your sleep . . . and your life."

81

Files, intel reports, news articles, and other folders were piled on his desk, but Beckner was going through the motion of work rather than making progress toward accomplishing anything. Every day a huge volume of information had to be pumped into the Vortax-4000 so Chalmers and DivKay staffers could analytically crunch facts and make judgments about virtually everything that now had a bearing on the strategic survival initiative and Operation Black Spade's Underground States of America.

Beckner was more than overwhelmed; he was sick and tired from his work.

He didn't know how Chalmers kept up *his* pace, but he continued to be impressed with his boss's analytical skill and foresight. As Chalmers had predicted, the USSR had collapsed and the Soviet invasion of Afghanistan had ended in a crippling defeat for the Red Army and humiliation for the Kremlin. Within a few months, the name of deposed Soviet president Gorbachev was replaced in newspaper headlines by Iraq's military dictator, Saddam Hussein, whose invasion of Kuwait prompted the first Gulf War that Chalmers told Beckner would result in, among other things, an escalation of terrorism waged by radical factions of the Islamic world. Beckner recalled when Chalmers had first mentioned Osama bin Laden, describing him as the architect of a new era of global terrorism.

Beckner shared both of Chalmers's key judgments about the future. First, that regional, asymmetric wars and ever-sophisticated destructive acts of terrorism would inevitably lead to the use of nuclear weapons or other forms of mass destruction throughout the world, with America a prime target. Second, that China would be the most aggressive, dangerous competitor the United States had ever faced in the global race for technological primacy, political hegemony, and economic dominance— particularly as the United States continued on a path of deficit spending while China increasingly bought American indebtedness through Beijing's loans to Washington.

Beckner hoped there was something about the UFOs, or Jack the Ripper, or discoveries pulled from the Roswell wreckage or from the Time Crystal that his boss could use to extract order from the chaos Beckner saw spreading around the world.

Mostly he hoped the Citations would be ready in time, though America's megascale bomb shelter against the Armageddon that Chalmers envisioned would not affect Beckner's life.

He checked his watch. It was time for his meeting with Paula, who no longer worked as his assistant since she'd decided to spend most of her time with Steven. She still had her K-RED clearances and worked part-time with other DivKay components. Paula was in the building today and had agreed to stop by Beckner's office.

⊷

Opening pleasantries exchanged, Beckner had quickly raised the issue he'd wanted to discuss with her.

"John may live another hundred years, but not me. I frankly don't know how I've made it to seventy-six . . . all that time . . . so quick. I've done my best to match his pace and lighten his load."

Seated in a sofa chair next to his, Paula tenderly touched Beckner's arm. "And he's appreciated everything you've done, Lee. I am *so* grateful that you've always been a friend even more than a colleague . . . for him *and* me. You are a dear man."

Head drooped and voice filled with remorse, Beckner said, "I could have retired and spent more time with my wife, children, and now my grandchildren. I gave those days and months . . . and all those years to John, and now I've run out of them."

Her face and voice conveyed her genuine sympathy. "Look, your own deputy can fill your shoes for a while. You *must* take a vacation, recharge your battery. You and Janice can—"

"Paula, I'm taking a leave of absence, a permanent one."

The abruptness surprised her. "Oh. Well, you've got your own special assistant. He'll hate losing you, but I'm sure Jonathan will immediately promote Joe Junior into your position."

Beckner nodded.

"Jonathan certainly liked having Joe Anderson Senior as an assistant back in the day, and I know how pleased Jonathan was when J.J. followed his dad's career path in the Agency. Remember, Jonathan brought J.J. into DivKay."

"And he'll make an excellent deputy. But assuming John does keep on working indefinitely he, perhaps even you, will have to explain to J.J. why the amazing Dr. Chalmers has more staying power than the Energizer Bunny."

Paula's face registered a moment's lighthearted glow, then tightened into seriousness. "Lee, as I've shared with you before, living with Jonathan is not easy. His . . . experiences, as I can best call them, are more unique than I can explain to you. I believe he has been places and seen things . . ." Her voice trailed off. She knew she could never reveal, even imply, what her husband had confided. "Well, the point is that he certainly could have spent more time with me and Steven, and he's definitely had plenty of time to mellow, but instead he's become even more driven to complete the Citations before, as he says, the forces of Malthus and Volterra collide. I don't know what I fear more, that there'll be an eventual catastrophe that requires us to take shelter underground, or that we won't and he'll have the same regrets about lost time that you do."

"I believe those forces will meet. I just won't be by his side when it happens."

"Then tell me, Lee, what *are* you going to do when you retire?"

He smiled with weak resolution. "Paula, I'm going to die."

Seeing the shock on her face, Beckner took Paula's hand, looked gently into her eyes, and softy said, "I've just been diagnosed with stage-four lymphatic cancer. Don't know how much time's left . . . only that there won't be nearly enough."

❖ 82 ❖

A couple of CIA security officers from DivKay picked up Dr. Walter Stern at his home near Cornell University and drove him thirty miles east to a proprietary trucking company owned by the Agency. From a private office there, the trio accessed a hidden elevator that took them down to the functional, though still-expanding, New York Citation.

Located in an previously unknown chamber of the Howe Caverns system, this was the last, and northernmost, station on the SpadeLiner's thirteen-stop rail system now running fifteen hundred miles under the Appalachian Mountains. With its latest technological advances in magnolectric engine propulsion, the SpadeLiner's current top speed was two hundred and ninety miles an hour.

After arriving at Washington's Langley Citation, constructed in a secret subbasement at CIA headquarters, Stern had been escorted to Chalmers's seventh-floor office where they and others would review some recent technically enhanced photographs from the Hubble Space Telescope. The HST's digital photos astounded and troubled Stern, especially when he'd compared frames taken when Hubble was launched some four years ago to the latest batch, whose resolution had recently been sharpened by a computer-driven pixilation program called anti-aliasing. Designed to remove signal components with frequencies unable to be properly captured by the recording device, the commercial anti-aliasing technology was modified by Chalmers, who programmed it into the Agency's Vortax-4000, which cleansed and relayered the photos into a virtual 3-D composite with unprecedented clarity and detail. Chalmers had arranged for the classified program and the top secret Vortax to be used by specially cleared NASA scientists and Stern's Astrophysics Department at Cornell.

❧

Joining Stern and Chalmers at the meeting this morning were J. J. Anderson, who had replaced Lee Beckner as Chalmers's deputy, and Dr. Nash

Hickman, as well as other senior strategic analysts from DivKay. Everyone here had attended Beckner's funeral a few weeks ago, and although
the sadness of his loss still hung in their shared emotional air, there was,
as Chalmers had said immediately following the service, "work to be done.
And the best way to honor Lee's memory is to get on with it."

Stern, who was as well-read about current events on Earth as he was
about the origin of the cosmos, had also said something after the funeral
that still resonated in Chalmers's mind. Stern had used the phrase "pervasive sense of haste" in referring to the current nature of world events.

Like Chalmers, Stern believed that the spread of terrorism and political
instability stemming from a complex tangle of ideological, religious, financial, technological, and other issues dangerously stretched the delicate
threads holding together a rapidly evolving one-world economy where
competition for everything from oil to freshwater was matched by the concern about the proliferation of weapons of mass destruction.

In addition to man-made dilemmas threatening the planet, Stern had
galactic concerns that he called Earth's jeopardy factor—potentially catastrophic impacts by asteroids, many of which were headed toward Earth
from deep-space trajectories currently being tracked by NASA as well as
his Astrophysics Department. However, what he'd come to Langley today
to discuss with Chalmers was a new development, a bizarre cosmological
event unlike anything Stern had ever before seen through a telescope.

It actually did more than just perplex him. It frightened him.

ta

"Here are the photos," Stern said, unzipping a large flat case and spreading them across the ample conference table. "I selected these from the
comprehensive array of imagery captured during the HST's four-year
scan."

"You ran all these through Vortax?" Chalmers asked.

Stern nodded. "And Dr. Hickman, as background for some of your
DivKay staffers who haven't been with us from the beginning, Hubble's
ultradeep scan has been directed toward, but well beyond, the Orion constellation."

"They're incredibly beautiful," Hickman said, tilting his head to get a
better view.

"We're all eager to hear their relevance to national security, Dr. Stern,"
Anderson said.

"Dr. Stern and I have discussed some of that on the secure phone,"
said Chalmers, "but based on the limited briefings even I've had from

Walt, I agreed with him that this needed to be handled here at Langley, so we could see for ourselves."

"Exactly," said Stern, continuing to arrange the photos. "We are looking back billions and billions of light-years in time with each photo array, and when we reverse the order, we have in effect a form of time-lapse photography. The past moving toward the present, with projective extrapolations ahead to the future."

"And here in this series, Dr. Stern, " said Anderson, pointing, "looks like a . . . ?"

"Massive cosmic cloud. A nebula of stellar gas. Perhaps a solar flare from a long-ago imploded or supernoviated sun. It begins to intrude *here,* at this point," he said as he pointed with a pencil tip to one of the large photos, "and clearly starts to whirlpool into itself over the time span of this photo sequence."

"Disappearing, as if through an invisible door. A black hole," said Chalmers, as much to himself as to anybody else in the room. He turned to face the windows, not wanting to see any more of what he now knew these photos depicted.

"Exactly, John," said Stern, "or a wormhole of time as my friend Asimov and some of the other science-fiction writers have called it."

"Dr. Chalmers told us earlier that you'd discovered something unique about this particular gaseous matter," said Anderson, noting that his boss seemed strangely distracted, giving more of his attention to the view of the sky beyond the windows than to the meeting.

"Indeed," said Stern. "It doesn't hang in space like normal accretion material but seems to have a clustered swirl—not from gravitational pull but from independent propulsion, like a swarming movement . . . like something with a direction."

And with a purpose, Chalmers mentally whispered.

"Looks like it extrudes back out here," said Anderson, pointing to another photo.

"And this disappearing act followed by reemergence," said Chalmers, again facing the table and waving his hand over the photographs, "is a repeating pattern across this panoply of digital images. Across an expanse of space and time."

"Yes. Across billions and billions of light-years," Stern said.

"Dr. Stern, you mentioned extrapolation and the future," Anderson said. "Have your computer jockeys at Cornell been able to ascertain a celestial heading, so to speak? Do you have a sense of where this . . . this cloud or swirling flare is headed?"

"Yes, everyone at the Planetary Studies lab is on it." He slid a photo to the center of the table. "This is the last HST frame of the nebula entering an energy-absorbing schism in the dark matter. And given its previous trajectory, my analysts predict it will emerge here at the juncture of MV7-6793 and KJ2-6909, two star systems believed currently trapped in the orbital death throes of a black hole. If our 'conundrum cloud' indeed pops out at that point, we can postulate it will be on a direct heading for our solar system."

"Good Lord," said Hickman. "That's astounding."

"What could that mean to our neighboring planets?" asked one of the staffers.

"Well, it'll undoubtedly mean something to Jupiter," said Stern, "since that seems to be the direct heading."

"When will it hit?" Anderson asked.

"What do you think it means to us?" added Chalmers, who'd once more redirected his line of sight out the window.

Stern shrugged. "*When* is hard to say, J.J. It could reach Jupiter sooner than we might expect. A decade, a century, a millennium . . . a month from now. Who knows?" He paused, looked around the room, and continued.

"As for *what* it means to us . . . C'mon, John, we don't even know what to make of the ominous clouds *already* casting shadows on us. You know more than I do about global security issues—Pacific Rim aggression, Middle East terrorism, social and political discord here at home. Not to mention preparation for probable war with China. You've been ringing that bell for years and everyone's starting to hear it all of a sudden. And everyone in this room knows about the UFOs and USOs building what we all agree must be undersea colonies."

"USOs?" one of the DivKay analysts asked.

"Sorry," said Stern. "Unidentified submarine objects. Turns out the flying saucers also go diving now and again."

Pausing for breath, he again looked at everyone and waved his hands in a fashion that signaled disbelief . . . or just more despair. "And then of course there's an alien life-form currently on a murder spree in the very caves I rode your train through to get here."

Turning to face the others, Chalmers tossed one of the photos he'd been holding back on the table. "You seem to be saying that the galactic issues of time and space you've just outlined have less priority than all the other security issues?"

"It's up to you and the CIA to sort through national security priorities. But I'm telling you, John," Stern said with a sigh, "that this nebula is larger than anything we can fathom and that if it strikes Jupiter you better believe there will be shock waves, radiation dispersal, or other released-energy consequences that undoubtedly will affect our atmosphere in a substantial, perhaps catastrophic fashion."

Looking pained by the thought, Chalmers said, "I do believe that . . . and more."

"But if we've already blown ourselves to kingdom come in a third world war," said Anderson, "or terrorists do it for us, then the cloud raining on what's left of our planetary parade at some point in the distant future won't much matter, I guess."

"Not exactly a time for flippant dismissal, Joe," Chalmers snapped. "You said it could be here in a decade or sooner, Walt."

"Based on everything that's happening in a world spinning with a pervasive sense of haste, I'd have to say yeah, anything is possible. I'd also advise not quitting your day job, John. There's a lot of work left to do on your underground cities, and before it's over everyone in this room may be living in one of them with you. If we're unlucky."

The meeting over, Chalmers now stood alone in his office, his knowing eyes angled high into a peaceful sky, rethinking what Stern had said about an atmospheric impact on Earth if the cloud slammed into Jupiter.

"If only it were going to be that simple," he said softly as the mental image of the Samaritan's message flowed forth like lava from a caldera, its molten madness cascading downward in destructive horror.

Then taking Stern's advice, Chalmers went back to his day job. But this time, even more than previously, he was driven by a sense of haste that was very perverse.

He was already more than a hundred years old—a fact his appearance still masked and a secret that only Paula knew—but he had no idea how many more years he might live. For all he knew, his chronological time span was as erratically unpredictable as the arrival of the nebula.

He began to think about when it would become necessary to relocate the Crystal.

Part VI

DUSK

83

Paula Chalmers sat in her husband's office waiting for him and his deputy, J. J. Anderson, to finish a meeting in the director's conference room just down the hall. She had started working full-time again with DivKay some years ago after Steven—the highest-ranked honors graduate from a private academy in Washington—enrolled as the youngest freshman ever admitted to Cornell University.

Along the way Steven had also become the youngest single-engine pilot in New York State. He had already logged hundreds of hours toward his next goal of earning FAA instrument and multi-engine ratings. As he'd always told his parents, he had a true passion for aviation. While as brilliant, motivated, and focused as his father, the son's style was more casual and his temperament more congenial. Handsome, charming, and witty, he had none of the demons in his head that darkly whispered in his father's.

With Uncle Walt's mentorship in Stern's Astrophysics Department, Steven had excelled in every subject. And later, in graduate school, he'd become the youngest person at Cornell to earn a PhD in astrophysics.

Immediately after receiving his doctorate, it was not surprising—though it'd been very disconcerting to his parents—when young Chalmers had enlisted in the Air Force. His father as well as Stern had assumed Steven would pursue a research career in academia or a private think tank. Indeed, the young Chalmers had always wanted to study space—and he intended to—he just wanted to fly into its outer reaches to conduct firsthand research.

His parents had understood and even encouraged Steven's quest to become an astronaut; they just hadn't imagined that his preparatory safe stint in the Air Force would result in near tragedy on a simple training flight. On their way back to base, the jet trainer piloted by Chalmers had suffered total engine failure, and his instructor gave the command to eject.

The instructor was killed when his head hit the canopy during ejection. Chalmers exited safely and his chute deployed, but strong winds aloft drove him into the high-altitude tree line of a snow-covered mountain. Breaking his shoulder and sustaining deep lacerations in the landing, he then fought to survive the frigid temperature. It was eighteen hours before the SAR team located him.

The uncertainty and fear for her son's life she'd experienced during that terrible episode were still in Paula's memory, and she was pulled from one of its periodic flashbacks when her husband and Anderson returned to the office.

After a few pleasant exchanges with Mrs. Chalmers, Anderson had excused himself and headed for his own office. Chalmers had recounted to Paula the general essence of his and Anderson's meeting with the director, who was getting ready to brief Congress about security issues stemming from the new spate of nuclear weapons tests taking place in China and several other of the so-called nuclear club countries.

"I'm sure he must share your main concern, a smuggled conventional nuke or dirty-bomb terrorist attack here at home," said Paula.

"Of course, but military-grade weapons testing by official state sponsors opens a huge can of other political worms, and the director has to weigh in on that tangled mess."

"I gather you still haven't given him a full, K-RED briefing?"

"He certainly knows about CRYPTOS, Black Spade, and the final phase of Citation readiness, but the Committee hasn't granted him a clearance for the CONUNDRUM file."

"Why not?"

"Probably because he doesn't have a W in his name."

Puzzled, she was poised for the next question about what that meant.

"Doesn't matter," he preempted.

"Well, what he *will* hear, if he eventually gets the K, will be its own kind of blast, not to mention what he'd think if he knew the rest of what you know about crystals and aliens."

"True enough," said Chalmers, "but there is a CONUNDRUM-related aspect of the director's and my own concern about atmospheric radiation from the test detonations, as well as the increasing incidents of nuclear accidents around the world."

"You mean the two latest events reported in DivKay's intel assessment."

"Yes. I didn't write them, just made some editorial changes before dissemination to the director," Chalmers said. "The heavy water leak from India's Rajasthan Atomic Power Station and the accidental venting of radiation-rich steam from Japan's uranium-processing plant have drawn them out again."

"As you always say, darling, those kinds of incidents are chum for the sharks."

"Definitely. UFO and USO sightings have skyrocketed. Even the International Space Station took high-resolution digital photos of seven extraterrestrial ships perfectly contrasted against the Pacific Ocean."

"I assume you arranged for the ISS pictures to be K-crypted and sealed?"

"Of course; they were confiscated immediately. Apart from NASA, only two of the other five space agencies had personnel on board, and fortunately last week's *Soyuz* shuttle had to bring back the Russian cosmonaut for medical reasons and the Japanese scientist for a family matter."

"Only Americans left. I'm sure that made security simpler," Paula said.

"It did. Our astronauts couldn't come down if they didn't sign the K-waiver. And they'll never go back up if they talk about the UFOs or photos. Pretty simple."

Her head tilted at an appraising angle and with a challenging demeanor to her voice, Paula asked, "And is that how you and NASA and our Agency will handle Steven when he completes the Air Force's astronaut-training program? He's bound to learn about or even see the ships for himself somewhere along the way."

"Well, maybe he'll do something else for NASA besides fly on the shuttle when his service commitment is up," replied Chalmers, not believing his own words for a second. "In any event, I'm more concerned about the alien craft harvesting these radiant ions. It seems somehow to tie in with the accelerating pace of all the other events that suggest we're headed toward some kind of ultimate closure."

"Because of our world's own penchant to wage war, or the otherworldly intuition you have about what's out there swirling through space?"

Chalmers shrugged. "Either way . . . both ways. What's the difference? All of it's like the Maya calendar business and its apocalyptic prediction that the world will end in 2012, and similarly, the end times prophecy some biblical scholars are starting to talk about with regard to escalating problems in the Middle East."

"And novelists are writing about it. Actually, some of it is pretty good. Do you ever look at any of Joel Rosenberg's work, like the Last Jihad series?"

"Are you kidding?" said Chalmers, shaking his head. "I'm too busy dealing with *real* sci-fi to read the fictional kind."

"Yes, dear, but the way you laser through a book, it'd only take a few minutes."

"True enough," he said, giving her a kiss on the cheek as he grabbed his briefcase, "but the few minutes I'm about to spend now are going to involve lasering my way into the Crystal. I'll see you home later tonight . . . maybe," he said with a smile as he hurried off to catch the noon Spade-Liner to CSC.

Paula noted that his stride was still long and brisk, especially for a man who looked to be in his early seventies. *Not bad for one hundred and thirteen years old,* she thought as she blew a mental kiss to the remarkable man she was still very much in love with.

84

Reviewing the CET's latest video dump with Pete Peterson, chief of the Crystal Exploitation Team at CSC, Chalmers was pleased to witness first-hand that the Loch Ness Monster really *was* what he and a number of others had always suspected—a plesiosaur. Chalmers felt a strange comfort knowing that somehow this long-necked Cretaceous era marine reptile had escaped extinction in the cold depths of its Scottish lake.

"Imagine that," said a wide-eyed Peterson, "a dinosaur *still* roaming Earth, or at least swimming in one of its lakes."

"And to think," Chalmers added, "that dinosaurs once ruled Earth."

Answers to other mysteries emerged from additional CET reviews. Some had to do with people. Others with places.

One video session provided Chalmers with an actual perspective on the murder of President John F. Kennedy, who was *not* killed by Lee Harvey Oswald—a dupe who many alleged had been set up by the Soviet KGB and who apparently had fired from a building window *behind* JFK's motorcade traveling through downtown Dallas. Instead, the assassination was carried out by two shooters positioned *ahead* of the presidential limousine. Based on other videos pulled from the Crystal by the laser probe as well as collateral research by the CET, Chalmers now knew that the prominent Greek shipping tycoon Aris Ouranassus had arranged the assassination of JFK.

Chalmers realized it made sense for Ouranassus to have been in league with Russia during that time frame. There had been many intelligence reports back then that the KGB had wanted to kill Kennedy, but lacking the chops for the task, Soviet operatives had resorted to the same outsourced assistance the CIA had used when it tried to knock off the Soviet's puppet dictator in Cuba, Fidel Castro. Because the CIA director had asked Chalmers to compute a risk-versus-gain assessment of odds for success in the planned assassination of Castro, Chalmers knew firsthand that Agency operatives had used Sicilian Mafia based out of New York for President Kennedy's approved wet work against the Cuban leader. The KGB, Chalmers figured as he'd watched the Vortax monitor, had made similar calculations for their retaliation and had chosen to use an element of the Greek Mafia handling organized crime in Texas.

Though it'd taken thousands of hours to piece together the whole story through randomly downloaded snippets of collateral data from the Crystal, Chalmers's CET staffers eventually discovered why Ouranassus had agreed to use his Greek pals to murder Kennedy. As Chalmers surmised, it was a business deal—an *actual* one that guaranteed Ouranassus a multibillion-dollar contract for his tanker fleet to transport Soviet oil to international ports.

The emotional motivation Ouranassus had for getting Jack Kennedy out of the way also made sense to Chalmers. It was so Aris could openly court and eventually marry Jacqueline Kennedy, with whom he had long been infatuated after meeting her years earlier at a political event.

Chalmers marveled that some people possessed such arrogance, and at the same time he found it operationally admirable they had the will *and* the power to fulfill their ambitions, whether for good or evil intent. He seldom thought about the psychological rationale for his own operational drive on behalf of the CIA, never wanting to know one way or the other if he was divinely inspired, pathologically disturbed, or simply compelled by a Machiavellian temperament to achieve order and control . . . whether for the good or evil that was inherent in everything about the Cryptos Conundrum.

Chalmers was captivated by every frame pulled from the Crystal, wishing he could devote his full attention to its exploitation.

He was amazed by the connection between the stone heads of Easter Island and the lesser known but equally legendary Carnac stones—the three thousand megaliths arranged in perfect lines over a distance of twenty miles on the modern-day French coast of Brittany. As the CET video had shown, at one time both sets of stones had faced each other in what looked to be game pieces positioned on a playing field located on part of a young planet that two hundred and fifty million years ago still had only a single continental landmass.

Who could have sculpted the stones? People who had already evolved on this world when Earth's own breathable atmosphere was still forming?

Chalmers did not think so. Perhaps the stones were cut by the CONUNDRUM-file extraterrestrials currently here, who'd perhaps always been here, or who had been preceded by countless other galactic visitors since the dawn of Earth's formation? The revelations. The questions they raised. It was all staggering . . . and it made Chalmers's mind spin faster.

Believing that their technological expertise may have been behind the amazing underwater construction of the pyramids, Chalmers was particularly excited by the Vortex video's undeniable connection between the legendary lost continent of Atlantis, which eleven thousand years before Christ had been an advanced civilization on an island nation located in the center of a section of the North Atlantic known during recent decades as the Bermuda Triangle, where countless planes and boats mysteriously disappeared.

He wanted to have the Agency, under its special national security directive empowerments, conscript elements of the U.S. Navy and Scripps Institution of Oceanography, forming another exploitation team that would pinpoint the ruins of Atlantis. From what he'd seen in the video, Chalmers believed that buried in the deep silt-filled rift was an ancient magnetic power transmitter whose leakage had for decades, perhaps centuries, been pulling modern mankind's sea and air conveyances into the briny depths.

He talked himself out of that plan, recognizing that higher national security priorities were already set against a clock ticking down to midnight's toll. But he could not lessen the frustration he felt about being unable to design an algorithm to change or tune the Crystal's chronological channels to specific eras, and ideally to exact dates, in order to capture and exploit more current, relevant, and actionable intelligence—as it was called in Agency vernacular.

He hated having to wait for whatever random events of recordable video Peterson and the CET stumbled across when scanning into the Crystal's infinite depth with the Vortex laser. Using the computer's laser optic as a forensic scalpel, his intellect wanted to believe it was possible to slice into actual real time of the past, surgically implanting something into it so that careful modifications to—or new information learned from—the past could solve problems about the present. Or even preempt those forecasted for the future. But based on what he knew now, the future was caught in countervailing forces—with white and black clouds as nimbus purveyors of good and evil.

With so little of it left, time was all that mattered now in this stern world swept along in a perverse sense of haste.

85

ATLANTIC OCEAN. NIGHT

Inbound from Europe, the United flight had started its descent toward Washington, D.C. With coastal lights still nowhere in view, the dark void of cold water far below seemed to have the visual interest of only one passenger staring vacantly out his port-side window seat in the last row. Hence he was the only one to see them, their trajectories having been too acutely angled off the aircraft's tail section for the pilot to spot, even with his peripheral vision.

Amed Karami wasn't even sure what he'd seen. Not lightning flashes, for there were no clouds below. Not surface vessels, for nothing could have moved so fast across the waves in what he knew to be a southerly direction down America's East Coast. But those strange greenish lights . . . they had streaked almost in the blink of his eye down what seemed the entire length of the coast. He even thought now it seemed like the seven coruscated rays had been diffused, as though they were shining up through the water rather than on its surface.

And as Allah was his witness, the light beams even looked to be traveling in some kind of formation.

Karami did not plan to inform the flight attendants of what he'd seen. They, along with some of the passengers, had already taken second looks at the prominent crescent scar than ran from his forehead through the center of his nose and across his cheek. Not wanting to call further attention to himself, he would share the incredible event he'd witnessed, if he bothered with it at all, only after joining the others who'd traveled ahead and waited for him in America's capital.

BENEATH THE ATLANTIC. SAME TIME.

He was oblivious of any flight craft above that might be monitoring their path through this liquisphere. Moreover, he was disdainful of all but one of the puny machines that often flew over or around and even sometimes under them as they maneuvered on this world.

He was Wul'ya-Qox, former deputy and now chief commander of the Fiverian fleet. Or what was left of it after Kul'da-Zak, the supreme leader, and his family had been lost in a crash, and a second Fiverian craft had been destroyed by militant inhabitants of this planet using a crude weapon expulsing the very energy source the Fiverians harvested continually to maintain their temporary status on this inhospitable world.

For a short while after Kul'da-Zak's death, the Fiverians collectively felt, through their genetic $\Phi\eta\iota\chi\eta\alpha\mu\vartheta$, a process of mentosynchronicity based on a Fiverian's unique bio-aura, that one of their brethren had survived the crash. Though still searching for him, Wul'ya-Qox feared their clansman's bio-aura had changed through body adaptation to this world, or that he had been killed. Either way, he was probably lost to them forever.

Wul'ya-Qox had another, far worse fear.

A brief $\Phi\Xi\phi\Xi\Phi$—a synchronic *vuezur* message sent from the Fiverians' home world shortly after they had departed for this voyage of discovery and colonization—had finally arrived after a long delay caused by a miscalculated tracking route. Even if this world's inhabitants had been receptive to the idea of visitors and settlers from another galaxy, Wul'ya-Qox knew it was all pointless now. The errant message, now finding its mark, struck with the numbing news that even as the *vuezur* was being sent originally, it was to inform the vanguard flotilla that Fiveria was being totally destroyed by an invading force of cosmic scale.

Realizing he worked off a thin margin of error, Wul'ya-Qox would search for his fellow Fiverian during the remaining time that he planned to continue with his harvest of this planet's useful energy required to accelerate out of this solar system. And into the next closest dark matter mass—a time portal that was his only escape from what he now knew pursued them.

As an immediate first measure, he was making one more pass through this unique energy field he'd discovered during his earlier explorations of this world's liquisphere. At the bottom of this silt-filled abyss, over which his seven ships now hovered, were the remains of what Wul'ya-Qox had previously determined to be a lost civilization, its level of technical sophistication impressive even by Fiverian standards. Particularly in view of the fact that whoever had lived down here, and perhaps on the surface at some point, had been around long before this current, indigenous population had taken root.

ᴋᴀ

Guiding everyone through the turgid depth, the various sensing screens on Wul'ya-Qox's helm control projected *halomodals* of the enormous construction maze through which his formation maneuvered. The interwoven arches, as viewed in quadra-dimension, resembled the skeletal chest cavities of dead and desiccated creatures he'd seen on surface land above. Suspended within this bony and briny cathedral was a massed flotilla of other craft—whose integrated images on his thermorphic screen Wul'ya-Qox recognized as hostile conveyances . . . the so-called ships and planes he'd seen used above by the militant forces that had attacked him.

This place is a ψασ δφαλ, he thought . . . *a graveyard—with arches as death markers.*

Like a sea nymph's siren, these deadly magnetic arches seductively sang to Wul'ya-Qox.

He was mesmerized by the hauntingly beautiful chorus of these vibrating pulses, for they reminded him of the symphonic hum made when a Fiverian windstorm swirled through a sulfuric ice canyon.

He wondered what this ribbed place had been. Probably a city. Perhaps a machine? The skeletal remains of a large creature who'd also come here trying to escape from someplace, or from some other *thing* somewhere else in the cosmos?

The answer to those mysteries didn't really to matter to him.

But one question did.

Would he be ready and able to lead the few survivors of his once magnificent world onward in their journey to find another home, obtaining the remaining fuel needed to depart before time ran out on this little blue planet?

86

VIRGINIA CAVE—INWARD PASSAGE

He watched as the circular alien craft swept over the city, firing bursts of devastating light that reduced structures to fiery gas and people to ionized dust. Relentless and cruel, the invaders were out not to conquer but to destroy Earth—and would have, were it not for the planet's own defense measures. Suddenly, the aliens were made ill by bacteria, suffering the only defeat they'd ever experienced in their cosmic reign of terror . . . all of them killed by this planet's own germ warfare retaliation.

Kaj'a-zar had seen enough of what he knew earthmen called moving pictorials. This one, evidently drawn from something known as an *HG-Wells,* had depicted events that seemed real but that his intuition said were purposeful departures from other pictorials actually occurring around the planet—authentic actions called news by certain screen heads he could identify when he now routinely saw them perform as newscasters.

He pointed and engaged the vision gun, which he'd eventually figured out made the screen images change. In this command post built from electronic items he'd taken on foraging missions, there were several pictorials now on display that he'd found to be most useful in his ongoing tutorial about this world. One was a screen called Fox, which visually reminded him of Ξαχ—the Fiverian word for something that rotates or spins.

In teaching his sisters about the world outside this cavern retreat, he'd found other pictorials to be helpful, and he had them stand with him in front of the screens to observe. One such learning outlet was something he would describe as ϑιεδατεφ in his tongue, which he found ironically meant the same in this world's language—a path or channel of Discovery. Everything he saw there intrigued and informed him, as well as his sisters.

And since it was time for one of these ϑιεδατεφ sessions, Kaj'a-zar went to find the females, now fully adult and carrying out responsibilities in an adjoining chamber.

As he left this room, he noted with pride his many technical and infrastructural accomplishments over the years. Multiple cables, intruding like root vines from surface plants, had been snaked through natural rock fissures, connecting dozens of large plasma monitors and banks of neon lights to solar panels and satellite receiver antennas camouflaged among vegetation high atop an Appalachian ridgeline.

Entering the next chamber, he noted with equal pride his two beautiful sisters attending dozens of youngsters being fed and groomed. When they were mature, the young males being cared for here today would join him in mating with the next brood of maturing females.

In the interim, Kaj'a-zar had already started a second generation with his sisters. Walking into another part of the cave, he surveyed dozens of their eggs incubating in bathtub bassinets, while in a separate chamber he'd already begun making preparations for the hundreds, and later thousands of eggs that would follow as he and his progeny repopulated this dark rock world with Fiverians.

He planned for them to remain here until the destiny of their true time beckoned to the light from above.

Part VII

NIGHTFALL

❖❖87❖❖

Today was a special news day on Fox, CNN, and all the other networks. Some aired extensive "anniversary" coverage of the al-Qaeda terrorist attack on New York's twin towers, and others also reviewed the ensuing decade of related troubles that had appeared on many fronts. Most citizens of an embattled and dangerously weakened America feared that the nation was on the brink of collapse.

It was a good time for reflection. Better still for planning.

Already knowing every detail about everything being discussed this morning, Chalmers nonetheless was surrounded by plasma screens in his office, each broadcaster loudly rehashing the decade's tumultuous history. As usual, Chalmers navigated through his computer monitor while simultaneously digesting piles of books, file folders, and intelligence reports scattered across his massive desk.

Watching Chalmers were two muscular security officers, Mike DeLorno and Quan Shantu—paramilitary specialists who'd been assigned by the director a few years ago to safeguard Dr. Chalmers at all times, and at whatever cost, in light of mounting security dangers across the country and especially in Washington, D.C.

DeLorno and Shantu had great respect and affection for the Agency's legendary icon they felt honored to serve and whose curmudgeonly humor they enjoyed . . . though frequently couldn't understand. They had stuffed napkin wads in their ears to mute the newscasters, whose cacophony of chatter was somehow being mentally processed, the men noticed, by their boss as though the TV commentators spoke to him individually.

ᵗ⌐

Never looking up but occasionally voicing a response to the talking heads, Chalmers nodded in agreement with their recount of events that had crippled the country, social problems involving illegal immigration; recession

driven by skyrocketing fuel prices and the collapse of the mortgage, banking, and automobile industries; widespread unemployment and inflation;
and grave security threats stemming from foreign and domestic terrorism,
to include gangland violence by narcotraffickers.

"And far more other issues than you know," Chalmers muttered.

"Were you talking to us that time, sir?" asked DeLorno.

Chalmers peered over his glasses. "I guess. Said maybe you guys should
go."

"Can't do that, sir," Shantu said.

"No, guess not. Just continue to sit quietly, then. I'm trying to work
here."

҉

On the domestic terror front, the major problem was with the Hispanic
Liberation Movement. The HLM's emergence years ago resulted, according to Chalmers, from failed federal policies on illegal immigration and
illicit narcotics. "From initially peaceful demonstrations to violent ones,
from demands for concessions to demands for political recognition, it will
become a full-blown Hispanic separatist movement that employs guerrilla tactics and paramilitary attacks consistent with the politicized drug
lords supporting it," he'd said during a congressional hearing years ago. In
fact, the labor strikes, political protests, and even gun battles in the streets
Chalmers predicted would erupt in certain southwestern border states had
become commonplace and were billed by some in the U.S. press as a civil
war to create a free-spirited, independent nation.

"Alphabet soup," a disgruntled Chalmers said hearing the term "immigration issue."

"Say again, sir," Shantu said, leaning forward. "Is that what you'd like
for lunch?"

This time Chalmers removed his glasses. "I've had enough HLM, UJF,
PC, BS, and the rest of A through Z to last *two* lifetimes . . . literally. In
fact, boys, if I live *ten* lifetimes, which I worry might be the case given my
physical circumstance . . . oh, never mind about that. In fact, forget I said
it. The point is that I will never understand the destructive stupidity of
politicians . . . and as to the other point, uh, your question, it's no, I don't
even like soup. I'd like that new chef in the executive dining room to make
me a cheeseburger. A take-out. For here," he added, his finger tapping the
desktop.

Exchanging a look and shrug with DeLorno, Shantu left for the kitchen.

҉

As Chalmers and many others had feared, foreign-sponsored terrorism continued and had increased in frequency as well as intensity in the years since 9/11. Based on CIA intelligence, it was clear that the brilliant but psychotic Afghan Amed Karami had replaced Osama bin Laden in the wake of the CIA operation that had enabled Navy Seals to kill al-Qaeda's chief operative several months ago.

Karami had created an even more daring, imaginative offshoot—the United Jihadist Front. Using alias identities and sophisticated disguises, Karami traveled the world at will, entering the United States apparently a number of times to mount UJF operations.

Bill Casey was right, Chalmers reflected. *We should have drafted Jack and sent him over there, turned that slaughtering bastard loose in* their *caves for a while.*

One TV commentator recounted how over the last two years Karami and his UJF killers had remotely detonated sarin gas canisters in several subway stations in London, Paris, and Berlin. A similar UJF assault in Manhattan had killed nineteen people, injured seventy others, and caused a major disruption to a business district whose economic coffin was already dangerously close to being nailed shut.

Still a Long Islander at heart, Chalmers worried about the Big Apple's fate.

ᵗ⊖

As with terrorism, the assault on American politics was also split between foreign and domestic fronts, each representing challenges serious enough, Chalmers calculated, to jeopardize the country's national security, if not indeed its democratic foundation.

Domestically, the country was weary of protracted wars in Iraq and Afghanistan that cost taxpayers too much money and the nation too many lives from its military ranks. Fed up with traditional partisan politics, voters shunned Democratic and Republican presidential candidates in the last election.

Raul Averez—an independent from the new American Party and a chamber of commerce "business community" organizer for the past eighteen months in a small Arizona town—popped out of the political woodwork and won the 2008 presidential bid by a surprise landslide. Handsome, charismatic, and eloquent in Spanish and English, Averez was like a rock star whom everyone called *lo elegido,* the chosen one.

With grand teleprompter speeches, he outlined a long-term plan of positive reform, but instead, almost overnight he had galvanized the country.

His ardent critics decried his "blatant Socialist agenda and staggering deficit spending." America's silent conservative majority called the Averez administration "an inept, naïve debacle and an unwelcomed shift toward European socialism."

"As politically feckless as he is factually clueless," muttered Chalmers when he heard the president's name mentioned by one of the commentators. It was an opinion that pollsters believed a majority of voters now shared.

On the international political front, most Americans who read or watched the news were alarmed by the spread of weapons of mass destruction. Chalmers had watched—and prepared countless intelligence assessments about—a problem he and the Agency knew had been under way since the end of World War II. The problem had only worsened.

Fox described some but, as Chalmers knew, by no means all of the threats.

With massive aircraft carriers under construction and plans for a global, blue-water navy soon to launch, China was also now conducting frequent nuclear weapons tests, and owing to its aggressive espionage activities, had stolen U.S. technology enabling the Chinese military to develop sophisticated rocket guidance systems. India and Pakistan, at political loggerheads for decades, had increased the tempo of their nuclear testing. Iran had the Shahab-3, a medium-range missile capable of hitting Israel and Saudi Arabia, and North Korea was developing its midrange Taepodong 1 missile into a full-purpose ICBM delivery system. There was still a significant ICBM threat from Russia's new-generation Topol-M nuclear missiles with multiple warheads. Cuba still had old Soviet missiles and had even sold some to Chávez in Venezuela. Brazil, too, was developing a weapon.

An unstable stack of dominoes, Chalmers thought, *just waiting to topple itself.*

He knew that stability, more specifically the lack of it, was a key concern for policy makers at the Departments of State and Defense, where there was disfavor with retired Chinese General Zhang Lao, who, after winning an election supported by the Chinese Communist Party, had not only seized total control of the CCP but also appointed himself grand premier. That surprise move consolidated what had been a division of labor between the former president, responsible for the politics of designing government policy, and the premier, in charge of implementing those policies.

Worse than his destruction of Beijing's system of checks and balances was Zhang's strident vow to infuse the CCP with "an even more rigid style of military governance and an aggressive policy of promoting China's new international posture."

Based on intelligence reports Chalmers had seen, Zhang intended to move quickly toward total reunification of Taiwan and to promote political as well as economic hegemony over the rest of the world, particularly the oil-rich Middle East. And based on his own biographic analysis of Zhang's personality, Chalmers knew the general would not tolerate any resistance from Washington on any of China's agenda items.

This was far more than self-serving saber rattling. Chalmers heard the rolling thunder of what he feared preceded the Chinese lightning flash he had always known would strike America someday.

But before that could happen, another kind of flash occurred.

88

The program on the 9/11 attack ten years ago was interrupted by breaking news about the 9/11/2011 attack that had just occurred ten *minutes* ago. Chalmers and his two security escorts watched in stunned silence as reporting, including aerial footage from news choppers, streamed across the screens.

"The Department of Homeland Security has just issued an emergency Red Level threat alert," said the reporter, "following a series of explosions in Washington's Metro system. A deadly chemical agent, believed to be sarin gas, has been released and there is concern it could drift upward and into the streets. Fire and rescue teams in hazmat suits are on the scene, with initial reports indicating there are a number of dead and many more wounded victims in the stations below . . . Just a moment," she said, pressing her finger against the earpiece speaker. "There's been a new development. District and other Metro police units have begun coordinating an evacuation of the nation's capital and surrounding Beltway areas ordered by DHS, this on the heels of an FBI announcement that UJF terrorist Amed Karami has claimed responsibility for the attack—the *first*, evidently, of others that the UJF promises will occur today and, as Karami threatened, every tomorrow that follows."

Phones began ringing on Chalmers's desk. First Anderson, then Paula, burst into his office. Coming from the Operations Center just down the hall, they'd heard some interagency chatter on secure comm systems that had preceded the news releases.

"Bridges are jammed and the Beltway's completely clogged," said Paula.

"Yeah, the White House has been sealed off, the Pentagon's locked down, and Congress has scattered," Anderson said. "There are already reports of widespread looting. It's a madhouse out there."

"And we can't have one in here," said Chalmers, who immediately be-

gan to issue directives for the ways he knew his DivKay staff could, and
had to, weigh in operationally to support the Agency's broader role in this
crisis. There was no time for him to consider the obvious question of why
CIA, FBI, DIA, NSA, DHS, and the rest of the alphabet soup had not learned
of Karami's plan in time to stop it.

It was just like his former deputy and departed friend Lee Beckner had
said years ago: "We have to be right every time; they've only got to do it
once." This one had slipped through the operational cracks.

֍

One of Chalmers's phone calls alerted him to what he'd already known
would happen next. The presidential helicopter, Marine One, was ferrying
Averez to Langley, where CIA director Craig Weaver, Chalmers, and other
designated federal officials would accompany the commander in chief on
the SpadeLiner's spur rail to Mount Weather—the bunkered command
center for a Continuity of Government emergency and a safe site for the
White House in Exile.

By the time everyone departed, Chalmers had more details about the
attack.

So far, the number of known dead was four hundred and fifteen. Those
closest to the exploding backpacks and briefcases were killed instantly.
Many more of the additional eleven hundred wounded were expected to
die from their grave injuries.

Knowing the effects of sarin gas, Chalmers could envision the subway's
chamber of horrors. Those trapped inside lost control of bodily functions
from inhaling the nerve agent, which caused them to vomit, defecate, and
urinate in metabolic concert with their spasmodic bodies. Unless injected
with antidotes and administered oxygen quickly, victims suffocated from
collapsed lungs or died of heart failure.

֍

During the SpadeLiner's quick run to Mount Weather, Chalmers briefed
the president on some probability statistics he'd computed after hearing
the UJF's threat about further attacks. Chalmers did not think Karami
could strike again every day, but he did believe there was an eighty-five
percent likelihood of additional attacks during the next thirty to ninety
days in other U.S. cities.

"Also from sarin gas?" the president had asked.

"Not exclusively, sir," said Chalmers. "It's more likely we're finally going to see what we've been spared thus far—sleeper cells carrying out
homicide bombings in public places. It's one of the UJF's goals we learned

from electronic surveillance on Karami. These will be high-value targets intended to disrupt our economy even more, using high explosives to slaughter thousands more."

"Good Lord, that'll be horrific, won't it?"

Chalmers nodded. "As our briefings and intel reports have been telling you all along, Mr. President."

89

Following the "Metro Massacre"—as Washington's subway attack six years ago had become known—Chalmers had relinquished further presidential briefings on subsequent UJF incidents to CIA and FBI officials who dealt exclusively with terrorism. Karami had certainly given them plenty about which they had continued to inform the White House—virtually monthly, since that was how often the UJF had struck the United States, as well as other foreign targets.

Suicide bombings at shopping malls had dramatically slowed an already torpid economy that'd gone into a total tailspin when Premier Zhang—openly critical and contemptuous of President Averez—had restructured China's economic policies. With Beijing carrying much less of America's debt stemming from continued deficit spending, the United States had finally cut back on its many social entitlement programs and had enacted forceful measures against illegal immigration. All of that had inflamed certain ethnic groups, principally the HLM, which had started to copy the terrorist tactics of the UJF to express social grievances.

The administration's inept handling of one physical and financial crisis after another resulted in an outraged electorate sweeping Averez out of office after one term.

Chalmers and Paula were glad that Steven had transferred out of the temporary billet he'd been filing at the Pentagon only weeks before the Metro Massacre. Dr. Steven Chalmers, now thirty-eight years old and a colonel in the Air Force, had been detailed to NASA's Spaceflight Training Program at an air base outside of Houston. In the intervening years, he and his wife, Alena, and their three-year-old son, Steven Junior, had been living in a secluded suburb.

Though she missed them terribly, Paula was glad her son, daughter-in-law, and especially the grandson she and Jonathan called Stevie were at least somewhat removed from today's madness around Washington, New York, Los Angeles, and many other trouble-torn cities and regions across America.

Chalmers missed everyone, too, but he was glad to be spending most of his time with Paula here at CSC, where Pete Peterson and the CET—incorporating some of the new programming features Chalmers had designed for the Vortax-7000—had made a major discovery about the Time Crystal.

In addition to the fascinating views of Earth's history that the CET continued to retrieve and study, Chalmers and Peterson had, while working alone late one night, inadvertently opened a separate compartment in the Crystal, which held an intriguing discovery. The discovery came about solely as the result of an incredible, serendipitous act—what Chalmers had labeled the supreme example of a convergence of coincidence. And it consisted of nothing more than misplaying a musical tune.

Vortax was still translating what Chalmers and Peterson believed were instructions about the discovery—whose apparent internal file name, they'd already determined from the computer, was Collabros—and whose purpose seemed to be to perform some kind of general, though still imprecisely defined, function. For now, Chalmers called it a functional service modality, a term he'd drawn from his research into semiotics—the study of signs and symbols, especially those used as elements of any system of communication composed of semantics, syntactics, and pragmatics.

Chalmers had always believed the Crystal Tabula—as he alone knew was its Tutorium name—held the answer to every question that could be asked. If the gorgon-sized byte of math formulas and schematic drawings they had discovered was what his initial assessment indicated, Chalmers felt that Collabros was the answer to one of the most important questions he envisioned could be raised about the future—whatever it might look like.

As with everything he did that involved the CRYPTOS CONUNDRUM, Chalmers feared it could take more energy than he might have to understand and exploit the full potential of Collabros. For one thing, he already knew that far more powerful, sophisticated generations of computers would have to be designed in order to pull the deeply embedded secret from Collabros.

And in the rapidly diminishing time he felt was left to save his country, even the world, he watched as almost overnight the sense of haste became even more perverse.

90

After his ineffective one-term administration, President Averez had been replaced by a Democratic apologist who had wanted to make diplomatic peace with the UJF fanatics and politically accommodate the HLM separatists. Knowing that agenda was doomed to fail, Chalmers and everyone else watched as terrorist and guerrilla attacks not only continued but increased.

The political base that had narrowly elected this Democrat turned against him. The press called for his resignation. An attempted assassination by the HLM had reinforced his voluntary decision to step down. He was succeeded by the vice president who, while more capable and well-meaning, suffered a combination punch that knocked him, too, out of the political ring. Those two events, each a dramatic escalation of UJF terrorism, also put America's time-honored democracy on the canvass.

The first terrorist incident, details of which Chalmers learned from the subsequent investigation, was carried out by some of Karami's sleeper cell members who had earned FAA licenses and established patterns as private pilots—routinely renting single-engine planes for personal aviation purposes. On the appointed day, and flying in from different small airports throughout New York State, they had rendezvoused at another rural airstrip, loading explosives that Karami had prepositioned in a storage hangar. The pilots then took off for their final destinations—two other airports in New York City.

By the time control tower personnel at each airport had noted the unorthodox approach of closely clustered planes, it was too late to respond. The UJF kamikazes dive-bombed and detonated themselves into fully fueled commercial airliners in the process of boarding passengers in the morning rush at JFK and LaGuardia. A deadly domino effect of exploding jumbo jets and aviation fuel trucks shattered the terminals' massive plate-glass windows, shredded the tightly packed awaiting passengers, and instantly incinerated adjacent departure terminals.

ᔰ

When he'd later viewed airport security cameras, as well as ground-mapping satellite and Google Earth coverage that inadvertently had re-corded the attack, Chalmers saw a disaster of Gothic proportions. To him, it looked look like a string of road flares popping in red-hot rhythm along an accident-strewn expressway. More than sixteen thousand people were killed and thirty-five thousand injured at both locations.

In the UJF communiqué that followed the attacks, dubbed by the me-dia the "twin airports," Karami said, "We pledge our lives that more at-tacks with even more visceral terror are imminent. Targets will be New York and other undisclosed cities."

More than three million panicked New Yorkers made a ground trans-port exodus from the city within a two-week period. The first wave of panic induced even more frightened departures. The local economy, still reeling from the recession that'd begun several years earlier, quickly col-lapsed and civil disorder ensued among the criminals and other distraught doomsayers who'd stayed behind.

ᔰ

The second attack took place after the UJF hijacked gasoline fuel trucks making routine deliveries to gas stations located near Karami's designated first-tier sites, which were high-traffic anchor stores in strip mall shopping centers. During thirty minutes of coordinated assaults, seventeen com-mandeered tankers—each carrying ten thousand gallons of gasoline—crashed through plate-glass entrances at the malls, plowed into the interior, and detonated.

As Chalmers heard one newscaster describe it, "Billowing blackish-orange clouds of fire have melted the flesh from thousands of shoppers."

That was nothing compared to what followed at the second-tier sites.

A half dozen of those tankers had been driven into the sides of school buildings and crashed into cafeterias packed with youngsters at lunch-time. It was so unconscionable and ghastly that it defied description.

ᔰ

All across America, most people simply stayed home as families cowered with the fear and the terror of profound uncertainty in the aftermath of both attacks. Having lost faith in politicians, law enforcement, and the intelligence community, citizens were all the more demoralized to think that perhaps even the military, which had now been directed by Congress to govern the nation during the all-out war on U.S. soil, might not be able to save the country.

91

VIRGINIA CAVE—INWARD PASSAGE

Kaj'a-zar's adult sisters no longer had their tutorials in front of the viewing screens, for as they'd seen with their brother and clan leader, all that flashed now when he pointed and fired the control gun were more violent pictorials of events happening above. Lacking their brother's ever-improving language comprehension, the females were not exactly sure what the strange sounds coming from the talking heads meant, but they knew that the }{λδυζα)δσ, or surface world, was an alien and dangerous place for them and the other Fiverians.

Though at first only a survivalist in this subterranean realm into which he'd been forcibly birthed by the human Chalmers, Kaj'a-zar had quickly become a student of his new environment—not just the dark inward passages he'd traversed throughout his lifetime but especially the lighted region above once he'd discovered it. There he had foraged . . . and flourished through the acquisition of knowledge and the power it provided.

Unlike his sisters, as well as the new emerging generations of Fiverians, he did not see the realm above as alien. Kaj'a-zar saw it as the land upon which he and all like him would eventually roam free. He saw it as the world his father intended him to rule, wearing the Tyrannical Crown the Fiverian patriarch always meant for the son to have.

And unlike his sisters, Kaj'a-zar was not apprehensive because he lacked complete information about what was happening above. He knew enough to understand that a new time was near—one that his intelligence and intuition told him would bring disruption and perhaps destruction of this strange species called mankind.

And he definitely knew that the key to his longer-term plan was to move deeper still into the rock world and wait for the troubled dust to clear.

PACIFIC OCEAN—THE LIQUISPHERE

Wul'ya-Qox had left the magnetic arches of the deep trench and relocated to another of his underworld domains. Current events on the hardscape above did not concern him, though he was very interested in certain of its physical structures—especially those from which he could obtain the fusion power this planet's inhabitants were capable of producing. Soon he would have enough of it stored to propel his fleet across this galaxy toward the next time portal.

It would be through one of these $((\alpha))\delta\alpha\zeta$—compressed-dimension holes scattered throughout the dark matter of cosmic space—that Wul'ya-Qox planned to outrun the threat that trailed him. At the same time, he knew his upcoming departure would spell the end for Kul'da-Zak's offspring—if the sole Fiverian on the Earth world was still alive.

Wul'ya-Qox also knew that even if such an offspring had managed to survive up to now, the arrival as foretold by the *vuezur* message was soon to occur . . . and with it the death of any Fiverians remaining on this planet.

On his command, the ships rose from the depths and headed inland, navigating well above but along the great rock wall that was the only civilized structure visible from beyond this planet's orbit. From there, on a new heading, were the smoking towers of the site that produced what he needed.

ᛏᛖ

Taking advantage of the environmental circumstances his instruments showed at the site, Wul'ya-Qox guided his seven craft into the thick nimbus that engulfed the target structure and at the same time served to visually mask their arrival. From his console, he fired a single blast that cut a perfect hole in a strategic location. From it spewed a debris stream that was immediately harvested.

TANGPIEN, CHINA. 1645 HOURS

Officials at Junglopau, China's largest nuclear power plant, had never seen such a black-clouded thunderstorm. Its high winds, hail, and lightning strikes represented a real danger to Beijing's major supplier of electricity. Suddenly, their worst fear materialized.

The turgid sky crackled with a deafening rasp and spewed out a laser stream of torchlight that cut into a crucial external part of the reactor. The resulting explosion ruptured the core and released a contamination cloud more powerful than the one showering rain and mere lightning from nature's minor tempest.

PREMIER ZHANG'S OFFICE. 1700 HOURS

When briefed by his senior military adviser and handed the accompanying report, Zhang's reaction to the Junglopau incident was more electrified than the thunderstorm raging outside. Radar had picked up seven blips inside the eye of a weather system with the size, shape, and force of a cyclone. Though the adviser said radar probably spotted nothing more than clusters of compacted hail, Zhang concluded that U.S. stealth bombers had attacked the power plant in retaliation for the otherwise peaceful deployment months ago of Chinese troops into Taiwan as part of Zhang's internationally stated plan for the forced reunification of the island.

Knowing that America was under near constant terrorist attacks—as well as domestic violence, state-separatist movements, and other nationwide social and financial problems—Zhang further assessed that Washington had planned for this thinly masked covert assault on China for propaganda purposes. And to generate a new wave of press coverage that would distract Americans from their many problems and somehow reunite them in a common front against Zhang.

"How stupid can they be?" Zhang had asked rhetorically after sharing his assessments with one of the advisers. But he smiled, knowing the chessboard's political configuration favored him checkmating his opponent.

He explained that now would a good time to send Chinese troops— peacefully, of course—into California to guarantee the security of millions of Chinese expatriates living there in dangerous circumstances. Coincidentally, he planned to use the opportunity to seize what remained of the Silicon Valley computer chip industry and otherwise to establish a "beachhead" presence before the West Coast collapsed into total anarchy and ruin.

Figuring that Californians had always wanted to have a Communist state, he knew he'd be welcomed there to provide them with one.

Zhang ordered his staff to draw up such a plan immediately.

HIGH STASIS—TIMELESS

Won had tried repeatedly to mentalate with the Headmaster, but there had been no response—a likely indication that his professor had been wrathfully cashiered.

Though he could not recall where his last assignment had been, nor how he had become a Samaritan in the first place, Won drew upon some remnant of a faraway memory as he felt what he assumed must be the metaphysical effects of the Hastening. He was becoming vaguely disembodied, even in his already celestial nonbody form.

Since there was nothing he could do about it anyway, Won gave his essence willfully to the pending disengagement from High Stasis and to the journey that would take him to whatever fate he'd encounter at the mysterious Iris Portal.

It was not in his Samaritan duties to say good-bye to the human Chalmers, with whom he had already communicated more than was allowed. It was, however, his responsibility to remain vigilant over the chosen human, and all of humankind, even as these final sectics ticked down to the midnight toll of his workday.

92

Chalmers had wrinkled skin and walked slowly, but he nevertheless looked like a robust man in his early eighties, though he was now one hundred and thirty years old. He remained the family's patriarch, as well as a central figure in the CIA. He and Paula, now seventy-six, were still very much in love.

Their son, Colonel Steven J. Chalmers, was NASA's senior command pilot for the Aurora Space Flight Program, which had continued to be funded even with all the nation's problems, especially its financial ones. Today, he was in Earth orbit on an ASFP mission, training for an upcoming manned flight to Mars. His son, Stevie, was in McLean with his mother Alena and grandmother Paula.

These aspects of life for the Chalmers family seemed normal.

Nothing else was.

The Oyster Bay mansion that had been home to Chalmers families for more than two hundred years had been abandoned months ago. There'd been no alternative.

DeLorno and Shantu had handled the salvage and transfer to Chalmers's McLean residence of any remaining valuables not stolen or destroyed during looting and rioting that had erupted throughout New York City and across Long Island. Widespread lawlessness continued even now in spite of strict martial law.

Chalmers had instructed DeLorno and Shantu to check the attic for what he'd described to them only as a "uniquely framed painting." One of many stored there, it was the portrait of a youthful Chalmers—the painting that he felt contributed to his schizophrenic thoughts and that stoked his paranoid fears . . . one of which was that his framed likeness, just like the satanically possessed Dorian Gray's, would have aged hideously over the years, while he himself had changed relatively little and at an unusually slow pace.

に

Now back at headquarters, his security men said they'd located the particular ornate frame, which had been placed on an easel adjacent to a stack of other paintings.

"What did it . . . the painting, look like?" Chalmers asked, revealing an apprehension, a nervous behavior they'd never seen before. Sensitive to it, DeLorno described smoke and fire damage to part of the attic, as well as water damage to some furniture and other items from rain that had entered through cracks in the slate roof.

"The *painting*," Chalmers emphasized, his voice agitated, his eyes on Shantu.

"Sir, the oil painting in question . . . you never really said, but I'm guessing it was some kind of abstract thing, or something else that must have melted in the fire."

"More like it softened, then sagged and cracked," added DeLorno. "Looked to me like it was somebody's face at one time. Ugly mess now, though. Sorry, sir."

"Yeah, too bad, Dr. Chalmers. We left it, just like you instructed," said Shantu.

His face ashen, Chalmers nodded, turned his back on the men, and walked to his large bank of windows—his mind still burdened with the heavy uncertainty that had characterized every aspect of his life . . . and every facet of the CRYPTOS CONUNDRUM.

93

DeLorno and Shantu were helping Chalmers pack up everything in his office. They noticed he seemed to be having difficulty deciding what to put where and had finally walked over to the window, where he stared into the sky. Exchanging worried glances, the two men joined him.

Still looking outward but aware they'd quietly flanked him, Chalmers spoke in a soft, reflective voice. "A good friend and astrophysicist named Stephen Hawking said just before he died that mankind's longer-term survival would depend on humans colonizing outer space . . . my Steven's pioneering mission to Mars . . . it could be . . ."

His words vanished into a distance even farther than his view beyond the window.

"Sir, everybody's pulling for Colonel Chalmers and the ASFP," said DeLorno, "but when it comes to survival . . . hey, you've already set up things underground, at least for now, with the Citations and all."

Shaking off the mood, Chalmers shifted his thoughts and focus down into the courtyard between the two headquarters buildings. In the middle stood the enigmatic *Cryptos* statue, sculpted by an artist now dead and long forgotten by all but Chalmers.

Their security assignment to Chalmers meant that DeLorno and Shantu had received K-RED clearances and selected briefings on the CRYPTOS CONUNDRUM files.

Highly disciplined professionals and strict adherents to the need-to-know principle, the men had never asked Chalmers additional questions about the incredible things they'd learned since coming to work for him, but they were always eager to listen when he volunteered anything new.

"You fellows know I put a secret message into that artist's sculpture down there."

They both nodded. "Everyone says it's never been decoded," said DeLorno.

"Oh, the sculptor's message, his cryptographic challenge to the work-force, was eventually figured out, at least for the most part, but *mine* certainly hasn't been. No one even knows there was, or *is* another message . . . except now, of course, you two."

DeLorno and Shantu recognized the consequence of what they'd just been told.

Shantu couldn't resist. "Gee, why would anybody have ever thought to look for another message? So are you like, going public with this now?"

"Sir, if I may," said DeLorno, "I think the real question is why you've told us?"

"The existence of another code and its decryption will be an issue only if I am *not* around. Then, at the right time, perhaps with help from you two, either my son . . . or my grandson will have that responsibility."

Glancing at each other, DeLorno and Shantu's eyes reflected mutual agreement that they should refrain from further questions. They did, however, have work to do and they set about packing the remainder of Chalmers's files, books, and other personal effects that were being transferred from his Langley office to the CSC.

෴

With anarchy spreading across the country—as much from the now to-tally collapsed economy as anything else—everyone feared for their lives and had taken to shooting first and asking questions later. Even the CIA was closing its doors at Langley, which required Chalmers to vacate the premises. Many officers had already retired or simply left Washington for someplace less dangerous, although such locales were increasingly hard to find.

Based on recommendations from Chalmers, the Agency had been reorganized and renamed, and it was now relocating as part of the Continuity of Government contingency plan. A streamlined workforce that relied primarily on overhead platforms, nanobotic drones, and other laser-based technology to collect national security intelligence was being transferred to the underground facility at the CSC.

With Steven now on his way to Mars, Chalmers had decided some time ago to send Paula, Alena, and Stevie down to CSC. They were safely quartered in base housing, where they waited for Chalmers to join them.

෴

"That's the last of it, sir," said DeLorno, placing a box on his flatbed cart. Shantu was already pushing his fully loaded cart out the door and into the hallway. "It's time to go now, Dr. Chalmers."

"Give me one last look at the courtyard. I'll meet you at the elevator."

DeLorno nodded and left.

As he had planned from the beginning—and like everything else having to do with the CIA—*Cryptos* was a lie to create a deception to hide a secret. Now the sculpture would stand as a sentry for the future. When the time came, the steel slabs of alphabetic letters would spell out the final code, the one that revealed the ultimate truth hidden in the core of the Crystal Tabula—which Chalmers would soon transfer to a special vault beneath the CSC lab. It was a wondrous compartment deeper in the cavern Chalmers had discovered a long time ago when the mysteries of the CRYPTOS CONUNDRUM had first cast secret shadows over his life.

And the ultimate truth that Chalmers had stumbled onto even deeper within the Crystal was a set of instructions about a celestial machine called Collabros.

Even more interesting was the fact that Chalmers had figured out how to build the device—but only after he or someone using his blueprint first designed and constructed a computer with more technological sophistication than at present existed.

That would take time, more of it than Chalmers now believed he had left.

But once the new computational tool—the key—had been cut, Chalmers was certain it could unlock and engage the Crystal's embedded machine. And he knew that the productive capability of Collabros would make all the difference in the new world . . . whatever was left of it.

☙

Accepting that his work at Langley was forever finished, Chalmers turned away from the window, headed for the elevator, and went down to the sub-basement station.

There he boarded the SpadeLiner for the CSC, the last bastion of defense and the only hope of survival he had for his family, for his country . . . and now, he feared more than ever, for the world.

Part VIII

DEEP DARKNESS

94

CSC LEVEL II. MARCH 15, 2021, MORNING

Watching the powerfully built and intellectually impressive man read the sitrep, Chalmers thought about how many times he'd provided situation reports or given briefings to presidents, CIA directors, generals, and other senior officials at the federal and state levels. He'd just never briefed anybody who, with a congressionally designated title of homeland governor, had held all those positions at the same time.

But in these times and under current circumstances, Lieutenant General William Walston was now the exception to every political rule American democracy had ever known. And as Chalmers knew, these were exceptional, complicated times—in fact, more bizarre than anything the general realized or could even imagine. But Bill Walston was going to hear about it, at least for the most part, from the briefing he'd soon receive from Chalmers.

With the nation continuing to come apart at the seams and full tilt anarchy raging in many large cities, Congress had passed an euphemistic National Security Decree that implemented martial law and ceded federal control to a new, and true, commander in chief. That individual was General Walston, chairman of the Joint Chiefs of Staff. Though Congress tried to stick the newly minted homeland governor badge on his lapel, Walston would have no part in wearing a pin-striped suit or sporting a fancy civilian title during a time of war. And he had no sufferance for foolishness nor any patience for indecision. For him, no measures were too draconian if they would save the nation.

"I'll always take the lead," he'd said once at a meeting, "but I damn well expect everybody to line up behind me." Back in the day, Walston had always been a regular in the Pentagon weight room where he had posted a large sign on the gym wall that said more about his philosophy on life than his credo for pumping iron. *Work out or get out.*

In his new appointment and by whatever name, rank or serial number he chose to go by, Walston's first official action today was to get a K-RED briefing from Dr. Chalmers. It was a private, one-on-one session that lasted a long time and involved spirited interchanges between individuals whose respective personal style and professional substance were different, but equally strong. In the process, both men established an immediate sense of mutual respect, which in turn set the stage for their strong friendship that quickly followed.

Though amazed by revelations in the phenomenal CRYPTOS and CO-NUNDRUM files, Walston nonetheless absorbed details about the Roswell alien, Time Crystal, Strategic Survival Initiative, underground Citations, and everything else he'd learned while exhibiting the disciplined composure reflecting his military rank.

"As a solider, I'm forced to be more concerned about the nuclear war and survival aspects of CRYPTOS than the technical details of the CO-NUNDRUM business, though I do have a few questions about your Jack the Ripper alien and that Time Crystal," he'd told Chalmers.

Emphasizing its intelligence and proven show of force, Chalmers said the alien, including those presumably like it on the seven spaceships, could have a goal other than mere survival. "We believe they've established undersea colonies and may plan to remain here permanently," he'd told Walston. "It's likely we'll cross paths with at least Jack should a full-fledged war force us into the Citations, probably for generations."

Regretting he had no time to explore the Time Crystal himself, Walston then asked Chalmers, "What's the most gripping piece of history you've witnessed so far?"

"Watching a carpenter from Nazareth walk across water and divide a single loaf of bread among a sea of hungry humanity." Chalmers's reply had sent cold shivers down Walston's spine and opened a floodgate of new questions. But time was short. The general needed answers and solutions for secular, combat issues rather than spiritual ones.

"Those might be the same," Chalmers would tell him later.

CSC. SEPTEMBER 27, MONDAY

Subsequent events with China and General Zhang had accelerated Walston's preparations for what he now knew to be an *unavoidable war with the Chinese.*

Washington had repeatedly stated it's policy of support for Taiwan, emphasizing American refusal to tolerate the intervention of outside forces in the democratic island nation. Following the CIA's earlier reporting that a takeover was imminent, Zhang had done more than send "peacekeeping" troops into Taiwan. He had also begun to annex parts of Indonesia and North Korea, stating publicly that South Korea was next. Moreover, learning of General Walston's assumption of martial power in Washington, Zhang had vowed to launch a preemptive nuclear strike on America, or maybe just invade California, if Walston interfered with Zhang's "Great March"—his version of China's Manifest Destiny for the Pacific Rim.

He had sent a cable to Walston: "Do not stand in my way."

"Then do not head in my direction," responded Walston, who in turn had said to Chalmers, "that slant-eyed son of a bitch is really crazy, isn't he?"

Chalmers had nodded, sharing his observation that the entire world was gripped by insanity. He also admitted his angst about the triage of decision making during war, providing details about his process for selecting several million people based on genetics, intelligence, and technological and practical continuity skills . . . those who'd be allowed to take refuge in the Citations while those above were condemned to fend for themselves.

"You're not alone in making life-and-death decisions, Jonathan," Walston had replied. "We're on the brink of civil war and nuclear war at the same time, and I intend to win them both . . . or at least kill everybody wearing a different uniform in the process of defeat."

SEPTEMBER 28, THURSDAY MORNING

Finishing today's sitrep, Walston tossed his reading glasses on the table. "Israel bombs another Iranian nuclear plant. The Tehran tyrant who finally knocked off that asshole Ahmadinejad, and who is currently very busy killing everyone trying to assassinate him, in turn, has managed to find time to announce another counterattack against Jerusalem." Now he dropped the sitrep on top of his glasses and looked at Chalmers, who could see the weary frustration in the general's eyes.

"John, even though you've said it'll be another year before everything underground is completely online, I think we've got to go full plus on the final selection of candidates."

"I agree. It's going to be a lengthy process to brief and then transfer, perhaps even forcing the selectees to their designated shelters. The country's plenty spooked already."

"Well, the race is to the swift and the battle to the strong," said Walston. "I hope we haven't run out of time and that things don't get any more complicated."

"Bill, I'm afraid you've misquoted Ecclesiastes."

"Oh, and you know the Bible that well?"

Chalmers smiled. "Chapter and verse. Nine, and eleven through twelve in this case."

Walston nodded. "Have me stand corrected, then. Let's hear it."

"The race is *not* to the swift *nor* the battle to the strong," Chalmers cited, "and in paraphrase it goes on to say that time and chance happen to everyone, with the sons of men snared by evil times that fall unexpectedly upon them."

"For a so-called Good Book it has a lot of bad things to say, doesn't it?"

"Yes, and unfortunately something *unexpected* is about to dash your hope that things don't get any more complicated." Chalmers slid across the table a folder he'd been handed minutes ago by his deputy who'd stepped into the briefing room and immediately left. "Some NASA photos we need to discuss."

"The Mars mission? Nothing serious about your son, I hope."

"No, but thanks for your first thought being a concern about Steven."

"With reason, he's a soldier and explorer. A national hero. Certainly for me."

Acknowledging the general's comment, Chalmers immediately moved on. He explained that the photos involved exploration *and* discovery—as well as another kind of briefing, one that Chalmers believed Walston would find more amazing than anything he'd heard up to now about the CRYPTOS CONUNDRUM. And one that Chalmers knew he simply could not explain fully to the general.

95

CSC. MOMENTS LATER

Walston studied the photos while Chalmers explained the background of the cosmic cloud—or massive nebula of stellar gas, as Dr. Stern had called it when his Astrophysics Department at Cornell analyzed the Hubble Space Telescope's first photos of the transient deep-space anomaly taken many years ago. Bringing Walston up to speed brought back personal memories of Stern. Chalmers still missed his friend, long ago lost to a painful battle with cancer.

"So Stern and you watched all these years as the HST tracked this cloud pop in and out of different black holes, and now NASA has suddenly discovered—"

"It's ahead of the arrival schedule Stern originally calculated but still on the course he projected."

"Jupiter."

Chalmers took a breath. "Yes, sir . . . to start with."

"What does that mean?"

"That the cloud . . . or the swarm, as I know it, is headed for us, for Earth."

" 'Swarm'? What's *that* mean, and how'd Stern calculate it was coming our way?"

"I alone know the destination and purpose of this thing."

"So now it's a thing, you mean like something—"

"Yes, alive and undoubtedly sentient, well fixed on its purpose and intent."

"Dr. Chalmers, it's not like everything else I've learned since meeting you hasn't been fuckin' bizarre beyond belief, but I've gotta tell you, this is more rattling than all the other CRYPTOS CONUNDRUM stuff combined. As my intel chief, I want you to give me the five *W*'s in one sentence."

Chalmers knew that Walston wanted the who, what, when, where, and why of the NASA photos. Chalmers also knew there was a sixth *W,* the source of the information that he did not want to reveal because just as he himself had always worried, Chalmers thought General Walston might believe his chief adviser had delusional thoughts and hence untrustworthy judgment. Now was not the time to lessen any confidence Walston had about being commander in chief.

So to answer that question, Chalmers resorted to standard CIA tactics. He lied.

He explained that he had focused the DMT-9000—a DigiMiscible Tezarmetric modality Chalmers and his staff had engineered from the CIA's now outdated series of Vortax computers—into a new region of the Crystal, where he'd discovered, and the DMT had subsequently translated, the Roswell craft's historical journal.

From the beginning of the Crystal's appearance in the laboratory, and with everyone who worked on its ultra–top secret analysis, Chalmers had always said the Crystal had been found at the Roswell site. Only Paula knew what Chalmers believed to be the Crystal Tabula's true origin at the Tutorium, as well as the revelations about Chalmers's life and the tragic fate of the world that the number one Samaritan had shared the night Won diffused through Chalmers's bedroom window.

ка

"So you're telling me this cloud is a living creature, some kind of *what* . . . a galactic hit squad that's been on Jack's, or the rest of his alien pals', trail, and that they, or whatever kind of comic monster it is, will engulf our world to assassinate someone from their own otherworld—and all of this is only ten to twelve weeks away?"

"You did want all the *W*'s in one sentence."

Making a hapless gesture with his hands, Walston said, "I guess it's safe to assume this represents a *major* complication to the mess we've already created for ourselves on Mother Earth."

Recalling how the Samaritan had mentally pictured it for him, Chalmers nodded.

"General Walston, nothing you've learned in recent months that has seemed unbelievable or impossible will compare with what we'll face even if we somehow avoid the looming apocalypse of a third world war. I cannot reveal my source, but I have seen . . . call it a special kind of visual portrayal of this swarm, and I tell you it's ghastly beyond articulation."

"John, I believe you, but we are close, *very* close, I'm afraid, to the only kind of war for which I, too, have a visual portrayal, so let's deal with first things first—the mushroom cloud. We'll press ahead as planned, and if God is on our side, and everything you've done in creating the Citations holds true, then maybe there'll also be a fighting chance to duck the dooms-day cloud headed our way."

Yes, if God is on our side, Chalmers thought as he left the command center.

Not knowing exactly how much time was left now, he wanted to spend as much of it as possible with his wife and grandson.

96

Stevie had accompanied his grandpa down to the office built more than seventy years ago following the discovery of this cave beneath Building W01. Though redecorated several times since then, Chalmers's sanctuary—as he'd always called it—was still on the elevated catwalk above the cryogenic tank where the alien cadaver egg had been hatched.

But now, instead of facing a massive chamber of stalactites formerly lost in the depth of darkness, the sanctuary's windows overlooked a huge lighted train station. Looking beyond it and into the cavernous distance, Chalmers and Stevie surveyed a high-rise city also alight and bustling with workmen putting the final touches on stores, apartments, and manufacturing sites even as selected citizens arrived.

"Lot of changes since last time we checked on the construction, huh?"

"Still looks to me like a Z-D holomaz on my digavu game pod," said Stevie with a casual tone of technological sophistication reflective of the youngster's keen intelligence. "So are we going to be down here the whole time Dad's in space, Grandpa?"

"For a while, bud, that's for sure, but your dad won't be gone too long."

"C'mon, Grandpa, he's going to Mars, not taking the SpadeLiner to Oyster Bay." The kid was reflective for a second. "You know, we haven't been there in a long time, I mean the whole family and all. I miss the beach and that old lighthouse."

"Times have changed a bit up in New York . . . and so has the round-trip travel to Mars since your gramps here, along with my technical staff, helped NASA boost the speed on your dad's rocket engine."

"The Aurora Pulse Engine," the boy said with pride. "Dad explained it to me."

Chalmers tousled the youngster's hair. "Yep, shows you're as smart as he is."

"Thanks for making his trip shorter, Grampa," said Stevie as he hugged Chalmers tightly. "I love you and I'm glad to be here with you and Grandma."

"Love you, too. We'll stay busy, have some fun, and I'll bet my boy will be back to see his boy quicker than a wink."

❧

Aware of strange sensations in his heart, soul, and bones—functions of timing, as he'd regarded them lately—Chalmers had suddenly instructed DeLorno and Shantu to take Stevie to the surface. He'd then gone to the lab, and after dismissing everyone there, he removed the Time Crystal from its metal cabinet.

Then, with considerable effort—because in recent days his old bones had in fact begun to cause him pain and he'd felt his physical strength also diminish—he slipped into an obscure rock corridor just beyond the lab and made his way down a path illuminated by a hand lantern. He was the only one, for now, who knew this walkway existed.

He knew it would take just a few minutes to reach the bottom and get back.

❧

Aboveground, on the small patio of their temporary quarters in the heavily guarded CSC compound, Paula and Alena made plans for tomorrow's picnic.

"This might be our last one," said Paula, "before we all move into the Citation condo. I want this to be a real memory maker, especially since the forecast is for more sunshine."

"Definitely something to be held outside, which is where Stevie needs to be now, out here playing while he can, instead of down there with Grampa. They and we and everybody else will get plenty of that, possibly a lifetime of it, when the siren goes off."

Paula patted Alena's hand. "Jonathan has spent so much time down there all these years, getting ready for this moment. God bless his aged bones, he's likely to make me a sad widow soon enough."

"Don't say that, Paula, it'll make me sad, too. Besides, I'm already a space widow. You know how little time I've had with *my* husband the last five years. And how much of his son's precious life the famous Colonel Steve has missed flying for NASA. I know he's a hero, to none more so than me," Alena said with a sob, "but he should be here with his family, especially now with us on the brink of Lord knows what."

Equally frightened by the future, Paula embraced her daughter-in-law. "Sweetheart, our only choice is to get a good grip and hang on for dear life."

97

CHALMERS'S OFFICE. SAME DAY, 1615 HOURS

With Stevie now topside and his squad—as Chalmers thought of DeLorno and Shantu—back below at his side, he and the two stout men had left the gantry office and taken the escalator deeper below, where Chalmers had another private office. This was a smaller one next to the massive Command Center where General Walston was currently coordinating with still-active U.S. military bases aboveground.

Entering his office, Chalmers was met by his new deputy, Clifford Monroe, who'd been sent by Walston to find Dr. Chalmers. In his hand Monroe held a sealed, red-striped folder marked SCI/ZARZ—*Eyes Only*—CHALMERS—SSPL/NY.

"For you," Monroe said, handing his boss the folder. "Came in from the astrophysics lab at Cornell. The general wanted me to update you on the latest development on another issue. Should I do that, or do you want to read your document first?"

"Walston's information."

"A Chinese carrier has left Singapore headed south," said Monroe, glancing at the piece of paper in his hand that contained Walston's notes. "It's loaded with S-80 Dragon Claw stealth bombers and a support fleet of destroyers packing Tang missiles . . . nuke-tipped." Monroe added that Beijing had given Walston a last-minute heads-up they'd be conducting training exercises in the Timor Sea, just north of Australia. And Zhang had emphatically stated he would broach no interference from Walston. "Sir, Red Storm ICMB silos throughout the Chinese mainland are showing activation telemetries," Monroe continued. "Hopefully it's only more chest puffing like we've seen before."

"Last year Zhang said his navy was conducting training exercises in the Malaysian Straits, and China wound up with a permanent base in Singapore," said Mike DeLorno, trying to be informative and helpful.

"Will General Walston put an end to the tumbling dominoes this time, Dr. Chalmers?"

"Too late for that now, Mike," Chalmers said, opening the folder. "The Aussies will probably have . . ."

Seeing what was inside, he abruptly stopped and sat down, his face ashen.

"Sir, what is it?" asked Monroe.

"Are you all right?" added DeLorno, stepping to Chalmers's side, where he could now see there were pictures in the open folder.

Chalmers looked up, not at the two men but *through* them, and when he spoke his voice was distant, like dull thunder in a storm cloud still far on the evening horizon. "Another photo array. The nebula ripped through Saturn on its way to Jupiter."

Monroe and DeLorno exchanged looks. "Sir, a nebula . . . what are you talking about?" asked Monroe, who even though he was Chalmers's deputy had not been briefed on the doomsday cloud headed toward Earth. Walston had made the decision to keep that compartmented until the very last moment.

Chalmers read the accompanying written report from the Stern Space Physics Lab in a matter of painful seconds. Much of the ring system around Saturn had been dislodged—or chewed apart, as Chalmers alone would have known—by the cloud. Comparative simulations were being run by the SSPL to determine what kind of orbital or gravitational anomalies might occur, and whether they could someday cause asteroid strikes here. There was also the related issue of giant rips in Jupiter's deep gas layers when the cloud passed by it—also having gorged, Chalmers figured, on anything edible.

ꝯ

"Voracians," Chalmers said hoarsely.

"I'm sorry, Dr. Chalmers . . . *For a shuns*?" said Monroe. "I don't understand . . ."

"Oh, Steven, dear God, no," Chalmers moaned in raw anguish.

"I'm going to call the medics," DeLorno told Monroe.

Chalmers suddenly made direct eye contact with both men and squared his shoulders as he took in a deep, calming breath. "No doctors. You'll learn about all this later."

"What can I do for you now, sir?" DeLorno asked.

"Go find Paula, bring her down to me, but say nothing of this to her, make sure Stevie stays with his mother and don't alarm her, either." He looked at Monroe. "Cliff, tell the general I'll be in to see him in a few moments after I've spoken with my wife about . . . a grave family issue."

❧

As both men left the room, Chalmers took a final look at the remaining photos on the bottom of the stack. Taken by the Aurora crew and transmitted seconds before the ship's hull was breached, they provided magnified details of the Voracians. And they confirmed what Chalmers had learned from the Samaritan: these creatures were an unstoppable, insatiable sludge of cosmic terror, a feeding force that was galactic death incarnate. Worse than in his analytical mind, he knew in his seldom expressed but profoundly emotional heart what had happened to Steven and the crew.

He would never tell Paula the horrid details, but neither could he ever expunge from his soul the vivid description of a Voracian conveyed to him that night by the Samaritan.

Chalmers knew the Aurora astronauts had been consumed by microscopic organisms—Voracians with the feeding fervor of piranhas capable of stripping bare anything animate or inanimate, regardless of size. The Voracian method of savaging human flesh was gigantically horrific. Contact with these aliens caused their victims' bodies first to fester into a million pustules, spewing out liquefied remains that had no time even to puddle before being consumed by the frenzied invaders.

❧

He sat, unable to feel anything now, having done what Paula had always chided him for often resorting to in his professional life—focusing on an empirical task at hand to such an extent that he shut the emotional doors to his heart. He needed the numbness now, though he knew from experience it wouldn't last.

But he could better afford to fall apart later.

Quan Shantu knocked and entered the office tentatively, already informed by DeLorno that their boss had suffered some kind of emotional incident minutes earlier. "Some additional but . . . uh . . . unrelated information," he said, handing over a file with reports that he explained had come from radar stations from several U.S. air bases and had been confirmed from control towers at some commercial airports still handling international passenger travel.

Chalmers opened, read, and closed the file within seconds.

"Thank you, Quan. That'll be all."

These new pieces of information were of no consequence to Chalmers in light of his son's death, but they were a timely distraction. He noted that some of the final puzzle pieces now fit into the overall mosaic. They had to do with a rash of UFO sightings—a seven-craft formation streaking across the sky and beyond Earth orbit.

Rats deserting the sinking ship, Chalmers thought. Fiverians getting up from the dinner table before the Voracians arrive to gorge themselves.

Apart from the gut-wrenching fact that Steven was dead, Chalmers knew that everyone in Roswell, New Mexico, and Tidewater, Virginia, would be, too, because that's where the Fiverians originally crashed and where their remains were taken, where the "scent" trail had now led the trackers.

Stroking the keys on his DMT-9000 keyboard, Chalmers recalculated that the Voracians' killing force was nine days away.

And for one of the few occasions in his one hundred and thirty-one years of life, Dr. Jonathan Chalmers was wrong.

98

Walston was still processing the updated nebula information and photo array. Stunned by the loss of Colonel Chalmers, the general's heart ached, too, for the father's grief. He searched for words of condolence, knowing there were none.

"The sky is darkening like a stain, something is going to fall like rain," he said on impulse. "I don't know a lot of quotes, but that one seems to cover all the bases."

"I'm impressed, Bill. Do you know who wrote that line?"

Walston indicated he did not.

"For reasons that aren't important here, I'm partial to names with a *W*."

Not knowing what that meant, Walston simply shrugged.

"The poet W. H. Auden often wrote about the relationship between human beings and the impersonal world of nature. You picked an appropriate and most appreciated quote—for me and everyone else who will be affected by what the sky brings . . . one way or another. I've already resolved the personal pain about my son, so let's get back to work."

"Agreed. I'm rescinding the caveats on K-RED compartmentation. It's time to bring the entire staff up to speed. Everyone's already in double-duty mode for a nuclear attack. The nebula will just be one more critical ball to juggle in this last-minute circus."

99

There had been long days and nights of hasty new preparations. As everyone knew, in the process everything on every front had deteriorated even further.

"Increased attacks this morning already by the UJF and HLM, nuclear war with China any day now, and America facing imminent invasion by space alien assassins," said Monroe, still dazed like everyone else by the updated K-RED brief they'd received. "It's like a Hollywood movie—a goddamn horror story."

"Jack and the Fiverians have been with us in remarkably low-key fashion for over sixty years," said Chalmers. "There's probably always been a ticking-bomb reality to the situation. I believe everything happening now was inevitable . . . probably planned."

"Before I'd ever heard of the CRYPTOS CONUNDRUM," said Monroe, "I'd seen documentaries and read books by Stern, Asimov, and others. The idea of space aliens was fascinating but only seemed like scary grist for sci-fi movies, never a real threat."

"Part of the design plan," Chalmers said. "Propaganda, disinformation, mind control. Things the old CIA did rather well."

Finishing his phone call, Walston swiveled around in his chair to face the others. "National Guard is experiencing more relocation resistance from some of the selectees than we anticipated."

"I knew from the outset this would be like keeping the family pet calm and comfortable prior to euthanasia," Chalmers said. "The prima facie absurdity, if not insanity, of the premise is clear—but still and all, our goal is to make these preparations, even the event itself, as nonalerting as possible."

"Avoid panic and save as many folks as we can who are not already in, and *cannot* now have access to the Citations," Walston added.

"Exactly. We can do it by repeating the ploy used at Roswell in 1947."

"And that would be what, Dr. Chalmers, for those of us whose parents hadn't even been born yet?" asked DeLorno.

Chalmers smiled. "Calling the new alien arrival by a benign scientific name."

"A weather balloon," Monroe said.

Chalmers shook his head. "A borealis space dust anomaly."

"Brilliant," said Walston. "BSD . . , bullshit deception. Linguistically brilliant."

"General, I also recommend handling BSD civil defense as if it were an auxiliary part of the current final-phase activation of the Citations. Even though most people were not selected for underground safe havens, they nonetheless have accepted their second-class exclusionary status."

Walston nodded his agreement.

Chalmers continued. "The public's current mind state is denial—a belief that America will somehow sidestep nuclear war with China, and those UJF terrorists, HLM separatists, and panicked looters will finally regain their senses. Everyone topside believes the undergrounders will return to the surface and life will again be normal."

"A harsh assessment, although I certainly agree with it," said Walston.

"I believe there's also a more empirical self-defense measure we can try, but I defer to your war-fighting expertise, General."

"I'm open to any and all recommendations, Dr. Chalmers."

"How current are you on Norse mythology, specifically Thor's hammer?"

"Walstons are Scandinavians bred from Germanic pagans. I know all about Thor, and I know exactly what you're talking about. And I'll be a son of a bitch if I don't think it just might work."

As Chalmers and Walston knew, Thor 2MPD was a multipurpose, multiple payload delivery system originally designed as a strategic ICBM weapon, satellite killer, and deep-space asteroid buster—the latter tactic originally conceived by Walt Stern.

⋈

Walston understood what needed to be done, and he gave the order.

"I want a dozen Thor 2s reconfigured faster than yesterday. Program 'em to spread a defensive wall of coordinated nuclear blasts that'll destroy the 'space dust' before it enters the atmosphere. Launch sequencing will occur over NATSECLINK. People, there's zero tolerance for delay or failure."

Unable to provide further technical assistance to Walston on this initiative, Chalmers could only trust that the gears of coordination would mesh among the missile launchers at the National Security Command and Control Communications Link. There was, however, a strategic analytical role for him as Walston's intelligence adviser . . . and a new piece of intelligence—intercepted from the Chinese—that Chalmers needed to brief him about.

Chalmers felt it best to have *that* discussion in private.

&

"It's amazing. No other countries seem to have discovered the inbound alien mass, and it's pointless to inform them now," said Chalmers, "because no country technically capable of helping defend America from the Voracians is likely to curtail its ongoing national effort to destroy us."

Walston snorted his disgust. "Time for the other quote I know: the enemy of my enemy is my friend."

"Right. The Chinese wouldn't help us now, but what you need to keep in mind is that China believes we've done more than build a national fallout shelter, a *defensive* shield for some enemy's future attack."

"What do they think it is, if not defensive?"

Referencing today's intercepts of China's 3C grid—command, control, and communications systems—Chalmers explained to Walston that General Zhang believed America's outward defensive measures had nothing to do with UJF terrorist attacks, HLM insurgency, or other domestic violence. Zhang believed the defensive bulwark was a support element in Washington's—and now General Walston's personal—agenda to stop China's continuing incursions through Indonesia by launching a preemptive *offensive* strike against Zhang and his forces.

"The bastard is already headed toward Australia, he's already threatened to nuke us or invade us. Exactly what does he think we might be thinking about him?"

"This is the first real issue. Zhang *wants* us to attack him and he *wants* to attack us . . . doesn't care who makes the first move, but he's definitely planning his now. We have it all on tape, and I have just listened to it—ran his voice through the DMT's psychometric evaluation matrix. Bill, the man is totally insane . . . socially suicidal, at least in the sense of leading his country into a war where everyone loses."

"Okay, the shithead's crazy. Got it. Anybody is who wants to fight a war, and right now that includes me. So if that's the *first*, then what's the *next* real issue?"

"That if we launch the Thor 2s, Zhang will think—neither knowing nor caring about the nebula—that we've made the first move, which will prompt him to make the second one."

"Well, John, either way we're screwed, so I say, *Game on.* You and I will divide and conquer the clouds. You focus on the alien one, I'll handle the mushroom."

100

CITATION COMMAND BUNKER. DECEMBER 7, 2021, 1600 HOURS

Chalmers surveyed his CCB dominion—a glass atrium bathed in neon green light and built within a giant cavern, its cathedral ceiling adorned with chandeliered stalactites.

Also hanging down, and reminiscent of a center-court scoreboard, was a four-sided xenon gasmic monitor. A phalanx of ITPs, information technology processors, analyzed data at their workstations, which Chalmers had originally designed into the existing rock terraces to maximize vertical space. Other work pods hung from cantilevered crane assemblies drilled into the rock walls. All of the elevated stations were connected by a system of crisscrossed foot gantries serviced by a central-core open-cage elevator.

The CCB's computational power was the acme of absolute technology—much of it designed by Chalmers and all of it the result of his prescience about the future . . . and his quest to be ready for its arrival. With such technology he should be able to monitor, assess, and respond to any requirement. Yet at this late moment, Chalmers questioned if he had tools enough to handle the Voracians, to save the country from their swarming death.

Additional technicians, whom Walston and Chalmers had cleared for BSD defensive countermeasures, coordinated last-minute activities over NATSECLINK, which included the CIA, FEMA, and the SMLC, the Department of Defense's Strategic Missile Launch Command site at Fort Madison, Iowa.

1620 HOURS

Caught completely by surprise, the NATSECLINK scrambled to activate the national civil defense alert system, planned for tomorrow when Chalmers had calculated there was an additional seventy-two-hour window for abovegrounders to seek shelter.

Fortunately, more than ninety-five percent of the selectees—those twenty million who had qualified for contingency admission to the Citations—were already in place. Left, however, were more than three hundred and forty million to scramble in the panic Chalmers had for decades sought to avoid, even as he secretly had prepared for the worst.

1635 HOURS

The Thors were primed for launch, but suddenly the alien invader was already in a maelstrom's spiral descent through the outer layer of Earth's atmosphere. Walston barked the order to "throw the hammers," but it was too late, as everyone could see on the CCB's overhead monitor.

The live video link was 3-D composite imagery from mapping satellites, intelligence collection platforms, NASA atmospheric monitors, commercial TV relay orbiters, Doppler weather, and FAA radar, even MapQuest and Google Earth.

For Chalmers, the view was satanic, the sheer scale of its horror surpassing anything he'd steeled himself to witness. Both repulsed and amazed, he watched the Voracian magma split into two monstrous funnel clouds— their impact points calculated by the DMT to be Roswell and Tidewater, just as he'd correctly surmised earlier.

1642 HOURS

Chalmers suddenly thought of the twin masses as buckets of black sewage water that had been dumped off a balcony and splashed onto a patio. Instantly responding to Chalmers's tasking, his DMT monitor grid-rendered the clouds into a 3-D holomast overlaid with a spiderweb matrix of quantum computations.

"It's like all the water from the Great Lakes pouring down in two stupendous cascades of infectious sludge," he told Walston.

Chalmers continued to stroke the glowing red virtual keyboard that floated in front of him. His fingers brushed at clusters of laser-lit holographic keys as he conducted additional analytical probes into the Voracian mass. A virtual Aurocom halo transceiver electronically ringed his head and gave him full telemetry and communication linkage with every ITP console.

"Full-phase integration," he commanded.

He and everyone else watched interpretative AIQ data flashing across an additional bank of gasmic screens embedded in the glass walls. Chalmers was particularly interested in the invading force's biometric composition.

"Bracket a single organism and give me a five-x tactic focus."

The overhead video screen blipped, then fuzzed over.

"What happened to OptiCon?"

"Sorry, sir, optic control lost signal stability," said one of the technicians.

"We're registering an atmospheric disturbance," said another IP tech.

Assessing it to be some kind of anomaly caused by the electrolic velocity of the funnels, Chalmers ran the numbers and gave technical operations a potential solution. Fortunately, the DMT-9000, already loaded with data, continued to project information.

"It's a virus," Chalmers told Walston, "probably of subatomic-particle-size originally. I imagine that after ingesting the Fiverian civilization, it gained enough strength and mass to pursue the few remaining Fiverians who fled here . . . perhaps, it now seems, to warn us."

"Well, I wish the hell somebody had listened back then," said Walston.

Chalmers continued to refine the input he received from his IP staff.

"I believe that even as they tracked their prey here, the Voracians continued to feed in outer space," said Chalmers, watching a holographic rendering materialize on-screen. "But look at that, even as they spiral down on us, each cellular alien is only the size of a flea."

"So how bad can they be, then?" asked Walston.

Chalmers stroked more keys and read the new output. "Very bad. Each one has a compressed viral toxicity equal to a ton of *Staphylococcus* infection."

"Like a necrotizing fasciitis," said Monroe. "A flesh-eating disease."

"Will it grow now that it's here?" asked Quan Shantu.

"God a'mighty, look," exclaimed Walston when live-feed video suddenly popped back on the overhead screens.

♦101♦

"The landscape in both impact zones is completely denuded," Walston said.

"Buildings, vehicles, and everything man-made is pockmarked. Like it's all been sand-blasted," Monroe said.

"Those are all microbial feeding pits where minerals and other digestible trace elements have been acidized away," said Chalmers, punching up more screen images. "But this is post–ground zero, where the Voracians *have been*. OptiCon, give me a three-point radial boost. Let's see where they are now."

"Roger. Bumping three, sir."

Remote cameras scanned, locked on new GPS coordinates, and caught the first images of unsheltered people being overrun by Voracians.

"God have mercy," Walston exclaimed. "It's roiling like black fog across no-man's-land." The images affected even the battle-hardened Walston.

Everyone else in the CCB felt their own skin crawl as they watched the front-line Voracians blanket their prey with a buzzing shroud of death. Those victims screamed until their throats clogged with gobs of black matter. Eyes melted and dripped from their sockets. Bodies twisted in agony and shook violently as tiny blood geysers jet-streamed from skin pores as alien organisms bored in to infect, then feasted back out to dissect. People, animals, birds—all blistered, bled, and dissolved away.

Those in the CCB who'd not already closed their eyes to the horror were in various stages of shock, with some gasping, gagging, or sobbing. Everyone was praying for mercy. "Dear God, deliver us from evil . . ." "The Lord is my shepherd . . ."

"Dr. Chalmers, we've reestablished focus lock," OptiCon reported.

"Good. Plus up the new imagery to biometrics," he instructed.

The Voracian ground mass was about three feet thick and instantly reminded Chalmers of "Leiningen Versus the Ants," a classic short story about a South American coffee grower whose plantation was overrun by trillions of swarming ants eating everything in their path.

"Holy shit, they're already the size of army ants," said Walston as one of the cameras zoomed in on a single Voracian.

Chalmers figured this was part of the advance column that fed first—and based on the new biometric information he now had, it grew faster than the mass of creatures slugging behind as they scraped every living insect, bacterium, and mineral from the desiccated soil.

1650 HOURS

"Look at that," said Monroe. "Frontliners are starting to feed off the back-benchers. The ugly bastards are cannibals to boot."

"And fast movers, even on the ground," said Chalmers after glancing at his DMT screen's latest update. "In the first ten minutes, the two mac-romass organisms scoured one hundred and sixty-four thousand square miles, the combined landmass of New Mexico and Virginia."

"Like a cancer that's metastasized throughout a body," said Walston.

"Exactly," said Chalmers. "Every plant, animal, and insect consumed. Minerals leached from soil and rocks. Pollen, dust, and even bacteria vacuumed from the air."

He composed himself for the next revelation. "And more than fifteen million people have been metabolized . . . ingested."

"Yea, though I walk through the valley of the shadow of death, I shall fear no evil, for thou art with me," said Mike DeLorno softly. It was the first thing he'd said all day, but he'd been at Chalmers's side the entire time. Quan Shantu had left earlier to be with Chalmers's family in the Citation condo.

Chalmers continued to work at the holographic console.

"Cannibalism has reduced each mass by twenty-three percent, but the remaining individual organisms are a thousand percent larger. I believe we can now rightfully call them creatures, if not monsters," he said, pointing to a close-up view of a rat-sized alien.

"Looks like a combination of spider, cockroach, and ant," Monroe said.

Everyone watched the creature's mandibles and multiple spidery legs move in frenzied harmony as it carried out the imperative to kill and consume. Unable to find indigenous prey, the cosmic predators continued to turn on each other—the black muck of their innards spewing out as they slaughtered and feasted upon themselves.

"John, there's a new problem," said Walston, who'd just received a separate military channel message on his own Aurocom transceiver. "They're starting to burrow into cracks and crevices. Right now that puts us, and the other Citations very soon, at SitFive-level jeopardy."

"You're the army general," said a trembling Monroe. "How do you stop them?"

"I can't. No one can."

❖102❖

"We're the only ones who know this, so far," said Chalmers, "and I doubt anything's to be gained by sharing it."

"I agree, John," said Walston. "Based on what the entire CCB has been monitoring above, this would be like hammering in a final and fatal nail."

"So do we just shut down and cower in a corner?" asked Monroe.

"Not at all," said Chalmers, his fingers returning to the keyboard. "There's new data to post, and dealing with it will keep our team, and everyone throughout this Citation, clinging to a shred of hope . . . hopefully."

The CCB's huge center core screen split into multiple panels as even more data-polling projections flashed from the DMT-9000's ruby-laser hard drive. Chalmers provided a summary announcement over his Aurocom transceiver.

"Fifty minutes from now, forty-three states will be completely denuded and an estimated two hundred and forty million people will have perished. Ten minutes after that, the continental U.S. will be a barren wasteland, and the remainder of the aboveground population will have been consumed by billions of multilegged, alligator-size aliens."

Many in the CCB who'd earlier retreated into stunned silence began to sob again.

Chalmers's life work had been to create the safe haven Citations. Knowing that everyone and everything in America was gone, he found no satisfaction that a few thousand or so might survive for a while longer in special, vaulted security sections of the deepest Citations. After the fully matured Voracians burrowed down to discover the Citations, Chalmers was uncertain how intelligent and resourceful the creatures might be at gaining entry to those vaults.

But he knew the answer even as the computer continued to forecast the final projections, which were truly Armageddon. He wasn't sure he had words grim enough to describe the situation, but everyone listened anyway.

"Several hundred million creatures approximately half the size and generally the shape of a Jurassic period *Stegosaurus* with a raptor's temperament will rule North America. They will comprise the *alphagenetrons*—the largest, most intelligent of the mixed-gender Voracians who will have survived and stabilized during their intro-evolutionary period on this planet"

A biometrically extrapolated video of the heinous creature flashed on the screen.

"They will procreate, migrate across continents, exhaust new indigenous supplies, cannibalize their own ranks, and then reestablish a new pattern of Malthusian balance somewhere else in equally short and ever-repeating time periods," said Chalmers.

"How much time?" Walston asked wearily.

"They'll bring about total global destruction within nine days."

The revelation was profound. So was the stunned silence . . . for a moment.

1700 HOURS

Suddenly, the command bunker shook violently.

Ripped from its mooring, the overhead screen crashed through the gantries, severing the terraced workstations from the high walls. Bodies were flung into free fall, the sharp screams of panicked descent replaced with the dull thud of death's impact.

"Here, Dr. Chalmers," DeLorno shouted as he pulled Chalmers to safety under a heavy metal bench. "Stay close, sir. I'll take of care you."

"Paula. Stevie. I've got to—"

"Quan's with them. They'll be fine. You'll all be together soon, I promise."

From their CCB vantage point, Chalmers, Walston, Monroe, and the others looked through the large windows and saw tons of rock and earth debris cascading down on Tidewater Citation and its trembling citizenry.

"God save us," someone cried out, "the creatures are coming in."

That wasn't true. Something else was happening, and Chalmers believed he knew what it was. And as he imagined, the best—or perhaps the worst—view of it was from high Earth orbit.

SPACE—SAME TIME

The crew had not received any transmissions about the nebula, nor had their angled view from the portals enabled them to see its funnel cloud descend through the atmosphere. Hence, blissful in their lack of current information, astronauts aboard the United Earth Space Station *Solidarity* first watched in awe as a brilliant sunset spread a blanket of wintry darkness across North America.

"How could there be trouble down there when it looks so beautiful from up here?" asked the *Solidarity*'s commander.

A second later, he and the crew watched in mesmerized uncertainty as the black night provided a backdrop for bursts of enormous chrysanthemum-shaped lights.

"What the . . . Houston, this is *Solidarity*. Do you copy? Houston, do you have a problem?"

And then the space station's lighted bank of ground-link communications instruments went black. The astronauts pressed their faces against the windows, immediately realizing it was a deadly vantage point from their now permanent imprisonment.

Far below, they saw more lights blossom as one Chinese nuclear warhead after another exploded across the land of the free and the home of the brave. Everything within an immediate radius of the several hundred impact zones was cratered and vaporized; everything else was shattered or charred by thermal energy that raked across the countryside as a concussive windstorm.

ᗏ

Thinking the Thor missiles America fired only minutes ago were a preemptive attack on China, General Zhang had ordered an immediate counterstrike on the United States.

And now, across the planet's arced horizon tinted with pale blue atmospheric light, the astronauts saw other bright flashes, which indicated to them that every other member of the nuclear club that had a beef with a fellow member had suddenly started to tip global dominoes.

Until the satellite links had gone dead—one after another due to electromagnetic pulses from nuclear detonations—Chalmers and Walston had been monitoring NASA, DOD, and other communication systems from nations around the world, and thus they had a clear picture of what had happened.

CCB. 1709 HOURS

They knew the United States had been battered and flash-fried.

Walston knew that China, if also not totally destroyed, had sustained massive damage from the counterbarrage of U.S. ICBMs that NATSE-CLINK had been preprogrammed to launch in a last-ditch retaliatory effort.

Chalmers correctly surmised that ironically China's attack had killed the Voracians—atomically sautéed in their own feculence—but it had rendered America a pile of burned rubble.

Walston's last source that had reported from the surface confirmed that China had also been devastated by Russia, which in turn was obliterated by nuclear counterstrikes from the Chinese, Iranians, and others. There was also confirmation that the Middle East could now truly be called a sandbox, and South America was a denuded wasteland, awash in radioactive water that'd been melted off the Andean glaciers.

The list of who struck whom was long and complicated, just like global circumstances that had stacked the dominoes . . . and the odds . . . in the first place.

Chalmers was now sure that voracious spacemen would not cause global destruction in nine days. Vanquished earthmen had just done it in _nine minutes._

He suddenly felt a strange sensation sweep through his body.

It was more than fatigue from the ordeal he'd just been through. It was knowledge, emotion, and the consequence of a pending event—and it frightened him more than any nightmare he'd ever experienced.

103

THE AFTERMATH. JANUARY 1, 2022

Walston and Chalmers, accompanied by DeLorno and Shantu, snaked through the rubble of Tidewater Citation. Cleanup and repair were already under way here, as well as in the other twelve colonies, whose subterranean communication systems were still operational. However, with many portions of the SpadeLiner's track now buried, transportation between them was impossible.

Walston had already appointed military-rank governors to administer the other safe havens, with democratic elections to be held later once the regional centers were repaired, and rail service, manufacturing, and commerce were reinstituted among the underground colonies.

"John, reconsider the offer," said Walston. "As a birthday gift, maybe?"

"How did you know it was my birthday, General?"

Walston nodded toward DeLorno, who quickly held up his palms in defense.

"Sir, your wife told me."

"Come to think of it, Dr. Chalmers, how old *are* you anyway?" asked Walston.

"It's like Paula has told others. Old enough to know better, but youthfully spirited enough to be impetuous, willing to make mistakes . . . and to continue making her happy."

The other three men laughed. Chalmers did not join them.

"Bill, I told you before, I'm flattered by the offer to be Tidewater's governor, but it would be a mistake I'm unwilling and, frankly, unable to make—precisely because of my age . . . and what I sense to be my failing health."

"Whatever your age," said Walston, "you're obviously still strong and robust."

Chalmers shrugged and gave a little snort. The truth hurt him. Literally.

"Sometimes age is what you think, even more than what you feel. And right now I think I'm tired of scrambling around with you guys and I *know* I want to get back to the condo. It's Stevie's birthday, too, and I want to spend time with him, make a memory and share some I have about his father. Today is also Steven's birthday. Seems like Chalmers men have always been born on the first day of a new year."

Aware of the personal, introspective comments Chalmers had just shared with them, Walston felt he needed to add some appropriate final words before returning.

"It is a new year, and this is a new world for us, John. One that affords promise for a future we'd never have were it not for the decades you spent creating the Citations."

"Bill, you need a new quote, and one from Albert Einstein works perfectly."

"And that is . . . ?"

His legs suddenly trembling, Chalmers took in a deep, obviously painful breath.

"'The distinction between past, present, and future is only a stubbornly persistent illusion.'" Chalmers looked at DeLorno and Shantu. "I need some help, boys. Please take me home to Paula." He was already missing her more than he could bear.

104

CITATION CONDO. LATER

After they'd escorted him to the bedroom, DeLorno and Shantu had set off to run other errands Chalmers assigned them down in the Level II laboratory. DeLorno had then returned with Stevie, who had remained for some time thereafter with his grandfather.

When Paula had arrived, she was immediately distraught by how her husband looked, and even more so by the things he said—and especially *how* he said them . . . to include his firm insistence that he didn't need or want a doctor, since it was too late anyway. She protested, but he was intractable.

She'd given him water and checked his temperature—hoping he was *only* developing pneumonia. Chalmers had alternated between talking with her and slipping suddenly into unconsciousness, which she more gently had thought of as a nap. But as she watched his eyes grow more fatigued each time he awoke—and sensing, too, what he'd told her about the feeling in his own bones—Paula's eyes remained full of tears throughout the day, knowing that her husband's life was ending.

2230 HOURS

She and Stevie were seated at the side of Chalmers's bed.

"You'll be here a long time," he said slowly. "This cavern is your new world . . . with a promise for sunshine again someday."

Paula smiled bravely at Stevie. "Grampa's right, you have many hopes and dreams still to be realized."

"And there is someone you must become . . . and many important things you must do," said Chalmers, his voice now more labored. "I gave your grandma some envelopes, they're in . . ."

"The desk drawer," she finished for him.

"Yes. Give them to Mike and Quan in the morning."

Stevie nodded, tears washing his face as his grandfather's eyes slowly closed.

2345 HOURS

A thin smile stretched across his sallow face as he reopened his eyes and found Paula and Stevie still holding his hands. He gave no thought to whether his life would flash before his eyes in the last second, but he wanted to tell them all he could in these final minutes.

"Your love has been everything . . . a blessing that will be in my soul forever."

"Jonathan, no, my darling," she cried out as he closed his eyes again.

"No, not yet," he said, eyelids lifting slowly as he clutched Stevie's hand tighter. "There's something special only a very smart and strong young man can handle for me."

"Yes, Grampa."

Chalmers slowly placed his hand on the left side of the boy's head, covering his ear. "You have me in here now. The headache will go away soon and you'll forget about it, but remember, my boy—the clue and key, the Crystal . . . and Collabros."

Stevie wiped tears and nodded. "I'll remember, Grampa. All of it."

"They're your entrustments, son. You must do everything I've prepared you for," Chalmers said as he glanced over the youngster's shoulder at the stainless-steel roller-wheeled table—its contents covered by the cloth De-Lorno had draped over it before he'd left Chalmers and the boy earlier this morning.

"Yes, Grampa," he said as he squared his shoulders. "You are my grandfather now, and I am your Steven. I'll do everything you said."

2355 HOURS

His tired eyes managed to twinkle, as they'd always done when focused on her.

"You've been the sole star in my galaxy, Paula. My only fear is the darkness of my next world without you. I'm more frightened about leaving than I imagined."

"Oh, my love," she sobbed, "there's been no greater joy in my life than you."

2359 HOURS

Chalmers placed his wife's right hand over his heart and his grandson's left hand over his forehead. "Heart and Soul . . . always as one . . . forever."

They fell into his embrace and held on tightly.

2400 HOURS—MIDNIGHT

God, look over them, he prayed. Then Chalmers exhaled his last breath.

105

Continuing to carry out his list of instructions, DeLorno and Shantu now stood by Chalmers's side in a final moment of silent respect.

♠

As Chalmers had informed them on the morning of his death, he long ago had discovered that a narrow fissure below the SpadeLiner's arrival platform at Tidewater Citation led to an extraordinarily beautiful geode—a hollow rock cavity infused with crystal, mineral, and dripstone formations, one of which was a prominent snow-white stalactite hanging dead center from the chamber's ceiling. Crawling into it back then, he'd discovered that the chamber walls consisted of pure kyanite, a silicate mineral whose name was derived from the Greek word *kuanos,* meaning "deep blue."

Mesmerized by the magical aurora of blue light that had filled the chamber when his lantern's beam struck the walls, Chalmers had immediately decided this one spot represented the theme of the entire CRYPTOS project—that in a cave's dark retreat there still could be found a blue sky's promise.

And as he'd explained to DeLorno and Shantu, Chalmers was also drawn to the interesting convergence of coincidental similarity between the Greek words *Cryptos* and *kuanos.* He had decided that day this was the place he wanted to be buried if ever he died in the Citation he'd been driven to construct and was forced to occupy because of circumstances at the time.

♠

Following this morning's public eulogy delivered by Governor General Walston in Tidewater Citation's main-cavern chamber, DeLorno and Shantu had maneuvered Chalmers's stainless-steel casket down to the kuanos geode.

"What do you think is in it?" DeLorno finally said after he and Shantu had finished Chalmers's second instruction—the placement of another small stainless-steel box under the metal stand that supported the casket, which was located directly beneath the stalactite.

"No idea. Everything about the guy was some kind of mystery. I mean, the way he looked when we took him out of the room the next morning . . . it was like, or at least reminded me of . . ."

"I know. The painting in the attic," said DeLorno.

"Good thing Mrs. Chalmers didn't see him in the casket like that."

"Maybe that's why he left orders that it be closed, no viewing at the service."

Shantu nodded. "Yeah, it's spooky, don't you think?"

"I think it's ironic."

"What does that mean?"

DeLorno looked around the small chamber. "That Dr. Chalmers spent a lifetime making unbelievable preparations for us to be able to survive a nuclear war. In fact, he said he'd spent two lifetimes at the task, which I thought at the time was only a joke. But now I'm not sure it was."

"So where's the irony?"

"That he made the preparations for the wrong kind of attack, but it turned out that we survived the second one because he had originally anticipated war anyway."

"Like I said, Mike, it's all spooky. Let's get outta here."

On their way to the top, they heard rumbling from below.

"Sounds like a cave-in," said DeLorno. "Better go back down and check."

"No way. Earthquake, demolition derby, or a poltergeist rampage . . . I'm not going back, and according to the instructions no one is supposed to until the so-called designated day arrives—one the kid will know. The envelope, remember?"

DeLorno gave a reluctant nod and both men made their way to the high cave.

Having ripped a wider opening in the fissure to accommodate his bulk, Kaj'a-zar burst into the geode, his faceted eyes seeing everything in iridescent hues of glimmering yellow-green.

"*Ch'al-murs,*" he growled in his rough version of human speech with which he had gained impressive comprehension skills over many years, though lesser talent at articulation. =ηακψυ= Continuing in the convenience of his own language, he added, =φ λφαζ ατε= *For you and yours I told you I would come someday.*

Paying no attention to the small box, he picked up the larger one and carried it deeper into the cavern's endless depth, where Kaj'a-zar believed it really belonged.

Part IX

THE MIDNIGHT
BELLS TOLL

106

He glanced at his m-comm, a multiplexed computation and communication device also worn as a wristwatch. "You whitecaps ready to pull a transit?"

The two gray-haired men nodded. They were, as he also called them, his squad. Chalmers activated the switch.

In moments, the SpadeLiner's single tubular coach had reached full speed and was automatically controlled by RIMS, the rail integrity measurement system that ensured the track ahead was sound and the tunnel unimpeded.

"How do you feel about this? Apprehensive? Excited, maybe, like me?"

"I'd say both," said Mike DeLorno.

"I'll let you know on the return trip, Dr. Chalmers," said a cautious Quan Shantu glancing at the Level-A hazmat suits draped on the seats across the aisle.

"You guys have known me over forty years. Ever going to call me just Steve?"

Both grinned and shook their heads.

Director of Tidewater's Institute for Substratic Research, Dr. Steven J. Chalmers had refined the ISR's science of underground survival and designed future plans for surface emergence when the world above was finally safe from radioactive contamination. Chalmers had recently undertaken an a'bounder—an aboveground atmospheric test using ISR's newest DMT computer, the 11000X series, which he'd engineered from his grandfather's first-generation DMT. He had decided that radiation levels were low enough for the first sustained surface excursion since the war'acian.

Everyone in all thirteen colonies knew there'd been a war, but it was not until afterward, when Voracian stories had begun to circulate, that Walston officially confirmed they had also been invaded by aliens. In view of everything that had already happened, the big reveal caused little more than a ripple. However, the combined events became known as war'acian, another new term to emerge in a rapidly evolving vocabulary.

ᴋᴀ

"Glad you're with me today," said Chalmers, "and I promise I'll get us back to Tidewater without anybody glowing too brightly."

DeLorno and Shantu spoke in unison. "Okay." "That'll be good."

"Let's check the gear again, we're almost there," said Chalmers.

DeLorno removed the Autovolt from his hip holster and checked the charge. *Thirty plazers, each with 1000 kV,* he noted.

One plazer, or a plasma laser burst, packed enough electrical wallop to shatter a piece of thick timber and to knock out a man instantly. He couldn't imagine any a'bounder threats, but he'd brought it along figuring it was better to be safe than sorry.

Shantu reviewed the checklist for various atmospheric instruments to be used.

Chalmers recalibrated the master radametric dial and the other radiation detection instruments on the suits.

He also thought again, as he'd done every day, about the four trusts empowered to him by his grandfather: the clue and key, the crystal and Collabros. And he was becoming more anxious by the minute, knowing that soon he'd undergo a unique test involving one of the four trusts. The others, he knew, would unfold over the days and years of many tomorrows—time that his grandfather had said passed exactly as his friend Einstein had calculated: *relatively fast.*

Exactly how I got from yesterday to today, Chalmers reflected.

ᴋᴀ

Under Walston's disciplined military rule and Cliff Monroe's technical management skill, the original fifteen-hundred-seventy-five-mile length of the North–South SpadeLiner Express was repaired and fully functional less than a decade after the war'acian. For the past twenty-five years, a new east–west boring operation had been under way; when finished the Bicoastal SpadeLiner Express would continue past Carlsbad Cavernation, now the fifteenth and largest Citation. The other new Citation was Missamec, an expansion of the Meramec cave which had been the largest tourist cavern in the then-state of Missouri.

Chalmers hoped that one day soon he'd visit Nava'darnia, which had become the new west coast after Chinese nukes triggered the San Andreas Fault that in turn unleashed the earthquake separating the former aboveground states of California and Nevada. As Chalmers knew from satellite photo images, the Cali'waiian Islands were now prominent landmarks on the Pacific horizon. The old island of Santa Catalina was gone, swept away by a three-hundred-foot-high tsunami.

Tidewater Citation had been monitoring surface information for years through the only orbiting surveillance platform still functioning. Chalmers had reprogrammed one of his grandfather's old DMT-9000 computers to communicate with a CIA cold war–era reconnaissance satellite. Hard-wired with dated but resilient components impervious to electromagnetic pulse damage, the tough old bird had survived the EMP bursts that'd de-stroyed other higher-tech video-communication platforms in orbit dur-ing the global hot war.

Chalmers had taught himself, in part from the countless technical and other research notes his grampa had made. More significant, he *literally* possessed his grandfather's knowledge, because on the day of Jonathan Chalmers's death, Mike DeLorno had brought a small portacart version of the old BK-PULSE instrumentation up from the Level II laboratory. And with Jonathan's supervision, DeLorno had lasermetrically copied selected portions of the cerebral wiring diagram of the elder Chalmers's remarkable mind . . . and then pasted them into young Steven's.

A double-dosed savant, Steven Chalmers had ultimately assumed Tidewater's mantle of knowledgeable leadership. He had become not only the founder of the ISR but also director of the Task Force K technical-security group after Clifford Monroe had died of a heart attack. Walston had lost his battle with cancer. Grandmother Paula had simply died of a broken heart.

These, and so many other events—all in Chalmers's eye-blink life un-derground . . .

SHORT TIME LATER

They had arrived at Old Langley Station, directly below what had been the CIA.

"Ready?" Chalmers asked, looking up through the debris-strewn ele-vator shaft and feeling the historic consequence, past and future, of this moment.

Nodding, DeLorno and Shantu shouldered their gear.

"If we're not back down here in fifty-two minutes," said Shantu, check-ing his m-comm readings, "these suits will turn into old-fashioned micro-wave ovens and we'll be fried and good-byed."

DeLorno adjusted one of Chalmers's straps. "Mind the sharp edges while climbing. Torn suit's no good either."

Chalmers took the lead as he spelunkered up through a fractured shaft of concrete, metal, cables, and granite boulders.

The climb was hard and consumed half of their surface time.

❖107❖

Emerging from the shaft, they turned in all directions, taking in the panorama of a truly alien world. It was a surreal landscape—everything beneath a canopy that didn't even remotely resemble how they remembered Earth's sky.

"Ten times more bizarre than the grainy satphos we've seen," Chalmers said, referring to the old generation satellite photos.

He didn't need instruments to know the air was unbreathable—not just because radioactive toxins were still chemically welded to normal atmospheric gases but also because the air was supersaturated with soil, concrete, and other grit that had been pulverized in the chain-reaction blasts that had atomized the planet. Sandblasting in their effect, these particulates blew in the incessant wind that formed part of a hot jet stream that now swept low across the scorched wasteland.

The three men watched long streamers of brownish-orange clouds snake rapidly in higher currents across a pale yellow sky still ripe with the bruise of atmospheric disaster. The blurry sun cast jaundiced shadows across the mound of rubble that once was the Agency's twin headquarters buildings.

But this was a time for clue searching, not sightseeing for Chalmers.

He made a visual sweep of the nearby ground area and immediately spotted it.

The discovery struck him as amazingly simple or a fateful convergence of coincidence. Either way, DeLorno and Shantu followed as Chalmers headed for the aluminum columns, badly pitted and leaning slightly but still attached to the trim, right-angled slabs of rusty steel punctuated with thousands of alphabetic letters.

Based on what his grandfather had told him, Chalmers knew this sculpture had been made for a farsighted purpose in the past—but now, here in the present, the artwork once known as *Cryptos* was about to deliver, or so Chalmers hoped, an even greater and farsighted message about the future.

ॐ

"This was the last thing we looked at from your grandfather's office window before we evacuated him," said DeLorno. "How in God's name can it still be here?"

"He told us no one ever figured out the code," said Shantu.

Letters reflecting off his faceplate, Chalmers stared in silence at the mon.

"This trip's not about radiation testing," said DeLorno, remembering the envelopes he and Shantu were given a long time ago. "It's about decoding *Cryptos,* isn't it?"

Thinking for a second about how to answer, Chalmers remembered all the stories he had learned from his grandmother—the truth of his grampa's age, the divine revelations the old man believed he'd experienced, and the psychological as well as brutal physical experiences he had endured throughout his remarkable life, especially in the First World War.

"This sculpture contains *two* secret messages," he finally said. "One created by the artist as an intellectual game. The other embedded by Grampa as intellectual and technical insurance for the future."

"So, based on what happened the morning he died, I guess you already know what the message is. And if that's the case, then why are we here?" asked DeLorno.

Chalmers paused, scanning again the vast destruction around them and checking the radiation reading on his m-comm. "Mike, as improbable and dangerous as this journey is," he said, making direct eye contact with DeLorno, "I believe my grandfather intended it to be a rite of passage for me . . . the actual gut feeling of a challenge rather than just the memory of one artificially inseminated into my brain."

"You're probably right. I don't think he knew for sure if the procedure would transfer feeling along with fact," said DeLorno, remembering how reluctant he'd been to conduct the application in the first place. "It would be like him, though, to analytically deduce this was the right thing to do."

"And he may have given me only certain of his mental files in any event."

"I don't have a clue what you guys are talking about," said Shantu, who had not been present for the BK-PULSE memory transfer that Dr. Chalmers had ordered DeLorno to administer to young Stevie at his grandpa's deathbed vigil. "But we're burning valuable time here."

Since Chalmers did not already know the sculpture's message, he was going to have to study it for however long it took. He believed, however, that he was ready for any challenge this a'bounder might present.

The minor vibration he felt under his feet and the slight rumble he thought he heard through his helmet told him he might not be ready after all.

108

"It's truly artistic," Chalmers said, dismissing the minor rumbling beneath him as he began to trace his gloved fingers and focus his savant's eyes over the letters. Like DeLorno, he, too, thought it was rather interesting that the sculpture was the only thing still standing.

Recalling everything his grandfather had ever told or otherwise passed along to him, Chalmers quickly worked the mathematic cipher and read the first-tier message.

"The enemy of my enemy is my friend," he read aloud. "I don't know what the artist meant at the time, but now, in retrospect, I'd say it's a perfect allusion to the Chinese burning down our house even as they exterminated the Voracians infesting it."

"Front and back follow each other," he continued. "That's an aphorism from the ancient Chinese philosopher Lao Tzu. Perfect for a fortune cookie, perhaps even a prelude for what Grampa layered underneath."

"But there's something else, right?" asked Shantu.

There was, and within seconds Chalmers had found it—his grandfather's clues for locating the entrustments. There, in plain alphabetic sight, for Chalmers's eyes only, were the directions to the box and the mallet sequences for both sets of tritone notes. He kept that information to himself.

"Well, that's it," he said with simple softness. "Let's go home, guys."

"Whoa, what's *it*? What's the rest of the message?" DeLorno blurted.

"Let's discuss it on the train," said Shantu firmly, looking at his m-comm. "We're almost out of time."

As they headed for the shaft, the building debris began to vibrate and rumble beneath their feet. This time everyone sensed it.

"What the hell?" said DeLorno.

Suddenly, an ugly living *thing*—an appendage or tentacle of some kind, Chalmers immediately assessed—exploded through the rubble. Before anyone could move a step or utter another word, the approximately ten-foot-long tentacle whiplashed Shantu's body. It cut him in half and splattered Chalmers and DeLorno with bloody viscera.

They started to run but were knocked to the ground when the rubble pile shifted and the rest of the deadly appendage emerged. Scrambling back to his feet, Chalmers saw that what had killed Shantu was a tail, and it was attached to an alien beast that towered over him and DeLorno.

"Run, damn it! Get down the shaft," yelled DeLorno, drawing the Autovolt.

He pumped all thirty plazer rounds into the prehistoric-looking creature. Stunned, it roared, clawed at its skin, and slung slobber from its hideous mouth. DeLorno fumbled for another magazine.

"Not without you," said Chalmers, grabbing DeLorno by the arm.

Breaking free, DeLorno shoved Chalmers in the direction of the shaft just as the monster lunged toward them. Now running, Chalmers heard behind him the hissing spit of the plazer strikes and the angry howl of the demonic creature. He turned, expecting to see DeLorno a few steps behind, but instead he saw the creature swallowing the last of his body.

Chalmers was only steps away from the safety of the shaft, but he could hear the pursuer closing on him and felt its breath on his back. Suddenly, Chalmers stumbled and on his way down caught a glimpse of a shadowy blur as he fell onto a large chunk of granite. Immediately scrambling backward on his haunches and looking for another venue of escape, he was surprised to see that the marauder had vanished.

An instant later, Chalmers heard the sound of crashing rocks. Looking to his right, he watched as that creature tumbled head over horned heels, locked in fierce combat with a second one, which Chalmers figured was the blur that had come out of nowhere and tackled the first one an instant before it would have devoured him.

The new monster—clearly a different species, Chalmers noted, but no less gigantic and equally ugly—quickly slaughtered the other one.

Before he could get to his feet, the victor turned on the still-cowering Chalmers, whose escape route in any event was blocked by the slab of granite behind his back.

Chalmers braced for death as the new creature leaned forward and opened its jagged-tooth mouth. A putrid stench steamed out. Amazingly, so did what an astonished Chalmers believed could only be words. It was talking to him. What the hell was it?

Wide-eyed, he listened to its guttural articulation . . . one cluster of sounds being something he could not have mistaken, one recognizable *word* that sent chilled plazers down his spine.

109

THE RUBBLE. SAME TIME

"Ch'al-murs," Kaj'a-zar said in graveled human-speak.

It knows my name? Chalmers thought. *How can it speak my name?* Before he could think further about whether, when, or how this thing that seemed to know him was about to slaughter him, his bizarre interlocutor continued.

=ηακψν,= Kaj'a-zar said, less roughly in his own phonetics, which Chalmers noted with interest—if not as a sign of optimistic hope—were accompanied by agile, demonstrative hand movements. Though his huge fingers were talon tipped and bloody, the hands nonetheless gestured in a manner that suggested to Chalmers the creature was communicating something . . . well, almost sensitive, maybe peaceful, he let himself wish.

=ηακψν ℏϖιεδ ωηιθζ,= added Kaj'a-zar, then repeated coarsely what he hoped was a comprehensible translation: *"tank far-mah lay'va."*

Chalmers wanted to think there was something to understand, wanted to believe he was hearing this creature, this being, try to communicate with him in English. But it was incredible, so impossible . . . and he was, he realized, in such a degree of shock that he could not form his own words, truly though he wanted to—especially now that he recognized an unmistakable intelligence in the eyes of this alien entity.

"Where . . ." Chalmers hesitated as he struggled to finish the sentence *Where are you from?* that he was trying to ask the creature who he now believed might actually also understand English.

=ηιχη= *There,* Kaj'a-zar said in his Fiverian tongue, pointing to the nearby elevator shaft, which he believed this cowering human creature had been trying to enter in order to escape from the now-dead Voracian.

In the second Chalmers had glanced to see what was being pointed toward, and in even less time than it had taken him to turn his head around, Kaj'a-zar had stood and taken a step backward.

"*Guh om,*" he said as he pivoted and leaped onto his former adversary's carcass, ripping off a hindquarter and feasting as he stomped away.

⊷

Disappearing into a jagged crevice, Kaj'a-zar hoped he had been able to express his sentiments in comprehensible fashion. He had always wanted to convey a proper ηακιψυ, to say even more than *thank you for my life* to the human Chalmers.

As Kaj'a-zar had vowed long ago, *I will someday come for you and yours.* Today was that day.

He had just killed the marauder that had intended to kill the ωαελ—the egg-spore offspring of the first, parental Chalmers. Without that human's initial life-giving experiments, Kaj'a-zar knew he would never have been birthed from his own dead mother's womb and could never have subsequently produced his own extended family of Fiverians. His debt now paid, Kaj'a-zar descended into the crack that led to a deep kingdom where he reigned as lord of a new, though only temporary, Fiverian world.

⊷

With no idea what this mind-boggling event he'd just gone through had actually meant and with his legs still shaking from the brush with death, Chalmers nonetheless had managed to get up and make his way to the shaft moments after the alien persona departed.

Though he'd not understood all the English-like utterances, Chalmers had definitely known what "*goh om*" meant.

Astonished to be alive, he struggled down the elevator shaft and boarded the train, still shaken but now at least confident he would return home safely. Riding in silent sorrow, he mourned his friends and vowed, as a commitment to their lost lives, that he would never waste a single opportunity his own life still afforded him.

⊷

It seemed like only a moment later that he stepped off the coach at Tidewater Station, ready to follow directions sleuthed from his grandfather's clues. Chalmers walked a relatively short distance to a narrow passage that adjoined the very chamber where his grandfather's, and now his own, CSC office and Task Force K laboratories were located.

Back where I started.

He smiled. It was just like his grampa to send him on a scavenger hunt.

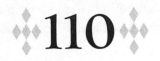

110

TIDEWATER STATION. EVENING

Finding the lantern where he knew it would be, Chalmers entered the obscure passage and navigated deeper down the walkway. It led to a mineral-encrusted geode with a single stalactite hanging from the ceiling. Although the stalactite was radiantly white, it was the extraordinary blue radiance of the small chamber that most impressed him.

Knowing from his grandmother that his grandfather had requested to be buried somewhere deeper within the cave, Chalmers half-expected to find his casket here, and indeed it looked like one might have rested on the two metal brackets at one time.

It was also just like Grampa, he thought, to have disappeared from his own sarcophagus. No matter. What he was supposed to find was here.

In a small metal box directly beneath the stalactite was an old five-bar pitch-tune xylophone and percussion mallet. When Chalmers struck the three musical notes for *bing-bong-bing*, he watched something magical occur.

The stalactite began to emit a soft bass hum that grew in intensity as the calcium carbonate formation became exceptionally brilliant, flooding the geode chamber with a surreal celestial blue light. The stalactite also began to melt, dissipating as a white mist into the chamber's blue ambience.

Suddenly, a pear-shaped crystal—which the elder Chalmers had known how to embed, probably with instructions from the Samaritan, Steven figured—tumbled from the formation's open bottom. It came to an abrupt stop and floated, Chalmers could see, a few inches above the cave floor. He knelt and took it in his hands.

He felt no discomfort as he cradled the cold Crystal and stared into its deep clarity. He knew from his grandfather's description, as well as the old man's inserted memory, that this was the Crystal Tabula—the divine instrument of limitless knowledge the elder Chalmers had explored extensively and from which he had made many discoveries.

ᚹ

One of them, a secret compartment within the Crystal, contained the blueprint for a machine his grandfather knew was called Collabros, which could be built only when Earth's technology had evolved to the degree required to bring forth a heavenly miracle. Such, it had seemed to his grandfather, was God's ultimate definition of human evolution, or so it was that Chalmers had explained to his grandson during the deathbed revelations.

As his grandfather had told him that day, Steven and only Steven was entrusted with the responsibility to take the elder Chalmers's countless records and his many advances in computer science to the next evolutionary level—building a computational tool that was able, in turn, to assemble Collabros.

The grandson's DMT-11000X was such a tool. And by reversing the xylophone's tune, a simple *bong-bing-bong* had revealed within the infinite Crystal Tabula yet another eternal door behind which Collabros waited to be technologically brought to life.

ᚹ

Dr. Steven Chalmers knew from his grandfather, who had learned it from the Prime Samaritan called Won, that Collabros was a gift to Earth, like fire and the wheel had been, and it was entrusted to mankind through the evolutionary lineage of one man. That man's progenitors, Steven knew, had included his grandfather and now him as well as other of his own descendants still to come.

If properly built and used for collaborative goodwill, the instructional gift would serve as a celestial energizer that converted light into any solid building material or product imaginable, whereafter it would generate an endless source of power to drive any and all other things that could be *conceived to be constructed.*

~*All you have to do to make anything happen,*~ Won had shared with Chalmers, who had detailed the event to his grandson, ~*is truly believe, to have faith that you can make* everything *you imagine happen provided it is for a good and noble cause.*~

ᚹ

The simple truth—as Steven Chalmers realized and that his own son learned over the course of advancing time—was that believing in truth and goodness, of oneself and in the divine power of a singular almighty force, could always achieve what seemed to be miracles.

And as time continued to unfold, Steven and subsequent generations of Chalmers sons presided over the building of a new, one-world civilization that was rich in comfort, free of pain, and spiritually luxurious. Green plants and a blue sky were again seen on the surface. Along with new cities beautiful in design and full of robust people whose lives were tranquil and devoted to goodwill.

It was a Noble outcome considering all the ignoble events that had preceded it.

111

For more than two thousand years, every Chalmers descendant had been an only child, and always a male savant. Considering it a rite of passage and definitely an honored family tradition, each of the successive sons—first with his father and later as an adult perhaps seeking a thoughtful, escapist moment—had traveled to a sandy beach where he would remain long enough to witness the Perseids meteor shower that obligingly had fallen the same time every year since the beginning of time.

That was the case this evening for the only member of the Chalmers lineage left on Earth. With no son of his own to pass along the importance of this event, Chalmers nonetheless looked forward to seeing again what his own father had shared with him many years ago.

But he was also out here waiting for the onset of a darkness that he hoped would provide its own brand of illumination about an array of other things he'd long had on his mind, to include solitude and loneliness.

Like all his predecessors, Chalmers knew that these meteors, when they'd first rained down on Earth, were thought to have carried fire-borne seeds of life from outer space. Would the streaking fire trails for which he waited this year deliver the same stellar material that comprised his genetic makeup? What exactly had he and mankind actually amounted to after countless evolutionary millennia . . . after the endlessly predictable deluge of Perseids?

What, he found himself wondering all the time, was the point of living a serene and gentle life whose every natural challenge had been obviated by the universal ease and goodness of having achieved true Nobility?

Collabros had long ago made obsolete the need to perform physical labor. Like everyone else, Chalmers's thin arms and elongated fingers served only to point at lighted activation buttons that made virtually anything that needed to happen actually occur, usually in near-instant fashion. Seldom did he even use his willow-reed legs to walk, instead aero-ambulating as he'd done down this beach using the contour jet pulsers that comprised his levitational footwear.

Expecting any moment for the first meteor to sketch its lighted line across the darkened sky, Chalmers suddenly thought of mankind's age-less question about what remains after the sentient nature of having been alive is supplanted by death. The answer was simple, really. He realized that the only way to know what followed something that had already pre-ceeded itself was to *be whatever it was that came next.*

And ironically, a mere second later, he witnessed an unmistakable message being scribbled across the heavens. He watched in awe as a con-vergence of consequence spelled out what was going to happen next, while also providing a definitive answer about the meaning of Chalmers's life . . . and the fate of mankind.

Having long accepted that in his Noble world truth was always good and beautiful, Chalmers realized he'd just caught a glimpse of the ugly reality about almighty power . . . and what it could do when driven by an-ger and vengeance.

112

OUTSIDE. MIDNIGHT

The knowledge of ancient war'acian history was barely a drop in the sea of information coffered within his savant's mind, so Chalmers instantly deduced that the magnitude of meteoric light streaming down came *not* from the Perseids, which were composed of relatively small chunks of widely dispersed celestial debris. The Perseids were definitely in the sky tonight, though lost in the convergent coincidence of an altogether different-scale celestial event simultaneously unfolding.

Calculating the unavoidable outcome and realizing the futility of fleeing from the massive cascade of huge asteroids, he simply stood mesmerized as countless chunks of Saturn's rings—which had been torn free when the Voracians had ripped past on their infectious rendezvous with Earth more than two thousand years ago—now belatedly and with a predator's intent lunged toward the peaceful blue planet.

Flaming trails of death lit the sky, setting off thundering compression explosions as the thin, overmatched atmosphere put forth a pointless defense to repel this wave of cosmic invaders.

Chalmers knew that moments from now he would experience either the meaningless *End* of everything sentient . . . or the limitless vista of a new *Beginning* that would surely be surreal.

Calm and resigned to his choices, Chalmers inhaled his last breath of refreshing night air, holding it as a savored treat until the impacts destroyed everything.

HIGH STASIS—TIMELESS

Measured even by the standard of his own Samaritan realm, everything was accelerating almost beyond his comprehension as Won felt the star-blurring pull of the Hastening. It was Ga'Lawed's almighty force that Won knew hurled him toward the unknown Meg'etheral and some form of

Ascension he would experience once he had reached his destination at the Iris Portal.

He was saddened to see, though he'd suspected as much from the outset of today's unique mission, that humans and their humanity had just become extinct—scorched from the residue of a saturnine firestorm ignited earlier by voracious hatred.

Willing to depart, he nonetheless struggled against the Hastening's grip, for he wanted to see every remaining sectic of this world's evolutionary process he could.

His last glimpse of the planet—which by his knowledge of its time measurement he knew would be the year 10,000—revealed the emergence, as always had seemed to be the case with Earth, of new forms of life. Won knew by the time anything of interest happened to the newly evolved inhabitants that he, and today as it applied to him, would be over.

In less than the partial sectic of Won's final moment in High Stasis, he was able to see that a colony of Fiverians had been bred from Kaj'a-zar. They had flourished deep in their own underground enclave, where they still worshipped at a special shrine. It was a stainless-steel casket bearing the body of their collective Father, the Chalmerian who had given life on Earth to Kaj'a-zar and all who legend proclaimed had been destined to come from him.

They had long ago come to refer to the Father as *Hez'a-Dod*, for He who delivered our destiny.

Won was able to witness Kaj'a-zar's clan rise to the surface and follow their King. He wore his long-awaited Tyrannical Crown and trod powerfully across yet another new landscape foliated from the seeds of time.

Similarly, a few Voracians, whom Won had seen burrow belowground prior to the atomic fire, had also flourished. And after eons, they, too, came to the planet's rehabilitated surface in search of the Fiverians . . . their genetically encoded adversary.

Always fascinated by the way Ga'Lawed employed his carefully crafted convergence of coincidence, Won strained long enough to take a fading glance back at the two new Earth species. He knew that as warriors they would—for at least some time—possess their own Nobility and time-honored traditions.

Won found it ironic and appropriate that they would call themselves

Tyrannosaurus and *Stegosaurus*. As he knew from his Headmaster's syllabus taught earlier today, these alien dinosaurs would be locked in a titanic battle. And they would again rule Earth, as he knew they had in a previous beginning.

But even as Won blinked into his new trajectory toward the Iris Portal, so, too, had time winked its cosmic eye toward Earth, fast-forwarding the dinosaurs through a hundred-million-year life span and to their ordained extinction once again.

Wondering if perhaps they would be replaced by something different tomorrow morning when Ga'Lawed awoke, Won dismissed himself and spiritually dissolved from today's working realm.

EPILOGUE

IRIS PORTAL—EVENT HORIZON

Having made the journey in no time at all, Won already hovered in a new High Stasis even as he had left the old one. Though the travel was instant, there had been ample time for him to analyze his circumstance and to draw what his own faith told him were correct conclusions about the Meg'etheral—the new realm he would enter by Ascension through the Iris Portal. He looked now upon that portal.

It was a hazel-blue accretion disk at the core of a celestial body unlike any he'd ever witnessed—a Divine Galaxy, as he knew it to be in his heart and soul—that dwarfed the horizon of any GoodWill journey he had ever taken for Ga'Lawed.

It was clear to Won that a convergence of galactic circumstance had brought him to this moment so he could see and be seen by the Eye of Ga'Lawed. Now he was poised to accept Ga'Lawed's will, good or bad.

Suddenly, Won had an overwhelming sense of the Eye's presence. He felt its magnifying focus on him and, in turn, his sensation of being drawn to the Eye.

Indeed, he had been pulled into the vortex of a crystal tube. Glancing back as he accelerated into the tube, he saw that all the galaxies in the cosmos had worked their way around full circle during the eternal day, compressing now into a single dot of light. It was like a punctuation point at the end of time's sentence, he thought, or like the last lamp's bulb to be flicked off at bedtime.

Then there was nothing but profound darkness.

He figured Ga'Lawed was now asleep . . . but he was wrong.

Abruptly exiting the tube, Won saw a strange new light and experienced a shocking epiphany. As part of being stripped of his Samaritan title, Vor had been sent to a hellish imprisonment through this same portal. The sensation was more than just a shock.

For the first time in his existence, Won felt fear of the unknown.

THE SANATORIUM, DAWN

Having worked through what seemed to her like an eternally long night of peering through the research monoscope, Dr. Savantha Gahlaud suddenly looked up—her singularly beautiful hazel-blue eye wide in excitement. Returning to the eye lens portal, she directed the micropipette, a crystal extraction tube, into the dark liquid matter on the glass slide. The slide held more than dark energy, it contained a galaxy of curative possibilities for her.

Miraculously, her search had ended. She had found what she'd been looking for. It was the start of a new day for everything she had in mind. So much to do. So little time.

"I have won," she said with pride, knowing she had just discovered the one true antibody she needed in the race to save her patient—a demented victim of insanity who threatened to infect everyone with his virulence and voracious appetite for evil.

Gahlaud placed the tube's contents in a small centrifuge and prepared her serum. She glanced for a moment at her comatose patient, lying naked on the examination table with his arms firmly strapped down.

She finished her work, filled the syringe, and turned again to face the prone body.

She cried out in disbelief as she stared at the table—for her patient was gone, at least for the most part. All that remained were bloody arm stumps that had been ripped from the missing body's shoulder sockets as the patient had torn himself free.

Gahlaud trembled with fear. Not from the scene before her, but from the unknown apparitions that she knew would again confront her and her world. She and the good souls who served her had worked long and hard to contain this crazed individual here in the Sanatorium where he could be treated. Gahlaud had spent forever trying to find a cure for his illness.

She had been seconds away from effecting the greatest cure of all time. And now he was free again.

Suddenly, Gahlaud saw a shadow loom large on the wall in front of her. It was her worst nightmare. Gahlaud's patient had managed to get behind her and was poised to infect her heart and soul with his vile intentions.

Syringe in hand, she turned to face her archenemy.

His name was Lucifer Sa'tan.

As he rose to his full, maniacal stature, vulture wings unfolded from

Sa'tan's blood-soaked shoulder blades, and his horned head turned blackish-red as smoldering sweat dripped from the enlarged pores of his hellish face. Now towering over her, his ghoulish mouth twisted into a hungry, voracious sneer.

It was his place to consume her, body and soul. It was her spiritual will to resist.

He was Evil. She was Good.

Only time would tell if Gahlaud had marshaled a Samaritan to assist her in restoring Nobility, and only at war's end would she know if she actually had won. In the interim, she braced for another eternal battle for supremacy between antithetical forces.

And as it always did, today's round of timeless conflict would again herald . . .

The Beginning.

∞ ∞ ∞ ∞ ∞ ∞ ∞ ∞ ∞ ∞ ∞ ∞ ∞

APPENDIXES

APPENDIX 1.

THE BIBLE

With the Lord one day is as a thousand years, and a thousand years as one day.

The heavens existed long ago, and the earth was formed out of water and through water by the word of God. But by the same word the heavens and earth that now exist are stored up for fire, being kept until the Day of Judgment and destruction of the ungodly.

The day of the Lord will come like a thief, and then the heavens will pass away with a roar, and the heavenly bodies will be dissolved, and the earth and the works that are done on it will be burned up.

—Excerpts from 2 Peter 3:7–10 (NIV)

APPENDIX 2.

ADAMS'S THEOREM

There is a theory which states that if ever anyone discovers exactly what the Universe is for and why it is here, it will instantly disappear and be replaced by something even more bizarre and inexplicable. There is another theory which states that this has already happened.

—Douglas Adams
The Hitchhiker's Guide to the Galaxy, 1979

BRIEF AND TRUE HISTORY OF THE SURNAME CHALMERS

❧ *Chalmers* ❧

Chalmers is a Scottish variant of the English occupational name Chambers, a derivative of the Old French *de la chambre* as well as the Latin *camera*.

In medieval times, servants in royal households were held in high regard, and frequently those with senior positions received certain privileges, with the position in turn being passed from one family generation to another. It became popular for such people to adopt the name of the occupation as their surname.

Hence the surname Chalmers socially evolved from the occupational description of someone who served a nobleman and later came to bear a noble administrative title.

Eventually Chalmers carried the standard of Nobility itself.

The Chalmers coat of arms includes a helmeted warrior, and the clan motto originally was a war cry that morphed into *Spero*, the definition of which is "I hope."

Today, Chalmers family records are held at the Edinburgh University Library.

APPENDIX 4.

CHALMERS GENEALOGY—*CRYPTOS* VERSION

Name	Era/Life-span	Notable Facts
Shar	Pliocene epoch—4.1 million years ago	First *Australopithecine* to look with wonder at the night sky.
Sha'fyer	Pleistocene epoch—1.8 million years ago	First *Homo erectus* to strike flint and make a controlled fire.
Kar'penta	Paleolithic period—100,000 years ago	First *Homo sapiens* to build a roofed living structure.
Kha'landers	Paleolithic period—30,000 years ago	First *Cro-Magnons* to make a calendar based on seasons.
Shumers	Holocene epoch—6,000 B.C.	First "modern man" to write on clay tablets in Sumer.
Shulmyrus	Golden Age of Greece—500 B.C.	Geometer who postulated that the shortest distance between two points is a straight line.
Suwan Calmeros	A.D. 750–814	Chief strategist for Charlemagne, who was *Imperator Augustus*, the "Father of Europe."
Jean de Chalmier	1300–1376	Wrote *Treatise on Ecclesiastical Exigencies and Temporal Reality*.
Strom Jonnas Chammler	1560–1640	Founded the *London Tablet,* later called the *London Times*. Wrote widely under the nom d'plume William Shakespeare.
Jonah S. Chalmer	1730–1799	Sea captain and scout for General George Washington. Chief of staff for President Washington, "Father of the United States."

Severn Joseph Chalmers	1830–1906	Botanist. Founded Megatherium Club, group of Washington, D.C., scientists at Smithsonian Institute.
Jonathan S. Chalmers	1860–1930	Immigration lawyer; wrote speech for 1886 Statue of Liberty dedication. Wall Street legal counsel; financial advisor to top corporations and prominent families.
Jonathan S. Chalmers Jr.	1890–2022	Dean of Mathematics, Columbia University. WWI war hero. Classmate of William J. Donovan and Franklin Roosevelt. Director of Office of Strategic Assessments. Father of USA, Underground States of America.
Steven J. Chalmers	1980–2018	Youngest fighter jet pilot in U.S. military history; Gulf War II combat hero. Killed in 2nd Aurora space flight to Mars.
Steven J. Chalmers Jr.	2010–2110	Emerges from USA in 2055. Journeyed to the rubble of Langley. Solved the CRYPTOS CONUNDRUM. Located the Crystal Tabula, and built Collabros—a Divine machine that will Enable and Ennoble all broken nations to work together to rebuild a once wonderful world.

Then in what seemed mere seconds, Time hastened forward to the moment when even though Nobility was imbedded deeply in the soul of the people and the soil of the planet, everyone and everything—the Chalmers lineage and Earth itself, abruptly perished in a rainstorm of cosmic fire.

AUTHOR'S END NOTE

A long-held rumor at Langley is that Wayne W. Wondelman, the deceased CIA cryptographer who provided guidance to the sculptor of Langley's CRYPTOS artwork, was also an expert on the Maya calendar. Some say he claimed to have found computational errors in the *so-called expert's* translation of the calendar date for the "End of Times" prophecy. Always insistent that the translation was off by two millennia, Wondelman maintained that instead of the year 2012, the Mayas believed that time on Earth would end in the year **4012.**